# READER BEWARE

This novel MAY CONTAIN depictions of sex, assault, murder, blood, gore, taking candy from children, multiple phobias, and other questionable acts.

# A MESSAGE FROM APEX ACADEMY

Welcome back to Apex Academy. The second semester of your education will be starting soon. We do hope that you will struggle to succeed as you did in your first semester with us. Be aware that our curriculum increases in difficulty with each passing term. We do this in order to push our students into becoming the very best version of themselves, whatever that may be. We do not shun away from our true selves. Instead we encourage you to embrace it. And inside of that embrace we ask that you seek out the truth of who you are versus who you wish to be.

Sincerely,
C.C.

# CHAPTER 1

Inside of her hotel room, Safia lay on the bed. The white sheets covering her naked body, shielding her from the cold sterile air around her. Next to her, she rested her head on the arm of David, whom she had spent the previous week alongside. Cutting the peaceful serenity of their unconscious embrace came the sound of a buzzing alarm clock as it made itself known to the soft mumbling complaints of those in the bed.

"Do we have to get up?" asked David, as he snuggled in close behind her.

"You know we do," moaned Safia with a smile. "We both need to head back, so come on. Let's get up."

"But it's so cold and you're so warm," said David as he kissed her on the back of her neck allowing his hand to slide down over her, his finger grazing her nipple before taking her breast in his hand. "Hmmm, so soft."

Safia smiled before rolling over in bed and giving David a kiss. "You've had your fun. Now come on. Get up," she said before lifting the covers off them both and exposing their bodies to the chilling air. The only thing she wore were the fuzzy pink handcuffs that locked around her left wrist. The other dangled and grazed against her hip as she stood up to get dressed.

"Oh, so mean. How does your boyfriend deal with you?"

"I don't have one, remember? He wanted me to go to college, so he did something incredibly stupid and broke up with me, and now I have to deal with the mess he put me in."

"Isn't college supposed to be where we find ourselves.? And looking at you topless now, I imagine you must have a hard time fighting off the guys who find you."

"What? Are you jealous?"

"A little. Especially now, looking at you."

"What, are you going to tell me that no girls approached you while in California?"

"A few have. But it's nothing serious. I meant what I said about us being together after graduation. That is, unless you've found a new guy already."

"Stop that, you know I haven't. And besides, if anything, it's more girls than guys."

David sat there for a minute and looked at her. "Oh! And what type of girls?"

Safia frowned as she turned to him. "I don't like that stupid smile on your face right now."

"What!?" said David, unable to hide the smirk across his lips as he sat up in bed. "There's nothing wrong with same-sex love."

"Why do I think you're fantasizing about something inappropriate right now?"

"Well, seeing as we're both naked, I can hardly see how it's not appropriate."

"Oh, just be quiet," said Safia as she slid into her panties, then looking down at him. "Calm your dick down and hand me my bra. We don't have time to fool around anymore." She shook her wrist at him, the chains of the fuzzy handcuffs clinking together. "Now, help me find the keys to these things."

"And here I was, trying to be a sexy and supportive ex-boyfriend," said David as he slid out of bed, scooping up Safia's bra off the counter and handing it to her, before searching around for the key. "And I don't suppose you wish to tell me about those girly acquaintances who have taken an interest in you."

Safia sighed. "Mostly just Mallory, and there was this girl named Amanda. They kissed me. Oh, and there was this girl named Addison." *I could tell him about Dario and Jericho, but I'd rather not think of them. Especially that jackass, Dario.*

David's face twisted in confusion. "What kind of college life are you having?"

"What? You're the one who asked?"

"Yeah, but I didn't...ah, found 'em," said David after running his hands under the sheets and coming back out with the key. "Here you go." He then passed it to Safia.

"Thank you," said Safia as she unlocked the handcuffs and sat them down on the nightstand. "I much more prefer it when you wear them."

"That's because you get off on having power. I'm glad to see you've learned some control now."

"That's not exactly true. It's... it's different when it's with you."

"So, you just want to feel powerful over me. I guess in your own way, that's romantic," said David, placing his hand to his chin. "But wait, back to the topic of that girl Mallory liking you. You mean as in Mallory next door, the one who came with you? The one who's all soft spoken and has trouble looking me in the eyes?"

"Yes, but it's weird. And I can't really talk about... Stop fantasizing about it. I can see it on your face."

"I'm not. I swear. I'm… I'm just considering… things."

"And how would you feel if I fantasized about you being with other men?"

"Whatever it takes to get you off. The mind is a playground, after all."

"Just get back," said Safia, swinging her bra and playfully hitting him with it before sliding her arms in and placing the cups over her breasts. "I swear, men are just idiots."

"Hey, the wire in those things hurt," said David while laughing."But being serious. You're not taking advantage of her are you. I know you can be when you get excited."

"No I am not. And it's not like I get off on having power over other girls.If anything I feel more protective of her because…" Safia saw David face studying her and instantly frowned. "You weren't being serious, were you?"

"Not at first, honestly I was just teasing you. But I am certainly interested now. And besides, this is the most you've talked to me about college since you've come back. Of course, I am going to listen to you when you talk about stuff like that."

"I told you I couldn't talk about it. I want to, but I just can't."

"And I accept it. That doesn't mean it's still not a little frustrating," said David as he slid on his boxers. "It's not like I can blame you for keeping secrets after what Yago and I did. Speaking of which, why haven't we heard from him this week? You'd think he'd call home, or at least call back after seeing that you weren't there."

"My mother said he called when he landed there, but they only talked for a minute or two. I'll find him when I get back. But come on, let's get ready. Our flight leaves at nine."

"Alright, alright," said David as they both dressed while continuing their flirting. When finally finished, they exited the room and headed downstairs, where they found Mallory and Hashmi awaiting them.

"We were wondering if you two were ever going to come

out," said Hashmi with a knowing grin as she turned to David. Safia got the chance to spend a whole week at home, yet somehow, she never once slept in our room. Don't you feel that may have been just a little-bit selfish on your part, David?"

"Hey, you two get her for the next six months. The least you can do is give me a week," said David, his eyes slowly drifting over to Mallory.

"Do I have something on my face?" asked Mallory, rubbing the side of her cheek, seeming somewhat self-conscious about David's attention settling on her.

"Huh? Oh, ahh, no. I was just thinking about... Oouf!" David coughed as Safia elbowed him in the stomach. "I mean, I hope you both... have a fun trip. Take care of my abusive partner here. She can be a handful."

"Ah! There they are, honey," said Safia's mother as she stepped into the hotel lobby, followed by her father and Mr. Smith, the man who had first taken her to the school. "Are you ready to head back, honey?"

"Yes, Mama," said Safia, taking note of her mother purposely walking slowly to match pace with her father as he paced himself on his crutches.

"Well, when you get back. Can you tell Yago to call us? I know he's busy with school. But he hasn't called us since he got there."

"I'll tell him."

"If you're ready to go, Miss Safia. I have the car waiting," said Mr. Smith gesturing towards the doors.

"Yes, I'm ready."

They all headed out to the car as David and Mr. Smith placed their luggage cases in the trunk.

"Be good, my little girl," said her father. "Don't get too involved with the snooty types up there."

"Hector, stop that," said her mother.

"What? You know what I mean. Some of them college type act all snooty and look down on us hard workers, ya know."

"I swear, sometimes I wonder why I married you."

"Oh, you know why you married me. I can perform them magic tricks, and I don't need a deck of cards to do what I'm talking about."

"Papa, please!"

"Safia," said her mother, shaking her head. "Just take your friends and go before your father poisons their minds. And Hector, you behave yourself."

Safia hugged her parents. "Bye Momma, and Papa, take your medicine. I don't wanna see you on crutches when I come back." She then turned back to the car as Hashmi and Mallory got inside. Placing her hands on the hood of the car, she turned around and reached her hand out to David, grabbing him by the collar and pulling him to her. She lifted herself up on her toes, planting her lips against his. "Just a year and a half left. You better not be married when I get back or I will come and find you."

"Is that a threat?"

She gave David a playful slap on the face. "Damn right."

Safia sat down in the car, closing the door behind her. As Mr. Smith drove off; she had to take a deep breath, attempting to hold back tears as she watched her parent's and David waving at her in the rearview mirror.

"Did you enjoy your trip home, Miss Safia?" asked Mr. Smith.

"I did. But I guess it's time to head back."

"Oh, I assumed you would be overjoyed to be heading back to campus," said Mr. Smith as he looked in the rearview mirror and saw the solemn faces of Hashmi and Mallory. "Oh my, are classes really that difficult there?"

"It's not the classes, it's the people," said Mallory. "The school isn't exactly a bastion of goodwill."

"Ahh! I see. Well, think of it this way. You girls met each other in college, right? You all probably never would have met each other otherwise. So, no matter what, college allowed you three girls to become friends."

"You know how to look on the bright side, Mr. Smith."

"Ha! Really? Well, I met one of my best friends, Nathon, while I was in college. We still hang out from time to time now when I'm in New York. But it's not just college. I'm sure there were some people in each of your high schools that you didn't get along with but may have eventually found a more redeeming quality."

"I'll try to remember that the next time I see Dario," said Hashmi. "But I find it hard to believe that man has any redeeming qualities."

"He doesn't," added Mallory. "He's just a liar."

"You girls sound like you've really had it rough on you," said Mr. Smith. "Hopefully, everything works out for you three. Who knows, maybe one of you will become valedictorian and end up being president or something."

"Or in my case, Prime Minister," said Hashmi looking out of the window. But I doubt that since there has only ever been one female prime minister in India, and it didn't end well."

"Then you can be the second."

Hashmi laughed, "You really are a hopeful person, aren't you, Mr. Smith?"

After a while of traveling on the highway, the girls arrived at the airport where Mr. Smith would escort them to the terminal and down the aisle until they reached the last door. They exited out, following the stairs downward. The clanking of their feet on the metal was barely audible over the roar of the engines of nearby jet liners. Placing their feet on the tarmac, they walked over to a nearby hangar where they saw their own private jet just recently exiting.

Upon their arrival, it slowed to a stop where the door opened and out came a flight attendant, who waved at them as they approached. Instantly Safia thought about the first time she had gotten into the plane.

*That was Addison. I guess this one is a student who also*

*needs the points. I still don't understand how all this...*

Safia squinted her eyes as the person in the flight attendant's outfit smiled and waved out to them. She stopped in her tracks as she realized who it was. "Amanda?"

"It's about time you all got here," said Amanda, placing her hands on her hips. "We woke up hours ago. I was starting to wonder why I even took this trip. Now, come on, I'm not allowed to leave the plane."

Safia and the rest made their way onto the plane where she saw Ricardo sitting down in one of the seats having a drink of water. He also was in a male's stewards' outfit.

"Hello, Miss. Safia."

"Hello, Ricardo," said Safia as she stepped forward, taking a seat next to him. "When I saw Amanda. I knew you had to be in here somewhere."

"I've found that it's best for me not to leave her alone. She tends to get into trouble without me."

"I think she does that even when you're around. Maybe more so then."

Ricardo smiled. "Just so. But I am impressed that you managed to get the school to allow you to come home."

"Yes, well. Things happened," she said, looking around the cabin. "Where's your other discarded, did you leave him back on campus."

"Yes," said Amanda as she walked past Safia and sat on Ricardo's lap, her exposed legs pointed out towards the aisle. "I have him running a few errands for me while I came all the way out here to visit you. While most at school prefer to use their as followers as pseudo-slaves, I prefer to let them handle things as they wish. Ricardo is enough to hold my interests.

"How did you get the school to allow you to come out here?" asked Hashmi as she and Mallory came by, sitting down in front of Safia.

"Oh this! I merely bribed the poor girl who they had planned on giving it to. A dark-haired girl; homely looking thing. I think I fit this uniform far better than she ever could." She placed her hands on her chest and shifted the bra beneath her clothing a bit. She then tilted her hat so that it hung over the front of her head a bit. "What do you think? Am I not just simply adorable?"

Safia just shook her head, a smile across her lips. "Why are you even here?"

"Oh, yes. The pressing matter at hand. I've come to warn you. I figured it was best that I do so before you land."

"Warn me? About what?" *Has something happened to Yago?*

"Your little vacation has gotten the attention of the second and third years."

"Okay?" said Safia, not sure what that meant. "But, aren't you a second year?"

"Yes, but I'm not overly curious. Okay, well, I am, but I'm not obsessive or malicious about it, like they are."

"I... I don't understand. Why would they care about me?" asked Safia as the jet shook and began making its way down the runway.

"Seriously? Are you really asking me that? Oh!" yelped Amanda as she bounced in Ricardo's lap and in quick response, he stuck his arms out to catch hold of her before she fell to the floor. "Thank you. That was a bit of a surprise."

"Amanda," said Safia, regaining the girl's attention. "Why are they after me?"

"Because you have done something that they are not allowed to do. You've gone home. Did you really think that little detail would go unnoticed? And that's not to mention what you did to Dario by taking Miss Mallory from him. And let us not forget that you beat Killian. Why, that's all anyone has been talking about since word got out."

"And how did word get out about me going home?" asked Safia, narrowing her eyes at Amanda. "I only told you, Hashmi, and Mallory." *I told Jericho also, but he would have no reason to tell anyone.*

Every Student has their Truth

"Hey, I see that look in your eyes. I'll have you know I was as quiet as a mouse about your travels."

"Fine," said Safia as the jet tilted and they began to ascend. She found herself unable to keep from looking out the window as the airliner lifted off the ground. "I still don't see why they're interested in me. I don't even have many points."

"Safia," said Amanda with a sigh. "Do you remember what I was doing the day you met me?"

Safia thought back to her arrival at the school. "Harmony took me around the school, showing her the campus. We met you there, and you were with Dario, and you had Ricardo playing in the fountain."

"Playing in the fountain? Is that what you call it? Then what about your friend Mallory over there? Would you refer to what she endured as playing?"

Safia turned to see a saddened look on Mallory as she herself remembered how Dario treated her like a slave. Suddenly, Safia felt a small piece of anger dwelling up within herself.

"There, maybe now you understand," said Amanda, seeing the change in Safia's face. "We were bored, Safia. And because they are bored, they look for things or, most importantly, people to play with. So, can you guess who just jumped to the top of their things-to-fuck-with list?"

"You can't be serious. All because I got to go home?"

"No, it's because of everything else on top of going home. Which none of them have been able to do, no matter how many points they have. Really, Safia, we weren't even allowed to step off the plane, or else they could have expelled us."

"What?"

"I don't understand?" said Hashmi, chiming in. "Even if they are after Safia. It's not as if they can make her bet or anything, and you can't hurt anyone on campus without their permission."

"Oh, you sweet child," said Amanda. "There are plenty of ways to force someone to do something against their better judgment. Considering what you went through before, I'd assume you'd know that just as well as anyone."

"Okay, okay," said a man as he stepped out of the cockpit holding a carton housing several bottled waters. "All of you take your seats. We're in the air now, so it's time for you to go to sleep."

"Excuse me, sir," said Amanda. "I'm not trying to be complicated. But out of curiosity. What would happen if we decided not to drink these drinks?"

"Then we would turn the jet back around and the school will decide what to do with you. But probably expulsion or something like that. I've never had someone refuse before." He tilted his head, lifted his hand, and smiled. "It's up to you. I'm just the pilot." He turned to Amanda, who was still sitting on Ricardo's lap. "But you take a seat and strap in. We don't need you sprawled out on the floor when we land. You can be all lovey-dovey after that."

"Oh, so forward." said Amanda and slid from Ricardo's lap, over to her own seat. "Well, bottoms up, I guess." And she took a few gulps of the water, handing it back to the man who placed it back into the holder.

The others did the same, all handing their half-drunk bottles back to the man.

Safia sighed. "Why does this have to happen to me? Can't you just convince all your friends to just leave me alone?"

"Wish that I could, darling… but… but… it doesn't work like that. Your friend there probably understands this just as well as I do."

"It's… it's true, Miss Safia. Dario… Dario is friends with a," Mallory yawned trying to stay awake. "He has a lot of friends who he plays with. They have a lot of points. He probably told them things about you."

Safia's eyes began feeling heavy. "I don't have time… for this. I need to find my brother before they do."

Every Student has their Truth

"Brother!" yelped Amanda, her eyes blinking hard as she tried to focus. "You... you could have said somethi..."

And just like that, they were all fast asleep in the jet's cabin. The pilot shook his head, before securing their seatbelts and made his way back into the cockpit.

# CHAPTER 2

Safia awoke to some type of bright light above her head. Feeling drowsy, she rolled over, trying to shield her eyes. She blinked several times, keeping her eyes lids low to stave off the ping sensation behind them as she took in a breath of the cold sterile air. Through the blurry world in front of her she could see someone sitting at a desk, two computer screens near them as they picked up a mug to drink from. As a hint of a soft coffee now tingled her nose, she heard the squeaky wheels of their rolling chair fighting their weight as they moved from one monitor to the next. Safia moaned as she tried moving her body but found it more difficult than she assumed it would be.

"Oh, you're awake." Came the familiar sound of Abigail's voice as she slid over into Safia's still blurry vision. Reaching over her, she moved the light from above her face.

"Ahhh," moaned Safia, her body feeling stiff as she

tried to blink away the spots in her vision left by the light. "What... what... Where am I?"

"As your teacher, I guess the right answer would be back at school. Which is odd, since I wasn't even aware you had left. But imagine my surprise when I arrived here to greet another student and I find you sleeping here."

"Sorry. I didn't... really tell anyone."

"I figured. But the school rarely allows people to leave early like this. Is everything okay at home?"

"Yes. Remember when I told you about my father? He... he was shot, so they allowed me to visit him when he left the hospital."

"I see. I can certainly understand your frustrations in wanting to make sure he's okay. But I suspect there's more to it than that."

"What... what do you mean?"

"For you to go home is one thing. But I also tended to Miss Hashmi and Miss Mallory. For them all to leave campus and for them all to be associated with you. That goes beyond suspicion and reaches out towards something more secretive."

"Ah... well," Safia looked down at the floor as she bit her lip.

"And I suspect that it's not something you can tell me, is it?"

Safia sighed. "No, it's not."

"That's fine. We all have our secrets we must keep for one reason or another. And after everything you've tried to do for me, I'd be a fool to doubt you."

"Is... is everything okay... I mean with you and Killian?"

Abigail shook her head. "It's going as well as could be expected. He spends most of his time painting like he used to. In all honesty, it feels like we've just gone back to when we first met. I bring him some art supplies and watch him as he paints."

"I see."

"Enough about me," said Abigail, lifting Safia by the arm. "Come on. Let's have you stand and see if you've gotten your legs yet."

Safia lifted herself, feeling a bit woozy as the blood rushed from her head. Her feet dangled in the air for a moment before she lowered her weight to the floor. Her legs felt wobbly as her body forced itself to stand, but she could feel herself shaking off the last bit of the induced sleep.

"Has anything happened at school in the last week?"

"No, not especially," said Abigail as she let go of Safia's arm and watched her find her balance. "There ya go. Seems like everything's in working order. Let's go and see your friends. I'm sure they're still outside waiting for you."

"Okay," said Safia, now feeling sure-footed as she followed Abigail out of the room and into the checkered-patterned hallway. They headed down the corridor. To each side of her were the same rooms as before; rooms behind glass walls that housed exercising equipment and large puzzles that Safia had never actually entered before and hoped that she would never have to.

They made their way down the hall until finally reaching the door.

"I guess the proper thing to say is 'welcome back to Apex Academy,'" said Abigail, holding out Safia's badge to her. "Your second semester awaits."

Safia looked down at the badge for a moment. The jewel in the center looked beautiful as it reflected the light from above. In any other setting, she might think of the jewel as quite lovely, but here it didn't give off such a thought. Instead, she took the pendant from Abigail, rolling the rope that was attached between her finger and thumb, feeling the coarse thickness of it. *They returned my leash to me,* wondered Safia as she stared down aimlessly at the brown rope.

"Safia? Is everything okay?"

"Oh," said Safia, brought back to reality. "Yes, sorry. I

was daydreaming for a moment." She then took the rope in both hands, lifted it over her head, and placed it down around her neck. "I guess I'm ready."

The doors to the outside opened as the cold air around her rushed past her, ruffling her hair as it left the building. Following it, she stepped forward into the light. The campus ground appeared before her as her eyes adjusted to the sunshine and outside, waiting for her were her roommate Hashmi and her discarded, Mallory.

"Oh, there she is," said Hashmi as Safia appeared out of the door. "We were wondering when you would show up."

"It's still morning here. What should we do?"

Safia turned back to Abigail. "Thank you. Will you be teaching our classes again?"

"Yes. I look forward to seeing you again in class, Miss Famosa and Miss Hashmi."

"Okay, I'll see you there." Safia then headed off into the campus with her friends.

"Where are we headed?" asked Mallory.

"First, we are going to head to our room and change our clothes. Enough people apparently already know we left the campus. But for those that don't know. I don't want to just inform them." They all then headed out following the spiraling walkway of the campus towards Yennefer House. On the way, she tapped on her badge. "I, Safia Famosa, would like to know the location of Yago Famosa." The light around the badge began to glow white for a moment.

"Yago Famosa is no longer in our system," spoke the badge.

"No longer what?"

"What does that mean?" asked Mallory. "Does that mean he's not at the school anymore?"

"I don't know. It's never said that before when looking for someone." Safia tapped on the badge again. "I, Safia Famosa, would like to know what happened to Yago Famosa."

"That information is inaccessible. You do not have the

proper privileges to access that information."

"I don't like the sound of that," said Hashmi. "Do you think he's okay?"

"I don't know. I mean, you can't hurt anyone here. But… I need to be sure," said Safia as she began to feel even more uneasy about returning to the campus.

As they made their way across the campus, they saw that it was mostly empty, as everyone had yet to get up and head out for breakfast. There was only the occasional student heading to their area as they passed.

"Location Denied," spoke Safia's badge.

"What was that about?" asked Hashmi, looking over at Safia's badge as it glowed.

"I don't know. I didn't ask it a question that—"

"Location denied," spoke Mallory's badge, glowing the same.

"Why would someone be looking for me?" asked Mallory. "You think our badges are broken?"

"I don't think so. I mean, it's never broken before. And they've just returned them to us. It would be weird for it to break the moment we—"

"Location denied," spoke Hashmi's badge.

"Okay, I think it's fair enough to say that someone is looking for us. Or at least one of us, and they are going about it in a very desperate fashion."

"But we've only just gotten back. Who would even know we're here?"

"Oh! You think it's your brother?" asked Mallory. "Maybe he's looking for you."

"No. That would make sense if it was just me. But how would he know your names?"

"Oh yeah, that does make sense."

"Who then?" asked Hashmi. "And it seems that the school is blocking the information on your location. Beforehand, it would ask you if you wanted to tell people where you were. Now it's not even asking you."

Safia lifted her badge from around her neck, holding it up in the morning light. The crystal at the center shined, reflecting a deep reddish color down on her cheek. "I already don't like being back here. I feel like this thing is just watching me."

"Don't try to break it or anything," said Hashmi, placing a hand over her own pendant. "I think that will either get you expelled or fined a lot of points. Or at least that's what I've heard."

Safia sighed before wrapping the rope around her hand, letting the pendant dangle beneath her fingers. "Come on, let's just head on back."

"Location denied," spoke Safia's pendant once more.

"I wonder if this thing has a mute option," said Safia, getting frustrated by the pendant as they made their way back toward their dorm. It didn't take them long before they reached Yennefer house. The same purple plants were outside by the steps but as they made their way upward. There was no one at the door. Heading up the stairs, the girls made their way to their room unimpeded.

They opened the door to their room and stepped inside. Everything looked the same as when they left it. Mallory stepped inside, grabbing her blanket from the closet.

"I just want to rest. I still feel tired. But I should... what?" asked Mallory, looking over at Safia, who was staring at her.

"We should get you a bed since you're living with us. We didn't do it last time, because of the points it would cost. But now we should have more than enough."

"You don't have to. I mean. I know how important the points are."

"No. There's enough room here for three beds. We'll buy another."

"Everything does look the same," said Hashmi as she inspected the room. "But it is weird, I mean. Yago talked to your parent's, right? He should have known you would come back, eventually."

"I've been thinking about that. But what day is it?"

"What do you mean?"

"I mean. All we know is that we went to sleep," said Safia as she walked over to her closet and picked out a set of clothes. It was still a bit cold outside, so she chose the pleated long skirt and vest. "We don't know exactly when we woke up. For all we know, they could have kept us asleep for days."

"That's true. I didn't think of that," said Hashmi. "I'm surprised you thought of that."

"I need to take this place more seriously now. So, I'm trying to think like my brother would. If I had done that from the start, I probably wouldn't be in the mess I'm in now. Did either of you see Amanda when you woke up?"

"No. We haven't seen her since we got back."

"I should look for her too. This stupid school tricked me when I first got here, because I didn't know what they were doing. But I'm not going to let myself fall for it again."

"So, are we going to just go out and look for them?"

"That's the plan. But first. I think we should take a bath. I don't feel clean right now, and who knows how long it's been since my last one."

Together they all got out of their clothes, grabbing their towels, and made their way down to the showers.

The hot water felt like a much-needed cleanse over her still weary body as Safia stretched her shoulders.

*I have to be smarter if I don't want to get caught up in their mess this time. Thankfully, I have a lot of points now. So, I should be fine as long as I don't bet anything big. But I still need to be careful about the people Amanda warned me about.* Her mind went back to her time down below in game night, where she could still smell the burning flesh on those two that were strapped down to the chair as others watched, placing bets on them. *I don't want to end up like them. I just need to be careful. The first thing I need to do is find Yago. I doubt they would send him home. No, this place enjoys its stupid games too much. They must be planning something. Maybe Champ Champ would know something.*

Safia's mind circled as she kept going over the same ideas.

"Safia," said Mallory. "We're done. Should we just meet you back in the room?"

"Oh, ahh, no," said Safia, turning the knob until the constant stream of water turned into nothing but a drip. "I'm coming out now." She grabbed her towel from over the stall and wrapped it around herself, opening the door. Together, they made their way back to their room and got dressed. All adorned the standard pleated skirts with Hashmi slipping into her favorite purple Hijab.

After getting dressed, they left the room, headed downstairs to the front door. It was there that she met Jericho standing outside their building.

"Welcome back, Miss Safia," said Jericho with a smile. "I see you've made it back safely. And hello to you too, Miss Hashmi and Mallory. I am hoping I can count on your help again this semester. I have a lot of fun things planned around the campus."

"How did you know we were here?" asked Mallory, her face not hiding her hesitance to approach the boy before her.

"Safia's badge is linked to mine, remember? In case she needs me, she will always be able to find me. From my side of things, it told me that Safia was back on campus, so I just came to say hello. And of course, make sure I can count on you for helping me with my next campus project."

"Jericho," said Hashmi with a smile as she made her way down the steps. "Why do you go around building things on campus? That seems like an odd hobby to have."

"I just like to help people. It's good points, and as long as we get enough people, then it's not much work. But I admit that not everyone wants to help build things. Most of the students here have never held a hammer and nails in their whole lives. So, they'd rather just gamble their way into servanthood."

"Yes. And since you know that we don't gamble as much, you thought to come to us for assistance?"

"Well, you and Nasir both have your religious exceptions, so I just assumed you both would be keen on the idea. And Safia now has Mallory, so I figured it couldn't hurt," said Jericho, scratching his head. "But maybe I did jump the gun a bit. Have you three changed your mind about helping me?"

"No. I was just curious. And as you said. It's a good way to gain points. But what about you? Why have I never seen you bet?"

"Oh, I bet," said Jericho with a smile, shaking his head. "Just not so much as to get myself in trouble. And I don't bet nothing big, maybe just a couple of points a month. The people around here start acting funny when they get too many points. Speaking of which, Safia, I came to tell you that a bunch of people have come to me asking about you."

"What? Why?"

"I don't know. They were mostly a bunch of second or third years. I'm not sure what they want, but I've heard about them, and I don't think it'd be anything good. If I were you, I wouldn't bet anything with them. I heard they use fancy tricks," said Jericho as he waved her finger at her, trying to seem spooky.

"And that's really all you came here for? You don't want anything... else?" asked Safia, looking around suspiciously.

"No, that's it, unless you want to go out on a date later. I still have a few things I need to check up on around campus before classes start."

"No thanks. There's still a lot I need to do since I got back. But we can meet up later if you like." *I know he wants to talk to me about something. I can see it in his face.*

"Okay," said Jericho with a smile before turning and walking off ahead of them.

Every Student has their Truth

After watching him leave, all Safia could do was shake her head with a sigh. "He's going to ask me for something soon. And it's not like I can just say no since he's blackmailing me." She bit her lips for a moment, trying to think what it could be, but the number of things was too vast. So, she just took a deep breath and stepped forward, headed off into the campus beside her friends.

The walkways were still quiet for the most part as the girls made their way around the confusing path. The sun was fresh in the morning sky, peeking out over the distant mountains behind the school.

"Do you trust him?" asked Mallory as they stepped past a few students on a bench. "I mean, didn't you say he was blackmailing you to do stuff?"

"Yes. But he hasn't ever asked me to do anything yet. Really, I don't know what he's thinking. After telling him I was going back home, he just smiled and wished me luck."

"Well, I don't trust him."

"Agreed," said Hashmi. "What will you do?"

"Nothing I can do at the moment, except wait," said Safia with a shrug. "He'll eventually try to force me into doing something, then I'll know what he wants and why he helped me. I just have this uneasy feeling with him just being nice to us now. I don't know how to describe it, the way he looks at me. Actually, it's the way he looks at everyone. It just feels off."

"Hey, you think he was the one who was looking for you?" asked Mallory with a snap of her fingers. "You know, with the pendant talking?"

"No. It's part of our deal. He can find me if he wants. And I can find him."

"Oh, I thought it was a good guess, since he was outside of the dorm and all. It shows that he was looking for you."

"That's a fair guess," added Mallory, nodding her head.

"Come on, I want to find Yago. Let's go look around the campus." They headed off through the winding roads of the
22

campus.

"If he's a new student, then at least that means he hasn't started betting yet," said Hashmi. So, that's good. We still have some time before classes start, so that we have some time to warn him about how this school is."

"He already knows," said Safia. "Or at least I think he does. I'm not sure anymore. Did you two know anything about this school before you joined?"

"No. My sister got me in. I was completely lost when I got here," said Mallory.

"I knew about as much as the both of you, I'd assume," said Hashmi with a shrug of her shoulders. "I mean my father asked me a few times about what college I wanted to attend, but I'm not sure he meant this.

"You think your father also went to this school?"

"I'm not entirely sure, but all signs are pointing to that conclusion."

"Location denied," spoke the pendant again.

"This thing really is annoying. I should have brought my bag so that I could stuff it in there."

They made their way through the campus, stopping at several places on the way. But there was no sign of Yago. As the day went on, and the campus filled with more people leaving their dorms, Safia couldn't help but feel that more and more people were looking at her. The feeling wasn't malicious, but now and then she would catch a person staring at her a little longer than normal. When passing someone on the walkway, she would see them turning around to glance at her.

At first, she assumed them to be nothing more than the normal veers of the boys checking them out. But she would notice more and more girls doing the same. This would be followed up by hearing whispers when they thought she was out of earshot.

"Come on. Let's go in here," said Safia as they passed by the left library of the campus. Walking up the steps, they opened the large wooden doors, heading inside. The cool air of the building flowed over her as they made their way through rows of bookshelves.

"I do think we are being watched," said Hashmi as they sat down at a table. "And not by only a few people."

"I've been thinking the same thing. But we haven't done anything. You think it's what Amanda warned us about?"

"That would be my first guess. But it's not like we can—"

"Safia Famosa, where are you?" screamed a feminine voice that bellowed through the halls of the library. "I know you're here somewhere."

Safia, Hashmi, and Mallory just stared at each other for a moment in confusion as they heard several footsteps coming closer. Through the opening in the bookcases, she could see a decent amount of people making their way through the aisle.

"I know she's here. I saw her enter with her friends," came the voice of a young man.

"For your sake, I hope you're—"

"There she is," said a blonde-haired young boy with purple accents in his clothing that Safia recognized from her dorm. He pointed his finger out toward Safia after spotting her. "I told you she was here."

Safia frowned at the boy but narrowed her eyes at the group. *I'm going to guess that this is what Jericho and Amanda tried to warn me about. Maybe we should have stayed in our room.*

"Oh! So that's her?" said the girl, walking up to her table and giving Safia a look over. "So, you're the one who has everyone talking?" She glanced over at Hashmi and Mallory. "And I take it you both are her friends."

"I'm sorry, but do I know you?"

"Not yet. But my name is Frilla Santiago. And you are Safia Famosa, right?"

"Yes, that's me. Why are you looking for me?"

"Oh, it was part of the game. We had bets going to see

who would find you first, and it seems I've won this round."

"You were betting… to see who would find me first?"

"Yes, amongst other things."

"Is that why our pendant kept flashing so much today, saying someone was trying to find us?" asked Mallory.

"What?" asked Frilla, looking annoyed. "We all agreed not to use the locator. It's a good thing I asked Champ Champ to disable that feature of those involved. Tell me, who was it? I'll see to it that they lose points for trying to cheat in the game."

"We don't know. It never said who it was."

"Well, it doesn't matter. I'll soon find out who it was."

"You can disable things in the system?"

"Me? No, not alone. But together we can change almost anything as long as we can prove that it is in the interest of fair play here at the school."

"Excuse me," said Hashmi, chiming in. "But why were you looking for us?"

"For the games, of course. We've had several bets going around the school on you three ever since we were informed of your disappearance. It is quite the mystery after all. Three students disappear from the campus at the same time. One perhaps, but three. Oh yes, there is a mystery there." She clapped her hands. "And look at me for being fortunate enough to find all three of the golden eggs together. I certainly have won, haven't I?"

"Okay, you all placed a bet to find us. But who told you we had left the school?" asked Safia.

"I have no idea who started the rumor. But you certainly brought some life to this dull place. Many thought they had expelled you three, but there simply was no one who understood why. And you know how it goes from there, speculation turns into an investigation." She gave a gleeful smile at Safia. "And that's when we found out who you were, or is it more precise to say what you've done?"

"Frilla Santiago has been awarded six-hundred thousand

points," spoke the woman's pendant that she wore on her wrist. It was attached to a golden bracelet, shaped in the image of a cat that wrapped around her arm.

Safia's eyes fluttered at the ludicrous amount of points.

"Six... six hundred thousand?" asked Mallory in shock. "You bet that much on just being the first to find her?"

"Oh, it's not that much. Just two hundred thousand per person. We plan to bet far more than that now I've found you. Tell me, what do you have planned for the coming days before class?"

"I'm still getting used to being back," said Safia, knowing that there was no way she would tell her about her brother. "I have to buy supplies for the new semester and have them delivered to our room."

"Yes, I suppose you do still need to go to class. Sorry, I forget that you're not one of us," said Frilla, biting her lip, then waving any caution aside. "But no matter. You must come visit us on the second form of the main building."

"Who is... us?"

"The second and third years, of course. We've been bored for some time, and we've made a lot of plans in the event of you returning."

"What if she doesn't want to be involved in your plans?" asked Hashmi, her voice a little harsh. "We've got other things to do."

Out of the corner of her eye, Safia caught a glimpse of Austin over by a bookshelf, shaking his head at her.

The girl looked at Hashmi, a slight grin on her face. "Are you sure? While I do admit that this is purely for our entertainment, I think it would serve you all as well. She then turned to Mallory, her eyes looking her up and down, taking stock of her as if she were an animal of some sort. "You're Safia discarded, aren't you? We've heard about you. Tell me, does your caretaker there know why you ended up with Dario? Or are you just playing the victim?"

"What? That's not—"

"Oh, so she doesn't know. Well, that's a bit of fun that will come in handy later, I'm sure." She looked over at Hashmi. "You're the daughter of—"

"I'll come. What time do you want me to be there?"

"Oh, now that's a good girl. Not too early. I'll contact you when I gather everyone to attend," said Frilla, with a smile as she patted her hands on the table. "Oh, this is going to be so much fun. I can't wait until the start of classes when you're allowed to bet again. It must be so hard being a first year and having your points locked away."

"Hey," said the blonde-haired boy from earlier. "I'm going to get paid for leading you to her, right?"

"Yes. You are still here, aren't you? Do not worry, all wagers and bets must be upheld. You will receive your points shortly, I am sure. Come on, everyone. We have so much to do before tomorrow's meeting." And with that, just as suddenly as she appeared, the woman left, followed by her entourage, which Safia wasn't sure who in the group was and wasn't her discarded.

"Why did you agree to meet them?" asked Mallory.

"Because if I didn't, I was going to end up in a mess like last time. The moment she thought I might not come, she started looking over at the both of you and I'm not dragging you both into this if I can help it."

"I couldn't help but see that as well. While I'm sure they will have some trouble getting me involved in anything. That doesn't mean that I am immune from them annoying me wherever I go," said Hashmi with a sigh. "So, I don't think we, or you, are going to have much say so in this matter, if we wish to attempt to have something of a peaceful existence here."

"Yeah, it'll be best to just go and see what they want."

"You know they are going to try and involve you in their games. Safia, you don't exactly have that many points to experiment with, especially considering you and Mallory's monthly burdens?"

"I don't plan to get involved in their games. It's not like they can make me bet. I just gotta go there and tell them I don't want anything to do with their games."

"That sounds very hopeful, considering what you went through the last time."

"It's not like I really have much of a choice. I've seen what they do to the ones who they dislike," said Safia, thinking about the boy and girl that were burned while strapped to their chairs. "I'll be careful this time. I won't go risking my points and sending Mallory back home. That's not a mistake I plan to make again." She turned back to where Austin was but noticed that he had left. "Come on," she said with a sigh. "Let's go."

"Are we going to keep looking for Yago?"

Safia lifted herself from the table, now feeling more tired than when she first sat down. "Yeah, let's search around a little longer. I understand what he's saying, but that doesn't mean that I have to like it."

# CHAPTER 3

For several passing days, Safia would traverse the campus aimlessly in hopes of spotting her brother. But along with periodically checking her pendant for his location and trying to send him messages, her efforts went unrewarded.

"The second years still haven't contacted you?" asked Hashmi, sitting in their dorm room brushing her hair.

"No. And tomorrow's the first day of class."

"Maybe they changed their minds and decided to leave you alone."

"I doubt that. They might wait until classes start. They were all excited about me being able to bet again."

"Well, I don't like the looks you get around campus now," said Mallory. "It's like everyone is either too interested in you or too afraid to talk to you."

"They probably don't want to get themselves involved in whatever mess they have planned, seeing as how Safia has all these rumors floating around about her now," said Hashmi with a laugh. "I think the best one was how they are grooming you to be the next head mistress of the campus."

Safia laid herself down on her bed and began looking up at the ceiling. "Great! I could be the next Champ Champ. I'm so excited."

"I really don't think I will ever get used to that name. I mean really, Champ Champ of all things. It sounds like a cartoon character. And all because she lost a bet, she has to be called that. I wonder what her real name is."

"She wasn't too thrilled with it either, if I remember correctly."

Safia's badge began to glow. "Champ Champ would like to see you. Would you like to know her location?"

Both Hashmi and Mallory turned to Safia in surprise.

"You don't think she was listening in on us, do you?"

Safia tapped the pendant with a smirk at Hashmi. "Yes, give me her location."

"Location has been sent to your device."

Safia reached over across the bed, picking up her glass tablet. Recognizing her, the tablet unlocked, opening up a 3D model of the school. It was more detailed than before, but still displayed the location of people in red and blue dots.

"I guess I should go then," said Safia, rolling out of bed and placing her feet on the floor.

"Do you want us to come with you?"

"No, it's fine. It says she's just down by the lake. And I want to just take a walk by myself for a while and think. You two just stay here."

After getting dressed, Safia headed out of the dorm, making her way across campus and down toward the lake. There she saw a large orange and white umbrella staked into the ground, where underneath it, on a blanket, sat two people wearing matching swimsuits.

Taking her time, she made her way down to the lake.

There was Champ Champ, sitting on the blanket in a bikini with her shirtless husband, his head in her lap with his eyes closed.

"Do you drag him everywhere? I don't think I've even seen him awake," said Safia with a smirk, being playful knowing that she had indeed seen him awake, although it was only once.

"He's awake when I need him. Until then, I will provide him comfort."

"You make him sound like a pet or a guard dog."

"Is that not what men are? Some are smarter than others, but they all know their purpose."

"And what's your purpose?"

"To be his good little wife and act in his stead while he sleeps. And that brings us to why I have asked you here. I wish to warn you."

"Yeah well," said Safia, sitting down on the blanket beside Champ Champ, looking over the water. "If it's about Frilla and whoever those second years are, then I think you're a bit late on that. They've already invited me to one of their meetings. And judging from how they spoke, I didn't really have much of a choice."

"No, you didn't," said Champ Champ with a sigh of her own as she stroked her husband's head. "I did try to shelter you from this school's upper dealings as much as I could. But some secrets were bound to be found out eventually."

"So, what do I do now? Everything is turning to shit, and I've only just gotten back."

"The same as before. Struggle and survive as long as you can."

"That is the plan," said Safia as she dug her hand into the sand beside her, watching beads of sand fall back to the ground. "Can I ask you a question? Do you know if my brother Yago is here? I tried to find him, but the pendant—"

"Yes, he's here."

"Then why doesn't my pendant allow me to find him?"

"Because he doesn't want to be found, most likely."

"What? But, he's my brother. Why wouldn't he want to see me?"

"I don't know. I haven't met him myself. In the interest of my own enjoyment, I tried to find him myself. But no one has told me anything other than he is here."

"But aren't you the Head Mistress here? Aren't you able to make things happen?"

Champ Champ just smiled. "Do you really still believe that after everything you've been through? I was told you spoke to that person over the phone after figuring some things out."

"Who is she?"

"Now that, even I am not allowed to say. You must figure it out on your own. But I don't think it will be as surprising as you think it will be."

"Then why try to help me at all, if it's going against what that person wants?"

"Because it's what he would want me to do," said Champ Champ, smiling down at her husband. "And as I said, I wish to give him good news when he wakes up. So, I will tell him about our conversations."

Safia placed her hands to her face in frustration. "This is all just so ridiculous. It's like everyone here is speaking in riddles."

Champ Champ laughed. "And you're just figuring this out now? Then I feel for you if you do not adjust fast, because this small world that we are living in has its eyes keenly set on you at the moment."

"And there's nothing I can do about it, is there?"

"We all have our role to play. It just appears that now it is time for you to figure out yours."

Safia just closed her eyes and laid back on the blanket, her head next to The Husband's.

"Oh, will you be joining us for a while?" asked Champ Champ, smiling down at the two as the hair mingled together.

"I'm honestly still just tired and I need a place to think," said Safia as a cool breeze rose from over the water, sliding over her skin. "And this seems like a good place to relax."

"Go on then. I shall wake you if anything of note appears. I wish for you to be in good mental health and rest is a large part of such things."

"I appreciate that," said Safia as she closed her eyes, embracing the sound of the wind as it roamed over the grass. *Why am I even here? Why did I come back? Was it for Mallory? Maybe, I can ask Mama and Papa to let her stay with us for a while? But it's not like we have a lot of money or an extra room. And the school is paying for my father's hospital bills. Will they stop that if I drop out? Knowing this place, they would. They'd use that against me. Everyone here is always looking for something to use against someone else. Where the hell are you Yago? I could use your help now.*

Safia's thoughts circled in her mind until she began losing them to the passage of time. Hours passed by as the sun moved across the sky above them. But like all dreams, it needed to end. This one came to a halt with the vibration of a pendant over her chest.

"Frilla Santiago has sent a message to you," spoke the pendant, repeating its message as Safia slowly roused from her sleep.

While the effect of the much-needed sleep on her was pleasant enough, the opposite couldn't be said of the extremely shiny sunlight on her eyes after waking from it. Safia rolled her head over as the pendant repeated its announcement. Her face was on something soft and warm. She stretched out her legs as her eyes slowly adjusted to the light. As her vision cleared, she was surprised to see a smirk on the face of Champ Champ looking down at her.

"Welcome back to the land of the living."

Safia frowned as she looked around, realizing that she had taken the place of The Husband, resting on the headmistress's lap. Safia quickly sat up and began looking around.

"How... how long was I out for?"

"About five hours. You must have been really tired?'

"Five hours? You let me lay there for five hours."

"Well, no, it was more like four hours. You only took the place of my lover after he had awoken. You were rummaging about so much that we began to think you would just roll off into the water. So, hubby and I both figured it best that I look after you till you came too."

"But... five—"

"Frilla Santiago has sent a message to you," spoke the pendant again.

"You may want to get that. I'm afraid it will not stop until you do."

Safia tapped the pendant on her chest.

"Hello, Miss Safia. So sorry it took so long. But our members are busy people who have had prior arrangements to take care of. However today at six p.m., please come to the second floor of the main school building in the last room on the hall, marked 'Council,' where we can share everything with you. Have fun 'til then."

"Oh, so it was Miss Frilla who contacted you. I guess it could have always been worse. Although she does sound rather excited."

"Well, I'm not excited about meeting any of them."

"No, I suppose you're not."

"I had a dream where I quit the school and took Mallory home to live with me."

Champ Champ laughed. "Oh my, that would be a sight to see. I'm sure that would certainly leave a few sour faces amongst their group."

"But I'm sure that I wouldn't be allowed to do that without paying for it, would I?"

"That is true. You are indebted to us, after all. But just because something isn't true, that doesn't mean that it can't be used as leverage. You're in the game with us, Safia. I suggest you try your best to adapt to it."

"I'm trying. It's not as if I'm used to this."

"Well," said Champ Champ, standing up. "I suppose... ohhhh!" Her legs wobbled as she lost balance and went falling forward. Safia, on reflex, stepped to the side, catching her before she fell. "Oh my, it seems my legs have fallen asleep, haven't they?"

"Are you okay?"

"No. It would appear not. Would you mind helping get my legs back under me? I'm sure..." said Champ Champ, wincing as she tried to take a step. This... is quite the uncomfortable... position to be in."

Safia held the woman's arms as practiced walking again until she had a solid footing.

"Okay, that seems to have done it. Thank you."

"You do know that you're a weird person, right? You must have been told that before."

"Oh, I've been called many things around this campus. If all it amounts to is just being thought of as weird, then I shall count it as a compliment. But I'm okay now, so I suppose you should be on your way. It is almost six p.m. now."

Safia shook her head as she watched Champ Champ begin a sort of stretching routine out on the sand.

"I'll be on my way then," she said as she made her way back up the hill and onto the winding walkways and through the campus. It wasn't long before she reached the main school building. Classes hadn't started yet, so everything was quiet around her. The marbled walls and patterned design on the floor were so polished that it reflected the arched ceiling and chandeliers above it.

Her steps echoed as she made her way down the hall, the barely visible image of herself becoming distorted by the small imperfections on the marble. Placing her hands on the cold railing of the steps, she climbed upward to the second floor.

After reaching the top, she realized she'd never actually come up to the second floor before. Sure, she'd visited the rooftop of the school with its spires pointed high into the sky, but she'd never visited the second floor beneath them.

There were several rooms, but fewer than there were below. Whereas the bottom floor had six rooms, three on each side, the top floor housed only four rooms, two on each side. And up ahead one of those large rooms had a sign that had 'Council' etched across a wooden plaque on the door.

Safia stepped forward, knocking on the plaque.

"Come in," said the voice of Frilla, muffled through the door.

Placing her hand on the plaque, Safia pushed it open and stepped inside. The room wasn't what she expected. Instead of a classroom filled with chairs, it was instead an oval shaped room. Inside was a large room with a split level. Marble stairs lead up to the second level where ten figures sat. They each wore a mask of a different animals and were spread out."

And at the center, atop all the steps, standing proudly, was Frilla, looking down on her with a smile on her face. The backdrop behind her was of a stunning mosaic-stained glass piece that allowed light to shine through in a bevy of colors that spread across the room.

*I don't like this. Why the fuck are they wearing masks? This feels like some cult stuff.* Safia glanced back at the door, thinking she might need to escape.

"Welcome, welcome, Safia. I am so glad you came to visit us," said Frilla from her perch ahead.

"I don't think I had much of a choice," said Safia, turning back around and cautiously stepping forward, looking at the people sitting on the steps in their masks.

"Nonsense. There is always a choice. Why, what we have planned will be proof of that. Now come, step forward. We don't mean any harm to you. We simply wish to have you entertain us. To relieve us of the ever-present boredom that this school has us locked inside of."

"I'm glad you all are having fun, but why would I get involved in this? I just want to graduate and go home. I'm not like all of you. I don't even have that many points." *I don't think telling them about my points should matter. I mean, if they have millions, what would it matter to them?*

"Oh, fuck this," said one of the boys, ripping the rabbit mask from his face. He was a good-looking, brown-haired boy. His brown pleated vest did nothing to hide his physique, stretching over his biceps as he tossed his mask.

"Dammit, John," said Frilla. "We went through all the trouble of disguising ourselves, and you just had to spoil it."

The mask spun in the air before sliding across the floor and bumping into Safia's feet. The boy leaned forward, placing his arm across his knee with a smile. "Just tell us how you beat that point freak. If none of us could beat him, I damn sure wanna know how you did it. The only fun we had left was finding ways to keep him from getting that bitch, Abigail."

"Well, that hardly matters now," said a woman in a deer mask from across the room. "He's beaten us again, and now that he has her, he's just become boring. All he does is paint with his little toy standing beside him."

She was a larger woman, wearing a pleated dress. Her hair, like all the other women Safia noticed, was hidden by a brown cloth that wrapped around their heads. It reminded Safia of the Hijab Hashmi used on her hair. Their coverings were all so well done that she couldn't identify any defining characteristics about them.

*Why are they hiding themselves? Is there a reason for me not to know who they are? I dislike this even more now.*

"I did try to warn you all about John. He's a brute through and through. Why did you ever invite him?" asked another woman in a goat's mask.

"Oh, piss off, all of you. I agreed to be here. I didn't agree to be part of your 'eyes-wide-shut party.' Let's just start the games and see who comes out ahead."

"Now, now," said Frilla, trying to lessen the tension between the two. "I won the contest of finding her, so that means that I get to organize the games we play."

"Yeah, only after you bought out her whole dorm. How many points did that cost you?"

"More than you were willing to sacrifice, but don't worry, that is also a part of the game that will play itself out. Remember this is for our enjoyment, so try not to pout too much when you lose."

"Enough with the suspense, Frilla," said the larger woman. "Tell us what the game is. I'm absolutely feverish to find out what you have in store for us."

"Okay. So, the first game will be simple. Safia Famosa, your first goal is to find out who we all are under these masks over the course of the next six months."

"What?" said the larger woman. "But I've already spoken. She knows my voice now. And it's hardly as if I'm not recognizable?"

"Such is the way of this, I'm afraid," said Frilla with a smile. "I did warn you all before she arrived that it would serve your interest not to speak. You should have heeded my advice."

"Well, that's hardly fun, now, is it?" asked the larger woman, as she placed her hands to her face, removing her mask. Her long blonde hair flowed freely from its wrappings, falling and hanging down to her elbows. "I guess there is no need for this now, is there?"

"Don't be like that," said Frilla. "There are plenty of heavier students on campus. You could have simply blended in."

"Watch your patronizing tone. Be that as it may, there are not so many that I wouldn't be found within a day. And given the look on our guest's face here, she isn't likely to forget anything about today's meeting anytime soon. No, I shall simply bow out and join in on the other games."

"What other games?" asked Safia.

"Oh dear. There will be many games during your time here. But do not worry, I can see that you are fond of your classes. So, we will limit the games to a reasonable amount. There is such a saying as 'too much of a good thing' after all. And we need proper time to plan, not just the week since your return."

"I'm sorry, but what if I refuse to play your game? I have to ask, even though I'm pretty sure I can guess what you are going to say."

"Oh yes. Occasionally we meet someone who says they refuse to play. But at least you don't seem as self-righteous about it as they did. I'll humor you with a few examples. First, we could simply send word out that anyone who bets you will come under our direct attention, and we could crush them until they are expelled. And as you know, if you do not place at least one bet a month you will be penalized and the following month, if a bet is not placed, you will be expelled."

"Yeah, we've got a lot of fun ways to make people play even if they don't want to," said John with a smirk that made Safia think of Dario.

"Or we could just target your friends and go after them, even if you are expelled. But really Miss Safia. This whole thing would be a lot easier for you if you just decided to be a good girl and play along. Less hassle on both our sides really, since there really is no fun in just outright having you expelled through alternative means."

"And what happens if I lose these games?"

"Huh? Well, nothing really. You just keep going about your life as usual. That is, unless you lose all your points, then you and any discarded you have accumulated will be expelled. But you already knew that."

Safia nodded her head. "I get it. I'll play along. But if

possible, I'd like to ask for something."

"Oh, really. Well, considering that you are our newest pet. I suppose it would make sense to allow you a treat. Tell us, what would you like?"

"The first is that I'd like to cut the amount that I must find in half. From ten to five, then I ask only that I find one per month. I think that's reasonable."

"Hmm. I can accept that. It may even force us to become more active in seeing which ones you will get and which ones you won't. Okay, five will do, and points will be rewarded based on who you find. This is actually more exciting than before. And what else do you have in mind?"

"May we start next month? I've just gotten back, and I would like to get some things in order before I really have to start thinking about all of this."

"Well, I don't see why not. That is a very reasonable request, and I'd like to think that we here are all understanding people," said Frilla raising her hands while looking around to see most of those wearing masks nodding their heads in agreement.

"Thank you."

"No, thank you for making this as painless as it needed to be," said Frilla as she tapped on her pendant, as all those in attendance did the same. "So Safia Famosa, I humbly invite you to play a game of 'Finders Keepers'. In this themed game, you will be asked to find who is under these masks. Over the next six months, we will come and try to befriend you, giving hints as to who they are; the fox, the rabbit, the parrot, the snake, the turtle, the deer, the pig, the panda, the sun, and the moon."

Safia looked over the room cautiously as everyone just stared at her. The white glow of her badge circled around the jewel in the center. "So, I just need to find out who some of you are. What will I need to risk?"

"We will start out with thirty thousand points per person."

*Thirty thousand? I don't have points like that.* Safia tried not to show her emotions. "I don't mind, but you all must realize I'm not as rich in points as you are. After a few failures, then I'll be out of this game."

"Oh, no need to worry about that. It seems two of our members have inadvertently decided to give you a handicap by removing their masks. So, their points are literally up for grabs. That should start you off nicely, and only means you actually need to figure out three of us for this semester."

Safia tapped on her badge. "Then I, Safia Famosa, accept this game of 'Finder's Keepers."

"That's a good girl," said Frilla as the badges of the other masked member glowed in unison. "Is there anything else you would like to know before we start?"

"No, that's all. Can I go now? I really need to get back."

"Yes, of course," said Frilla, a little taken aback by Safia's lack of reaction. "You are able to leave whenever you wish."

"Thank you. I guess, I will see you all when the game starts then," said Safia as she turned around, calmly walking out of the room. The moment she closed the door, she turned on her tablet and opened up a writing app. *The Fox, Turtle, Deer, and ahh.... Dammit Safia, remember. This is important. It was... it was... Yes! The Snake and the Eagle were also girls. The rest were boys then. Except for the Sun and the Moon, I couldn't tell who they were.*

Remembering all that she could, Safia leaned up against the wall, rubbing her arm with her free hand. *The boy in the Rabbit mask. What was his name? John, I think it was John. I can't let them just have their way. But I don't know what I can do. There must be something. Something I can do to get them to leave me alone.* She pulled herself from the wall, making her way back down the steps. *I need to get back.*

# CHAPTER 4

Safia stood by the window of her dorm looking outside the window over the side of the campus. Her eyes felt heavy as she wasn't able to get much sleep the night before. *I have a month to figure out what I'm going to do.* She sighed. *So much for coming back to school and just focusing on schoolwork. It's not enough that I have to worry about whatever Jericho has planned for me. But now I have to worry about a whole other group of idiots. Maybe if I tell him, he'll think of something. It's not like he's not affected by this.*

The door to her room opened and in walked Mallory, holding her bathing items and a towel wrapped around her hair and body. She smiled, spotting Safia by the window.

"You're still thinking about it. Have you decided what you're going to do?"

"No, not yet. It's not like I can do much anyway, except play along. I think I'll tell Jericho. He might have some ideas."

Mallory frowned, "I still don't know how I—"

The door to the room swung open again as Hashmi entered the room, already fully dressed.

"Where have you been?" asked Safia.

"Just went for a morning walk. After what you told us yesterday. I thought it would be a nice habit to start in order to clear my mind. And given what you're into, it seems we are going to have a lot to think about."

"Do you think they would be mad if we tried helping you find out who they are?" asked Mallory.

"I don't think so. I mean, they didn't say that I couldn't have anyone help me. So, I guess it's okay."

"Yes, but how are we supposed to know who is who? You said they were wearing masks the whole time, right? I hardly see how we could be of any help with this."

"They said they would try approaching me and giving out clues as to who they are. I suppose that could also mean getting close to either of you as well."

"Well, that just sounds so roundabout that they seem intent on driving us all mad."

"Yes," said Safia with a laugh. "I can see how..."

Her pendant vibrated on the desk as it began flashing white. "The 'Finders Keepers' wager information has been sent to your device," spoke the pendant as Safia walked over, picking it up. "The 'Finders Keepers' wager information has been—" Safia clicked the jewel to make it stop speaking.

"I must admit that our pendants have the most annoying sound when it speaks. Makes me wonder if there is a way to use it as an alarm clock. It wouldn't be so hard to wake Mallory up then."

"Hey, I don't sleep that deeply. Do I?"

"Well, I believe I once tripped over you, stumbled over to Safia's bed and fell on top of her and somehow you still did not awake from your slumber. So yes, you are indeed a deep sleeper."

Safia reached over to her bed picking up the tablet. On it there was a new icon in the shape of a cartoon child's face. Clicking on it, it opened another page where ten cartoon icons slowly swayed back and forth. Each icon represented a mask that was worn in the room.

"I guess that means that the game has officially started."

"Safia. Don't take offense to this, but you seem a lot calmer about this than I expected you to be."

"Do I? Well, I can promise I don't feel that way. But I need to try to make as few mistakes as I can, I don't want to end up in a situation like last time with both of us almost getting expelled," said Safia, as she clicked on the face of the rabbit icon and a text field appeared, prompting her to enter a name. "If I remember correctly, they called him John." She typed the name in and pressed enter. The words turned white to gold.

"Safia has found one of the ten names and has been awarded points," said the pendant.

"You won. But it didn't tell you how many points."

Safia watched as thirty thousand points flashed across the screen. "Apparently it appears on the screen." She turned the tablet to face her friends.

"What? Really? For just typing in someone's name?"

"I guess they were telling the truth, then. They want me to find the names of four more people and each name will give me another thirty thousand points, I guess."

"And if you put in the wrong name."

"Then I'll lose thirty thousand, probably."

"And did you have thirty thousand points before you typed in that name?"

"Yes, but only barely."

"Goodness, that was reckless."

"It didn't seem as if she wanted me to lose. Well, at least not right away, since it would spoil their fun. So, I figured it would work. And if it didn't, I still would have had a few points to support myself and Mallory for the next month till

I figured out what went wrong."

"I have faith in you, Safia. I know you'll find a way to win," said Mallory, as she walked over to the closet to grab her clothes.

"I'm glad you do, because I sure don't."

"Come on, let's get ready for class," said Hashmi as she walked back over to her bed. "The few points we get there might still come in handy."

Leaving their dorm a few minutes later, the girls made their way about the campus. While not as obvious as before, Safia could still tell that more than a few of the students on campus were watching them closely as they passed.

"Do you suppose they will ever stop? Or are we just doomed to live the life of a sideshow attraction while we attend this school?"

"It's school. All gossip dies down eventually, and they'll just move on to whatever other thing they find to talk about."

"Yeah, but isn't it the first day of school? I thought I would see more people betting on things."

"Maybe things have changed," said Safia as they continued on their morning walk. Eventually, they made it to the front steps of the school and headed inside through the heavy wooden doors.

"I'll see you all later," said Mallory as she made her way to the second floor.

"Oh, that's right," said Safia, watching her friend leave. "Mallory's in her second year now. I forgot about that."

"Yes, I also forgot that fact. Also, she still hasn't told us about how she ended up with Dario before she met us. Have you asked her about it yet?"

"No. Things have always been so complicated that I never really got the chance. You think I should?"

Hashmi sighed. "It's an issue that I'm sure you will be force to confront eventually. You know how she feels about you, and you haven't addressed it yet, have you?"

"As I said, I've been busy. There really hasn't been

the best time to talk about it. And even if I did, what am I supposed to say?"

"I understand. But remember, when emotions get involved, you can never predict what someone will do."

"I know. You're right, I'll try to talk to her today. I guess it is better to try to handle it before school really gets started," said Safia as she opened the door to their class. Inside, she found half the class sitting down at their desks, with a few others standing about, chatting with each other. As Safia made her way inside, she could see a few familiar faces. Or a familiar head of hair in Jericho's case, since he was face down on the desk, face between his arms.

Safia and Hashmi found two seats next to each other, once again by the window. It wasn't long before Miss Abigail entered the class, and all the rest of the students took their seats.

"Hello, students. There are quite a few unfamiliar faces." She glanced at Safia. "And a few pleasant old ones. Welcome to Economics 102: World Manipulation. In this class, we will delve deeper into how the world truly works and how you are to navigate it. Now, this is unlike the last class module, so there will be six specific moments in history that we will look into. And those are King Mansa Musa's trip to Mecca; Genghis Khan and his Mongol Empire; the foolish king Neo Claudius; China's only female empress, Wu Zetian; and finally, the rise of bubblegum."

"Bubblegum?" asked one of the students in class. "How did we go from famous world leaders to damn bubble gum?"

"It sounds weird, but bubblegum has had a profound effect on the world economy in terms of its influence. Plus, it's a good idea to mix in odd topics for a bit of variety in class," said Abigail as she reached under her desk and pulled out a brown box, placing it on the table. "Let us reach and see what we will be discussing for our first month." She reached into the box, letting her hand rummage around for a bit before pulling out a piece of folded paper, before opening it. "Genghis Khan will be our first topic of discussion."

A large amount of the class sighed.

"What? Were you all hoping for bubblegum?"

"Yes," spoke up one disappointed class member.

"Sorry, but that topic will have to wait for another month. Now who here can tell me a little something about Genghis Khan?"

"He was Chinese like Kaori over there."

"I am Japanese, idiot."

"Oops."

"We must respect our cultural differences," said Abigail, shaking her head. "Please, try not to intentionally say anything others might find absurdly offensive."

"Hey," said another boy in class. "Did you really marry that point freak that everyone keeps talking about?"

Abigail sighed. "In particular, things like that. And to answer you and the rest of the classes' curiosity, yes, I did."

"So, are you like his discarded now or something? Do you have to do whatever he tells you?"

"Is what your definition of what a wife is? Someone who does whatever you say? If so, then perhaps you and Genghis Khan have a lot more in common than you think."

"It's not like that," said another girl, turning around in her seat to the boy. "I just became a discarded to my friend, and he's not trying to make me do anything stupid like you're talking about. And now, I don't have to worry about all this betting nonsense. If you find someone you trust, all you're essentially doing is just sharing points."

"That certainly is true, Miss Derks, but trust in this school is in limited supply and not so freely given. Tell me, how long have you known this friend of yours?"

"What, Richard? We've known each other since we were in pre-school."

"Then I'd hazard a guess that you are in a very unique situation."

The young woman looked around the class confused at

all the other students nodding their heads in agreement, while at the same time Safia couldn't help but be reminded of Mallory at how naïve the girl appeared to be.

*I wonder if I was like that when I first got here.*

"Okay, so back to our original question. What can anyone in the class tell us about Genghis Khan?"

"That he was the warlord of the Mongol Empire," said Kaori. "Although classifying him as Chinese is debatable. That is like saying Hitler was Jewish because he took over Jewish lands. Or the Americans who stayed in Japan after the second world war are now technically Japanese."

"Ha! So, you are Chinese," said the boy from before. "How else would you know all of that?"

"It is called reading and educating oneself. Something I encourage you to try. That is, if that brain of yours can ever get past 'one plus one equals dumbass.'"

Safia found her covering her mouth, trying to hold back her own laughter.

"Okay, no need for insults, no matter how well deserved," said Abigail, looking over at the boy. "And let's continue our discussion. Just this in a more civil manner."

The class continued for the most part without interruption, except to ask questions on the topic.

"Okay, that's the end of class," said Abigail as all the students rose from their desks. "At the end of the month, I'm going to expect a twenty-page report from all of you on your opinions of the leader Genghis Khan."

The class moaned again.

"Don't you think twenty pages is a bit much? We do have other classes to attend."

"We will be spending the coming month in discussion on this. So don't worry, you will learn a lot by just attending class."

As the rest of the class left, Safia stood with Hashmi and made her way over toward Abigail, who was stuffing her notes back inside of her tote bag.

"Excuse me," said Kaori, stopping Safia before she could meet with her teacher. "You are Safia Famosa, correct?"

"Ah, yes," said Safia, surprised to be stopped by the young Japanese man. "Can I help you?"

"Good, I would like to speak with you if you have the time."

"Well," said Safia before watching her chance to speak with Abigail slip away as she left the room. "Okay. What can I help you with?"

"Thank you. May we go for a walk?"

"Sure," said Safia, confused by the boy's invitation. *Is this part of the game? Was he one of the people in the room?* "Let's go for a walk, I guess." She turned towards Hashmi. "We can meet up later then if—"

"No, your friend is welcome to join us."

Hashmi shrugged her shoulders, and they all left out of the classroom and down the hallway. "Should we wait for Mallory, then?"

"Her classes usually last a bit longer than ours. So, we can meet up with her later."

"I was hoping I would find you in class today. Given all that has happened, I was not certain that you would appear," said Kaori as he led them through the marbled hallway.

"Why would I miss class?"

"Because of your situation with all the second years. It has been much of the talk of the school these last few days," said Kaori as they exited out of the school and onto the steps. "Come, we can walk over to this tree."

They all stepped off the path and headed towards the tree by the school until they were safely under its shade and out of the mid-day sun.

"So, what is it that you wanted to tell me?"

"It's about your brother Yago."

"Yago!" yelped Safia, unable to conceal her surprise. "He's here? Have you seen him?"

"Yes, but he asked that you not try to find him."

"What! Why? Is he in trouble?"

"No, not at the moment. But after getting here, he realized that he would be a burden to you if others found out that you were related."

"What! No, he wouldn't. He's my brother. How would he--"

"Perhaps I misspoke. Burden may not be the best word. The way he described it was that he would become what Mallory is to you. That people would try to use him as an attempt to affect you."

"But... but," said Safia, trying to think of something to say. "Can I not at least see him and talk about it?"

"I do not think so. But he has said for me to tell you that he misses you and that he loves you. But it is best for him to stay away for a while."

"Safia," said Hashmi. "You may not like it. But I think this makes sense."

"What? But how?"

"You do not know this. But even I have been approached because of my association with you. People have tried goading me into giving up my religious exemption. I would suspect this is because they are looking for ways to affect you."

"But... but that's just stupid."

"And is this school not filled with stupid scenarios like such?"

"Why have you never mentioned this to me?"

"What purpose would that serve? To provide you with unneeded worry? And besides, I am more than capable of taking care of myself. You should worry about yourself and Mallory, not me."

Safia placed her hands on her forehead in frustration. "How am I even supposed to keep all of this straight? I've barely been back a week, and it feels like everything is my fault." She looked at Kaori, "Will you just tell Yago that I could use his help? It's not as if this is easy for me."

"I will tell him. Take care, Miss Safia," said Kaori before turning around and heading back off toward the school walkway.

"Well, at least you know your brother is here now. That should provide you some relief," said Hashmi as she leaned her back against the tree. "But I must admit that I would like to meet this brother of yours. After the stories you've told me of him, he seems very interesting."

"Great," said Safia, watching Kaori make his way through the walkways. "And what good does it do me? He won't even let me see him."

"Maybe he will appear eventually. I mean, this is a campus. How long will it be before we run into him?"

"It's been a week so far, and even looking for him, we couldn't find him. So, I don't have much hope that he will just randomly pop up."

"Come on, classes are done. We might as well go and have another look around campus while we have the time."

Safia shook her head and headed off with Hashmi while tapping on her pendant. "Message for my discarded, Mallory. We're headed out, you can meet us in the cafeteria if you want. We may end up there."

Both girls stepped onto the path and made their way down the winding roads.

"Cafeteria? Is that what you call the lunch hall?"

"Yeah, why. What do you call it?"

"I suppose a canteen or a refectory."

"Refectory? I've never heard of that word. I don't even know what that word means."

"Really, I guess it's a cultural thing then. You suppose Miss Mallory calls it something else also?"

"She is from Florida, so it's possible."

They continued on their way with Hashmi, trying her best to keep Safia's mind off of her situation as best she could. Their discussion would swap back and forth through many topics as they made their way across campus, before standing in line waiting to be allowed entrance into the dining hall.

"Oh, it's that same fellow from before in the chef's hat. I guess that's his official job for the school then."

"Have you ever seen him in any of your classes?

"No. Never."

"Maybe he's a second year then. But I think I remember seeing him selling things in the stands when they held the skating competition."

"Maybe he's like Jericho, always doing odd jobs around the school for points."

"Okay, next up," said the boy in the chef's hat. "Oh, it's the girls everyone's talking about. Where's your discarded? Is she not with you today?"

"No. But she should be coming soon. Can I pay for her now?"

"Sure. That's no problem, as long as you agree to the withdrawal of the monthly food points for both of you."

"I do."

"Awesome, He waved the metal wand over Safia's and Hashmi's badge and they both flashed white."

"Monthly food budget has been accepted," said both their badges.

"Hey, can I ask you something?"

"Sure. What's up? Why the chef's outfit?"

"Why not. I think it makes me look dashing. What? Do you want me to come over and cook something for you?"

"Depends. Can you cook?"

"Not at all, but maybe you can teach me. I like learning new skills. My names Mauricio, Mauricio Astudillo."

"That's an interesting name. Where are you from?"

"Caracas, Venezuela, senorita, and you."

"America, Michigan."

"Really, I had thought with a name like Famosa that," he shrugged his shoulders. "You know."

"My father's Cuban."

"Ah, I see, that makes sense."

"Hey, go flirt on your own time," said a boy behind them. "We're hungry back here." A sentiment that was echoed by a few of those behind him.

"Oops," said Safia with a smile. "I'll head on in then," said Safia as stepped up into the building with Hashmi.

"I'll see you around Miss Famosa," said Mauricio, giving Safia a smirk before turning back to scan in more students.

"What was that?" asked Hashmi with a grin on her face. "Have you taken an interest in the chef boy?"

"No, not especially. But I am remembering everyone that was somewhat nice to me before all of this mess started. And since he works in line with everyone, he probably knows a lot of people. Which might help me learn some of the names of those people who were inside of that room."

"You're starting to sound like one of those detectives in the mystery novels I used to read as a child."

Safia looked around at all the faces as she entered the eatery. "Yeah, well, I can't think of a time in my life when I needed a mystery solved more than now."

"So, what are your plans, now that you've apparently found your brother?"

"Knowing Yago, he's not just sitting back doing nothing. What I really want to know is how much he knows. The least he could have done is visit me once. Would that really have hurt him so much?"

Safia sat down at a table with her food, joined by Hashmi. But it wasn't long before Mallory came in.

"Sorry I'm late," said Mallory as she sat beside Safia. "Classes went a lot longer than I thought they would."

"Is being a second year that stressful?" asked Safia with a smile as she saw Mallory's flushed face.

"It is for those of us that attend class. Mr. Hennig seems like the type of professor who is going to make us do a lot of reports."

"Hennig? I've never met him before. Wait!" said Safia,

tilting her head. "What do you mean, those of you that attend class? Do some students not have to?"

"No, some students can buy an A out of their classes if they have enough points."

"Why am I not surprised?"

"It's not cheap. I've heard it's like one hundred thousand points or something."

Safia began rubbing her face. "And these are the people I'm going to have to deal with."

"And who are you going to have to be dealing with?" asked a familiar but unwanted voice from behind them as Addison appeared, taking a seat at the table on the other side of Safia. "You three hiding more secrets? Care to let me in on them? I might be able to make some points by spilling them, since you're so popular now."

"No!" said Mallory, disgusted. "Why are you here? Go away."

"I second that sentiment," said Safia.

"Oh, am I not welcome? And here I thought I had joined your little group. A shame for you to leave me out after taking all your little friend's home with you," said Addison as she reached over, plucking a piece of food from Safia's tray and popping it in her mouth. She chewed slowly while smirking across the table at Mallory, who narrowed her eyes back at her.

"Why are you here?" asked Safia, trying her best to ignore the sudden tension at their table.

"What? Am I not allowed to come over and say hello to friends?"

"You are if we were friends. But I don't remember that ever happening. So, why are you here?"

Addison frowned before ripping another piece of food from Safia's tray. "Nasir started crying and asked me to try and make nicey-nice with little Miss Uppity over there. So here I am, doing my part for the man who makes me feel good."

"You really are such a vulgar woman," said Hashmi, the disapproval of the conversation clear on her face.

"And you are just some pissy—"

"No! Let's not start this again," said Safia, coming between the two. "Addison, I'm sorry, but I can't say that I trust you any more than they do."

Addison was silent for just a moment and Safia thought she could see the hurt in her eyes.

*I think I just made a big mistake.*

"Well, fuck it. I tried. You three can have your little prissy bitch group for all I care," said Addison, standing up from the table. She turned to go but Safia grabbed her by the arm, causing her to stumble, dropping her tray of food on the floor. "The fuck is wrong with you, let me go, or I swear—"

"Let me finish," said Safia, standing up from the table staring Addison in her eyes. "You're always so quick to speak. Listen!" They had gotten the attention of the entire room now, as everyone turned to stare at them. *I hope I'm doing the right thing.* "I was saying, but I would like to try to be your friend. I think you're a nice person. You just don't know how to show it, so you lash out at people."

Hashmi and Mallory stared up at Safia in shock, not knowing what to say. While Addison found herself red faced as she began looking around at the people staring at them.

"I like you, Addison, I really do," said Safia loud enough to make sure everyone could hear.

"Hey, keep your voice down," said Addison.

"I want us to be friends. But I want you to start being nice to Hashmi and Mallory. They've done nothing to cause you to treat them the way you do. So how about we all try again?"

"Let go of me, dammit," said Addison, snatching her hand away. "I don't know what game you're playing, but you should stop."

"So, you're going to start being nice to us now?"

"What? I didn't say that."

"You didn't *not* say that either."

Addison was quiet for a moment, but Safia could see that she was trying to think of something to say.

*Oh, no you don't. I'm not going to give you the chance to use that smart mouth of yours.* Safia outstretched her arms and stepped toward Addison. "I'm going to hug you now."

"What! Get back. Don't touch me," said Addison, before turning around. "I don't know what you…" She took another look at Safia before looking around nervously. "I'll see you later. I… I… I gotta go see Nasir." And with that Addison made a quick retreat out of the cafeteria, leaving Safia behind to clean up the mess. Which she soon found out was unnecessary as a student with a mop and bucket came out and began to clean the spilled food.

"Oh! Sorry about that," said Safia, as she knelt, grabbing a pan to help him scoop up the waste.

"Don't be. That was fun to watch," said the boy as he squatted beside her. "Do you always make friends that way?"

"Sometimes, when I think it will work."

The boy smiled back at her. It was a cute smile to match his green eyes. "Thank you. Not many people help me clean up the messes."

"Seeing as I am the cause of the mess. I really don't see how I have a choice."

"Then you're better than most. What's your name?"

"Safia."

"Hey Safia. My name's Dell."

"Hey Dell," said Safia as she smiled back.

"I should probably take this mess back. But I'll see you around, Safia."

"Okay. Thanks again," said Safia as Dell left and she sat back down at the table.

"What was that?"

"That was me, embarrassing Addison."

"I wasn't under the impression that she could be

embarrassed.

*Neither was I.* A smirk made its way across Safia's lips. *But that look on her face. It was fun watching her squirm for once. I can admit to myself that I really did enjoy that.*

"But the question on my mind is why? Why try to befriend her now?"

"I wasn't going to. But for some reason, I felt that if she were to walk away just then, as mad as she was, then I would have regretted it. Plus, she made me a little angry, and I saw a good chance to get back at her."

"And you didn't think it would backfire in some way?"

"I did, but I remembered that she's dating Nasir, and he's a good person. And no matter what she acts like with us, she might act a little different when it comes to being with him. So, I bet on that."

"Were you really going to give her a hug?"

"Yeah, Yago used to embarrass me like that in school all the time. He would run up to me screaming 'Saffy, Saffy,' and hug me after class and shout how much he loved me. It was the most self-conscious I'd ever felt in my life. And given how Addison acts, there was no way she'd be used to that type of affection being thrown at her."

"Maybe you are meant to be here after all. I'm not sure I could have done that. Although I will admit, it was fun to see her run away like that. Perhaps you should make signs next time."

"No, thank you. I never said I didn't feel embarrassed with everyone here looking at me like I'm crazy."

"You are ever the reluctant tactician now, aren't you?"

"Well, I can promise you that I don't enjoy thinking like this. I just can't help it now and—"

"The delivery of your new item has arrived and been installed," spoke the pendant.

"That must be Mallory's bed. Guess that means no more sleeping on the floor for you."

"Really, Miss Safia, I didn't mind."

"Well, I did. I got tired of almost stepping on you every morning."

"You two could have always slept together," said Hashmi with a smirk.

"The bed wasn't big enough for that. One of us would end up getting pushed off, or I'd roll off in my sleep," said Safia, standing up from the table. "Come on, let's head back."

Finishing their meals, the girls headed back through the campus. It didn't take them long before they arrived at Yennefer house and made their way upstairs. Opening their door, Hashmi stepped inside and smiled.

"Safia, what did you tell the people that you wanted?"

"What? I told them that we needed two beds, since Mallory and I were living together."

Hashmi laughed. "I do believe you should have stated that better. I think they may have misunderstood."

"What do you mean?" asked Safia, stepping into the room. She didn't speak for a moment. She just stared at the large sized bed over on her side of the room. And then at Hashmi's small bed on her side of the room.

"Because I do wonder if you said you needed two beds or a bed for two people," said Hashmi, unable to control her giggling. "Oh my. This does remind me of that conversation we had some time back about your luck with women."

"But I distinctly remember saying two beds. How could they mess this up?"

Mallory went over, sprawling herself out on the bed, rolling around on top of the sheets. "Oh, it's so soft."

Hashmi stepped closer to Safia to whisper in her ear. "Remember that conversation I told you to have with Miss Mallory? Well, I expect you're going to be having it soon, whether you like it or not."

Safia turned toward Hashmi, her lips bawled up and eyes wide.

"Oh, it seems Addison isn't the only one who will be

embarrassed today. I guess the world really does work in cycles," said Hashmi as she went to her closet, grabbing some toiletries, and a wash towel. "I suppose I'll leave you two alone for a while. Privacy is important after all." And with that, Hashmi left the room, closing the door behind her.

As Safia watched the door close behind her friend, she felt as if it was sealing her fate. With a deep breath and then a sigh, she turned back around to see Mallory with a smile across her face as she sat up on the bed.

"Mallory, we should have a talk."

"Yes."

"It's about... us."

"Okay. I wanted to ask you some things, but you know. It just never felt like the right time. With us going to your home and then with your brother, and everything else that's happening. I know you said you don't really like girls. But you said you are on a break from David, so since you don't have a boyfriend, maybe if you'd just—"

"I'm sorry. But as I've said before, I've had female friends before, but I've never thought of girls as lovers or anything like that."

"Oh," said Mallory, her gaze dropping to the floor. "I thought... that maybe... that maybe you wanted us to become closer."

"I do... just not like that."

Mallory brought her knees up to her chest and wrapped her arms around them. To her surprise, Safia saw the already small girl begin to appear even smaller. It was as if she could feel her going back inside out herself.

"I'm sorry. You've already done so much for me. I'm... you probably think I'm being selfish."

"No," said Safia, as she stepped closer over to the bed. "You're not being selfish. Maybe I am." She began scratching the back of her head. *Ahhh! What do I even fucking say to fix this?* "I just don't want to give you the wrong idea."

"Even if I told you that I think I love you?" asked Mallory, her eyes beginning to water. "I mean, you're nice to me. And you don't make me do stuff. I just... I just want to be around you so much."

*What the fuck am I supposed to do when you say stuff like that?* "I love you too Mallory, but just not the way you want me to. I hope you understand. I want us to keep being friends even if not in the way you would like me to." *Don't take advantage of her, Safia. This is why you and David broke up, remember? You can't hurt Mallory like that.* Safia bite down on the inside of her gums as she looked at Mallory. Somewhere inside of her there was a feeling welling up and she was trying her best to suppress it.

"I understand," said Mallory, removing herself from the bed and standing on the floor next to Safia. "I guess we can get rid of the bed then."

"No," said Safia, wrapping her arms around Mallory, embracing her. "It's here now, and I think the movers would get mad at me if I called them back. Let's keep it unless you mind sleeping next to me."

Mallory gripped the back of Safia's uniform, her head against her shoulder, refusing to show Safia her face. "Thank you. I... I'd like that."

*I don't know what I'm doing anymore. But at least this... this feels like I'm doing the right thing.*

# CHAPTER 5

It was early in the morning as Safia sat on a bench along the spiral walkway beneath one of the streetlamps. She'd sat here for some time just waiting as she watched the wind blow through the leaves of a nearby tree.

*I wonder if I just tried to run away, what would happen? Would they send someone to find me?* She gave a small laugh. *They would, and the person they'd send would probably have a gun with those sleeping things.* As she sat there in the morning's sun, she watched as a few students made their way across the campus. *I wonder if they think this place is weird or do they accept it as normal. I mean, there has to be a reason for doing this, right? Like, where do they get the money for all this? The buildings, the cameras, all of it must cost a fortune. Who—* Her thinking pattern halted as she saw another figure approach her.

"Hello there," said Jericho, as he came walking up to

her. "I was hoping you would be here."

"Why wouldn't I be? I mean, isn't that the game now? I have to do what you say?"

"Maybe, but you don't need to be so hostile about it," said Jericho as he squatted beside the streetlamp, looking down at its base.

"What are you doing?"

"Checking out this light. It has a crack down here, and it squeaks on the bolts what are supposed to be holding it down, so I'll probably have to replace it," he said before standing back up and taking a seat beside her. "But that's something for another time. Back on the topic of me and you, you do know that I really am trying to look out for you."

"You mean look out for yourself?"

"There's no reason they can't be one and the same. I am trying to build something, and I can't do it alone. And in the process of doing that, I think it would benefit you as well."

"Usually when people want help, they ask for it. Not blackmail someone into doing what they want."

"Well, looking at things objectively, if I didn't blackmail you, you would have been expelled and all of this would have ended anyway."

Safia was quiet.

"See. Even you can't deny that what I did saved you. So, how about we work together and build something great? And besides, don't you think I'm cute? I even brushed my hair for you." He ran his fingers through his hair, showing how bouncy it was. "I'd say you've done pretty well for yourself to have me telling you what to do."

"Just tell me what you want."

"There's this small gathering of first and second years today after classes in the Eco -101 room at four o'clock. There will be a few interesting people in attendance. I want you to be there."

"Is there a reason?"

"Experience. You're still not used to how things work

here. Before I can really use you, I need for you to understand what is happening around you."

"It's not like I want to get used to this. And you say we're in this together, but you don't have people looking at you funny every time you step out of your room."

"We are in this together. I've just always known better than to stand out. I let everyone here think I'm just a simple-minded guy who likes to build stuff and, for the most part, they can't even be bothered to look my way. Do you know why? It's because they think I'm boring."

"Well, congratulations. You've managed to fool them all."

"Even now. With us sitting here. What do you think people are thinking about when they see us?"

Safia glanced around for a moment, catching the several people glancing in her direction as they passed on their way to wherever they were headed.

"I don't know. Maybe that we're both idiots?"

Jericho laughed. "Close. Most of them think that you're the one manipulating me."

"What? How?"

"Think about it. You're the one who's mysterious. You have all this attention; you managed to escape the campus; somehow beat the unbeatable Killian; taken Mallory from Dario; and you've befriended Amanda, who is a mystery in her own right. And contrast to that, here I am, just some random first year who likes to build stuff for a few measly points. In their eyes, you might as well be the freaking Queen of the campus right now."

Safia shook her head. *This is ridiculous.* "And you couldn't pick anyone else to toy with?"

"I could have, but none of them were as smart or as perfect as you are."

"What do you mean?"

"You'll see. I'm not the only one interested in you."

"I know that. That reminds me. Some girl named Frilla

came to me. She's making me come see her in a few days. Do you know anything about her? I think she's in her second year."

"Yeah, I know her," said Jericho, as he rubbed his chin in contemplation. "I often build things for the games that only involve second-year students. It may be a good thing she's taken an interest in you."

"What? You want to become her friend as well?"

"Now there's an idea. But no, for other reasons I think it would be hard for me to be her friend. For now, I'll just continue to build those games for her."

"Fine, you said you wanted me to be in the Eco 101 room at four o'clock, right? Can I go now?"

"Of course. You're free to go," said Jericho as he leaned forward on the bench as Safia stood. "Wait, before you go. I want you to grab me by the collar, lift my head, and kiss me."

"What?"

"Don't argue, just do it. We have a deal, after all. There is a reason for it."

*Oh, fuck this.* Safia's anger bubbled up inside of her as she reached down, grabbing him by the tie, twisting it in her hand until it dug into the skin of his neck. He lifted off his seat as she pulled him up to meet her. With the momentum of her pulling him up, and his weight pulling her down, their lips met in a crash. The kiss was forceful, the two breathing each other in as they stared into each other's eyes for a long moment. Tolerating as much of their false intimacy as she could, she pulled away from him, tugging at his neck and tossing him aside as fell back to the bench.

Safia then turned around and began walking away, not even wanting to look at his reaction. But she made sure to audibly spit the taste of him from her mouth where he could see her.

*If there is a way to get you back for this. I swear I'm going to find it.* She made her way back across campus, her heart pounding in her chest. She could still taste him on her lips, a soft wooden taste, as if he'd been cutting lumber all day. But it disgusted her; and that disgust pumped through her blood and across her back, causing her to stiffen her shoulders.

With heavy feet, she made her way back through the campus toward her dorm. After kissing Jericho, she did notice people watching her. They're veering eyes silently judging her for things she had no control over. It didn't seem fair. But that was the point, wasn't it? It wasn't fair. It was never meant to be.

It wasn't long before she found herself standing in front of her room door, her hand trembling as she placed it on the door. *Calm down, Safia. Just try not to think about it. Just get ready for class.*

Opening the door, she was surprised to see a topless Mallory with her back turned to her. She was sitting down on a stool with a bucket of water beside her.

"Oh, Miss Safia, you surprised me."

"I surprised you?" asked Safia, stepping into the room and quickly shutting the door behind her. "Why are you in here with your clothes off?"

"The waters broken. Didn't you see the people outside working on it?"

"No. I... I must have missed them. I've had a few things on my mind."

"Oh, did your meeting with Mr. Jericho not go so well? You said he just wanted to talk."

"No," said Safia. "He wants me to go to some meeting today after class, that's all. Just the way he talks, it pisses me off. That's all."

"Okay. If you wish to talk about it. I... I'm here for you. That is... you know... if you want to," said Mallory as she tried to reach around her waist to scrub her back.

"No... It's fine," said Safia as she stepped forward, taking the wash rag from Mallory's hand. "Here, let me do it."

"You don't have to..."

"No, I want to... I want to focus on something else, rather than thinking about Jericho."

"Ah, okay then," said Mallory, resigning her back to Safia as she dunked the towel in the water, squeezing a large amount from it before placing it against Mallory's back. *Why am I doing this? She's such a sweet girl, but it's getting to the point where I can't help myself. I... I'm starting to feel like...*

"Ouch, Safia that hurts."

"What?" asked Safia, looking down to see she had dropped the rag and her hand was tight around the back of Mallory's neck, squeezing it tight enough that it was turning red. She quickly removed it, reaching down to grab the rag, before dunking it back in the water. "I'm sorry, I wasn't paying attention. Are you okay?"

"It's fine. It just made my neck feel stiff, is all."

*Dammit, Safia. Get a hold of yourself. You're better than this. Remember what happened the last time you went too far. You're better than that. Just... just think of something else. You have a million other things to think about.*

As she went about scrubbing, she found that her mind did indeed drift away from her thoughts of Jericho. Instead, she focused on her friend's shoulders, the way the water dripped down her back, or how her hair had grown since they'd met. Realizing where she was, Safia looked around the room.

*Well, if there was ever a right moment. I suppose it's now. It's not like she'll run out of the room half naked.* "Mallory, can I ask you to tell me something?"

"What is it?" asked Mallory as she lifted her hair for Safia to rub the cloth over the back of her neck.

"It's about Dario. I know I asked you about him before. But I want you to tell me about what he had you do while you were with him."

There was a long, long silence in the room as Safia felt Mallory tremble through the wash rag.

"Did he force you to have sex with him?"

"It... no, he couldn't. When I became his discarded. That... that was part of the deal we made. I... I didn't want to end up like my sister."

*Sister? Did your sister come to this school before you?*

"He... he wasn't that bad when I met him. Or... maybe he was, and I didn't notice," said Mallory, her voice breaking as tears began to flow down her face, mixing in with the small amounts of bath water still left on her face. "But he'd have me do other things. For his bets, he would have me strip naked in front of his friends. They would... they would then all try to paint a picture on my body, and whoever would come closest to it would win the points."

Once again, Safia felt her shoulders stiffen the way they did after kissing Jericho. But this time it felt different. It wasn't the slow-building dull feeling that turned her stomach. This time it felt quicker, thicker. It was as if she could taste it. The feeling seemed to eat away at her chest, and she could actually feel herself getting hotter.

"There were other times," said Mallory. "Like when he would just take his time taking my clothes off, make me put them back on so he could just take them off again. Then there were times he'd make me watch as he had sex with other girls or... or the time... when... when he'd—"

Mallory stopped as Safia's arms embraced her, wrapping them around the girl's waist as she brought her closer, the wetness of her skin soaking into her pleated school uniform.

"It's fine. I'm not going anywhere. Take your time," said Safia, barely able to contain her own trembling as Mallory began to sob in her arms. *And here I was thinking... thinking.* She shook her head. *I hate myself sometimes. But it's fine, now at least I know what I want to do. I'm going to kill him. No, not that. More than that. I'm going to break him.*

# CHAPTER 6

Safia and Mallory sat in the right library; several open books lay across the table as the girls went about checking their notes. The quietness was a welcome change to the chaotic nature of the past few days. Safia had missed the meeting that Jericho had asked her to attend, but he hadn't contacted her about it, and she wouldn't bring it up if he didn't.

"Why do I need to know any of this stuff?" ask Safia as she scratched her head. "It all just seems so frivolous and useless." She held up a book, pointing to a picture of a soldier on a horse. "Why do I need to know about how Genghis Khan maintained his supply lines? He killed people, so that makes him a bad guy. Does it really matter how many grains of rice he had with him as he traveled from region to region murdering people?"

"At least your answer is actually in the textbook," said

Mallory as she began rubbing her hands over her eyes. "For second years, they just give you speculation. How many people do you think it takes to squash a rebellion in the fifteen hundreds if the castle had a population of one thousand?"

"What?"

"Exactly. I don't know anything about the fifteen hundreds except that they rode on horses and swung swords like in the movies. My teacher is asking me to plan out food rations and armor costs, and all kinds of other stuff."

"I am *not* looking forward to second year. Not that I was before."

"It's all so stupid," moaned Mallory as she dropped her head to the table, placing it between her arms. "I just want to go home and go back to sleep."

"Seeing as you still have another class, I don't think that's a good idea."

"I know, I know, I still need to—" said Mallory, her words freezing in her mouth as she focused on something in the distance.

Confused, Safia turned to see what had caught her attention, and it was there she saw Dario and his company of friends that shadowed him walking past an aisle of bookshelves. But just as they noticed him, he also noticed them and a smile crept on his face as he took a step towards them. One of his friends tried to stop him, placing a hand on his shoulder, but Dario waved him off and continued on his way over.

*Why do we even come to the library anymore? Every time someone shows up to annoy us.*

"So, here you are. I was wondering when I'd run into you again," said Dario as he turned towards Mallory. "Have you been taking care of my old pet? Although, I doubt you're having as much fun with her as I did."

"If I could punch you right now. I would," said Safia. "But the school prevents us from hurting each other. Even if one of us is trash and deserves it."

Dario leaned forward across the table, looking Safia in the eyes, lowering his voice. "Oh no, bitch. You don't understand. This school prevents unwanted attacks. But if both of us agree to it, then we're free to fuck each other up as much as we like." He reached over, placing his hand over Safia's wrist, and slowly began to squeeze. "So, what d'ya wanna do? I promise you that slap was nothing compared to what I want to do to ya."

Safia winced as his grip slowly tightened. She tried moving her arm, but he held it firmly down against the table. Undeterred, Safia's face changed to a smile as she placed her other hand on top of Dario's arm, digging her fingernails as hard as she could into the skin of his wrist. Dario gritted his teeth as they both stared at each other, neither willing to give ground.

"I might not be as strong as you, but don't think it'll be as easy as you want it to be. I've fought boys before, and I'll rip your eyes out before you can do anything to me.

"Yeah, I'd like to see you—"

"Oh, Dario. It's nice to see you are getting along with our little pet project," said Frilla, as she stepped to the desk. She then smiled as she looked down and saw them holding hands. "Oh my, I hadn't realized you two were so close. But remember, Dario, you're not to reveal anything to her that would spoil our game."

Dario and Safia detached from each other as he turned to face Frilla.

"We were just having a nice little chat, is all."

"So I see," said Frilla, turning to Mallory, "And to think you've even given her your discarded. But you never said why you did. I checked the records, and she wasn't part of some bet. You just happened to transfer ownership of her in the middle of the day. That certainly was generous of you." She raised a brow suspiciously at Dario. "Do you both have such a close relation as to just give away your discarded?"

"We came to an understanding."

"Did you now? And does that understanding involve any particular favors? I mean, with the way you two were holding hands, it does seem as if you are sharing something I might want to know about."

*Wait! He's nervous around her? Why? What would happen if I told her about that night after the party? Could she get him expelled? No, that won't work. It might prove that I blackmailed him to get Mallory. She could get expelled too.* Safia tilted her head before smiling back up at the girl. "Dario and I have a special relationship."

"Do you now?" asked Frilla with a smile as she looked back and forth between the two. "Oh, I've had an idea. You both will do couples betting."

"With her? You can't be serious. She's an idiot."

"Couples what?" said Safia, her eyes squinting as her mouth twisted in confusion.

"Frilla, have you lost your damn mind? Sticking me with her. She doesn't know anything yet."

"Nonsense. She's handled herself pretty well so far. And even so, I'll expect you to train your playthings properly. Otherwise, what fun would it be if you always knew what games were coming next?"

"Then stick me with Mallory. At least she can be trained."

Mallory was visibly shaken by Dario's words as her eyes went wide.

"No. I'll do it," said Safia, standing up. "I think this will be a good opportunity for me and Dario to work on our relationship. I don't know if you've noticed, but he's always marching around the campus like he has a stick up his ass. This might do him some good."

"I can't disagree with you there," said Frilla with a laugh. "Then it's settled. I'll get everything started and find a few couples to be your opponents. This really shall be fun. I knew you wouldn't bore me, Miss Safia." She then turned and started to walk away. "Oh, and see if you can do something about that vulgar mouth of his, won't you? Granted, since it is Dario, I'm not really expecting miracles."

Safia watched Frilla walk back down the aisle and probably out of the door.

"You bitch, what have you done?" said Dario, his tone low and growly. "Why did you agree to that shit?"

"Because I don't have a choice. What's your excuse? I saw your face. You were scared of her. If not, then why didn't you say no?"

"Oh my god, you fucking dumb cunt," said Dario as he began rubbing his face. "It's not about refusal. It's about availability. You made yourself available to them. They can't force you to do anything yet. Especially if you have other bets going. Previous bets will always lay atop more current bets. They can overlap, but they can't erase. So, all you need to do is not have the time for it and you're safe."

"What the hell are you talking about?"

"For fucking... I don't have time for this. And much less, I don't have time for you. I've got to try and fix this mess you've gotten me into," said Dario as he turned to leave, muttering more words as he left. Although Safia couldn't hear them, she was sure they were more curses.

"What was he talking about?" asked Safia as she turned back to Mallory. "Is there some rule about when you can place bets?"

"I don't know. I've never heard him talk about it like that before," said Mallory. "I mean... when I was with him, he always had one or two bets going on. But I just figured he liked to gamble. It always seemed like he did."

"This school and its secret rules." Safia tossed her hands above her head. "What, do they expect me to just bump my way through the dark here? They say they want me to play their game, but they won't tell me how it works."

"Do you think anyone else would know? I mean, well, someone who would tell us."

"Champ Champ, maybe, but the school or whoever

probably won't let her. She only tells me so much or tells me to go find out some other way."

"What about Miss Abigail? She's a teacher, right? She might know."

"No. She doesn't even have points, and she didn't even know we were gone. We need someone who's a—" Safia sighed, before reaching up and tapping on the pendant hanging from her neck, making it glow white. "I would like the location of Amanda Chastain."

"Do you think she will tell you?"

"Probably, but she'll want something in return. But at least with her, it's never anything really big or stupid."

"Location confirmed and has been sent to your device," spoke the pendant.

"Do you not like Amanda? She seemed nice on the plane. And she didn't seem so bad when I met her before. She always tried to take me from Dario, he just wouldn't bet her for me."

"No, it's not like that," said Safia as she stood up from the table. "Maybe I'm just tired of all the games, is all. I just wish for once; someone would just act like a regular person and help us out because they are a good person and not just doing it to get something out of it."

"You mean like you did for me?" said Mallory, a heartfelt smile across her face.

"Yeah, I guess I do," said Safia, unable to hide her own smile.

"Well, we do have Hashmi."

"Yeah, I guess we do," said Safia as she grabbed her bag from the table. "Can you put these books back for me? I'll go see my good friend Amanda and beg for some information."

"Okay," said Mallory with a laugh. "I'll clean up here."

Safia then walked down the aisle and out of the library, pulling out her tablet and navigating to the map screen where she saw the two dots representing their locations. Amanda was one of the buildings on the map that she'd never visited before. But following the path she eventually made her way there. It was a large flat-top, stone building with two impressively large mosaic windows in front at either side of the door. One depicted a woman dancing in a classical evening gown and the other showed a male bard playing a flute.

Stepping inside, there was a red carpet that led the way forward and split itself, laying atop a set of twin stairs that spiraled up to the second floor. Across either side of the room were brown and red drapes, along with a podium that stood in the center of the steps.

"Hello, Amanda. Are you here?"

Safia heard footsteps and saw a young man making his way down to her. As he appeared fully, Safia realized it was Ricardo.

"Hello, Miss Safia. Amanda said that you would arrive soon," he said with his usual smile.

"Hey, Ricardo," said Safia, unable to stop herself from smiling back at him. He was still as good-looking and well-mannered as he was on the plane. She thought she could see the stubble of a beard on his face but didn't want to mention it. "Is everything going okay with you?"

"Everything is fine. Just trying my best to keep Amanda out of trouble for the most part."

"And how's that going?"

"About as well as one could expect with her," he said as he extended his hand to her. "Would you allow me to escort her to you?"

Instinctively she reached out, taking him by the hand and letting him guide her back up the stairs. "Yes. Thank you."

"Tell me, has everything been going well? I was a bit worried when Amanda mentioned that the second years had taken an interest in you. But you seem to be in good enough spirits. Maybe I was worried about nothing."

"I wish it was nothing," said Safia honestly, as they made

it to the top of the stairs, where the red carpet found its way back together and extended down a hall with golden lighting. "That's actually the reason I am here. I wanted to ask her some questions."

"I see. Well, I hope she can help. Amanda has taken a liking to you. I'm sure she will do what she can."

"But at what cost? It's probably going to be something silly again."

Ricardo laughed, "Probably. But it won't be mean spirited."

"Actually, maybe you can help me?"

"Sure. Although I doubt I know as much as Amanda, since she does all the betting and things for us."

"It's fine if you don't. But do you know if one bet is able to cancel out another bet or how they overlap?"

"Hmm. I can't say that I really understand. I do think I've heard that bets can be overlapped, but I'm not sure in what way. Perhaps like a double bet, like how at the roulette table, a person is able to bet on both black and red chips. Is this what you mean?"

"Not exactly. Sorry, I know I'm not really making any sense, am I?"

"Very few things in this place make any sense, anyway. So, I think we're both lost in the same way. But you have arrived at a decent time. Perhaps you will enjoy today's show."

"Show? What show?"

Ricardo smirked as they stopped in front of two large wooden doors with engraved doors. "Welcome to the dance hall, Miss Safia." He opened the doors and before her were rows of seats that spread out the width of the building, and they all pointed to a stage where dancers twirled and glided across a wooden floor in uniforms of soft brown and gold.

Safia stepped inside, watching as the ladies and men down on the stage in front of her practiced their routine. And while it was impressive watching them move float across the stage, the more surprising thing was the person who led them. It was the familiar face of the larger woman from the masked meeting. She stood on stage, directing their movements and correcting their mistakes.

"Oh, it seems our guest has arrived," came Amanda's voice from one of the rows of seats adjacent to the door. "Come, Miss Safia, and join us. It's certainly a wonderful experience to watch the show before the show."

Safia turned to see Amanda smiling at her. Sitting next to her was another blond-haired woman. Safia thought she had seen her before, but she couldn't place her face.

"Hello, Amanda," said Safia as she walked over, taking a seat beside them. "I didn't know they had things like this here."

"Occasionally yes. Are you a fan of ballet?"

"No, but I've never gone to one. So, I can't say that I'm not."

"Then you're in for a treat. Oh, that's right. Safia, you remember Miranda, don't you? You met her during game night."

"Yes," said Miranda, "I believe it was after you bet that Gabriel fellow that if he ripped off your manservants' clothing that he would get to have his way with you. Tell me, how did that work out for you in the end?"

"About as well as you would expect," said Amanda. "My man there protected his lady's virtue, and I spent the night kissing Safia on top of the lake."

"I guess the word 'virtue' can be subjective," said Miranda with smile and bite of her lip in jest.

"Everything is subjective."

"What are they doing?" asked Safia, looking down at the stage as the people shuffled about.

"They're changing scenes. Which is certainly odd for this moment in their routine? I wonder what they have in store this time."

The instructor turned around, waving at them as the

two women beside Safia waved back.

"Jaqueline was a good choice for their choreographer. You might not think it to look at her, but she's quite graceful on her feet. A shame she doesn't practice anymore."

*So, her name's Jacqueline? I'll put that in when I get back?* "Why not?"

"Who knows? We all have our reasons. But she does enjoy teaching, so having her here seems to be a good fit. Oh, it seems they're doing Cinderella now," said Miranda as a woman came gliding out onto the floor wearing a white dress and crown with a slipper in her hand. "I wonder what made her decide on that."

"I'm sorry, Safia," said Amanda. "You wanted to speak with me about something. What was it?"

"I want to ask about the betting system here."

"Oh?"

"About whether someone can find themselves in a situation where even if they want to bet, they couldn't. Like if they had too many bets already active or something?"

"Well, I must say that I am impressed. Look at you, figuring things out on your own."

"So, is there something like that?"

"There is."

"Will you explain it to me?"

Amanda turned to Miranda.

"Don't look at me. She's your responsibility. You invited her, after all."

"Safia, this information, or at least the proper instruction, will require something on your part."

"I figured as much. I just thought you wouldn't try to take advantage of me as much as some others would."

Miranda laughed, "Oh dear, she certainly does hold you in high regard, doesn't she?"

"So, it seems. Honestly, it's my own fault. I've taken a liking to her, so perhaps that's limited my ability to indulge myself for fear of hurting her feelings," said Amanda, turning back to Safia. "Alright Miss Famosa. For easy understanding, how about I trade you this information and in exchange you grant me a small favor or two of my choosing and you and I go on another date, since it doesn't seem that I will ever get tired of your company."

"Okay, and thank you," said Safia as she reached for her pendant, only to have Amanda reach over, playfully slapping her hand away.

"Please Safia, that pendant is for those of us who lack faith in each other. I trust that you will keep your word to me. No need to involve the school in favors between friends."

"Thank you."

"Now, as to your question. The betting process here is intricate. And much like this ballet before you, bets can weave in and out of each other. One bet can be layered on top of another. So, for example, let's say that you make a bet for five points and that bet has a time frame. And then let's say you made a bet for three points and that bet must also be completed in a certain time. The school is able to calculate a reasonable time between bets. So, it may extend one bet's time frame or deny a bet before it can be accepted."

"It can do that?"

"It usually doesn't happen, but yes, it can. Now, in the case where the three point and the five point bets are accepted around the same time, before the computer has time to reject one. It may decide to make one of the bets null and void. So, which bet do you think it will cancel?"

"Ah," Safia began to think. "The three point one, maybe."

"Bingo. That's because the five point bet carries more weight. Now, obviously you can't wait until you're about to lose a bet, then place a higher point bet to try to save yourself from a loss. By then, the systems already figured out you're likely to lose and will ask if you wish to forfeit and pay up."

"I see. But that still doesn't explain why Dario was so mad."

"Dario? What does he have to do with this?"

"Frilla," said Safia with a sigh. The girl's name rolled off her tongue along with the exhaustion she caused. "She wants us to join in a couple's battle and I said I would."

Amanda and Miranda both instantly began covering their mouths as they tried to hush their laughter. "Oh dear, you didn't."

"Why? Did I mess up?"

"For you? No, but I suspect Dario wasn't so prepared for it if his pendant didn't negate the bet."

"I don't understand."

"Well, you see, sweet Safia, the total needed for a couple's battle isn't split equally. Much the way many relationships work, someone is carrying more of the load than the other. Let's say that the buy-in for the couple's battle is one million points. And say, for instance, that you only have thirty-thousand points being the cute little freshman that you are. The system won't take more than eighty percent of your points. So, the load bearer, who is Dario, will most certainly end up footing most of the bill."

"Essentially Safia," said Miranda, chiming back in, "depending on how much that couples buy-in is, you might have our dear Dario bent over the barrel. I believe that is the saying."

"That's why most people reject couple's battles. Finding a spouse who is your equal can't be said to be the easiest thing."

"But I also would lose points?"

"Of course, but let me ask you: who do you think has the most points to lose, you or him?" asked Amanda, still smiling. "Poor Dario probably couldn't escape the bet because of his second-year status."

"What does that have to do with anything?"

"Second years don't play by the same rules as the first years, dear," said Miranda, wagging her finger. "When challenged by another second year, if there isn't conflict or the bet is deemed unfair, then we must accept. He couldn't escape, but you, being a first year, you could."

"I imagine Dario is, at this very moment, trying to prove that you are unfit to be taking part in the game so he can cancel the bet or, at the very least, change you as his partner. Which I doubt he will have any success with because you've already proven that you can beat a second year. That point freak win of yours has solidified you as a worthy opponent."

"Oh, this is going to be so much fun to watch unfold."

Amanda tapped on her pendant. "Message to Frilla Santiago. Hello Frilla, I have decided to take you up on your offer. I wish to enter into the couples' battle with my discarded."

"Really Amanda, seriously?" said Miranda, with a smirk on her lips. "You just revel in being a busybody, don't you?"

"You wish to watch the fun. But there is absolutely no way I'm going to allow myself to not be involved. Safia, you wonderful woman. You can be anything but boring, I shall give you that."

"Am I going to have to bet against you, then?"

"Depends on the couple's games. Some are direct bets. Others are not so direct. It changes during every event."

Safia slumped down in her chair. "How do you both remember all these unknown rules? How did you even find them out?"

"Trial and error mostly," said Miranda. "Losing a few points during experimentation and then selling the information to others for points. When a new rule is found and can be proven, there are a lot of points to be made if you can find a new rule before anyone else. You can sell that information to someone who wishes to try and exploit it."

Amanda just laughed at the frustrated look on Safia's face. "Don't think too hard about it now. Instead, I suggest you just watch the ballet. There's much you can learn about this school just by watching how it works."

"Great, just great," said Safia, turning her head toward

the stage as the woman below directed the movements of her students. "I guess I might as well ask you to teach me about ballet. Why is it so special?"

"It's about interpretation," said Miranda. "A display of emotion through form and Jaqueline has been fairly good at it since she took over the role."

"I've only ever done sports, stuff like volleyball and swimming. Have either of you two ever tried ballet?"

"Sadly not. It requires a commitment of time and patience I just do not have," said Miranda.

"I never had the energy to even try," said Amanda.

Safia watched as they finished another round of their routine and Jaqueline took the tiara from Cinderella and placed it on her own head before sending the rest of the dancers away. She then did a few stretches before performing a series of moves that seemed so graceful. Safia thought even a woman of a smaller size would struggle with the lifts and twirls, but here was this larger woman moving as if through silk.

"A sight to see, isn't she?" asked Amanda. "Form, grace, and to let it all go at the blink of an eye. Yet, here I am unable to even stretch my back without feeling sore. A truly wasted talent."

"She's wonderful," said Safia, still in disbelief at the sight ahead of here. One foot planted behind the other, feet turned. She lowered herself before lifting back up, raising one leg to the knee of another before spinning around on her toes. Then, stopping and using her arms for balance, the woman leaned back, extending her leg up and performing something near to a split. Then, bringing her leg back down, she began spinning on her toes before finally jumping into the air, posing in a full split before coming back down and striking a pose and a smile for the girls above.

Amanda and Miranda both began to clap their hands, with Safia joining in as the woman below them took a bow before exiting the stage to come up and see them.

"Very well done," said Miranda. "A pirouette, into chains, into a jump of the cat. I can see you haven't gotten rusty at all."

"Why, thank you. There was also a développé in there somewhere, but I'm a bit too tired to remember where. I swear ballet is just pure agony on the toes and knees," said Jaqueline as she took out a small cloth dabbing it against her face. "How are you three doing today? It's not often that anyone wants to come and watch us practice."

"I've taken an interest," said Miranda. "My mother was in the ballet before she had me. Watching you practice reminds me of a simpler time."

"Why the tiara, Jacqueline?" asked Amanda. "Have you decided to take the star roll away from your lead and dawn the tutu once again? Are we about to witness your renaissance?"

"Hardly," said Jaqueline, waving a hand dismissively. "I just figured what girl in their life doesn't wish to be a princess at one point and time. A simple dream, but here on this stage I can make my own, if only for a little while, that is. As I said, the knees aren't what they used to be. So, now I teach like a shepherd herding in her flock."

"So, you would be the fairy godmother then? Tell us, why exactly did you give up on ballet?"

Jaqueline laughed, "Really? Is it not obvious? I simply enjoy food, dear. And despite what Disney fairy tales would have you believe; ballet is not a gentle beast. It consumes your life. Many in the profession starve themselves senseless for the art form. I, however, am not willing to sacrifice so many of life's joys to be truly great. So, here I teach, and I am allowed to experience a simple piece of the joy, if not the full experience."

"So, you will simply live vicariously through your students?"

"In a manner of speaking, yes," said Jaqueline. "Hello again, Miss Safia. Have you been trying your best to find out who my other masked companions are?"

"Not yet, but I plan to start."

"Oh, were you a part of that, Jaqueline?" asked Amanda. "And you decided to just give yourself away."

"I've already been partially exposed, anyway. I shall allow Safia here the opportunity to figure out who the rest are, along with the theme of the game. She may have even figured out the game by now."

"I'm not as smart as you think I am," said Safia. "And I doubt that this will be easy."

"But that's the game, my dear. We've all been there before, and I look forward to seeing how you fair."

"It's not like I have much of a—"

"Mallory Polana has sent you a message," spoke the pendant.

Safia shook her head as she stood up from the seat. "I guess that means it's time for me to go. Thank you both for talking to me."

"It's fine, just remember our date," said Amanda with a smile. "And do take care of that discarded of yours. She does seem to be the needy type."

"I'll remember," said Safia as she walked between the row of seats and back out into the hall. She didn't see Ricardo anywhere and found that the hall itself was completely empty. Feeling alone, she clicked on her pendant. "Play the message."

"Hey, Miss Safia. I've finished with my class. Can I come see you?"

Safia shook her head. *Maybe she is the needy type.* She clicked the pendant. "Send this message to Mallory Polana. Hey Mallory, meet me by the gazebo near the school." She then headed down the hall and back down the stairs where she met Ricardo standing by the door, looking over a tablet.

"Oh. I thought you had left," said Safia.

"No, I'm merely going over a few of my studies. Have you finished with Amanda? Did you learn what you needed?"

"Yes, she was helpful," I'm headed to meet Mallory now. "I suppose I'll see you later?"

"I look forward to it," said Ricardo as she opened the door for her to leave.

The walk toward the school wasn't as filled with people since the evening sun was in the sky. Instead, most of the students that weren't in late classes or in their dorms were now just lounging about on the grounds, talking to one another.

*Hopefully, the gazebo isn't filled. Maybe I should have asked Mallory to meet me somewhere else.* Safia then made her way over to the school. As she approached the building, she saw Hashmi over by the small auditorium, standing next to a boy she didn't know. *Now there's a rare sight.* She looked over at the two. *I've actually never seen Hashmi talking to a boy alone.* But before she could call them, she saw the boy grab Hashmi by the hand and lead her inside the building. *Well, that's odd. She* glanced back over to the other side of the school where the gazebo was, before turning back to look at where Hashmi went. *Okay, I'm just too curious.*

Safia walked off the walkway and headed toward the auditorium. Through the window, she saw Hashmi and the boy grabbing some type of black cloth before heading past where she could see.

*Does she have a boyfriend I don't know about?* Safia smiled. *This might be the perfect chance to get back at her for all her teasing.* Unable to wipe the smirk off her face, Safia pressed her ear against the door. She heard the sound of a muffled voice for only a moment before footsteps, and then just silence. Confused, she placed her hands on the door and peeked inside, but the room was empty, except for a large black sheet that was now on the floor. Confused, she stepped inside, looking around the room.

*That's weird. I know I saw her, or at least I think that was her. They were in Hijab, so I just assumed it was her. Could it have been someone else? But I've never seen anyone else here in Hijab before. Maybe it was a new student.* She knelt down where she saw a lump in the black cloth and ran her hand over the fabric. It was soft and cool to the touch. *I wonder what this is for.* She let her fingers continue down the cloth until hitting a lump in the fabric. Curious, she grabbed the sheet, lifting it, and was surprised to see a parrot mask sitting on the floor in front of her.

Confused, she began looking around the room. *What's going on? Is this...* There was nothing in the room that she could see beside the rows of chairs that lined the room and the podium up ahead. *Where did they go?* Safia spotted a door to the right of the stage. She then stood, taking the mask in hand, and walked over to the door, but she didn't see a way to enter. Pressing against it didn't budge it at all. There was no door handle, no latch, or anything that she could see that would grant her access. Turning around, she took another look at the room, before bringing the mask up to her face to stare at once again. She was sure that this was one of the masks worn by the people that were in the room with her and the second years.

*Was that Hashmi?*

Confused Safia, searched the auditorium for a while longer before leaving out of the building and walking over to the other side of the school. There she found the gazebo, but Mallory was nowhere to be found.

*Maybe she got tired of waiting and headed back to the dorm.*

Sitting down, she opened her bag, sliding in the parrot mask and pulling out her tablet. Remembering that the tablet showed certain information, she began clicking around on the options till she found a tab that had 'Mallory' displayed on it. She clicked it, and up popped a slew of information that she had never looked at before. It showed Mallory's test results, class schedule, and showed that bastard Dario as her last caretaker. And below his name were the bets that he had Mallory taken place in.

And sure enough, at the top of the most recent were

the words 'Naked Painting.' Safia could feel herself grip the tablet harder as she began thinking of the things Dario had forced Mallory to do. Shaking her head, she couldn't force herself to look at the other items below and instead clicked on the location icon. The tablet screen transformed into a familiar image of the 3d rendering of the school. And down below she could see the image of her own blue icon, placed inside of the gazebo. But, while Safia wasn't surprised to see the red dot representing Mallory, she was surprised to see where the red dot was located. Instead of on the winding path again headed back to the dorm, Mallory's dot was back in the school.

*Did she forget something in one of her classes?*

Slowly the red dot began spiraling as if Mallory were walking in a circle. Then Safia realized she wasn't walking in a circle. It was climbing. She was making its way up to the top of the school. Safia stood up and stepped out from under the gazebo, looking up at the side of the building.

*What's she doing up there?*

Safia remembered her own trip up to the top of the school, where she wagered her freedom in exchange to save her father's life. Unconsciously, Safia stepped down on the grass and made her way back inside of the school. She went down the hallway to the end of the school where she knew the door was. Placing her hand on it once again, she felt its coolness flowing against it on the other side. But unlike before, the path ahead was closed to her. All she could do was stare at her tablet before looking up at the ceiling.

*What are you doing up there? Are you in trouble?* Safia clicked her pendant. "I would like to send a message to Mallory Polana."

"Please record your message," spoke the pendant.

"Mallory, what are you doing on t—." Safia stopped before she clicked the pendant again. "Please cancel that message."

"Message canceled."

*She's allowed to have secrets. I shouldn't try forcing her to tell me things right now or it'll end up like last time. If she's in trouble, I'll have to wait and hope that she tells me. For now, I should just worry about my own problems.* Safia shut down her tablet and placed it back in her carrying bag. Then, accepting she couldn't fix everything, she walked forward, leaving the school and headed back toward Yennefer House.

The evening sun was in the sky as Safia made her back through the campus. The grounds were livelier than before, as a few of the students were running around the campus, having themselves a race. Taking the time to lose herself in something else other than the mysterious school she was in, she stood and watched as several boys raced back and forth on the grounds.

"Hey there," said one of the boys after noticing that they had caught her attention and came over to Safia. "Don't... just stand there and watch," he said, a bit out of breath. "Come on over and join us." He was an African boy with a low haircut who had sweated through the top of his undershirt as he stood before her.

"You want to race me," said Safia, shaking her head. "I'm not too sure about my chances.."

"Don't worry. We'll give you a handicap. And it's a good way to work off stress. This school has a way of getting to you if you don't find an outlet for it," said the boy, reaching out his hand. "You're Safia, right? Wanna give it a go?"

"How do you know my name?" asked Safia, cautiously, but reached out, shaking the man's hand.

"How can I not? You're famous around school. My name's Olum," with a firm handshake he slowly pulled Safia forward off the walkway, escorting her over to the group. "And even if you weren't, he already told me about you." Olum pointed to a familiar face on the ground that was hidden by the group.

"Hey Safia," said a shirtless Austin as he lay sprawled out of the ground, his dreadlocks laying over the grass as the sweat slid down his body.

"You look like you're having fun."

"I don't think I'd call it that, since all I've been doing is losing."

"Well, don't worry. Safia here will run the next lap with us. I'm sure you'll probably beat her."

"You're saying you're going to beat me just because I'm a girl?"

"No. I'll beat you because I'm faster than everyone out here," he said, nodding to the other boys who were lined up about to run. "They will probably beat you because you're a girl. Well, maybe not the boy with the green accented pants. He's just slow all around."

"I feel like I should be offended."

"Well, there's only one way to prove me wrong."

Safia watched as four boys, and one girl with pink accents in her clothing lined up. She noticed that they never clicked their pendants. Instead, a girl beside them waved her hands downward signaling the start of the race and they just took off running, but one of the boys stumbled a bit to catch his balance at the start of the race. The woman beside him was very fast, though, keeping up with the boys at the start.

"They're about to start," said Olum.

Safia watched, their feet kicking up loose grass and, true to Olum's word, the boy in the green was indeed the slowest runner. And it was by no short amount. He was terrible.

The race barely took a quarter of a minute as they sprinted down the field. Two boys came in first and second with the girl coming in third followed by the boy who stumbled, and then the boy in green. They were all fast, but the other girl surprised Safia. She had almost beaten the boy who came in second when she finished.

"I don't understand," said Safia. "The boy with the green accented pants, why even enter if he's that bad?"

"You're misunderstanding," said Olum, gesturing over

the crowd. "The people here aren't betting on who will come in first. They are betting on all the positions."

"What?"

"To win here you will need to guess everyone's placement. And the more positions you get correct, the more of the percentage of the pot you win."

"I still don't get it?"

"Well, if everyone knows for sure who will come in last, then they no longer has to guess all five spots. They only have to guess three."

"Three? Why not four?"

"Because we can pick our own placement. But in essence, we are doing exactly that."

"But then, can't they just cheat by just trying to slow down in their own placement?"

"They can, but remember, they can't bet on themselves. So, in reality, if someone knows they will be first and they know who's the slowest, then they are betting on who they think will come in second, third, and forth. And if someone knows you bet on them, they could always sandbag it, but then they'd lose to those beside them. And there would be no need for the three of them to work together, because then no one would gain any points."

Safia just shook her head. "I can't say that I really understand what's happening. Maybe I'm just too mentally tired to think about this stuff."

Olum laughed. "Don't worry. I'll cover your bet. I think running is a good exercise for everyone. It usually helps clear the mind."

"You can do that?"

"Of course. There's no rule that says I can't. So, what about it? You want to have a quick run?"

"Why not? But I think I will pay for myself after all." *I need to start focusing on bets or else I'll never make it in this school.* "So, how much is the bet?"

"Five hundred points per race. A little steep for us

maybe, but seeing as you beat that point freak, it's probably not much for you."

*That's still a lot considering how much I need. But if five people race, that means it's twenty-five hundred points per person, but only the first three places will win. No... that's not right. I need to pick who wins.* Safia watched as a few people in the crowd began speaking into their pendants, and then those same people then lined up for the race.

"We've got to wait our turn. But I think we'll be up soon."

"How do I place the bet? I don't know anyone's names here besides you and Austin."

"Oh, I guess I didn't mention that part. Everyone racing must be of a different house, unless there is a boy and girl. Then two can enter. You can see that in the accented colors in their clothing. So, for betting, we just say the tree colors and gender, in which order we think they will place, and the pendant does the rest."

"Doesn't that mean that boys and girls can work together and try to cheat, or plan where they finish?"

"Yep, but that makes it hard because they must also plan where the other three will finish. It makes it really hard to plan something like that."

"But how does the... oh, it's the tracking chips they placed in us."

Olum nodded. "Yep, that's how we've guessed they manage it. Either way, it works."

Safia watched the other group line up to run. This time, it was three girls and two boys. *How am I supposed to guess how fast everyone else is? I don't know these people. Am I just supposed to look at their legs or something?*

The girl swung her hand down once again, and the group took off running. Much to her expectations, the two boys took a commanding lead and finished first and second, with the girls trailing behind battling for third.

"Alright," said the boy, coming in second. "I won that time."

"So did I," said the girl in last place.

"Ahh, for christ sakes. You're both in cahoots, I know it," said the boy who came in first. "How did I only get second place?"

"Maybe you shouldn't be so fast," said the girl who came in last.

Safia watched as the two celebrated. *They have on different colors, so they probably didn't cheat. Or maybe they did. It's not like being in the same house matters much.*

"Okay, it looks like we're up," said Olum, extending his hand down to Austin, who was still down on the ground. "Come on, one more race."

"Fine, fine," said Austin, allowing himself to be pulled up. "I guess I have one more left in me."

Sadia watched Austin get pulled off the ground and noticed the blades of grass in his hair. "Hold still," she said as she walked up to him. "You have grass in your hair. I see your hair is still messy. You still haven't found anyone to retwist your dreads?"

"I do them myself. As you can see, I'm not that good at it. I don't suppose you've learned how yet?"

"Sadly, I've been too busy to learn about managing a type of hair that I don't have," said Safia, plucking the last pieces of grass from his hair.

"We're joining in too," said the girl with pink accents in her clothing that Safia saw running earlier. "I want to see what she can do, since everyone is talking about her."

"I guess, I'll join in two," said the boy with green accents in his pants. "I still need the exercise."

"I'm not sure you should be wasting your points on exercise." said Olum with a laugh.

"You say that, but I think the girls watching me are giving me motivation."

"Well, can't say I didn't warn you."

"Then it looks like we have our five. Try to take it easy on Safia here. This is her first race."

They stepped away from each other and whispered into their pendants, which prompted Safia to do the same. Then, when ready, everyone walked over to the start of the race. Olum and Austin placed themselves at the end, beside one another, while Safia and the girl with pink accents in her clothing, were placed on the opposite end. This left the boy in the green in the center.

The starting girl swung her hands down and they all lept from the line. But Safia was slow on the start and stumbled low to the ground. Before she could get a foothold, the girl next to her fell down on top of her over, pinning her to the ground with a "Oof" sound. Quickly, they both got to their feet and continued on with the race. Each ran as hard as they could with the girl in pink, quickly out-pacing Safia as she ran down the field. Even with her struggling at the start, she caught up to the boy in green, but was unable to finish before him.

"Cool, I got... second place," said Austin as he finished and tried to catch his breath.

Safia's pendant blinked, but she couldn't hear what it was saying, as she had just passed the finish line and her heart was pacing in her chest. *Okay, that was bad. I didn't realize I was this out of shape.*

"Ahhh! What a mess," said the girl in pink as Safia came in. "You tried to trip me, didn't you?"

"I... I tried to win. But then you fell on me," said Safia, bending over, her hands on her knees as she caught her breath.

"I only fell, because you got under me."

"You and Austin must have had some type of plan. It's a little too weird that you both won."

"Don't be like that, we all played under the same rules," said Olum. "And you did say you wanted to see what she could do. It seems to me that you got the answer you wanted, if not in the way you wanted. And it's not like you're so innocent yourself."

The girl in the pink accents looked between Olum and Safia before shaking her head. "Fine, I guess I got what I asked for. But I won't be tricked next time." She tossed up her hands. "I'm gonna race again. Next time we bet," she said looking at Safia. "I'm going to win." She then headed back off to try to join another group of racers.

"Well done, Miss Safia, it seems you and Austin were able to figure out who would win. I guess Yennefer House is just lucky today. Care for another race?"

"No... no, thank you," said Safia, still catching her breath. "I haven't run like that in a long time. I don't think I'm cut out for it. And I should head back to the dorm."

"Ha!" laughed Olum. "Well, let me know if you change your mind. We often run races out here."

"Wait up!" said Austin, "I'll walk you back. I'm also done for today."

Safia waited for Austin to grab his clothing and together the two got back on the spiraling walkway and began their way back towards their dorm.

"Tell me, what happened back there? You two didn't just happen to fall over, did you?"

"I don't know. She fell on top of me. What else could it have been?"

Austin frowned. "Tell you what. If you tell me how you figured out how to win, then I'll tell you something as well. Would that be a fair trade?" He held out his badge, shaking it back and forth.

Safia looked at him while twisting her lips in contemplation. *I guess this is how it starts. Building relationships and what not. I can't just keep relying on Mallory and Hashmi all the time or bothering Amanda or Champ Champ. I need people to owe me favors as well.* "I'll tell you how I did it if you promise to either tell me something in the future or do me a favor."

"Deal," said Austin, clicking his badge. "I promise Safia Fa—"

Safia placed her hand over Austin's, them both stopping

in their tracks on the winding path. "I trust you," said Safia, looking up into Austin's dark eyes. "I saw earlier, during the first race, that the person by the other girl who wore pink had stumbled at the start of the race. That was because she bumped into him."

"What? If that's the case, then why did you both fall?"

"That's because I stayed low to the ground, so when she tried to bump me at the start of the race, I wasn't there, and she just fell over and landed on top of me."

"Wait. Okay, but then how did you know the race would turn out?"

"I listened. Olum said he was the fastest person there, and you were complaining about losing. Whether it was to him or anyone else, didn't matter, you seemed pretty fast. So, that just left the other boy who Olum has already said was slow. My main issue was if the other girl was fast enough after she got up to catch him, which she nearly was."

"Wow, you caught all of that. I should have been thinking that way. I just thought since he was a boy, he would be faster. And you're right, I can't beat Olum in a race. He's fast."

"See," said Safia as she started heading back off towards their dorm. "It's nothing special. No magic, it was just a pain to think about."

"Well, it's impressive to me. Most people don't think like that. I wouldn't suppose you have a boyfriend already, do you?"

Safia laughed. "What? You wish to deal with my problems?"

"No, I just figured you could teach me a few things, and I didn't want a jealous boyfriend coming after me."

"Sadly, I..." *No Safia, think before you speak. The answer to this might become important. Judging by how people treat each other here, the answer might mean more than I think it does.* Safia focused her thoughts on the relationship between Ricardo and Amanda. Then her mind went to the couple's battle that she had yet to take a part in, and finally, the kiss she had given Jericho. "Yes, sorry, I already have a boyfriend."

"Dang. I should have tried dating you when you first got here. My loss, I guess. Who is it? Do I know him?"

"I'll tell you if you promise to do me another favor," said Safia with a smirk and a raised brow.

Austin frowned, "No thanks. I'll wait to find out. Something tells me that given your reputation, the favor I now owe you is going to be a pain in my butt."

"Don't worry, I'll only bother you when I really need something," said Safia when she reached the steps of their dorm.

"That's what I'm afraid of," said Austin as he sat down at the table by the front door.

"See ya later, Austin." said Safia as she made her way up the stairs towards her room.

Feeling exhausted from the day's events, Safia opened the door, walked over and ran her finger over her soft bed, feeling the coolness of the blanket. *I haven't sweated so much in a long time. I should wash up first, then I'll take a small nap.* She tried to rest her mind as she walked over to the window but found that all she could do was think about the day's events. Her mind was on a cycle, thinking over everything that had happened. *Was that Hashmi? Why was Mallory on top of the school? She couldn't have been the only one up there, not after everything I went up there for. But I was invited up by Champ Champ. Does that mean only school faculty are allowed up there? If so, then who was she up there with? Was she making some type of bet?*

The frustration began to work its way down her neck and over into her shoulders. Her stiffness caused her to take deep breaths, trying to relax as she reached down and opened up the window. Then, grabbing her bag, she pulled out her tablet. *I hope I'm wrong. I know she wouldn't involve herself in another bet.*

Placing her finger on the screen, it lit up and just like before, Safia navigated her way over to Mallory's information and clicked on her name. She gave a sigh of relief as she saw that Mallory hadn't been involved in any recent bets. It was the same as before.

*Okay, that's good. Then I was just worried for nothing. Maybe... I still want to know why she was up there, but as long as she's safe, that's all that matters.* She shook her head. *I guess I should worry about myself. I'm the one who is also not safe.*

Closing out of Mallory's screen, she clicked around the tablet until she was on the panel with the Finders Keepers game from before. In front of her, the images of the masks jiggled around on the screen. The only mask that didn't jiggle was the gray out image of the rabbit mask, which she had given the correct name to. At the top of the screen, in green coloring, was the number thirty thousand. Startling her a bit, the door opened and in walked Mallory, holding a basket in her hand.

"Hey, Miss Safia. What are you looking at?" she said as she walked over to the bed.

"Just looking at the list of masks again."

"Oh. You said that they were asking you to guess the names, right?" said Mallory as she placed the basket on the bed before stepping over, next to Safia to look at the screen. "But it's good that you have all those points now, isn't it?"

"I don't have them yet. It just shows up on the screen. So, I guess I'll only get the points when the game is over."

"Oh, okay then. Have you found out any more names yet?"

"I think so. I think the deer mask is named Jacqueline."

"Is there any way to be sure before you type it in?"

"I don't know," said Safia with a sigh. "I was thinking about waiting before I type in the names until like the last day or something. But there may be some type of crazy rule that I don't know about that could mess that up."

"I see. Then it's probably best to just try it now. Are you

sure that's her name?"

"As sure as I can be, so here goes," said Safia as she typed in the name on the tablet next to the image of a deer's face. The tablet vibrated for a moment as the large red letter X appeared over the deer's mask. Instantly, the green thirty thousand number flashed red as the number descended back down to zero.

"Oh!" yelped Mallory as her eyes went wide. "Do you only get one chance?"

"It seems so," said Safia as she closed her eyes, raised her head, and took in a deep breath. *Of course, the name is wrong. But why was it wrong? I know that's—*

"What are you going to do now?"

"What can I do? I have to try to figure out the rest of the names."

Mallory just stared at Safia for a moment. "You seem so calm about this. I thought you would be mad about losing so many points."

"I want to be angry. But I'm tired of being angry. I'm tired of thinking so much about all of this. And honestly, I'm just tired of being tired. I think I'm going to skip classes today," she said as she laid down on the bed. "I just want to sleep. I'll wash the sheets tomorrow." Letting her head hit the soft coolness of the pillow, she closed her eyes. It wasn't long before Safia felt the warm sensation of Mallory snuggling up beside her. "You don't have to be here," she said without opening her eyes. Just go on to class."

"No, I want to. And besides, it might make you feel better to have someone with you."

Safia didn't fight her on the issue, as she knew Mallory was right. It did feel good having someone lay down beside her. Giving in to her body's need for contact, Safia rolled over in the bed, wrapping her arms around Mallory as they both fell into slumber.

# CHAPTER 7

Safia sat beside Hashmi as another one of her teachers, named Mr. Granier, paced back and forth in front of his desk at the top of the class. He wasn't a much older man, probably in his mid to late thirties with a hint of gray in his beard. He stood in front of the class with a book in his hand as he looked out over the class.

"Now, who here can inform me as to some one of the ways that information is distributed throughout the world?"

"The internet," said another boy in class.

"Yes, the internet is actually the main source that we use to spread information from one person to the other. It has even eclipsed cell phones to the point where cell phones have become no more than little tv screens, which we occasionally talk on. Now, before you came here, tell me, what did you spend all your time on your phone doing; searching through your newsfeed and surfing the internet or actually talking to someone?"

"Reading stuff on the internet or watching videos mostly," responded a girl. It was a message that was agreed upon by the rest of the class.

"Exactly. Have you noticed that we, as humans, have gone so far as to come up with our own varied, speakable languages, and each language is as diverse as the culture that it comes from? But now, here in the modern age, we have created almost every convenience we can think of in an attempt to not speak to one another."

"What? I don't understand. How can you say that when you're talking to us now?"

"Yes, but I want you to remember your days before here. Think about people you know, or people outside of your certain group. It is a common fact that most people send text messages over actually speaking with their friends. On an average, we make a little over two billion phone calls every day, but dwarfing those are emails, which turns out around three hundred billion are sent out every day. And if you double that, there a six billion text messages sent every day. We, as a species, are regressing from verbal speech back to pen and paper, except now its tiny electronic keyboards on our multimedia devices rather than drawing pictures in the sand with our sticks. Now, who here has an explanation as to why this is the case?"

"Because talking to people is hard?"

"Yes, that's one reason. Who has another?"

"It's just easier most of the time."

"Well, that is also probably true. But you skirt around the real answer. Come one, who wishes to have another go at it?"

"Because people are afraid of confrontation," said Jericho, raising his head up from the desk.

"And there it is: the answer I was looking for. Confrontation. Most humans and animals avoid it to the best of their ability, but we, as humans, are absolutely singular in our understanding of what violence is. And as such, we, as a species for the most part, have always shied away from conflict and all things that make us uncomfortable. And in-person communication is one of the main things that can affect the mind and put you in an uncomfortable space."

"That can't be true," said one of the boys. "Isn't this whole school built on making us conflict with one another?"

"Yes, that is a good point. But, also have you noticed what this school doesn't allow you to do?"

"Ahhh! I don't know. We're told we can do anything as long as we have the points for it."

"Really? Then can anyone here raise their hands if they have been allowed to send a single text message or email since they arrived at this school?" The class was silent as no hands were raised. "Exactly. To my knowledge, the only ones who are able to send messages in the form of text are the faculty here. All students must communicate verbally. And who can tell me why that is?"

"Because it forces us to come into contact or conflict with one another."

"Now there's a smart lad," said their teacher with a smirk across his face as he closed his book, pointing it at the student. "And to think, this wonderful conversation was started thanks to the young man back there who was asleep at his desk, which it seems he wasn't sleeping, only pretending. And that may also be a form of escaping conflict."

"Everyone always thinks I'm asleep. Am I not allowed to rest my eyes as long as I'm paying attention?"

"Hmm. Mr. Andrews may have given me the topic for another discussion. Is it easier to listen to someone rather than look at them? Given the equal ratio of men and women in this classroom, I would think that everyone was equally incentivized to keep their eyes open for a potential mate."

Safia looked around the room, curious if the man's words were true. And sure enough, there were twelve boys and twelve girls in this class. *I never noticed that before. I wonder if that is on purpose.* Safia shook her head. *No, of course it was on purpose. Everything here is on purpose.* She rubbed at her eyes. *Dammit Safia, you need to stop thinking in 'ifs' and start thinking in 'whys'.*

"Is something wrong there, Miss Famosa? Do you have a question?"

"Huh? No, sorry, I was just wondering... ahhh... if this school keeps track of the messages we send to each other. I mean, we all have these pendants, right? But we can't use them like phones, instead we send pre-recorded messages to one another. Isn't that like a mix of what you are saying?"

"How very astute of you. And yes, I certainly suppose it could be thought of that way," said Mr. Granier, rubbing his hand across his chin. "You would think that a compatible system would be to use the same system in which walkie-talkies use to communicate, but then you would come into the problem of narrowing down the specific receiver of the messages. But given the capabilities of this school, solving that issue would probably be trivial." He clapped his hands together. "Good questions Miss. Famosa."

*Was it? Because I think you just made it more complicated. I'm not even sure what half the words you just said were.*

The rest of the class began to murmur about themselves after Safia's praises. She turned to them, seeing them eyeing her suspiciously as she caught Jericho smiling back at her. Feeling a bit uneasy at his gaze on her, she frowned back at him.

*You're the last person I want looking at me.*

The class went on until the teacher signaled for it to come to a close.

"Okay, we will resume this discussion next week. Refer to your textbooks for chapter four. We will be discussing the effects of communication services on the modern economy."

Safia stood up to leave the class with Hashmi.

"Is everything okay?" asked Hashmi, as they entered the

hallway.

"Everything's fine... well, as fine as it can be."

"You sure? These last few days you've barely spoken to me and Mallory."

"Honestly, I've just been going back and forth trying to figure things out. But no matter how much I think, I can't seem to figure out what I should do about this. All I ever feel is just tired."

"You could always join me on my morning runs. Ever since I've started running with Harmony, it's been a great way to work off the stress that this school brings."

"If it gets that bad enough, I may end up doing that. I ran a few days ago as a bet and it did feel good to relieve some of this stress. What about you? Has everything been going okay with you?"

"Me?"

"Yeah. You and Mallory are always trying to make sure I'm okay, but I started thinking that maybe I'm not exactly looking after you two. I mean Mallory maybe, but you don't really tell me how you're doing. Can I help you with anything?"

"That's sweet," said Hashmi with a smile. "But I think we are in different situations. I have few concerns at the moment outside of trying to keep up with my studies. Some of our classes don't come to me as naturally as they do for you, so I find myself studying more."

"What do you mean?"

"How do I explain?" asked Hashmi to herself as they stepped off the walkway. Looking around, she spotted a tree over at the side of the school and led Safia over towards it. "Follow me for a moment."

"It's nothing terrible, is it?" asked Safia, looking somewhat worried as they walked along the grass, the morning sun to their backs as they headed over to the standing tree beside the school.

"As you know, I cannot wager points."

"Yes."

"Well, that also means that I must ration out my points a lot more delicately than the average student."

"Wait! Then are you low on points?"

Hashmi just laughed as they reached the shade of the tree. "Safia, I'm always low on points. Or, at least, I'm low compared to you. Most months, I'm barely able to afford my food budget. I imagine Nasir goes through the same, but in his case, I'd suppose he depends on Addison's help."

"But... you've never said anything. I... I would have—"

"What could you have done? You've had your own problems. And besides, your friend Jericho has gone out of his way to help me acquire points since you've been busy."

"He has? But... I don't understand. He... he wouldn't do that. He only wants to help himself."

"I'm sure he does and I'm sure he will come to me sooner or later, expecting something for all the help he has given me."

"But you won't have to do it. I mean, it's not like he can make you."

"Safia," said Hashmi with a sigh. "I don't think you are quite understanding exactly how this school tries to manipulate everyone here. Tell me, what's the difference between Mallory and myself?"

"What? I mean... you're not a discarded."

"Am I not? Then what happens if Jericho decides to not help me anymore? What would I do then? Have you seen anyone else on campus handing out points like that?"

"Well... can't you just ask the school itself to allow you to do something for points?"

"I've tried. All the lower suggestions have been denied or have already been completed. There was apparently a boy who just graduated who performed the same duties as Jericho, but he's gone, now. And the higher-level jobs require points to get started, and those are points that I don't have."

"Wait, you need points in order to clean up the school?"

"You don't recall your conversation with Killian? Remember that he said he needed to invest thousands of points for the winter festival in order to receive the points awarded afterwards. Even Jericho, when he built that gazebo and ice house, needed to pay points in order to receive the materials. It was only after its completion, did he and we receive the points."

"I never thought of that," said Safia honestly.

"Of course not. Neither did I, until I found myself in dire need of points. If not for him, I may very well have been expelled."

"I wouldn't let that happen... I mean you could always become—" Safia's words froze in her mouth as she knew what she was about to say and regretted even thinking of it.

Hashmi smirked with a raised brow. "Your discarded? Sorry, but that option does not apply to those who apply here under the religious exemption."

"What? Why not?"

"Because having a caretaker is the equivalent of having a master. And we are not allowed to serve two masters. Or so the school says, but I imagine it's just another way for the school to find a way to make us indebted to them or someone else on campus or to force us to find some type of moral conflict within ourselves."

"But then... how does Nasir get by?"

"Jericho often helps him out as well. You've seen them together a few times now, right? But I'm sure Addison buys his school materials and such."

"I can do that for you. I mean... if you would let me."

"I think you should focus more on both you and Mallory's wellbeing. I won't add myself to your burdens needlessly."

"But Jericho, you don't know—"

"I am not ignorant of the will of this school, Safia, or the people inside of it. Jericho has informed me that he will ask me for a favor one day and, if it comes into conflict with my beliefs, then I am free to refuse. Either way, I'll just have to wait and see."

Safia began rubbing her head. "I understand. I just hate to think that I introduced you to him, is all."

"I'm sure our paths would have crossed eventually, whether you had done so or not," said Hashmi, stepping out from under the shade. "Now, come on. It is still morning, and we might as well go and get something to eat."

Safia nodded her head and began walking along with her friend. *I'm an idiot. I didn't even notice she was low on points. I never even thought to ask. I just assumed that every-thing was okay. She turned to her friend.* "Hashmi."

"Yes."

"You'd tell me if you were in trouble, right?"

"I would. But only if I couldn't find a way out of it myself. Besides, it's not as if you told me about your situations the moment you found yourself involved in them, now did you?"

"That's true, I guess I just thought—"

"Frilla Santiago has sent you a message."

"I guess that means we won't be eating breakfast togeth-er then."

Safia sighed but clicked on the pendant.

"Hello, Miss Safia, can you come to the Montgomery building please? Everything is set up, and I wish to speak to you before the game gets started."

"The Montgomery building? Which one is that?"

"It should be the large building downhill from the right library. I've actually never been inside of it myself, but I heard they sometimes use it as a gymnasium."

"Would you like to come?"

"Am I allowed to?"

"Let's go find out. Unless you have something better to do? And I would feel better having you with me."

"Alright then. Let's go and see what they have planned."

Together, they both made their way over towards the

building next to the right library. In front, they saw Frilla standing outside with two boys.

"Ah, good, you've made it. I wanted to personally inform you that this building will be the structure where we will have the couples' game."

Safia looked up at the building. "What type of game will it be?"

"Oh, now that would be spoiling the secret," said Frilla, a wide smile across her face as she turned to Hashmi. "Oh, but be sure to come alone. This event will only be for those that are invited."

"That's fine, but may I ask you something?"

"Of course, as long as you're not trying to get me to reveal anything about the game. I wouldn't want to ruin the surprise."

"Can you tell me your opinion of Dario and Jericho Andrews, the guy who's always building things around campus?"

Frilla tilted her head, confused for a moment, but then smiled and nodded. "I'm actually flattered that you would come to me for relationship advice. Yes, well, picking a mate here is important if you wish for it to carry over into the outside world. Dario is a bit of a hothead, and vulgar, and a bit of a jackass if you want my honest opinion. But his family is wealthy, I've heard."

"He's a lot more than a 'bit' of an asshole," said Hashmi.

"Yes, well, I was trying to be considerate to your friend here since she's going to be partnered with him. But, as for that Jericho fellow, I've used him for my needs in terms of our games, but I can't say that I know him all that well, personally. I've heard he's quite the brown noser and does his little charity projects around the school. As long as he does what he's told. I never saw much need to take anything more than a passing interest in him." She took another look at Safia. "But I suppose he'd do fine for someone like you. I mean, I haven't heard anything else about him having any form of influence outside of the school, so in fact I'd say he's just another boy."

Safia took the insult in stride without flinching and pressed on. "So… if I were to seriously date one, who would you—"

"Oh dear, if I was of your status, I'd choose Jericho," said Frilla with quick certainty. "My family has enough status. I don't need Dario's. And why pick some frivolous bastard like Dario when you can build up your own man? Jericho has already proven himself capable of being a good little boy and listening with his little game night some time ago, I heard. So as long as he can be trained, I'd imagine I could make something out of him."

"You make it sound like you build your men," said Hashmi with a laugh.

"Oh, please dear, all women build their men. Well, the ones who are worth a damn, anyway. Why, look at Champ Champ and her husband. When he first arrived here, he was nothing. Now look at him, married to that little head mistress and struts around like he owns the place. An odd couple if you've ever seen one."

"I've only ever seen him awake once," said Safia, shaking her head. "So, I'm not sure he struts anywhere."

"Oh, that's probably just the pills he takes. Those scars on his face apparently cause him a considerable amount of pain, so she has to shepherd over him most of the day. Or, at least that's the rumor. But tell me, Miss Safia, have you figured out our mask game yet? The names of all the people, I mean."

"No. It seems I was tricked on one of the names, so I still have a lot to figure out."

"Really, I figured. Well, don't worry. just eight more to go. I'm sure you will figure it out. After all, I'm told you're a smart little girl. In fact, this game has been designed with that in mind. Anywho, it's time I must be on my way. So, if there aren't any more questions."

Frilla nodded her head and headed off toward the library, leaving the girls to stand before the building, staring up at it before finally deciding to take off and head back on the walkway.

"What was that about?" asked Hashmi.

"What?"

"You know what, asking her what she thought of Jericho and Dario. You can't seriously be thinking of dating one of them. Especially Dario."

"What? No, of course not. She already thinks I'm dating Dario, or at least she's pretending she does. And I'm pretty sure the word of me kissing Jericho has already spread around to her. You saw how she knew about both his and Dario's families. She probably already knows about both of us, too."

"But... how do they know this stuff?"

"At this point. I have to assume they are able to buy the information with points somehow."

"What will you do about the couple's game?"

"What can I do but play?"

"Yes, but you don't even know what kind of game it is."

"That's good. Hopefully that means neither do the others. But seeing as it's in a gym, then it's probably a volleyball or basketball game or something like that."

"If it were that simple, they wouldn't have gone to all this trouble, I think."

"Maybe, but since I can't do anything about it. I'd rather focus on what I can. I still need to find out the names on the list, especially since I know now that she's able to watch it. And more than likely one or two of them will be at this couple's thing."

"Did she say that?"

"In a way, yes. She said I had eight people left to find. And that's true, but I never told her how many I had left, only that I've been tricked by one. So, it could have been nine or five or whatever, but she immediately knew it was eight, and she said it with confidence. She didn't even question it."

"I think... I think you're starting to think like them now."

"If so, then I'm doing a terrible job at it. Because right now, I'm losing and they're winning. And all I can do is just play along with their games.

# CHAPTER 8

The night of the game had finally arrived as Safia and Mallory sat in their room, with Mallory brushing Safia's hair while she sat in a chair.

"Just a little longer until the couple's game."

"I just want to get it over with," said Safia. "I hate feeling nervous like this."

A knock came to their door as Mallory stopped stroking Safia's hair and walked over to the door.

"Who is it?"

"Ahh… Hello again. It's me, Ricardo. Is everyone presentable?"

Safia looked over at Hashmi, who was still in Hijab and her school clothes as she sat up on the bed. Her friend nodded her head and Mallory walked over, opening the door. They were all surprised to see Amanda standing in front of the door with Ricardo behind her. The two were both dressed in suits, with Amanda wearing a pure white suit with a black undershirt and Ricardo being her opposite wearing a black suit with a white undershirt. His hair was freshly cut and showed the hint of a shave while Amanda's was pulled back into braided twin buns on the back of her head.

"You see, I told you she didn't have anything else to wear. Hand me those and wait outside," said Amanda as she took two boxes and a case with a handle and latches from Ricardo, stepped inside, and closed the door behind her as he waited outside. "Now, come on. Let's get you dressed, shall we?"

"What's wrong with what I'm wearing?" said Safia, standing up in her chair. Like the rest of her friends, she was still in her school uniform's pleated skirt and button-up shirt.

"Dear, this is an event to stave off the boredom of the school's most pompous and pretentious," said Amanda with a smirk. "I know because I'm as guilty as they are. So, they're expecting you to look the part. Thank goodness, I had the foresight to see that you would try to skirt by as you are."

"And what did you bring her this time?" asked Hashmi, not even trying to hide her curiosity. "That last outfit was quite problematic to squeeze her into."

"For someone who talks about their own modesty so much, you sure do seem to enjoy it when I'm not allowed to have mine," said Safia with a frown.

"Oh hush, everyone there will be similarly dressed," said Amanda. "And besides, this outfit isn't as revealing as the previous one."

"Says the woman in a full body tuxedo."

"Oh, well, I'd be happy to strip down right here for you if you like, but only if you join me. You can even have your discarded join us if you wish. It has been a while since I've had the company of two beautiful girls at once."

Safia glanced over at Mallory and saw the gears behind

her eyes begin to turn as she began contemplating the idea. "No, thanks. Just show me what you want me to wear."

"Now there's a wonderful idea," said Amanda as she placed the box down. "This bed sure is larger than the one Miss Hashmi over there has. But I'll not pry into that right now."

"I appreciate that."

Amanda opened the box, reached inside, and through the fluffy paper pulled out a sleek black bib-necked, full-length dress. It was sleeveless, with the sides of the dress near the waist exposed. The lower half was more of a two-tone design as the black at the hem transformed into a fiery crimson.

"Oh, it's actually conservative compared to the last one with the breast window," said Hashmi as she peaked over at it.

"Exactly," said Amanda. "While the back is exposed a bit, I wanted something that would give her a bit of movement. We can't be too sure what activities they have planned for us tonight. So, inside the box I've provided a pair of low form heels as well."

Safia sighed, before looking off and seeing Mallory rummage her hands inside the box and pulling out a set of black and red bracelets to match the outfit. "Do I really need to do all of this?"

"Well, you don't 'need' to do anything. This is merely helpful advice to show the other second and third years that you are as involved in the game as they are. I'm sure you've noticed that at the moment they've, for the most part, left you alone. That is, unless you've felt anything malicious about their actions against you recently."

"No, they've left me alone so far, so that's true. I haven't even seen Dario since the library that day."

"Then I'd say that is a blessing in and of itself. All you'd need now is to get through the night and hopefully be done with it. So, come along, and let's do something about your hair, shall we?"

"What's wrong with my hair?"

"Dear, you do not wear this outfit and not style the hair to match," said Amanda as she handed Safia the dress and then knelt, flipping the latch on the other case she brought with her and opening it. They all took inside and saw a large selection of hair and makeup items. "Alright, ladies. Let's get to work and make our princess look the part, shall we?"

"Oh " said Hashmi, as she walked over to her closet and pulled out the same jewel box from the last time Safia went to a game night. Opening it, she rummaged around before pulling out a red and black butterfly hair pin. "For luck, right?"

Safia and Amanda both walked on either side of Ricardo through the night with their arms looped into his elbows, on the way to the gymnasium.

"This doesn't feel so bad. It really is a shame I wasn't able to make you my discarded. Then we could have spent more nights together like this."

"I appreciate the thought, but no, thank you. I'm not sure I could handle situations like this all the time," said Safia, but she couldn't help but look up at Ricardo. He was a fair amount taller than her and looked attractive with his hair kept in the moonlight. She was reminded of her night down in tunnels of game night with rolling the dice for her.

"Tell me, Miss Safia. Would you like to have sex with Ricardo?"

"What!" said Safia as she stumbled, caught off guard by the question.

"Really, Amanda?" said Ricardo in a dry tone, not amused by the question.

"You see, that is what I shall never understand about not going after what you desire," said Amanda as she took two quick steps and stood in front of the two. "Here we are in the prime of our lives, and you two are afraid to admit what you're thinking. I'm not saying you have to do it, but at least admit to it."

"I was thinking about how I will keep you under control tonight," said Ricardo, shaking his head. "But it seems that plan has failed before it has even begun."

"Yes, I'm sure," said Amanda with a smile. "You are the type to wonder about pointless things. I honestly think that's part of your charm. But the point was made for my darling Safia here. It's not as if I haven't seen how you look at my Ricardo."

"That's not true," said Safia, trying to avoid looking back up at Ricardo. "You have him escorting us. How could I not look up at him?"

"Is that so?" said Amanda, stepping toward the two. "Both of you, give me your hands."

"What? Why?" asked Safia, as Ricardo sighed and gave Amanda his hand.

"Now, Miss Safia, I do remember you owing me some favors. Will you deny me?"

"And this is one of those favors?"

"It is."

Safia took a deep breath before extending her own hand to Amanda.

"Good, now both of you. I want you to turn and look at each other. Look into each other's eyes and stay that way until I tell you to stop."

They both did as instructed, with Safia glancing away shyly for a few seconds, trying to look directly at him. *Just focus on his ears or something, Safia. Why is she doing this right before everything starts? I should be focusing on the game, not this.* Her eyes slid over, focusing on Ricardo's lips. *God, she's not going to make me kiss him, is she?* The thought itself made her heart tremble, but she couldn't help but slightly bite her lip; a bit of anticipation seeping through.

"Now Ricardo, do you find Safia attractive?"

"I do."

"And would you like to have sex with Safia?"

"I would, but I have you."

"I didn't ask you what you have. I asked would you like to do very fun sexual things with Miss Safia."

"Yes, I would."

"Good boy. Now Miss Safia. Do you like my Ricardo?"

"I... I do."

"And would you like to have sex with my discarded standing in front of you?"

Safia was silent. *Are you really doing this now?*

"Keep in mind our promise, Miss Safia. I like to think I've been a good friend. And you wouldn't want to lie to your friend, would you?"

Safia glanced back at Amanda. "Yes, I want to fuck your boyfriend. Are you happy now?" The frustration and embarrassment clear in her face as her lips quivered.

"Don't say it to me. Say it to him," her voice as calm as if she were talking to toddlers.

Safia turned back to Ricardo, her hand still a bit shaky. "I like you, Ricardo. I think you're nice and attractive. And I want to have sex with you. I know it's silly because you have Amanda. And I'm not going to try to force myself on you or anything. It's... it's just how I feel."

"Wait!" said Amanda. "Do you want to have sex with him, or do you want to fuck him? Because the two can be two very different things. And considering your pension for being a domanatri—"

"Really, Amanda!" shouted Safia, having had enough of the embarrassment.

Amanda released their hands and covered her mouth, trying not to laugh. "Okay... okay, I suppose that is enough teasing." She looked back up to Ricardo. "Safia just has a dominating personality, don you think?"

"I suppose so. She can be quite commanding, I think."

"Yes," said Amanda, blinking her eyes to keep from

laughing. "I could not have used a better word. She has a commanding presence about her. Especially towards those she really likes." But seeing Safia's face, Amanda nodded her head and took a moment to regain her composure. "I suppose even I can go a bit too far." She then reached forward again, grabbing both Safia hands in hers and softened her voice. "See... Doesn't it feel good to just admit what you want?"

"No... it feels embarrassing as hell. What am I supposed to do now? Just go back and pretend we didn't just say that."

"No, you both move forward, acknowledging what you both want and accepting it." She stepped to the side, locking her arm into Ricardo's and leaning her head on his shoulder. "Now come along, we don't want to be last."

They took a few steps in silence, neither one of them speaking.

"Oh, are you both mad at me?" asked Amanda, looking back up at her discarded.

"I am," said Ricardo. "You can push your interests a bit too far."

"I'm sorry. You know how I am. I promise to make it up to you later. How about tomorrow we sit down by the lake, and I'll let you lay in my lap as I feed you grapes? I promise to spoil you all day after we get through tonight."

"I'll hold you to that."

"I'll make sure you hold a lot more against me than that. But at the very least, it'll be a start."-

Safia couldn't help but give a small smile at the couple beside them as they continued their banter. While Amanda was somewhat forceful, and Ricardo was mostly stern, the two of them seemed perfect for each other. *But I really wonder how he deals with her twenty-four-seven. It must be exhausting.*

"And Miss Safia."

"Yes?"

"Don't think you can just have sex with my Ricardo

without my permission. You will have to ask me nicely first. So, no going behind my back trying to seduce him. There are rules to loaning out one's man."

"Oh, just shut up!"

They made their way through the rest of the campus, and despite the circumstances, Safia felt a little lighter on her feet. The night ahead of her didn't feel quite as ominous as it had previously. She didn't want to admit it, but perhaps Amanda's antics had removed the tension from her mind for the moment. They approached the gymnasium and saw two men and two women, both standing outside wearing their evening dress attire.

"See, we aren't overdressed at all."

"Oh good," said Frilla as she stepped out of the door. "I was fearful that you had decided not to join us, Miss Safia, and that all my careful planning for the evening would have gone to waste."

"Amanda brought me this dress to wear. I don't have anything fancy, so it took some time for me to get ready."

"Well done, Amanda. You do know how to dress someone up for our event's standards, miracle worker that you are. And I see you and yours as looking quite complimentary."

"Thank you. I wanted to ensure that we all enjoyed ourselves tonight."

"And that we shall, now that all the participants have arrived," said Frilla as she turned around. "Come along then. The others are already inside, and I can't wait to get started and see what you all manage to do with tonight's game."

Passing through the front doors and into the side corridor, they headed inside a set of black curtains that hid the way ahead. Stepping between the sheets of fabric, Safia was surprised to see the area up ahead. Inside the gymnasium stood a giant cube that almost reached up from the roof. It looked larger than a house and at the front it had its own doors.

"Okay," said Amanda with a whistle as she stared up at the structure. "This is the first time I've seen something like this here. How did this even come about? And is that a stepladder at the side of it? Do you intend to have us climb your little toy here?"

"Yes, it seems our little builder boy is able to create some interesting things when given the proper motivation."

"Jericho? He did this?"

"Him and a few others, one of them being that little Muslim girl you brought with you before. Them and their little entourage have been working through the night to finish it."

*Hashmi? She did this? I knew she would be out late but... Wait, is this what she was doing when she said she was running in the mornings?* Safia thought back, she'd never actually seen Hashmi get up in the morning to go run. She'd just assume that she may be left an hour before they woke up for class. But seeing this, she had maybe only slept three to four hours a night. "Why didn't she tell me?"

"Because she was forbidden to. I couldn't have her exposing the secrets of tonight's game, after all. I thought of banning her outright after seeing her, but Builder Boy assured me that she wouldn't speak a word of this to you. And judging by the look on your face, it seems to be true."

"Well, either way. Bravo," said Amanda as she walked up, placing her hand on the structure. "This must have cost a decent amount of your points."

"Not so much, really. We all chipped in together to foot the bill for it. We will be reimbursed, plus something extra after a successful evening, I assure you. Our entertainment is paramount, but it's as if we are doing philanthropy here."

"Then don't keep us waiting. Take us inside and show us around your new toy. I'm dying to play the game you have in store."

"Follow the leader then," said Frilla, with a wave of her finger before walking over and opening the doors, allowing them inside.

Stepping inside, Safia was surprised to see the roof above her being a lot closer than it appeared from the outside. The walls were a tealish blue with a white ceiling over their heads. At each side of the room were red doors and ahead of them was a large TV screen that sat above an illuminated bar with drinks spread out atop the counter.

"Okay, everyone, our final guests have arrived. We can start tonight's game."

Safia just looked around as the rest gathered at the center of the room. Walking over, she placed her hand on the wall, feeling how sturdy it was.

*I still can't believe they did all of this. They built an entire house inside of the gym. How did they...* Then Safia's mind drifted back to Jericho and how he appeared tired, and then to how Hashmi would often go out at night and stay out all night only sleeping after class. *Dang it, Hashmi. You could have said... No, I suppose not. They probably would have found out... and after she told me about how she's always low on points, I guess it makes sense why she didn't. But if that's the case, who was that boy she was with? Why did they have that parrot mask? Was I meant to find it? I mean, that was her, wasn't it?*

"Miss Safia," said Frilla, walking over to her. "Is everything alright?"

"Oh yes, sorry, I was just still in shock that they managed to build all of this."

"Oh, well, be a good girl and come over then. There's fun to be had in explaining that as well. I was just about to go over the rules."

Safia stepped back over to the crowd, standing in with Ricardo and Amanda as Frilla stood in the center of them. There were a few people that she'd seen around the campus before but had never spoken to. To her surprise, there were more than ten people in the room with her, perhaps even double that amount. But the one thing that stood out the most was the appearance of Addison, who stood over in a corner as if waiting on something. Safia's face twisted in disbelief as she stared at Addison, who was wearing what looked like a wide, fluffy white dress, like something out of a movie. She even had a tiara atop her head.

"Now. As you all can see. We've done quite a bit of work in our gymnasium over the last few weeks. But now that it is finally finished, I am proud to present to you an escape room of my own design."

"Escape room? You mean the room with all the puzzles? Is that what this all is?" asked another girl, looking around the room.

"Exactly. In total, there are ten rooms altogether. There is only one room up ahead. However, the second and third floors have four rooms, but they are larger and third-floor rooms are more complicated. Now that's not to say that you must complete them all. Each room leads into another, depending on the path you take, which will then lead you to a room on the third floor where you will complete the game and be brought back down to this room through the red doors you see on the opposite sides of the room there."

"So, it's about who clears them first, then?"

"Not exactly. Each completion of a room will award points to all those in the room when it's completed. So, you're welcome to team up if you like. But keep in mind completing a room will reward one hundred game points and those points you receive will be dropped by half for each person in the room. Then when it's all over, whichever team with the most points will win the majority of the entrance fees."

"And what if we get stuck and can't clear one of the rooms?"

"Then just click on your pendants announcing that you give up and someone will come and retrieve you. Then you can spend the rest of your time down here with us, watching the remaining contestants through the display on the screen ahead of us. We have installed monitors in each other's rooms to watch the contestants."

"Okay, this does sound fun," said a dark-haired boy, looking over at another brown-haired boy. Safia assumed they were partners, seeing as they were holding hands. "When do we start?"

"One moment, please," said Frilla, as she clapped her hands. "Assistants, please go in and take your spots if you would."

Safia watched as Addison and a few others, in costume, headed through the door. *I guess that's why there were more people than contestants. She's using them for the game. But Addison didn't look so happy. I guess she's doing this for Nasir.*

Then, after a few minutes, Frilla's badge began to glow. "Good, it seems they're all ready. Okay, everyone, go stand by your partners and hold out your arms."

Everyone did as they were told, as Dario walked over and stood by Safia.

"Let's just get this over with. Then you can get the hell away from me," he said.

"Okay, everyone," said Frilla, taking her pendant and raising it above her head, clicking on it. "I, Frilla Santiago, invite all the pre-registered couples in this room to the competition of couples game night. The entry fee is five hundred thousand points."

*Five hundred... that's half a million points.* Safia looked around the room as everyone's badges began glowing and they clicked on their pendants, accepting the bets. *Does everyone here really have that many points?* She turned to look up at Dario.

"Don't fucking look at me," he whispered as he stared around the room. "You're the reason I'm in this mess." With a sigh, he clicked on his pendant. "Let's get this shit over with. You'd better not cost me a win here, bitch."

Safia shook her head, still looking up at Dario. "Fuck you. I hope you choke on your damned points." She then clicked on her own pendant.

"Okay. Everyone's points have been deducted. Only the first two couples with the highest game points the goal will receive the entrance fee payout. The first to finish will receive seventy-five percent of the points gathered here today, then second will receive twenty-five percent." She then walked over to the green door and opened it, revealing another black curtain. "So, my lovely ladies and gentlemen. Let the games begin."

They all stepped past the curtain into a room with four doors and four clocks that hung on the wall. Each clock was made of something different. One glowed gold, and another looked wooden, and the other two, Safia thought, both looked silver. But at the center of the room stood a half-naked woman on a stand with a sheer cloth that draped over one shoulder covering one of her breasts.

"Welcome," said the girl as she smiled upon their entrance into the room. "Please come in. Everything is waiting on you."

"Well, isn't this a pleasant surprise," said Amanda, as she stepped ahead, looking up at the woman on the stand. "And what is your name?"

"I am a woman removed for her beauty. Taken from my kingdom, I was spirited away. You would see alongside the roads with Paris atop a false horse, but alas, I was already lost to men who wanted to test their metal."

"That's not confusing in the slightest," said another boy with accents in his clothing.

"Well, doesn't this look fun," said the brown-haired boy with the male partner as he walked forward, running his finger over the golden clock. "I imagine it's telling us that time is running out."

"Yes, but why are all of them set at twelve o'clock?" asked the dark-haired one.

"I'm sure we will find out sooner or later," responded his partner

"I think they wish for all of us to work together on the first one," said Amanda as she walked over to the side of the room where there was a science table with beakers of some type of clear liquid alongside eight balls that sat in a tray next to a scale. "Does anyone have any ideas?"

"Nothing so far," said another girl as she knocked on one of the four doors of the rooms ahead. "But I guess since there are four doors and there are four clocks. That each clock would open a door."

"You are beautiful," said the boy with blue accents in his clothing, walking up to the model and admiring her with Amanda. "Are you a first-year student? When this is all over, you want to go out on a date?"

The woman smiled back at him. "Be warned, touching the models without permission will force an immediate expulsion from the game."

"Oh, so there are more of you then. Are they as beautiful and naked as you are? Because if so, then I can hardly wait."

"Oh, there's something attached to her leg," said Amanda, leaning forward and peering into the gown. There was a white piece of paper that blended in with the sheer of the fabric, making it hard for them to see. It was lodged inside of a garter belt. "I suppose that exposed breast was there to distract us from that little detail. Would you mind if…" She pointed suggestively at the note while smiling up at the girl.

The half-dressed girl on the stand smiled back at Amanda before reaching down, sliding the sheer fabric to the side and exposing her leg to Amanda. "You are given permission."

Amanda took her time, sliding a finger up the girl's leg before plucking the note from the garter belt on her thigh.

"Thank you," she said before opening the letter and reading it aloud. "Of the ten, find the value thrice and only then will your fortunes be weighed."

"More cryptic shit," said Dario as he continued to look

over the room.

"Yes, but what do we have to find the value of? I'm guessing we should use that scale over there," said the boy in blue.

"Yeah, but a dozen of what?"

"Well, we've got eight of these little balls here. Perhaps we weigh those," said another girl in blue accents, who began fiddling around with the science stuff on the table. "I mean, they're different sizes, so it might be what they are talking about."

"Could be. But let's keep looking around the room until we're sure."

They continued to search around the room, but only found a few trinkets.

Safia began inspecting the clocks. One was wooden, two were of some type of silver metal, and the final one was golden. *There must be something special about the clocks. Why else would they all be made of different things?* She ran her hands over the surface of them, feeling the ridges in their shape, but didn't feel anything particularly off.

Amanda picked up one of the eight balls and began rolling it around in her hand. "These are quite heavy. But they feel coarse, you'd think for little rolling balls they would be smooth." She let it drop from her hand and fall to the metal table. The impact shook all the instruments nearby as the bang it created echoed across the room.

"Okay, it looks like we can move the clock hands around on these things," said the girl in blue as she walked up beside Safia, placing her finger on the hour hand on the clock and began spinning it around. The ticking sound it made was clearly audible.

"Hey, I found a ball," said the boy in blue, reaching into one of the cushions of a chair and pulling out a gold sphere and holding it out for everyone to see. "Although, it's not like the other ones."

Dario walked over, plucking it from the boy's hand and

rolling it between his fingers. "It's gold. And we have a golden clock. So, I'm guessing there are more balls in this room somewhere that probably match up with the clocks."

"Sounds like a reasonable assumption to me," said Ricardo.

"Agreed," said Amanda. "Amazing that it came from Dario."

"Just shut up and search the damn room."

They all agreed and proceeded to search every nook and cranny of the room and eventually came up with three more of the balls. But none of them matched the clocks, and instead were just like the ones Amanda had before. They felt rough and were gray.

"We're still missing one," said the boy in blue as he placed his back against the wall. "And we've looked over this room like three or four times."

"Yeah," said Dario as he looked around one more time, before his eyes focused on the half-naked girl in the center of the room. He walked up to her and began looking over her body. "We're looking for a small space where you can stick a little ball in."

"Dario," said Amanda. "As grateful as we all are from your brilliant skills of deduction. I'm afraid that your keen powers of observation may be pushing the limits of reason. And if you're thinking of searching where you shouldn't, then I'm afraid things are going to get very, very violent for you."

"Yeah, well, no one asked you. And besides, I wasn't going to do what you think." He turned to the half-dressed girl. "Get down from there. I want to see something." The girl extended her hand to Dario, and he accepted it, helping her balance herself as she stepped down to the floor. She was a little taller than Amanda, which allowed Dario to see atop her head, where he graciously reached into her hair and plucked out a small coarse ball, tossing it to Ricardo. "There," he said, looking at Amanda. "My brilliant powers of deduction at work."

"Yes, and the joys of being tall. Tell me, what does it feel like to be a man of your stature, looking down on us women? It must be quite the boost to your ego."

"Ask your little pet there. He's as tall as I am."

"True, but I doubt he needs the ego boost, since he has me. Even so, after all this time, I question what you really have that you haven't already started overcompensating for."

"Okay, not now, you two. How about you all bicker after we get to the next room? That way it won't slow you all down," said the boy with the dark hair. "But for now, how about you help us figure out the rest of this puzzle?"

"Fine," said Dario as he stepped past Amanda and walked over near the table, his eyes glancing across the room at Ricardo as he did so.

Safia saw the exchange between the two men. But instead of choosing to walk over to them, she walked over to Amanda, who was now back to giving her attention to the near naked model.

"Now, tell me," said Amanda, "what was that phrase you had said before when we entered the room?"

"I am a woman removed for her beauty. Taken from the kingdom, I was spirited away. You would see me alongside the roads with Paris atop a false horse, but alas, I was already lost to men who wanted to test their metal."

"Shouldn't it be renowned for her beauty? Not removed?" said the boy in blue.

"Honestly, dear, in this game, who can tell? But for now, let's take her at her word, shall we?" asked Amanda, turning back to the woman. "Shall we help you backup on your stage?"

"This is fine. The purpose of it has already been lost," said the girl. "You can go over to your friends now. They may need your help."

"Friends? Me and him?" said Amanda, turning back to

look at Dario. "Now, there's a loose definition of the term if there ever was one. But I do suppose you are right. Let us join the group, Safia." She then grabbed Safia by the hand as they headed back over to the rest of the group, as they placed all the balls into their respective slots on the tray.

"I still don't see what we are supposed to do now," said the boy in blue as he took the golden ball and placed it on the scale, showing that it weighed ten pounds. "Anyone else have any ideas?"

"Well, they must mean something. What did that note say again?"

"Of the ten, find the value thrice and only then will your fortunes be weighed," said Amanda, reading out the letter again.

"So, it's ten pounds and we have ten of those balls, huh?" said Dario as he closed his eyes, placing his back against the wall.

"Oh! Look, it's peeling away."

They all turned back to the end of the table to see that the girl in blue had submerged one of the balls into the beaker of the liquid that was on the table. And slowly, as she poked at it, the round surface coating began to peel away, exposing a shiny surface beneath.

"What the? Is that stuff even safe to touch if it does that?" said her partner.

The girl placed her fingers to her nose. "It doesn't smell funny, and I doubt they'd let us fumble about in here if there was something really dangerous."

"Okay, then," said the dark-haired boy. "Let's start cleaning some balls, shall we?" He then immediately shook his head. "That sounded way more inappropriate than I intended it to." He then looked over at his boyfriend as a smile crept across his face. "But it will be appropriate later."

They all gave a laugh and went about submerging each of the spheres into the beaker before cleaning them off. To their surprise, this method only was able to remove the coating of three of the balls, as the rest stayed the same grainy texture and gray color, no matter how long they stayed in the beaker.

"Okay, so of the ten, six of them were failures."

"Not failure. Just dummies. Look," said the dark-haired boy pointing to the clocks on the wall. "Each of the balls that we rubbed off, 'Again, not sexual,' correlates to a clock on the wall. Gold for gold, two silver clocks, and one wooden clock for one wooden ball. I think we are almost done with this part."

"Why is one of the silvers shinier than the other?" asked the girl in blue as she walked over, trying to inspect them further.

"That's because it's platinum, not silver. Silver is the duller one," said Dario.

"So, what do we do next?"

"I suppose we weigh them all," said the boy in blue as grabbed from the tray and placed them on the scale one by one. "Okay, so the wooden ball weighs one pound, the silver one weighs eight, platinum five pounds, and the gold weighs ten pounds."

"What are we supposed to do with that information?"

"Oh, the clocks. We can put them into the clocks. If gold is ten pounds, then maybe we should set it to ten o'clock," said the girl in blue as she walked back over to the clocks.

"That's a good idea. My partner is smart. Try it out and see what happens."

Safia walked over to join the girl in blue next to the clocks and put in the time in correlation to the weight of the balls. One o'clock for the wooden ball, five and eight o'clock for the two silver, and ten o'clock for the gold. They then stepped back as they heard a clicking sound and they all watched as all the clocks reset themselves back to twelve o'clock. Curious as to what the noise meant, the group all then looked around the room in anticipation, but nothing happened.

"I think that means our little guess was wrong," said the dark-haired boy.

"Then I don't know what to do next. I really thought that was—"

"Fuck!" said Dario, so loud that the entire room turned to look at him.

"Was there a reason for that outburst," said Amanda, "or have you just grown so fond of that particular vulgarity that you're just shouting it at random now?"

"Don't you get it?" said Dario, pointing his finger to the half-naked model still standing in the room watching them. "That bitch over there is Helen of Troy."

"Yes, I had assumptions as to that, but I fail to—" Amanda's eyes went wide as she balled up her lips and began shaking her head. "Fuck! He's right."

"Do you care to enlighten us as to this revelation you both seem to be privy to?" asked the dark-haired boy.

Dario looked over at the scale, a look of disgust on his face. "She's Helen of Troy, metals are measured in Troy ounces, not pounds. Gold, Silver, and platinum are all metals. I bet my ass if you check that scale over there, there is a way to set it to Troy ounces."

"He's right," said the boy in blue, fiddling with the settings on the scale. "So, I guess we should try again." They repeated the process, but this time measuring the spheres in Troy ounces. "Okay, so the gold clock should be set to one forty-five, the platinum clock should be two eighteen, the silver should be one sixteen, and the wood needs to be set to—"

"You won't need to measure the wood," said Dario.

"What, why?" asked the boy in blue.

"That woman's message said that men would test their metal. Wood is not a precious metal. That is probably why it only weighs one pound. It wouldn't give you a high enough number to be put into the clock."

"Sadly, I must agree with Dario again," said Amanda,

shaking her head with a sigh. "As disgusting as the appeal of that is, even the note says to find the value thrice. Thrice means three and we only have three metals on the wall."

Safia walked over to the clock and began putting in the times on each of the corresponding clocks. And sure enough, there was a loud click after inputting the time on the platinum clock as all four doors opened up simultaneously.

"Well done, Dario," said the dark-haired boy. "If not for your vulgar mouth, terrible attitude, and overall Dario'ness, you might actually be useful for something."

"Yeah, well, I'm just here to win. And your dumbasses probably won't even clear the next rooms. So, I'm happy to be rid of you."

"So, which door do we take?" asked the girl in blue.

"I don't know," said her partner, peeking his head inside of each door. "It looks like they all lead upstairs."

"Then I vote for the one ahead," said the girl in blue as she walked forward, locking arms with the boy in blue. "I shall see you all at the finish. I'm sure we will be first." The two then disappeared behind a curtain and after a few seconds, the door closed in behind them and they heard it lock.

"I guess that means we're on our way, Ricardo. We can't let them get a head start on us," said Amanda as she and Ricardo headed towards the other door on the left. She then turned back to Safia. "Have fun, Miss Safia. A shame this game wasn't more cooperative, but what can you do? Try not to have Dario rub off on you too much." And with a smile Amanda and Ricardo exited through the door and disappeared, only to have the door close and locked itself behind them a few seconds later.

"I guess that we shouldn't dawdle as well, honey," said the brown- haired boy to his partner as they both headed toward the second inner door.

"Come on then," said Dario, as he nodded to the last door.

Following Dario as he stepped through the curtain, Safia saw the outside of the structure. She was able to see the bleachers and the inside of the gymnasium but looking upward as she took the steps to the second floor, she could see that it looped again, doing the pattern from the second floor to the third floor. *I hope this is safe.* She felt a little afraid of the height above her. Taking a closer look at the upside of the build as they went up the steps towards the second-floor door, she realized that each floor was just giant boxes set atop metal beams.

*How did they do this? Wouldn't they need some type of machines to lift all this heavy stuff? And Hashmi has been doing this every night?* Following behind Dario, she entered the second-floor room. *What does all this mean?* The room had four lights at each corner of its walls and in the center were four statues forming a square and in the center of them was a sundial.

Continuing to look around the room, she saw a large wooden machine against one of the walls with a sheet of cloth lying between it and a press above it. Over by another wall she saw Dario inspecting what looked to be a replica of a ship that sat on two mounts. And the final piece in the room was a portrait of a woman holding a cross in her hand as fire roared around her.

"What do we do here?" asked Safia, looking over the artwork.

"I don't know. But I'll figure it out. You just wait and—"

"Well, isn't a lovely room," said a voice from behind them as they heard the door close and lock.

They both turned around to see the dark-haired boy with his back against the door.

Dario narrowed his eyes. "What do you want? Go back to your husband."

"Sorry, the door's locked. Seems as if you both are stuck with me."

Safia twisted her lips in confusion. "But why? Why

would you follow—"

"You both should have paid more attention to Frilla's little meeting. She never said that we had to stay with our partners, only that the points would be divided between those in the room when it's completed." He stepped forward with a smirk on his face as he slid a finger across one of the statues. "And seeing that, I'm now stuck in this room with the both of you. I guess that now means that your points will now become my points."

# CHAPTER 9

"You son of a bitch," said Dario, as he walked over, grabbing the dark-haired boy by the collar and pulling him forward. "You think you can fuck with me and not pay for it?"

"Yes. That's exactly what I think," said the dark-haired boy, seeming unfazed by Dario's hands, gripping the collar around his neck. "It's really your own fault. You showed such aptitude in the previous room that I simply had to follow you. My boyfriend thought we should just follow Amanda, but no, you proved yourself to be more formidable. It's actually quite a compliment if you think about it."

"Dario, let him go," said Safia, walking over and grabbing him by the arm. "We don't have time for this."

Dario looked at Safia before turning back to the dark-haired boy with a snarl on his lips before he finally released his hand from the boy's neck and turned around.

"You're not even worth it." He then walked back to the area with the statues and began inspecting them.

The boy fixed his collar, loosening it from around his neck, before turning to Safia. "Thank you for your concern. But I don't think we've been properly introduced. My name is Arthur Sinclair, second year here at this fun and fabulous school."

"Yeah," said Dario, as he looked at a painting on the wall. "And he also enjoys bending his partner over and sticking a cock up his ass."

"Well, that's not true at all," said Arthur, with a smile at Dario. "I'm more of a bottom personally. All of the pleasure and none of the work. Tell me, Dario, have you ever tried to dominate a man? You seem like the type that wouldn't mind getting off in such a way. The way you huff and puff around is the standard trait for a top."

"Keep you fucked up fantasies to yourself."

"Hmph, what a shame," said Arthur, turning back to Safia. "Well, you can't win them all, now can you? Although I'm sure not many would refer to anything that has to do with Dario as 'winning.'"

"Okay? But are you alright?" asked Safia, pointing to the fresh imprints around the boy's neck.

"Don't worry about me, Miss Safia. Dario knows better than to hit me. He's just blowing hot air, is all. Physical violence isn't allowed unless both parties agree to it. That is, of course, if he wishes to wind up twitching on the floor like so many others. And that too, would serve my purposes just fine."

"But I don't get it," said Safia. "Why leave your partner alone? Wouldn't it have been better to work with him than to follow us?"

"What, Henry? No, he's always been good at puzzles. I'm sure he will do just fine. I'm just here to slow you both down, that's all. As I said earlier, the points are divided by all those in a room when it's completed. And since my darling Henry will be completing the rooms by himself, that means he will get all the points."

"Forget him," said Dario. "Get your ass over here and help me figure out this damned game."

"Have you ever considered asking properly?" said Safia, "Why are you like this? Would it really hurt you to act like a regular person for once?"

Dario just stared at Safia for a moment, his eyes squinted as if he was trying to make out what type of animal she was. "Then just stay the fuck over there then. Who needs any of you?"

"Ahh!" groaned Safia before stepping forward. "Fine, what is this puzzle about?"

"Here," said Dario, handing her a card.

Safia took it and began reading. "The sun once shined brightly on these four stars. And though the night has set upon them, you have the power to turn back time and bring them together again."

"Leonardo, Donatello, Michelangelo, Raphael," said Arthur as he stepped forward. "The great artists of the renaissance."

Safia began sliding the paper back and forth between hand as she looked at the statues. Both Donatello and Raphael were facing inward, while Michelangelo and Leonardo were both facing outward.

"This one is easy enough," said Safia, looking at the disk in the middle of the room. "I think."

"Oh yeah? And how's that?" asked Dario.

"The stand in the center of the statues is a sundial."

"I see that. What about it?"

"But it's not meant for time. Look at the roman numerals on the sides. It doesn't go from noon to midnight, it goes from one hundred to three thousand. So, the only time these four were alive together was around the fourteen hundreds, so if you get the shadows on it or near it, then that will probably be your answer." said Safia as she walked up under one of the lights in the corner of the room reach-ing up for it but found herself about two feet two short. "I can't reach them."

Dario walked to another corner of the room and reached up, managing to place his fingers on the lower portion of the light, but no matter how much force he used, the light would budge.

"Oh my, they do seem to be stuck in place, don't they?" said Arthur.

"How are we supposed to move this shit then, if we gotta make the shadows move?"

"There has to be something in here that can…" said Safia as she walked over to Donatello's statue in front of her and gripped its head and began to twist it in her hand. Slowly, it responded with her force as the whole bust started to turn. They all watched as the light on the opposite corner of the room, where Dario was, started to turn in response.

"Well, it turns out you're good for something after all," said Dario as he walked over, placing his hands on the Michelangelo bust.

Safia removed her hand from the bust. "You are just the worst, you know—" the bust began rotating back on its own. Before Safia clamped her hands down back on it again.

"Well, now," said Dario with a smile, as he looked over at Arthur. "It seems this room requires the use of two people. I sure do hope that boyfriend of yours isn't trapped because he can't reach the other side of some puzzle."

"Yes, I'm sure you'd be all torn up about it," said Arthur with a shrug. "But if that's the case, then I suppose there's nothing that can be done."

Dario and Safia began turning the busts of the statues, trying to get the shadows to match up on fourteen hundred. But no matter how much they tried, the shadows would not overlap.

"Oh, I'm on the wrong one," said Safia as released the bust of Donatello. "The statues need to be all facing each other, maybe."

"Maybe?"

"Well, it's not like it's not like I can't be wrong. Do you have a better idea?"

"Just turn the damn head."

Safia sighed, trying not to let Dario aggravate her anymore, but stepped over, grabbing Leonardo's bust, and began turning. And as they once again moved the statues to face the dial in the middle, they both heard a clicking sound as the statues both locked in position in place and the lights at the corners of the room all froze in place.

"Is that it?" asked Safia, looking around the room.

"Well, seeing as that door isn't opened, I'm guessing it ain't. But I know I heard a click. So, that means something in this room opened up somewhere."

"I believe that sound game from the sundial itself," said Arthur, as both Safia and Dario turned to him in surprise. "What? Am I not allowed to be of assistance?"

"But I don't understand. I thought you wanted us to lose."

"No, I just don't want you both to win. As long as it's not first, why should I care if you come in second?"

"Yeah, whatever," said Dario as he stepped over to the sunlight and placed his hands on it, feeling the grooves of it. It shifted on its base as he put some force into it, so he placed his hands under the sides on the top, lifting it off its base. Looking into it, under the sundial in a circular pot were a bunch of small wooden blocks along with a note.

Safia picked up the note as Dario placed the top piece of the sundial on the floor against the stand. "This room has two doors. One represents the way of the hero, and one represents the way of the villain. But good and evil are all a matter of perspective. Tell us the name of yours."

"What the hell does that mean?" asked Dario as looked toward the exit. "There's only one door, unless they want us to come back the way we came." He then reached into the pot and pulled out one of the cubes and saw that it had the letter 'S' on it? "Great, now what are we supposed to do with these?"

"Hmm," moaned Arthur, picking up a cube himself. "It reminds of the games I used to play as a child, where I used to put the odd shape block into holes." He then looked over at Dario with a frown. "Shut up. Don't even say it."

"Don't need to," said Dario, turning his back to go and inspect the ship. "You know it's there."

"Come, Miss Safia, as much as it pains me to help Dario, I actually need you all to succeed in order for my plans to take effect." He took Safia over to the wooden machine, reaching over and slid off the top of the press revealing small square shaped slots, where he plopped down the cube in her hand into one. "And looky there, a perfect fit."

"How did you know?"

"It's a printing press," said Arthur, pointing to the picture on the wall. "And I'm assuming that picture is of Jeanne D'arc." But then he pointed to the replica ship. "I'm not too sure about the ship, though."

"If it's the fourteen hundreds, then it's probably Christopher Columbus," said Dario, listening in but not looking back at them.

"Well then, there we go," said Arthur, clapping his hand for Dario. "Although I'm sure who would be the hero in this case and who would be the villain, seeing as our lovely Jeanne D'arc was literally burned at the stake and Columbus is a much-celebrated figure."

"It doesn't matter. Both were murderers," said Dario, walking back over to the pot and picking out a few cubes. "Just because one claimed she could hear God and the other probably thought he was God; it doesn't matter in the end. Everyone is a villain to the people they're out there killing." Dario tossed one of the cubes to Safia. "Pick one."

"Why me?"

"Probably so he can blame you, if he can't solve the next puzzle," said Arthur. "But, let's try Jeanne D'arc and see what happens."

Safia agreed, and they both went back and forth, grabbing the cubes needed to spell out the name, then took the time to insert them into the blocks of the machine.

"Is this really how the presses used to work?"

"What? Like this? Goodness no, they used to be far more annoying to use. This is just a simplified version for the game. It's cute though." After loading the machine with the name, they closed the top and pulled the level to lower the press down on the paper. When it lifted, they saw a red light scan over the name and they heard the sound of another click as the door to the opposite side of the room opened.

"It's about time. Let's head out of here and get this over with," said Dario as he walked over to the door and through the curtain. Safia then quickly followed suit, walking through the curtain and back outside of the makeshift building. Once again, she was on the other side of the manmade structure and looked down about fifteen feet to the gymnasium floor beneath her. She made her way up the steps, passing by Dario who was leaning on the side of the railing looking up at the ceiling as a stupid smile came over his face.

"What are you doing?" asked Safia, looking back at Dario. "I thought you—"

Safia got her answer before she finished her statement, as Arthur walked through the curtain and Dario quickly grabbed him by the color of his neck, forcing him up against the side of the railing so hard that the whole staircase shook from the force.

"Gotcha, you fucker."

"What are... let me go, or I swear I'll—"

"You'll what? You think you can click that little pendant faster than I can throw your sorry ass down to the floor?"

Safia dropped to her knees, clutching the side of the railing as it shook under her feet. "Dario, stop!"

Dario smiled wide as he applied more pressure to the

smaller boy and then nodded up at the side of the building. "Ain't no camera's out here. I guess they didn't think about the fact that their little dollhouse would end up blocking them."

"You wouldn't dare."

Dario pushed harder, his eyes wide with excitement. "It's our word against yours and I can't rat her out and she can't rat me out. So, that means I can do whatever I want, and she'll go right along with it."

Dario now had Arthur's back arched over the railing to the point where only the tip of his shoes were still on the steps.

"Dario. Think sensibly. You can't do this and honestly think—"

"That's the thing isn't it," he said, the saliva dripping from his grinning teeth as he pushed harder, lifting Arthur completely off his feet. The boy's weight was completely on the railing. "I don't fucking care anymore. I kill you, then I'll go after—"

"Dario, stop," said Safia, grabbing hold of his arm. "You fucking idiot. Let him go, right now, or I swear I'll throw you over the side." She tried tugging at his arm and found that he was stronger than she'd thought he was. With every jerk, his arm barely moved.

"I can do whatever the fuck I want," said Dario as they heard the door beside him begin to click. He looked down at Safia and then down at Arthur. "You got lucky, but if you ever try to fuck with me again. I don't care how many boyfriends you have. They won't stop me before I break your neck." Dario pulled Arthur in, turning his back toward the door and pushed him back inside of the room as the door closed, locking him inside with the sound of another click and it shut.

"You idiot," said Safia. "What if you both would have fallen?"

"Then I would have landed on him," said Dario as he

stepped past Safia. "Come on. We got one more room before I get my points and I'm done with this shit."

Safia closed her eyes and took a deep breath. She could feel her heart racing in her chest as she stared up at Dario's back as he ascended the steps. *One more room; just one more room and I won't have to deal with this jackass anymore. Just a little bit longer. Just a little bit longer.* Safia nodded her head, accepting what was ahead, and made her way up the steps where Dario waited on her.

They both stepped inside the room to see nine suits of armor, each holding swords. Eight of them were spread out amongst the back wall, separated by a compartment door. On the opposite side of the room was a single suit of armor with a cloak draped over its shoulders that sat down upon a throne. Its hands were open, facing upward, and in front of it was a sword embedded in a stone. In the center of the room, between them, was a circular table that was cracked completely though in the middle. And upon the table sat a locked ornate box with a piece of paper taped to the side.

Safia walked over, taking it and beginning to read. "Hello, brave knights. You are in the presence of the most loyal of men. For they all bent the knee in service, and all did great deeds. Who amongst those in this room were the most loyal to Camelot? Search them out and place their swords upon the mounts. But be aware that to find the answer, to know the answer, you must know the truth of men's hearts. If you wish to proceed, then you are given the quest of seeking out and getting to the bottom of the magical treasures of Camelot."

"So, it's King Arthur then?" asked Dario, walking around the room inspecting the suits of armor. He squatted down before one of the knights inspected its blade. "Hey, this things have lettered engraved on them." He looked over the other blades. "All of them do."

"That card, does it have their names on it?"

"It does. On the back it has: Gawain, Percival, Kay,

Lancelot, then it has: Bedivere, Tristan, Mordred, and Palamedes. Do you know a lot about King Arthur stuff?"

"No, but I know the cliff notes. That'll probably do here. The last one was so easy even you could figure it out. I can't imagine this one will be that hard."

"Really? Are you really going to take every opportunity to try and talk down to me? Are you really that small and petty? No wonder everyone hates you."

Dario laughed, "That's everyone's problem here. I don't give a fuck who likes me. Everyone here is hiding behind their fake smiles. Unlike all of you, at least I'm not lying to myself. I know who I am."

"We're not lying to one another. You're just—"

"Really? So, you haven't been lying since you got here?" said Dario, standing up and walking over to Safia. "You don't get it. You don't even know who you are. Go ahead and pretend you don't see what is in front of you. But you're not gonna peddle your shit in front of me and tell me I'm wrong for playing the game the way it's meant to be played."

*No, don't argue with this idiot. Just finished the game and hope that I never have to see him again.* She turned away from him and walked over to the table. "Let's get this over with. I feel dirty just being around you."

"Best idea you had all night," said Dario as he walked back to the other side of the table and began inspecting it. He ran his hands over the side of the table. "It's got little holes inside of it." He he moaned as he knelt, inspecting the holes on the table. "Looks like they go all the way around." He then stood up, walking to a suit of armor, and grabbing the sword with the P engraved on it. Weighing it in his hand, he brought it back to the table and slid it into the whole. It locked in place as a jewel on its hilt lit up. "Alright then, let's fill this up."

Both Safia and Dario went back and forth, taking the blades from the knights and sliding them into the holes in the table. They continued until all the slots had been filled and every jewel at the end of their blade had lit up. But the problem was that while there were eight blades, there were only six slots in the table.

"Now what?" asked Safia. "Nothing happened."

"Yeah, I see that," said Dario as he looked over the room again. "Something's obviously wrong. Six slots, but if we count King Arthur over there, then that makes nine blades. Help me look around the room for more places where we can put those blades."

And once again, they began to search. There was an assortment of things that were attached to the wall, things like paintings, shields, a staff, a lance, and a crown, but Safia didn't see anything that gave off a clue. Instead, she walked back to the treasure chest on the table and picked up the clue again.

"Hello, brave knights. You are in the presence of the most loyal of men. For they all bent the knee in service, and all did great deeds. Who amongst those in this room were the most loyal to Camelot. Search them out and place their swords upon the mounts. But be aware that to find the answer, to know the answer, you must know the truth of men's hearts. If you wish to proceed, then you are given the quest of seeking out and getting to the bottom of the magical treasures of Camelot."

"Getting to the bottom of the treasures of Camelot," said Dario as he walked back to the chest and tried to shake it open, but it wouldn't budge. "Damn thing's welded to the table. It ain't moving."

"Wait, is there anything in here that looks like a treasure of Camelot?"

"Everything could be a treasure."

"No, I mean it said magical treasure. Anything like that?"

"How are we supposed to... Merlin. He used magical stuff."

"Yes," said Safia, looking around the room again and spotting the staff from earlier. "And don't magical people in the stories use sticks like that?" She walked up and tried to reach up for the staff but couldn't since it was too high up.

Dario walked up behind her and reached up, grabbing the stick. "It's your own fault for being short."

"I'm not short. I'm tall for a woman."

"And I'm tall for a man. Which still makes you short."

"Just give me the stick," said Safia, taking the staff from him and inspecting it. Turning it over, she saw something black attached to the base. Reaching in and pinching its sides, she pulled out a key and held it out before Dario. "I was right, again."

"Yeah, just like a broken clock," said Dario, taking the key and walking back over to the treasure chest and sliding it inside. With a turn, they both heard it click and saw the latch of the treasure chest release. Dario smiled as he lifted the lid of the chest, but his smile quickly faded after peaking inside. "Oh, you gotta be fucking kidding me."

"What?"

Dario reached into the treasure chest and pulled out another smaller treasure chest with a jewel embedded atop it, along with a note. He then handed the note to Safia as he placed the chest in front of himself and closed his eyes, trying to contain his frustration.

"You have found the magical treasure, but you have not discovered who amongst those knights are the most loyal in Camelot. Only within the hearts of men will true loyalty be found, and righteousness will be grasped by one's own hand."

"I'm getting sick of all these puzzles."

Safia stepped over and looked at the smaller treasure box. The jewel on the top reminded her of the ones in their pendants. Out of curiosity, she tried pressing it, and all the jewels on the swords around the table began to flash. Before going dull.

"What does that mean?"

"Either we got them wrong or something's broken."

They began removing blades from the table, shuffling the around the eight blades into the six slots in the table. Each time they clicked the jewel on top of the box, only to have the lights on the sword's light up before fading back again. The sword with the L on it was never one of the six to be placed, as it lay on the floor by Dario's foot.

Safia placed a hand on the table, wiping a bit of sweat from her face with the other. "I don't know enough about King Arthur. How am I supposed to know who's the most loyal? What aren't you using that L sword?"

"Nah, I know Lancelot fucked his wife, so I don't know how loyal that is. That's why I'm not using his blade. We had a class on it once but fuck if I remember all of it. He fought some wars and died because of—" He looked over the blade and found the one he was looking for. He pulled out the blade with the M and inserted the one with the P. Then he clicked the button on top of the treasure chest, and they watched as the lights on the blades lit up, blinking three times before they heard the smaller treasure chest click.

"It worked."

"Finally," said Dario as he opened the box, furrowing his brows as he pulled out two wooden rods with latches on them and a letter, and began to read. "It was by their own hands that they pushed forward, and their final acts of loyalty were committed."

Safia reached over, grabbing the wooden rod. "I don't get it. What do they mean by their own hands?"

They both looked forward to King Arthur with his hands open, facing upward on his throne. They then each took a rod and walked over to the suit of armor and there in his hand saw a latch that looked to match the one on the rod. Placing their rod in the hands and twisting them, the hands closed on the rods, locking them in place.

"It was by their own hands that they pushed forward," said Dario, repeating the words on the note.

He and Safia both pushed forward on the rods and felt

the statue give way from the wall and slide outward, revealing two sword mounts on a sliding tray above a table behind its back. Understanding what this meant, they both walked back to the table and grabbed the swords of Lancelot and Mordred. Then, coming back, they placed them into the mounts as both jewels on the swords lit up, then they heard the latch that held the tray as it disconnected. And with a heavy push, they slid the swords of both Mordred and Lancelot into King Arthur's back.

The room lit up in colors as the lights twirled and then focused on the door ahead of them.

"Finally, I'm out of here," said Dario as he and Safia made their way over and Dario pressed his hands on the doorknob and pulled it open. Inside, it was revealed to be some type of odd elevator. "Alright, get in."

Safia hesitantly peeked her head inside the room and saw the makeshift elevator. It was made of wood and had some bars on top of it. It looked like some sort of makeshift cage. "This doesn't look safe."

"Yeah, well too fuckin' bad," said Dario as reached forward and pulled Safia forward into the cage. She stumbled before crashing into him as he held her in place and pressed a large button on the inside that read down.

The elevator lurched as all the light inside of it went out. Above them sat a timer 'two minutes' and 'The elevator will start soon.'

"You jackass," said Safia, as she freed herself from him, taking a step back. Which was all she could take in the tiny cage. "What is wrong with you?"

"The same thing that's wrong with you. And finally, I won't have to deal with your ass anymore after this. No way, I'm going to be caught by Frilla like that again. Her and her damn games."

"I'm nothing like you. And it's your own fault. None of this would have happened if you didn't come over and start being your own asshole of a self. Why didn't you just leave us alone?"

Dario started laughing. "Do you even hear yourself? The same can be said for you and your little bitch group. You didn't 'just' leave me alone the night you took Mallory from me, did you? No, you tricked me and tricked her. Don't pretend we're any different."

"I did what I did because you're an abusive ass. And just because the school allowed it, doesn't mean I will."

"You, who blackmailed me and took what belonged to me?"

"She doesn't belong to you. And I heard what you used to do to her. Painting her naked in front of people like she was on display."

"Oh, fuck off, I did it cause she liked it."

"She did not—"

"Ohh, she most certainly did," said Dario, laughing. "Now, look at you lying to yourself. There's no way you're living with that girl, and you don't see how she gets off on being used. I bet she's asking to do things for you all the time. But the problem is, you just don't want to admit it. Oh, but it's there. The more you use her, the more she gets off on it." Dario reached his hand out and ran it across a piece of loose hair by Safia's face. "You might be pretty, but you're dumb as shit when it comes to people."

Safia scowled in disgust at the feel of Dario's hand against her face. "Don't... touch... me." She raised her hand, flicking his hand away from her.

"Or what? It's just me and you in this slow ass elevator," Dario raised his other hand showing Safia his pendant. "I challenge Safia Famosa to one minute, where we are allowed to hurt each other."

A few long seconds later, the pendant around Safia's neck began to flash. "Dario Burrows has challenged you to remove the safety restrictions of the campus for one minute. Do you accept?"

Safia was quiet as she snatched her head away from

Dario and folded her arms in front of her. "I'm done with you. Don't ever speak to me again."

"Of course, you are, and that's why I'm where I am, and you are where you are. On the bottom, you're lucky to get my points after all this."

The pendant repeated itself as the light began flashing faster. "Dario Burrows has challenged you to remove the safety restrictions of the campus for one minute. Do you accept?"

In disgust, she lifted the pendant from her neck. *I hate this place. I hate all of it. I hate this school; I hate the people, and I hate...* She looked over at Dario, who also had folded his arms in front of his chest and was shaking his head in as he stared ahead thinking about something. That stupid smile was still on his face.

Safia then reached up as the cabin of the elevator lurched again, grabbing the beams above her head. She then gripped the beams as hard as she slid the pendant up between them as she did. Lifting her feet, she allowed her left to hang from her arms as she brought her knees up to her chest.

"Dario," said Safia

"What do you want now, you—" said Dario as he turned to Safia, his words freezing in his mouth as he saw her hanging in the air, her knees up to her chest. "What the fu—"

Safia clicked on the pendant, "I accept," and with as much force as she could muster, she stretched out violently and planted both feet as hard as she could into Dario's chest.

He coughed as the breath left his body and he bounced off the back of the cage, rattling it before catching a foot to the face as Safia continued kicking at him, landing hits on his arm and the left side of his chin.

Safia's pendant dropped to the floor as she continued her attack, but Dario regained control of himself and began reaching out for her, grabbing at her ankles. Eventually, he forced his way in between her legs, wrapping his hands around her neck and pushing her backwards against the other wall, forcing her to release her grip on the pole as he did so.

He looked at her, his face showing the gnashes and cuts from where she had kicked him as his eyes twitched. "One minute," he yelled back at her as he pressed her up against the wall. "One... fucking... minute."

Safia slapped him across the face over and over as she tried anything to free herself as her legs wormed around his waist, trying to hold herself up. He placed his hands at her neck and ripped at the side of her dress, tearing the cloth as and exposing her breast as he took it in her hand, squeezing it as hard as he could.

"Get.. your.." but before she could finish her words, she felt his lips on top of hers as he pinned her against the wall. His hot breath flowing over her body as she turned her face away from him and placed her hand over his eyes, trying to gouge them out. He then released his hands from her neck, forcing her face into place as he kissed her again, his hands finding their way down to her ass as he hoisted her up. With her head free, Safia bit down as hard as she could on Dario's neck.

"Argh!" He screamed as he released her and took a step back, placing his hand to his neck and then pulling it away to see the blood on his fingers.

"You son of a bitch," screamed Safia as she swung at him, but this time he caught her arm and spun her around, forcing her face first against the wall, with his elbow planted firmly against her back.

"Just remember, you wanted this."

She kicked back at him but missed. In her struggles, she felt as he lifted her skirt, revealing her panties. And then came the ensuing hotness of his hand as he slapped her across the ass with his bloodied hand.

"You like that, huh?" He slapped her again. "Admit, this

is what you really want." He said as he leaned forward, his lips close to her ear, then slapped her on the ass again, then again, and again.

"Say you like it."

"Fuck you, ahh!" she screamed as he slapped her again.

"Say it!"

Safia screamed again on the final slap, but this time threw her neck back so fast that the back of her head collided with the right side of his face. He yelled as he stumbled back. Safia turned around, her hair falling to the side of her face and saw Hashmi's hair pin, now stuck to the side of Dario's head, embedded into his skin.

The elevator lurched as it reached the bottom floor. Safia screamed as she pushed off the wall and jumped on Dario, just as the doors opened and they both fell out into a room of people, with her landing on top of him.

"Restriction time is now up," spoke their pendants. As both Safia and Dario wrapped their hands around each other's necks and began trying to choke one another. "Safety protocols are now back in place."

Suddenly both Safia and Dario began twitching as a set of electric current ran through their body. Safia fell down on top of Dario, pinning him beneath her.

"Oh my," said Amanda as she stepped over, looking down at the two. "I think your couple's night has ended up with one less couple, Frilla. Either that or these two are involved in things I would have never guessed. Oh, my darling Safia, but then again, maybe I should have."

"Get... off... me," said Dario as his strength came back to him. He reached up, pushing Safia over off of him, and struggled to stand, falling back to one knee.

"Oh dear," said Amanda as she knelt beside a heavily breathing Safia and lifted the torn fabric of her dress to cover her exposed breast. "You really did have fun this time, didn't you?"

"Fu... fu... fuck Dario."

Amanda couldn't help but laugh, as she patted Safia on the shoulder. "Well, given how you both came in. I would be hard pressed to say that isn't what you were doing. I mean, really, the way you were convulsing on top of him looked pretty convincing."

Safia struggled, trying to lift herself, only to have Amanda hold her back down.

"Oh no, you stay there for a moment," said Amanda as she turned to her discarded. "Ricardo, if you would be so kind as to pick up our friend here and carry her over to the next room?"

Ricardo stepped forward and knelt beside Safia, sliding his arms under her back and knees, then lifted her up into his arms. He carried her back into the first room with the metal clocks and sat her down on the couch.

"Make sure no one enters the room, dear," said Amanda as she began trying to fix Safia's torn outfit. "Oh my, it seems you're missing a shoe."

"It broke," said Safia as she took a deep breath, her body still hard to move as she leaned forward.

"Yes, I'm sure a lot of things broke in there. But you seem to be okay, if not a little worse for wear."

"Hey! Let me in," said Addison as she was blocked at the door by Ricardo.

Ricardo turned to see Safia nod her head, and he stepped aside, letting her in.

"What the fuck happened to you?" asked Addison as she walked over holding a few opened bottled drinks and her broken shoe, the broken strap dangling from its side.

"I must admit, I'm curious about that as well. But since you're here, help me fix her outfit," said Amanda as she reached up into her hair and pulled out two bobby pins. "Not perfect, but I imagine you don't care much at this point."

Addison placed the drinks on the floor to her side as she tied the fabric together and Amanda finished it off with the bobby pins. "Here, drink this," she said as she handed Safia a drink.

Safia gladly took the drink, trying to wash the taste of Dario from her mouth for the second time. The first being when she after game night when he assaulted both her and Mallory. The drink was strong and burned at her throat, making her wince with squinted eyes as she took another sip. "What... is this?"

"Vodka and something else mixed in. Whatever you're feeling right now, you won't be feeling it long after drinking some more of that. And you look like you've been through hell."

Safia nodded. "Yeah, I have," she said before forcing herself to take another gulp of the alcohol.

"Alright, spill it. What the fuck were you and Dario up to that you both came out looking like that?"

Safia frowned, not wanting to think about it as she looked over at Addison, who was still in her princess dress. "You wanna tell me why... you're in that outfit?"

Addison stood up looking down at Safia, contemplating, "I needed the points. So, I took part in this game. I didn't know they'd have me in the getup until I got here. That bitch, Frilla, said she wouldn't let me take part unless I wore this damn dress."

"So, you really are doing all these jobs to help Nasir afford all his school supplies and stuff?"

"What! Who told you that? Was it Nasir? I told that bastard to keep—"

"Hashmi did. Remember she's here under the same rules as he is. She told me how hard it is for her to get points each month. Figured you were probably buying things for your boyfriend."

"Yeah, well. So, what if I am?"

"Oh, it seems even Miss Addison has the heart of a maiden," said Amanda.

"Fuck you."

"And the mouth of a sailor." Amanda laughed. "Our princess Addison here was a part of the games tonight. When Ricardo and I reached the third floor, she played musical notes on her violin that we had to match with items in the room. It was quite annoying, but thankfully Ricardo over there apparently likes to listen to the classics in his spare time."

"Oh, the game? Did we win?" asked Safia, as the sound of music began to play from the other room.

"Well, it seems they've started their little party," said Amanda, looking over at the curtains. "But as to the answer to your question, no. You lost horribly. Henry and his lover Arthur came in first, and Ricardo and I received second place. And the other couple, they quit on the second floor. Apparently, there was a bedroom puzzle they couldn't figure out. I'm curious if that's a metaphor for their love-life, but let's not get into that, shall we?

"So, all of this was a waste of time, then?"

"I wouldn't say that. I imagine you left a resounding impression on everyone in that room over there."

"Alright, I told you why I'm in this outfit. So, you gotta tell us what the fuck happened up there with you and Dario."

"Is that bastard still out there?"

"Dario?" said Ricardo. "No, I watched him leave. He didn't seem as if he wanted to stay. That makes sense since his face was all bloody."

Safia frowned, looking back up at Addison. "Fine, fuck it, whatever," she reached down grabbing the other bottle and took it to her lips and took a few swallows. "Help me up. If I'm going to remember this shit. I'm going to need another drink." Safia stepped toward the door as Ricardo stepped aside and peaked through the curtain to see everyone dancing and partying as strobe lights of different colors covered the room.

"Oh, no, you don't," said Addison, pulling Safia back into the room. "I told you my story, now you have to tell me yours. Then you can leave."

Safia looked down at her empty bottle and then looked back over to Ricardo, who smiled back at her.

"Do you have anything in particular you like to drink?"

"Anything sweet. Whatever this is, it tastes almost as bad as Dario."

"Yes ma'am," said Ricardo as he disappeared back into the curtain and returned a few moments later with a tray filled with colorful drinks for the girls. And throughout the rest of the night Safia and girls continued to drink as she told them all of what happened with Dario and how he almost pushed Arthur over the rail, along with puzzles of the room. Afterwards, Safia found herself dancing with both Addison and Amanda, trying to make the most of the night and forget everything that had just happened with Dario.

# CHAPTER 10

Safia awoke in bed with blurry vision as a migraine pierced the spot above her eyes. She moaned as the world struggled to come into focus. Slowly, as the wavy lines of color in front of her began to take shape into something actually recognizable, her eyes narrowed in on a portrait that appeared to be that of a man holding onto a jacket draped over his shoulder as he smiled back at her. She couldn't see the face of the painting as it was obstructed by a brown mound. Her mind puzzled on it for a moment until she realized it was a nipple.

Confused at the moment, she tilted her head upward and saw that the breast connected to the brown nipple was also connected to Addison, who she was currently lying on top of her, her face atop of her other breast. Safia frowned and closed her eyes.

*No... no... I'm dreaming. This isn't real.* She took a deep breath, feeling the heat of Addison's chest against her face. *Think Safia, think. What happened? How did I get here? I remember drinking with them and...* Suddenly, a rush of images flooded through her mind. Images of her dancing, a moment of her kissing Ricardo, and then talking to people around the room. She opened her eyes again and lifted the sheets covering them. *Fuck, we're naked. Okay... okay, think Safia. First... first I need to get out of—*

"Ahhhh!" yawned Addison as she rolled to her side, wrapping her arm around Safia's head, trapping her face between her breasts.

*I just know I'm going to regret this.* "Addison, Addison wake up?"

She yawned again, but this time blinking as she woke up. She had the same half-awake eyes as Safia as she stared around the room for a moment before looking down and seeing Safia trapped in her chest. Addison was quiet for a moment as she and Safia locked eyes. Then slowly she released Safia and, in a surprisingly calm voice, said, "Okay, what happened?"

"I don't know. I don't remember."

Addison raised herself up from the bed. "Fuck, you drooled all over my tits," she said as she began wiping herself on the sheets. "Listen, you can't tell Nasir about this."

"I won't and besides, we don't know what happened."

"Yeah, well, I have an idea what happened. I can't believe this happened again. Fuck, where are my panties?"

*Again? No, don't think about that now.* "We don't know for sure. I mean, weren't we with Amanda? She could be just playing a trick on us."

"Either way, this never happened," said Addison as she reached over, picking up her pendant off the floor and clicking on it. "Do I have any messages?"

"You have four messages from Nasir."

"Fuck," said Addison, clicking the pendant again. "Message for Nasir. I... ah... I overslept and missed your messages. I'll meet you at the library in an hour."

Safia slid on her underwear and grabbed the remnants of her torn dress from the floor and slid it on over her head. She then picked up her shoes, remembering that one of them was broken, and just dropped it back to the floor. She then turned back to Addison, who was struggling to get back into her overly flamboyant dress.

"Let me help," said Safia as she walked over, zipping up the back of her dress. "I'm surprised you're even putting this back on."

"Well, I can't just walk out the door naked, can I?"

"Where'd that stain come from?" asked Safia, who noticed the large orange blotch on the front of the dress as she buttoned up the back, before tying the string on the corset.

"Don't..." She heaved as Safia tied the string tight. "know. Don't care. Come on, let's get out of here."

They both headed for the door and back downstairs, through the room with the clocks and back into the main lobby. As they came through the black curtains, they stood frozen as they saw Jericho holding a broom and dustpan, staring back at them with the same dumbfounded look on his face as they now had on theirs.

Addison picked up her dress, and power walked over to Jericho, placing a finger on her check. "You didn't see nothing, Builder Boy. You got that?"

"Well, it's kinda hard for me to be scared of you when you're in that princess getup," said Jericho with a smile.

"If you utter a world of this to Nasir, I swear I'll—"

"Your secret is safe with me, my princess. But I might ask for a favor later."

"Fine, but it better be. Because if not, I'll find a way to make you regret it."

Safia and Addison left from the building, but as Safia passed by Jericho, she couldn't help but notice the smile on his face as he glanced back at her.

"Oh, thank god," said Addison as she looked around the campus. The sun was just about to come up and there were no students walking around to see them. "I'm headed back to the dorm before anyone sees me. And hopefully by tomorrow, both of us will forget whatever happened there."

Safia nodded her head. "I agree."

And with that, they both parted ways and headed back to their own dorms. Even barefooted, it didn't take more than a few minutes to make it back to Yennefer House, but that was mostly because Safia dismissed the time-consuming spiral walkway and instead just made a beeline over the cold morning grass, straight towards her dorm. Through the door and up the stairs, she went until she stood in front of her door.

*Please still be asleep. Please still be asleep.* Biting her lip, Safia opened the door to see Hashmi sitting on the windowsill, looking out the window. *Dammit!*

"I was wondering when you'd returned. Did the party—," Hashmi's words froze in her mouth as she looked at Safia. "Again? Every time you return from these game nights, you return looking as if you've been in a car wreck."

Safia looked over to her bed and saw that Mallory was gone. *Thank goodness. At least I won't have to explain what happened to her.* "It's a long story," said Safia as she walked over to the closet and grabbed her toiletries and a towel. She then pulled at her dress, lifting it over her head, throwing it on the bed.

"What?" said Hashmi, standing up and walking towards Safia. "Is… is that a handprint on your ass?"

"What?" said Safia, turning her head around to look, only to see Dario's bloody handprint on her panties. "Oh! For Christ's sake. Just… Just forget you saw that," said Safia as she wrapped the towel around herself, grabbing her supplies and heading towards the door before turning around to Hashmi. "Can you throw that dress away? And please don't tell Mallory that you saw me like this."

"Tell her what? I'm not even sure what I'm seeing."

"Good. Then that's perfect," said Safia as she left the room, closing the door behind her and heading out of the room towards the showers. There was no one in the bathing room when she entered. She walked over to one of the stalls and turned on the water before taking off her underwear. She took one look at Dario's handprints on them and walked over, tossing them in the trash.

Safia sighed as she stepped into the shower, letting the hot water ran over her body. Instantly, her body began to relax as she placed her hands on the wall, lowering her face and letting the water run over her head, dripping down her face, falling to the floor.

*That had to be the worst night of my life. He spanked me, that bastard actually spanked me. And he kissed me. Again! But at least he got what he deserved,* thought Safia as she tilted her neck and tried rotating the arm that he had locked behind her back. It still ached as she tried to move it. She grabbed the soap and began rubbing it over her body, trying her best to make herself feel clean.

*Just because he's stronger, he thinks he can do what he wants. I'll show him.* She ran the soap over her stomach, then around to her ass where Dario had stuck her. She grimaced from the pain of it. Her mind replayed the memories of the night, with him up against her and then the look on his face as the blood poured down into his eyes from where Hashmi's hair pin had cut him. She bit down on her lip as a smile curled its edges. Taking in another deep breath of satisfaction and letting the soap drop to the floor, her fingers slowly found their way down between her legs.

A little while later, Safia entered the room with her hair and body covered in towels to find Hashmi sitting on her bed reading a book. Not saying a word, she walked over to the bed, climbed up on it and laid down on her sheets, feeling the cool fabric against her hot skin.

"You know, you're going to get your sheets wet."

"I don't care," said Safia with a sigh.

Hashmi laughed. "Do you at least feel better now?"

"No, I'm actually feeling really disgusted with myself at the moment."

"Was last night really that bad?"

"Yes... it was."

"Well, at least you didn't come back with another Mallory this time, so it couldn't have been—"

"Dario kissed me, again."

Hashmi just blinked, her book falling from her hand down between her knees. She then turned to face Safia, their eyes locking on each other for a long moment, before Safia rolled over, looking at the wall.

"I'm going to go to sleep now."

"By Allah's name you are not," said Hashmi as she walked over to the other side of the room, placing her hands on Safia's back, then proceeding to shake her. "How can you just say that and expect me not to ask questions?"

*I'm pretty sure I ended up kissing a lot of people and places last night, but how am I supposed to say that? And of course, it turns out I lost the game. I wonder how....* "Hashmi, can you hand me my pendant, please?"

"Fine," said Hashmi, as she reached over, grabbing Safia's pendant and placing it beside her. "Now, are you going to tell me what happened last night?"

"I will," said Safia with another sigh. *Or at least, some of the parts I can remember.* She clicked the pendant. "How many points do I have?"

The pendant flashed, "You have one thousand eight-hundred points."

"I thought you had more than that?"

"We lost at game night."

"Oh, I'm sorry to hear that."

"Dario lost almost half a million points."

"Well, I'm not sorry to hear that. Serves him right. But why would you let him kiss you?"

"I didn't let him do anything." Safia thought about herself accepting the bet. "Okay, maybe I did cause it. Apparently, you can remove the restrictions to hurt each other. People do it so they can fight."

"And you did that? Why? You know he's bigger than you."

"I was mad. Oh, I broke the hair clip you gave me by smashing it against his face. I'm sorry."

"Wait! What? Did you say you smashed it against his face?"

"I didn't mean to... or maybe I did. I don't know anymore."

Hashmi shook her head in disbelief. "It's fine. Honestly, with you saying that I can't really think of a better use for it. But wait, if you were fighting him, does that mean those handprints on your bum are his?"

"He spanked me."

"I'm sorry," said Hashmi, squinting her eyes, and taking a moment to process the words Safia was speaking. "Did you say he... spanked you?"

"That was after I bit him so hard that he started bleeding."

"Wait... was... was this a part of the game or..."

"No!"

"Okay! But you do understand, I had to ask. The things you're saying, they all sound quite ridiculous."

*That's all that night was. Completely ridiculous.* Suddenly, the sound of Safia's rumbling stomach pierced the air between. Hashmi then laughed, patting her on the back.

"Come on. There's no classes today. I'll blow dry your hair and we can get breakfast. I should eat before the sun completely rises."

As much as Safia wanted to say no and just wallow in self-pity in the comfort of her bed sheets, her stomach wasn't exactly giving her much of a choice as it began rumbling again.

"Alright. I'm getting up," said Safia as she lifted herself

from the chair, getting out of bed, and sitting down in the chair Hashmi placed out for her. "Where'd Mallory go?"

"I haven't seen her," said Hashmi as she pulled out the blow dryer and the comb.

"Hmm," moaned Safia as she reached over, grabbing her tablet from the edge of the bed. She pulled up the map and, just like before, it showed the map of the school. According to the red dot, it showed that Mallory was down by the lake. *What's she doing down there?* She then tapped her pendant, "Message to Mallory Polana. Hey, Mallory, Hashmi and I are going to head to the cafeteria for breakfast in about thirty minutes. You can come join us if you like."

Just as Safia had said, around half an hour later, she and Hashmi were out on the campus in their normal school attire heading for something to eat. They found Mallory waiting for them by the steps leading up into the building. After a swipe over their badges, they were allowed access and walked in, standing in line to get their food.

"Where were you, Mallory?" asked Safia. "Hashmi said you were gone when she woke up. Have you taken up running in the morning too?"

"Huh? Oh no, I was in the library for most of the morning preparing for another test. Then I went for a walk, and I went to my old dorm to see if I had left anything since you didn't come back last night." There was a tone of bitterness in Mallory's voice as she said the last part.

"Yeah, sorry. A lot of stuff happened," said Safia, as she grabbed her food tray and made her way back toward the tables.

"Safia. Safia Famosa, over here," came a familiar voice over the room. "Come have a seat with us."

Safia turned to see that it was Arthur sitting at the table with his boyfriend, Henry. They waved the girls over.

"You know them?"

"They were at the game last night. They were one of the couples that were playing."

"I see. Should we go over?"

"Yeah. I'm sure not going over would just cause me more trouble than it's worth. Let's go and see what they want."

The girls walked over, taking a seat at the table with the two boys.

"It's nice to see you this morning, Safia," said Arthur. "I just wanted to thank you for trying to save me last night. For a moment there, I really thought Dario was really going to throw me over the edge."

"It's fine. I'm just happy nothing happened."

"So am I. Dario really is such an ass. I'm happy you broke up with him last night. He really doesn't deserve a woman such as yourself. I think you're much better off with that Jericho character."

"Yeah, that's what I have been told," said Safia, placing her hand over Mallory's to stop her from speaking. She wasn't even in the mood to try to correct the misunderstanding. But to her surprise, Mallory wasn't even looking at the boys. Instead, it seemed as if she was purposely looking away from them.

"Although I can understand falling for the bad boy," said Henry, looking at Arthur with a smirk on his lips. "They do have their appeal."

"Yes, well, I fail to see the appeal of myself dangling in the air," said Arthur, shaking his head.

"Anyway Miss Safia, to thank you for potentially saving my boyfriend here's life," said Henry. "I wanted to invite you to a party a little while from now with a group of friends of ours. You can even invite your friends there if you wish."

"Thanks, I'll try to join if I can. But we have a bunch of things going on around campus. I can't make any promises."

"Oh, of course. This is just a courtesy since you've looked after my boy here. And my mother always said to look after those that look after you," said Henry as he stood up. "You can have the table. We have a few things to take care of ourselves. You are Margetto, aren't you?"

"Yes, but I'd prefer if you called me Hashmi."

"Well, then Miss Hashmi. It was nice meeting you. You both take care. And it was nice to see you again, Mallory." And with those words, both boys left the table and headed out of the room, saying hello to a few others on their way out.

"Well, they seemed interesting," said Hashmi. "And you say they were at the games last night?"

"Yeah, they were the ones who won. I think they got over a million points."

"A million? Wow! It really is a shame you lost. You wouldn't have had to worry about points anymore if you had won."

"With Dario? I think we were destined to lose," said Safia, turning towards Mallory. "Are you okay? Did you know them?"

"Yes, I'm fine. I was just thinking about class," said Mallory, before taking a piece of food and putting it in her mouth.

"Well, since there are no classes today. What do you want to do?" asked Hashmi.

"Honestly, can we just go down by the lake and just relax? After everything that's happened, I'm just tired and we haven't really been able to just spend time together since—"

"You have a message from Champ Champ," spoke Safia's pendant.

Safia just dropped her face into her hands as Hashmi began rubbing her on the back, trying to comfort her. "A moment. Is that too much to ask for? I just want a moment to myself. A moment where I'm not studying for classes, or worrying about points, or dealing with fucking Dario, or any of it."

"Don't worry, it's coming," said Hashmi, "But if it's the headmistress, then it might be important. So you may as well go ahead and listen to it."

Safia looked over at Hashmi, her eyes weary and watery, before she nodded her head and reached down to her neck, clicking on the pendant.

"Hello, Miss Safia," said Champ Champ's voice. "I do hope everything is going well for you. We haven't spoken for some time, and I have an update on your father's treatment. When you have time, please come to the left library. I shall be here 'til three o'clock today."

"Sounds like you should go and make sure your father's okay?" said Hashmi.

Safia stood up, her hands still on the table as she bobbed her head back and forth, trying to work up the energy to continue. "I guess I'll see you all later."

"Bye, Miss Safia," said Mallory, absent-mindedly.

"We'll probably be at the dorm when you return," Hashmi added.

Safia nodded and grabbed for her tray, but Mallory took it before she could.

"I'll take it. You should just go and see after your father."

"Thanks, Mallory," said Safia, as she turned and left the cafeteria. She didn't want to admit it to herself, but she hadn't spoken to her father since she came back to the school. *How long have I been back? A month? A little less than two. I can't believe I haven't called home. I used to call home every week or so. Now... now, I just hope everything's okay.*

Safia made her way across the campus, the sun stinging at her eyes as she squinted. Everything seemed so bright today. Eventually she made her way into the left library and walked ahead to the front tables, but she didn't see Champ Champ. Confused, she began to wander around through the aisles. Walking up and down every aisle until finally stopping at a dead end, she stepped back out and tapped her pendant.

"Message to Champ Champ. I've come to the left library as you wanted. But I don't see you. Do you want me to meet you somewhere els—"

"Oh, Miss Safia, there you are?" said Champ Champ, appearing behind her.

Safia quickly turned around, startled by the small woman. "What! Where... where did you come from?" Safia looked over the small woman's shoulder, peeking around the corner, back into the dead end.

"I was there, Miss Safia. Did you not see me?"

"What? No, you couldn't have... I mean... there was no one there. I'm sure..." Safia just stared down at the smiling face of the headmistress of the school as she looked back up at her, confused. "No, I'm not thinking about this right now. I'm too tired. You called me here because you had news about my father? Is he okay?"

"Yes, he had an incident that forced him back into the hospital, but everything is fine now."

"What?" asked Safia, her hands beginning to shake. "What happened?"

"He just happened to fall down in the kitchen, I believe. The doctors said that he just over worked himself and will be keeping him in the hospital for a while. I wanted to inform you of this before you called home, unprepared for the news."

"Okay, okay. But my father, he is alright, right? There is no problem with where he got shot or anything."

"No, our doctors have properly checked him. Other than the weakness they say he'll experience for the next few months, he should be perfectly fine. They are just holding him in the hospital because it seems like that's the only way we can make him get any rest."

"Oh, thank god," said Safia, leaning her back against the bookshelf. "I really don't know what I would do if anything happened to him."

"You and Miss Hashmi really do seem to love your fathers."

"Of course, we do. I mean, why wouldn't we?"

"I don't think you know how much of a luxury you have,

Miss Safia. I, for instance, have never known my father and your discarded Miss Mallory perhaps wishes she had never known hers. Not everyone comes from such a loving environment."

"But... what about your mother?"

"Ahh, yes. My mother, I believe you've spoken with her. She was quite impressed with you figuring out part of the game here. But given your interaction with her, tell me, how do you think our conversations go?"

*What? I've never spoken with her mother. At least I don't think...* Safia's eyes went wide. "Your mother, she was the woman on the other end of the phone."

"That is correct, and she's taken an interest in you. Much like everyone on the campus, it seems."

"But wait. I don't understand. If she's your mother and she's here. Why are you the headmistress?"

"Yes, that is a question that she ponders about herself. But it was my grandfather who called for me to be headmistress over my mother. And let's just say she didn't exactly take too kindly to being passed over."

"But..." Safia's mind struggled to find the words to say.

"Just be thankful you have a family who loves you, Miss Safia. Not all of us can say the same."

"But... I mean. You have your husband. Doesn't he love you? So that's something?"

Champ Champ laughed, "Yes. I suppose, in his own way, he does. Granted, he does treat me well. So perhaps I shall have something of a normal future after all. But look at you, trying to cheer me up even considering the night you had."

"What? What do you mean?"

"Getting roughed up by Dario and that night with Addison. You've been a busy girl."

Safia just shook her head, "Why... why do you know that? Do you really have cameras everywhere? Are they in the showers, too?"

"Of course not. We do respect your privacy, but what

would you expect? In the middle of the night, we had a male and a female student both remove their security alerts we have in place. Of course, we would investigate. Poor Derrick was heading towards your location the moment the request was made. He stood outside of that building for an hour before turning back."

"Fine. I understand. But tell me. Did me and Addison, did we really—"

"Have sex with one another?"

"Yes," said Safia, taking a deep breath. "That."

"It's hard to say. You did kiss a lot of people that night. I believe you played some game which involved kissing Amanda's discarded, and by the time you made it to the bed with Addison, well, I didn't need to watch anymore. Some things are best kept private."

Safia began rubbing her face and shaking her head. "Great."

"Perhaps you aren't the best at handling your alcohol. You might want to stay with the softer beverages. I, myself, have the same limitations. I can only handle one or two heavy drinks before it begins to affect me negatively. Had I known this at the time, I probably wouldn't be in the situation I am in now."

"What do you mean? You're the headmistress of the school. Was your grandfather drunk when he decided on that?"

Champ Champ laughed, "Oh goodness, I'm sure my mother would certainly like to think so. But no, Miss Safia, I was referring to my current marital status. I wasn't exactly sober when the bet was made."

"I still have no idea how you all here just tolerate all of this. Doesn't this school and all its systems seem wrong to you?"

"Oh, that's right. I wanted to make sure I reminded you that the end of the month is fast approaching. And given your recent lack of points. I wanted to make sure you weren't forgetting your obligations to the school?"

*Oh, no. I forgot about the points. Why can't I get a break? It's like there is always something else.* "I won't forget. I still have a few days left to make sure I have the points." She began rubbing her face in aggravation. "I think I'm going to go now. I suddenly feel even more tired than I did before I came here."

"Of course. Perhaps some rest would do you good. Clear your mind of everything you've gone through."

"I really doubt that I'll be able to do that," said Safia as she turned and walked back down the aisle. She turned and headed out on the steps where she met Hashmi and Mallory waiting for her.

"What?" asked Safia, rubbing her face again as the light from the sun irritated her. "What are you two doing here? I thought you said you were heading back to the room."

"We were," said Hashmi, grabbing Safia by the arm and leading her down the steps and onto the spiraling walking way. "But we met someone and asked them for a little help."

"Met who?" said Safia, allowing herself to be led away. "I'm not sure I can handle any more surprises."

"Oh, I think you'll be able to handle this one."

They all stepped off the walkway and headed down to the lake where Safia saw a large beach umbrella where beneath it sat a large blanket. Safia frowned as they made their way down to the water.

"Okay. Who is it now?"

"No one," said Hashmi, taking a seat on the blanket to shade herself from the sun. "I was just thinking we could just relax by the water for the day since we don't have classes. And plus, you look like you could use a break."

"What?" said Safia, looking around. "But you said you ran into someone on the way back to the dorm. Where'd you get all this stuff?"

"We did." Hashmi laid her head back on the blanket. "We met Jericho and told him you weren't feeling well.

So, he took us to the school store and bought this stuff. He said it was in your best interest to rest and keep your mind cleared."

Mallory knelt beside a cooler, flipping the lip, and pulled out a cold drink. "We didn't have time to put on swimsuits or anything. But I don't really feel like swimming right now, anyway."

Safia shook her head, but with a smile on her face, she knelt down on the blanket beside Mallory. "Well, I was just going to go to the room and try to lie down, anyway. I guess I can do that here." She took in a deep breath as she took the drink from Mallory, taking a sip, and letting the coolness fall down her throat. Then came a gust of wind, taking the cool air from the lake, letting it wash over her skin. Safia couldn't help but just lay back on the blanket beside Hashmi. "Thank you two for this. I mean, really, I appreciate it."

"What are friends for, if not to try and help out their friends when they look like they've been through so much recently?"

The girls all relaxed next to each other and closed their eyes.

"The only thing that would make this better would be if we had us a nice gentleman to come and wave a big fan over us," said Hashmi with a laugh. "You think we can ask Amanda to lend us Ricardo? He looked strong enough to do it for a while. I thought about asking Jericho, but he'd complain and pass out after a few minutes."

Safia just shook her head, unable to wipe the smile off her face as she embraced the moment until the world drifted away in her sleep.

# CHAPTER 11

Safia sat out in the gazebo next to the school watching the morning sunrise. Ahead of her, she could see a few students heading into the building, perhaps to set up for classes or do some type of extra credit. In her hand sat her pendant as she rubbed her finger across the jewel in its center, feeling the smoothness of it and how it contrasted with the shaper pointy exterior it was housed in.

"Hey there," said Jericho as he appeared behind Safia, walking around and stepping up into the gazebo. "I didn't expect you to call on me so soon. What can I do for you?"

"I want you to tell me what you want."

"I'm not sure I understand. I thought I told you what I wanted: simply for us to be friends. I admit that given your reckless nature, I had to go about it in unorthodox means."

"You've been helping Hashmi get points. Why?"

"I help a lot of people get points. It's not as if I can build all this stuff by myself. I'm not Hercules."

"You bought all that stuff for us."

"Of course. What else could I do when I am confronted by Miss Hashmi and Miss Mallory, both of them with their little puppy dog eyes. I really do think men have an unhealthy weakness to the sympathies of the opposite sex. I'm sure those soft eyes you ladies have led many men to their demise."

"There's something you're not telling me."

"Of course, there is. It's not like I'm going to tell you my life's story. But all you need to know is that I'm here to help you."

"As long as I do what you say?'

"Yes, as long as you do as I ask. Otherwise, at this point, I'd imagine you'd burn this school down with the way you bumble about. Never have I ever seen someone so talented and so reckless all at the same time. It's actually really enjoyable to watch you. It reminds me of a television show with all its drama front and center."

"Is that what you were doing there during game night, watching me?"

"Oh, no, that was purely coincidence. I'll have to start taking down that escape room soon and I went to see what damage that might have been done. Imagine my surprise when I saw you and Addison poking your heads out. You must truly be a party girl. Did you and Addison sleep okay?"

"We slept fine," said Safia, a dry tone in her voice. "Just tell me what you want me to do."

"Now that's just an unfair tone to take with someone. You come out here to ask me for a favor and you find yourself unable to ask for it. It must be really hard for you to be so self-righteous."

"What? What do you—"

"Most times we've met, you've wanted something, either more points or when you wanted me to save you from being expelled. And seeing how you lost that couple's game, I figured you might be running low on points and wanted my help again.

"Did one of your so-called friends tell you that?"

"Nah! Dario was in a foul mood this morning, not to mention that cut on his face. It wasn't hard to figure out why." Jericho lifted his hands out toward Safia, "Alright come on, stand up. If you're going to do this, you need to do it the right way."

Safia stared at Jericho for a moment and then stood up.

"Good, now give me your hand."

Safia reached out her hand, letting him take hers in his.

"Now ask me what you've come to ask."

Safia sighed, "Oh great, a powerful master. Will you please help this little girl get some points?"

Jericho raised an eyebrow at Safia. "Really?"

"Isn't this what you want? To have me begging and dependent on you?'

"Well, yes. But your tone kinda takes the fun out of it," said Jericho with the same smile he always wore. "But I guess that will have to do. Tell me, how many points do you have?"

"A little over two thousand."

"I see. And you said that they take your points at the end of every month. So, since that's literally tomorrow. How much will you have then?"

"Maybe about four hundred after the food expenses."

Jericho laughed, "You don't make my work easy, do you?" he shrugged his shoulders. "Okay, give me a kiss and I'll see what I can do."

"What?"

"A kiss for your gallant hero. Oh, did you know that there's a rumor going around that you had a fight with Dario over me?"

"What?" asked Safia, her face twisted with an indescribable feeling.

"Yeah, I found that funny as well. But I should be able

to use that rumor to my advantage for a while. I'll have you play the role of my girlfriend for a few days and see what comes of it. But, at the moment, there are probably people looking out at us from the school window. Thinking that we've made some romantic reconciliation or something like that."

Safia just stared at him, not knowing what to say.

"Come on, step forward and give your pretend boyfriend another kiss so that I can be on my way."

She did as instructed, taking a step next to him and lifting her head. Jericho placed his fingers around one of the buttons of her shirt and pulled her forward, placing his lips down upon hers. She tried holding her breath, but this time their kiss was longer, and she found herself accepting it. His lips were soft, and he smelled of some type of wood and something else she couldn't name. Without her realizing it, she had begun kissing him back. After parting for just a second, she lifted herself upward on her toes to feel just a bit more of him and she squeezed her hands on his.

They then parted after what seemed like forever, with Jericho staring back down at her.

"You really do have soft eyes."

"You're going to help me, then?"

"Of course, I am. You're my most prized investment. I'll contact you in a day or two. Bring Hashmi and Mallory along with you. I'll have something for them to do as well."

"Thank you," said Safia, releasing his hands.

"Oh wow! That actually sounded genuine," he said as he tossed his hand up behind him to say goodbye, but not even taking another look at her.

And before Safia could think of a remark, he'd jumped down the two steps and headed on his way, back over to the school.

Safia took a step back, retaking her seat down on the stool of the gazebo. *I don't know what I'm doing anymore. Do I really like that idiot? He's using me and I can't believe I still like him.* Safia shook her head. *I guess he's right. I'm using him too.* Safia looked out over the school, watching students shuffle about inside through the large windows. *That's what we do here. We use each other.*

After a few moments to gather her thoughts, Safia stood back up, grabbed her bag, and left the gazebo, headed off toward the front of the school. Now, the hall was filled with the morning students making their way towards their classes. Outside her class, she saw Hashmi waiting for her.

"You didn't have to wait for me."

"I hadn't planned on it, but some of the people inside were watching you and Jericho from the window. I decided to leave before they turned their attention towards me and started asking me questions."

"Of course," said Safia as she shook her head and stepped into the classroom just to be immediately greeted with the stares of not too few of her classmates.

"Okay class, we're about to get started," said Miss Abigail before she turned to Safia with a smile. "And Miss Safia since you seem on friendly terms with Jericho, can you please inform him that while sleeping in class is frowned upon, skipping class altogether is just rude?"

"Oh, ah, yes ma'am. He said he had something to do today."

"Knowing him, he's off building something again," said another boy in class. "Just how does that boyfriend of yours get so many school projects? I've been trying to suggest things for the school for months, but they haven't accepted anything I've offered."

"I don't know. He just calls me when he has them," said Safia, choosing not to dispute the assumption of Jericho being her boyfriend as she and Hashmi walked to their desks.

"I'm just saying. Everyone's talking about you and that point freak and for some reason, only your boyfriend is able to get school projects. Something about that doesn't seem right."

"Then ask him yourself. He does whatever he wants to do. It's not like I control him."

"Calm down, you two," said Abigail as she grabbed a stack of papers from her desk and went to close the door. "You can discuss that after class. But for now, we have to move on with the lesson." She walked through each row of students and began handing out the papers one by one.

"I don't understand the question," said a student after reading the paper. "Name the way in which manipulation is used to control facets of society? Does this mean like television or something?"

"That's one way to think of it," said Abigail, returning to her desk and standing before the class. "You are going to write about a personal life experience where you have manipulated someone or have felt manipulated by someone."

"What? Don't you think that's a bit personal?" said one of the girls in class.

"That is what we are here to discuss today. We will examine different forms of manipulation and you will simply choose something that you wish to explore and discuss. So, who wants to go first?"

The class was silent for a moment as the student all looked around.

"Is this some type of trick?"

"No, not at all. But I can see that you all are very hesitant about this so, I suppose I'll start. When I was a little girl, my father would often ask me to look after my little sister because he had other things to do. So, he would come up to me and say that he needed me to be a big girl and look after my sister because he had important work to do. Now, I wanted to be a good daughter and big sister, so I did it and was happy to do so. But, in truth, he only said that so that he could go bowling some nights while our mom was out working late."

"That's not manipulation, that's just your father being lazy."

Abigail laughed, "True, but it is still a father manipulating his daughter. It's just not in a completely negative way."

"Wait. What about when my girlfriend starts complaining and being all kissy faced when she asks me to do her homework?"

"What? How can you say that?" said another girl in class.

"You should feel ashamed of yourself, manipulating me like that."

The girl threw a pencil across the room at the boy.

"See, you're doing your own homework from now on. I won't let you take advantage of me anymore."

"Then I guess you better practice kissing yourself in the mirror. Because you won't be kissing me anymore."

Abigail laughed, "And see, class, what we have here is a perfect example of manipulation. This time it just so happens to be with couples."

"That just sounds like blackmail," said another boy in class.

"Well, you're not completely wrong," said Abigail. "Blackmail is a form of manipulation, one that most certainly frowned upon. As you've seen from those two behind you. Other forms of manipulation are thought of as playful."

"Why are we learning about this in class?"

"Because what we are talking about here is just surface level manipulation. I wish to tie it back to events in world history where manipulation on a grand scale has taken place, and I wish for you to understand the basics of it."

"I don't get it," said another student. "Why is this even important?"

"Because the school says it is," said another student. "Between this and half the other stuff they are trying to teach us, I don't even care anymore. It's like they expect us to become like a third world dictator or something."

"Maybe not a dictator," said Abigail. "But keep in mind that this school does wish for you to succeed and become influential people. What you do with that success is up to you."

"Then what about you? Have you ever manipulated someone?" asked a girl in the class.

"I have, I manipulated my fiancé or as you all so loving call him, 'The Point Freak,'"

"Wait? I thought you were forced to marry him. That's what the rumor around the school is."

"Both things can be true. And that's what I meant earlier about a relationship. Usually both partners manipulate each other, but that doesn't mean it is malicious. Oftentimes, it can be for each other's benefit. Sometimes you may have to coax your partner into doing something for their best interest."

"That's a bit depressing," said one girl in class. "But my mom does the same thing to my dad. When his company was about to go under, she did a lot to try to keep him in high spirits. He kept his company but ended up having to pay off a lot of people. And he had to promise a lot to keep his main employees from leaving."

"I see. But if the company was about to go under. Then do you not think that the promises he made were a form of manipulation?" said Abigail as she gestured around the room. "The world is filled with this. Your parents, for example, probably used a bit of manipulation to have you attend this school. Perhaps made a few promises to be fulfilled at a later date. The world is filled with scenarios like this."

"So, when we leave here, will we just become like our parents then?"

"We all become like our parent's eventually. But that doesn't mean you can't make changes. Take our business example for starters. I'm sure you've heard stories of how mega corporations get caught in big deals or politicians getting paid off to vote a certain way in an upcoming election. This is the world you are living in, whether you wish to see it or not."

The class continued as they circled around the topic of manipulation until the bell rang.

"Okay, class, don't forget to do your homework assignment. And Miss Safia, do try to get your boyfriend to show up to class next time," said Abigail with a smirk and a nod.

"Yes ma'am," said Safia with a sigh. *What does that mean? She knows Jericho and I are not like that? I mean... doesn't she?*

Safia and Hashmi left their class and headed back outside.

"What are you thinking about now?" asked Hashmi. "Your face is all wrinkled again."

"Honestly, surprisingly, not much. I was just curious as to why Abigail said that about me and Jericho. She knows for sure that we are not really dating."

"Well, to be fair. If I didn't know any better, I would say that you both were. He does, in a way, remind me of your friend David, from the hotel."

"What! No, he doesn't."

"Really? Do you not see it? The way they both make small jokes. They even look to be around the same height. If anything, it just proves you have a type of guy that you prefer."

Safia stared at Hashmi for a moment, "That... that can't be true." But now that Hashmi had said it, she couldn't help but start comparing the two.

"Either way, I guess it doesn't matter if you're both just playing the pretend couple. But back to Miss Abigail. Maybe she just wants you to bring him to class, like she said."

Gladly pulling her mind away from the thought of Jericho and David, Safia latched on to the conversation. "Yeah, maybe. It just feels weird, is all. But, at least for once I don't really have anything to do for a while."

"What? No games to play or some great scheme for you

to join on."

"Happily, no. I'd rather not be put back—" Safia's words paused in her mouth as she narrowed her eyes, spotting Dario along with a group of his friends headed towards her, causing her demeanor to change immediately.

Dario's smile slightly dimmed as he spotted her as well.

As they got closer, Safia realized that he now had a cut on his brow above his right eye, where he was bleeding from during the game night after their fight. Safia gave him a smug smile as she tapped her own eyebrow as she walked past him.

Then came a slapping sound followed by an "Ow" from a girl in Dario's group as he slapped her on the ass, causing her to skip a bit as they passed.

"Stop that," said the girl playfully. "Dario, what was that for?"

"What? I thought girls liked to be spanked," he said as he made his way down the spiraling walkway.

"Oh, that ass," said Hashmi, catching on to Dario's action. "I wish it was me that had hit him."

"In a way, you did. Remember when I told you that I broke your pendant? Well, I happened to break it on his face. That's why he has that cut on his eyebrow."

"Then it was worth losing it and whenever I'm forced to look at him, which hopefully is never,-then I can take some solace in that."

"So, what do you wish to do now, since we have some free time?"

"Honestly, I'd just like to go for a walk, it's been a while since we've—"

"Jericho Andrews has sent you a message," spoke Hashmi's badge.

Safia was surprised as she turned toward Hashmi.

Hashmi made a face, before clicking on the pendant for it to relay the message.

"Hey Hashmi. Come see me over by the communication

room. I have something I need to talk with you about."

"What's that about?" asked Safia.

"I'm not sure," said Hashmi. "He doesn't usually call me. I guess I'll go and see what he wants. Maybe we can go for that walk later, or in the morning from now on. I kinda like getting up early and we did say something about going out together."

"Okay, then, I'll head on back. I should probably get started with our assignment before I get caught up in something else weird."

"Alright then. I'll see you when I get back."

They split apart at a path in the road. Safia felt weird about watching her friend run off to be with Jericho. It wasn't a nervous feeling; it was something else. Something she couldn't understand, but it made her uneasy.

*He wouldn't have Hashmi doing anything she doesn't want to do, would he?* Safia thought back to her own situation with Jericho. *Knowing him, he's trying to make her another one of his so-called 'friends'.* She began to turn and follow Hashmi but stopped herself. *No, I have to trust her. Hashmi would never let Jericho use her.* So, turning, she started her walk back to their dorm; the memory of Miss Abigail's lesson on manipulation repeating itself in her mind.

Safia took the long way home, trying to clear her mind. But as she took one step inside, she heard her own pendant speak.

"You have a message from Arthur Sinclair," spoke the pendant.

Safia just lifted her pendant and stared at it blankly for a moment. She let it repeat itself to make sure that she had heard it correctly before clicking on it.

"Hello, Miss Safia. How are you? I would like for you to come to us. Within the hour would be perfect. We shall try to wait for you. We have a surprise in store."

Safia continued to stare at the pendant with the same blank expression. *What? Why? And they didn't even tell me where they were.* A bit of frustration began settling back into Safia's mind as she closed her eyes for a moment. *Fine, let's just get this over with.*

She clicked on her pendant, "Can I have the location of Arthur... Arthur... What did it say the name was?" She waited for the pendant to reset itself, before clicking it again. "What is the name of the person who just sent me that message?"

"That person was Arthur Sinclair. He is a second-year student."

"Well, I guess that worked," said Safia, clicking on the pendant for a third time. "Can I please have the location of Arthur Sinclair?"

The pendant flashed again, before responding, "Location has been marked in the outside field."

*Outside field? Where is that?* Safia reached into her bag and pulled out a tablet, navigating over to the 3D model of the map of the school. The icons showed her near her building, but the red icon of Arthur was just out in the middle of nowhere. It appeared past the auditorium near the edge of the school grounds where Safia had never been.

Looking around for a moment, she turned around and headed off in that direction. The campus itself was not small; probably around a mile in length in terms of walking, but the trip to where Safia was headed was surely another mile out from the auditorium. While not excessively high, the grass was thicker as she made her way outward. She couldn't even see if they were ahead of her from the distance she was away.

*Maybe I should have waited on Mallory or asked Hashmi to join me. I don't even know what's out here.* Unsure about her situation, Safia continued her walk, the grass now tall enough to rub against the side of her stockings. Eventually, she would see two people sitting down near the rim of trees at the border of the school's campus.

"Hello there, Miss Safia," said Arthur, as he sat on the

grass, his arms hanging over his boyfriend's legs on the bench above him.

"Hey. Why did you call me out here?" asked Safia, looking around at the large field of nothing. The only things out here were two benches, one of which was occupied by the boys.

"To have a little chat is all. Henry and I often come out here to just look over the school from a distance and watch as the sun moves past the mountains. Go on, have a seat. You must be tired from your walk." He gestured over to the bench next to them.

A little suspicious of the two, Safia was feeling the effect of walking such a distance in her loafers and decided to do as suggested. She walked over, taking a seat on the bench beside the two and gazed out on the school far off in the distance. Instantly she understood why the benches were there. The view of the school looked like something out of a painting. Its tall arches beneath the backdrop of forestry and snow-covered mountains looked like something out of a fairytale. It almost seemed magical.

"Beautiful, isn't it?"

"Yes," said Safia, honestly.

"A stark contrast from what actually goes on there: the lies, the deceit, the manipulation. Really, if one had never actually attended the school, they would probably say that it is quite picturesque."

"Probably, but why did you invite me out here?"

"Oh, yes. I wish to thank you for trying to save me from that brute, Dario. Kindness is really a luxury around here. So, I think the luxury of it should be rewarded when it appears."

"Thank you, but it's okay. It's not like I'm a fan of Dario."

"Yes, so I saw. And here we assumed you were lovers, like us. I mean, it was a couple's game after all. But it seems we were wrong. So, making up for a loss, we wish to invite you to another game next month. One you may find interesting."

"Thanks, but I think I may need to stay away from games for a while. Especially considering what happened during that last one." *It's not like I can tell him that I'm low on points and probably can't afford to join the game.*

"Are you sure? I mean, it's actually more of a charity game. We know that your friends with that Muslim girl. And we know the games this school plays with its special projects. If you invited her, it would be a great way for her to earn some points."

"Sorry, Hashmi isn't allowed to bet. So, I doubt she would even show up."

"Ahh, so Hashmi was her name – forgive me for forgetting – and do not worry, this event won't become a betting extravaganza. In fact, there is no betting at all. Well, at least not on your part. You and your friend will be tasked with finding items around the school and solving puzzles. You solve the puzzle, and you win points. If you don't, then I promise you won't lose a single point. Think of it as a scavenger hunt. I've been told that in the past there have been one or two of the Muslim faith to play in this game, so I believe so there should be no conflict."

Safia gazed back out over the school before closing her eyes and taking in the surrounding sounds. There was only the wind. She didn't hear the sounds of insects or animals or anything she thought she would. She leaned forward, looking down at the tall grass, and slowly began sliding it forward on her shoes. "I'll ask her. But she may say no."

"Then that's fine. We still have time, after all. The event won't happen for another month or two. I just wished to ask for your involvement. You're both free to refuse."

"There's someone else. My friend Addison, her boyfriend Nasir, could he join as well?"

"That is up to you. But there is only one extra space left. You are free to invite either Hashmi or Nasir. But not both. You will need to make a choice of which you wish to help."

"And Nasir can't take my place?"

"Safia, since you've gained the attention of everyone in school, I'd hazard a guess that no one can take your place. Especially after that incident in the escape room. People have become interested in you and a lot of them are waiting to see what you do next."

"Can I ask you something?'

"Of course," said Arthur as he laid his head against his boyfriend's thigh, closing his eyes. "I can't imagine a better moment for us to talk than out here amongst the nothingness."

"Why is everyone so interested in me? I haven't done much since I've come back. I even lost that stupid game with Dario."

"But that's precisely why. Take, for instance, your victory over the Point Freak. Here you defeated the king of the campus, and you go on to lose the next few games. And that's not to mention your little vacation off campus; that still has us all puzzled. Goodness, you don't even participate in higher amount bets. You meek about with your little Muslim friend and Dario's discarded. Honestly, everyone has been making bets on what ridiculous thing you will do next. Will she adopt a new discarded, will she challenge one of the second years? Some are even wondering if you will host your own event."

"Wait! I can do that?"

Arthur just laughed. "See, that is exactly what I mean. How have you come so far when you know so little? You're like this campus's Golden Goose. You might even fumble your way into becoming the next headmistress for all we know."

Safia frowned. "I think everyone here has the wrong impression of me."

"Perhaps, but even if that is so. It is true that you have been quite the exciting ride, Miss Famosa. If it ends here, then so be it."

Safia stood up, taking in a deep breath. "I'll head back before the sun goes down." She looked around. "Are you just going to stay out here?"

"I prefer to be here sometimes and watch the stars when it's all quiet out. The school looks even more beautiful in the moonlight."

"Okay, thank you for trying to help, even if Hashmi doesn't take it."

"No worries, dear. But keep in mind that even though I'm not as bad as Dario, that doesn't mean that I'm a nice person. You should be wary of me as much as anyone else."

Safia looked back with a smile. "I'll try to remember that. But given all the people I've met here. You don't seem so bad in comparison."

"Then I suppose I'll have to work on that."

With everything said, Safia started on her way back toward the school. *This will be good. I can finally do something to help Hashmi. She runs out with Jericho most mornings, so this will fix that. I've just gotta—*"

"Mallory Polona has lost two hundred points in a wager," spoke Safia's pendant.

"What?" Safia stopped in her tracks halfway to the school. *What do you mean I've lost two hundred points? By Mallory? But why would she…That doesn't make any sense.*

Feeling a bit of panic, Safia hastened her steps as she made her way back to the school, but it wasn't long before her pendant began flashing red again.

"You have a message from Mallory Polana," spoke the pendant.

Safia pressed on her pendant.

"I'm sorry, Miss Safia," came Mallory's voice, sounding out of breath. "I didn't mean to. There was this game, and I didn't think it would cost anything. I mean… everyone was playing and… I'm sorry."

Safia pressed her pendant again. "Message to Mallory Polana; Mallory just go back to the room. I'll talk to you when I get back." said Safia, the tone of her voice harsher than she intended it to be. Or perhaps not. She was feeling a bit nervous, but surprisingly a lot angrier than she'd expected.

After picking up her pace, Safia made it back to the main campus quicker than when she'd left it. Cutting across the grass, she made her way into her dorm, up the steps, and to her room. Opening the door, she saw Mallory sitting on the bed with her head down. She didn't even turn to look at Safia when she entered the room. Looking at Mallory sitting there dejected, Safia tried her best to calm herself and before stepping inside.

"Okay," she said, her tone still harsher than she would have liked. "Tell me what happened. You know we don't have many points left." *I really don't want to deal with this. But I really don't think I have a choice.*

"It... it was a mistake. We were playing a new board game."

"What board game?"

"It was one someone had created. I was bored and thought it would be fun. We all would spin the wheel in the center and move our pieces from place to place. I didn't know it cost points. They never said anything about it."

"Where were you?"

"With the second years, at the school."-

Safia walked up to Mallory and sighed as she saw tears at the bottom of the girl's eyes. *Keep calm, Safia. Whatever it is can be fixed. Don't do* anything *that* you *know* you*'ll regret later. No matter how much you want to.*

"I'm sorry. Did I mess up?"

"You did," said Safia, clicking on her badge. "How many points do I have left?"

"You have two thousand nine hundred points available."

"Okay so, I owe the school two thousand points per month now and it costs us six hundred points to eat per month. That means I will have one-hundred points left. It's not much, but it will be okay as long as we don't make any more mistakes before Jericho can help us. Have you done any tests this week?"

"No, we haven't taken any."

"Then we need to hold out until then. So, let's both try not to make any more mistakes, okay?" said Safia as she reached forward, wiping the tears from Mallory's cheeks, which made the girl begin to cry more. "Hey, it's okay. We haven't lost yet."

"I know, it's just. Why am I like this? I'm trying not to mess up. I really am, but it feels like I can't help myself. I miss you sometimes and—"

"Hey, hey... it's okay," said Safia, placing the temple of her head against Mallory's. "It's going to be fine." *I'm just too tired to be dealing with this right now.*

Mallory nodded, rubbing her head against Safia's, but then leaned in, taking in a small breath, as their lips just slightly grazed against each other.

The door opened and in walked Hashmi carrying her bag, catching Safia and Mallory, their heads pressed against one another. "Oh, my. Am I intruding?"

"What?" said Saifa, turning her face toward the door. "No, we were just talking a bit. A lot has happened today."

"Has it really been that much of an eventful day?"

"I'll... I'll go take a shower," said Mallory, as she went to the closest to grab her toiletries and a towel and then headed out the door, her face covered by her hair.

Hashmi gave a smirk as she walked by her and left the room, then closed the door behind her. "She really is a handful, isn't she?" asked Hashmi, walking over to her closet and pulling out her prayer mat, spreading it out over the floor.

"You have no idea."

"I have a bit of an idea. I was listening through the door since you slightly left it open. So, she was caught playing a game and losing?"

"She says it was a mistake."

"So she says. But I was in the lounge when she came in. I guess she didn't see me behind the boys there. I saw her, running up the stairs with watery eyes and an unmistakable smile on her face."

"A smile?"

"Yes, I suppose she was excited to be seeing you again."

"Seeing me, but we're together all the time. We even sleep in the same bed now."

"Yes, but outside of sleeping. You've been busy, haven't you? I mean, at least we have classes together. She's alone for most of the day. And you've been busy most of the time. I think she feels neglected."

Safia began rubbing her face. "What am I supposed to do?"

"You know how she feels about you. And I can't imagine snuggling up to you at night is making it any easier on her."

"Easy on her? What about me? She's always so close and the way her hands always seem to find their way to my breasts at night."

"That's not something I was aware of. But something will need to be done eventually or the need for your affection will cause her to do something desperate. That little board game is probably just the start."

"So what? I should just have her expelled and send her back home?"

"I like Miss Mallory. But you must admit, she is quite a needy person. I wish I had the answer. But I've never been in a situation where another woman has fallen for me."

"I'm not even sure that's it," said Safia, remembering Dario's words from the couple's battle. Then immediately shaking them from her mind. *Damn that bastard. Mallory isn't that type of person, and neither am I. We're better than that. There's no way he's right. We're better than what he thinks of us.* She shook her head. *Don't think about this, now. I have to prepare for...* She looked back at her friend. "Actually

Hashmi, there's something I wish to ask you."

"Yes?"

"Do you think you could join a game with me?"

Hashmi just froze and stared at Safia for a moment. "Pardon?"

"There is another couple's game coming up, and I wanted to ask you to be my partner."

Hashmi narrowed her eyes on Safia. "I'm not quite sure I understand. You know that I do not permit myself to join any of the gambling games here. Why would you ask me that?"

"I was told it's not a gambling game. You won't have to put up any points. Instead, he said it was like a charity scavenger hunt game for students and points are given out to the one who finds the objects and solves the puzzles."

"So, it's not gambling then? Are you sure?"

"You don't have to decide now. And we can ask around first. But he said that Muslims in the past have done it for points. I know you are doing a lot of stuff with Jericho now and I'm sorry I didn't notice that you had your own problems with points. But if it's alright with you. I would really like to do something for you. I mean, if you're okay with it."

Hashmi just stared at Safia's face for a long moment and then sighed, "I think that I now know what you must feel when you placate Miss Mallory. It certainly is hard to turn down a sympathetic face, isn't it?"

"So, you'll do it?"

"Only if there is indeed no gambling on my part. Given this school and its reputation. I fail to see how I can claim ignorance if there is." Hashmi then closed her eyes taking a deep breath, but then open her eyes looked at Safia with a smile, before nodding over to her closet. "Actually, would you mind joining me in my evening prayers again. If we are going to do this, then I think we both are going to need to have a little faith."

# CHAPTER 12

Safia, Mallory, and Hashmi had just left the dorm and were on their way throughout the campus. They headed off over the grass where far ahead of them, in the field surrounding the school, were a decent amount of people moving about in the distance. The walk over took several minutes, where they found Jericho waiting on them.

"Welcome, ladies," said Jericho. "I was starting to have my doubts if you all would show up. Which was a bit unsettling, considering that this is all for our reckless friend there." He pointed at Safia.

"What do you mean?" asked Safia. "You said to get here at eight, and it's just past seven. Why is everyone so early?"

"Don't pay attention to Jericho," said Hashmi. "He just gets here hours before everyone else. So, we finally caught on to it and started showing up an hour ahead of his supposed time."

"And there goes Hashmi spoiling my fun. And after I've done so much for you, too."

"You only help me because I am Safia's friend."

"Is that really how you see me? And here I thought that our close mornings together in each other's arms would have strengthened our bond."

"You mean when you fell on me while building that escape room? I think that is the only time we have ever been close."

Jericho laughed, "You did do a great job of cushioning my fall though— oh!" He yelped as he dodged Hashmi's playful swing at him. "So violent. I knew Safia would be a bad influence on you."

"You're a bad influence on me," said Hashmi, swiping at him again, but still missing.

"Nasir," yelled Jericho as he ran away back towards the supplies. "Come get your religious companion. She's trying to inflict violence on me. Isn't there some tenet in the Quran about that?"

Safia was surprised to see Hashmi and Jericho so close, even engaging in playful banter. *What have I been missing during the mornings when you go out?* Hashmi had a genuine smile across her face as she watched as Jericho went skipping back towards the rest of the group.

"Hello, ladies," said Nasir as he approached. "I am glad you could join us."

"Hey, Nasir," said Safia. "Are you not with…" Safia's mind went back to waking up in bed with Addison, as eyes shifted away from him for a moment.

"Is something wrong, Miss Safia?"

"What? No, nothing. I was just wondering where Addison was. I don't see her around."

"She was tired and said that she would come join me later. I, on the other hand, would like to repay a debt, so here I am, able and ready to be put to use."

*A debt? Does Addison owe someone points? Is that even*

*possible? Can you borrow points here?*

"Looks like everything is ready," said Hashmi, noticing Jericho waving them over. "I guess we should get started."

They all walked over and Safia couldn't help but stare at the large, square concrete slab that was sticking out of the ground.

"What's this?" she asked, looking down at the squared concrete. In the center, there looked to be a door leading downward. "They put a basement all the way out here?"

"This is the other side of the shanty house down by the lake. You know, the one that leads down into game night in the tunnels. Well, this is another entrance to it."

Safia turned around, trying to peer across campus, but couldn't even see the top of the shanty house by the lake. *But that's like a mile or something away.* She then looked down at the ground. *Just how far do the tunnels beneath the school go? And how deep?*

"Today's a quick project. We just need to dig a hole around this thing, drop those pieces of lumber in it, and build a tiny house to stop the rainwater from leaking down inside. With so many of us here, it should only take a few hours if we all work together." Jericho stepped to the side and gestured back to their group. "Today we will be following the direction of my lovely assistant, Miss Hashmi. So, if our house looks like a boat by the time we're done, blame her."

*Lovely assistant?*

Hashmi stepped forward. "Let's all just forget Jericho and his silliness and get this over with. Curtis you and Terrell will do the cutting and the rest of the boys will do the boards. Us girls will stir the concrete until they're ready to place the boards into the ground."

"Yes, ma'am," said a few of the boys before they all set out on their assigned tasks.

Hashmi led Safia and Mallory along with two other girls over to a set of buckets that sat next to some type of pot machine with a handle on it. Beside them were bags of gravel, a few sticks, and a few chairs for them to sit on. Safia stepped over, looking inside the buckets, and seeing that they had water inside of them.

"What are we supposed to do here?" asked Mallory as she reached down to pick up a bag of concrete. But upon gripping it, she struggled to lift even half of it before dropping it back down. "Wow, this is heavy."

"Yes. Each one weighs about forty kilos. So, we'll just cut the bags open and use little shovels to scoop them into the buckets and the boys will come and get it when it's ready."

The girls got to work with Safia and Hashmi, scooping up the gravel, pouring it into the bucket, and then pouring the gravel into the machine. One girl began turning the handle, and they saw the machine start to spin the gravel inside. Adding water from the bucket into the mix, soon everything inside turned to a soggy, lumpy looking gray.

"This... is hard," said the girl with both her hands on the handle, pushing it up and down as the contents whooshed around.

"We will switch places as we get tired," said Hashmi.

"Okay."

"You and Jericho have become close," said Safia to Hashmi as she turned around to watch the boys' work. "When did that happen?"

"I don't know if we have become *so close*. But he said that he would depend on me since he was busy working on another project. I just accepted the responsibility. The hardest part was learning about construction. I wasn't allowed to talk to you about the escape room we built. But that was very difficult; all those supplies that were brought in. I felt like I was building a skyscraper."

"Hashmi, I know I asked you this before, but are you sure he's not taking advantage of you?"

"When he first proposed the idea to me, I also thought there would be some trick to it. But so far, everything has

194

been as he said it would be," said Hashmi, looking over at the rest of the group. "I know your worry, but he's more or less been pretty reserved with me. I wonder how he's been with you. Ever since you told me about that night in the snow, I have wondered about your situation."

"You mean outside of him having me pretend to be his girlfriend and those kisses he makes me give him? No. I think you see him more than I do."

"So, what do we do about him?" asked Hashmi. "On one hand, he has saved us numerous times with his projects around the school. But, on the other hand, I'm pretty sure he's just using us, and neither of us are exactly sure how or why."

"There's not much I can do since he's blackmailing me with being expelled. Either I do as he says, or Mallory and I are forced to go home."

"And I must admit, I'm not talking kindly to the idea of being left here by myself to deal with all of this. Without you, I might be forced to spend more time around Harmony and her accursed singing."

Safia laughed. "I thought you two were getting along now."

"We are, but that doesn't mean I enjoy her trying to convince me to sing on stage with her."

Safia turned around, stepping on the concrete block, looking at the door. "Can we go down there?"

"I don't see why not. It's not as if it's forbidden."

Safia reached down, pulling on the handle of the door, and lifting it open. The metal door leaning open on its hinges. Inside, she saw some steps leading down into the darkness.

"Are you off on another adventure?" asked Hashmi. "Care for some company?"

"Seriously? You don't mind coming with me?"

"Well, let's just say that I might feel a bit of jealousy when you come back from your adventures in from your late nights."

"Then let's have our own adventure," After taking Hashmi by the hand, Safia turned toward Mallory. "We'll be right back. We're just going to have a look."

They both held hands as they made their way down the steps into the tunnel. But unlike before, there were no lights illuminating the area. Instead, at the bottom, they were met with complete darkness that matched the unsettling mood of the stale air around them.

"You spent an entire night down here during that game night?" asked Hashmi, stepping forward and keeping one hand on the wall. "It seems like something out of a horror movie."

"I did, but it wasn't like this. There were lights on the walls and a bunch of people. Now it just looks like an empty subway. I wonder if there is a light switch nearby." Safia ran her fingers over the wall, along with Hashmi, in search of a switch. They didn't dare go much further into the darkness where the light from above them did not reach. "I can't find anything. Maybe the switch is somewhere else."

"I was hoping we could have an adventure. But I—" Hashmi paused as she heard something from up ahead in the darkness.

"What's wrong? Has—" said Safia as she heard the sounds of footsteps from inside of the shadows ahead of them. The sound echoed off the wall, the thick drumming steps getting closer and closer. Both girls stared off into the blackness as the sounds grew louder and louder. "Nope." Safia stepped over to Hashmi, grabbing her by the hand, turned around and headed back towards the entrance. One step after another, they made their way back up into the sunlight, slamming the metal door behind them.

"You move... fast when you... want to," said Hashmi, catching her breath.

"I already don't trust this school and its secrets. I'm not about to stay down there and see what or who that was."

"What were you two doing down there?" asked Jericho from the side as he tried to measure a wooden beam in the dirt around the concrete.

"We tried exploring a bit. But we heard someone down there. So, in the interest of self-preservation, we hurried back up."

"Oh, that's probably just someone cleaning up. I've run into a few people down there before. I've even done it myself a few times. All the trash from the drinks and food needs to be cleared out after a game night or gathering."

"So, you murk about down there in the dark?"

"Sometimes. It's not so bad when you get used to it."

"Well, you go on ahead. I'm not taking any chances," said Safia.

"Can I swap out now?" asked Mallory. "I'm getting tired."

"Oh, okay," said Safia, walking over. "I'll take your spot." She placed her hand on the handle and began to push. The concrete in the bucket continued its grindy whooshing sound. Turning the handle was a lot harder than it looked, and Safia quickly found her arms becoming weary. But she continued until the boys had brought over a few pieces of wood, planting them upward beside the concrete block. Then the other boys came over, taking the buckets and loading them up with concrete from the spinning tub and pouring them down into the crevice, sealing in the wooden boards.

The process repeated itself as the girls swapped with each other throughout the morning. The work was hard, but even though they were there for four or five hours, they all managed to finish laying the basic foundation of the little hut.

"Jericho," said Safia when it was all over, and they stared up at the little roofless shanty house. "Why is everything else here so well built, but both the entrances that go down into the tunnel made of these pieces of wood?"

"No idea. I just build what they tell me to build. But I

admit, you have a point.," said Jericho, placing his hand on the wood. "I would have preferred to build something better than this. But the instructions were just to build it out of cheap lumber. It's like they want it to come tumbling down one day. But I guess they will have me support the walls with something later. I mean, it still needs a roof and a door and stuff."

"They probably want it to look scary so that no one will want to go down inside of it."

"Well, considering how fast you ran out of there. I'd say they are on the right track."

"When are you going to finish it?" asked Safia as a few of the boys walked out of the opening after finishing nailing the boards from inside.

"The roof hasn't arrived yet, I think. But it'll be easy enough to put on when it gets here. It's not like there's anything down there to steal, anyway."

"Okay, that's it, Jericho, unless you have something else you want us to do," said one of the boys, wiping dust from his pants.

"Nah, that's it. Thanks for helping everyone. I really appreciate it."

"Don't worry about it. After everything you've done for us. It's about time you let us repay you for once," said the boy as he took a hold of his pendant, clicking it. "I forfeit any points from the current construction project."

"What? Why?" asked Safia, as she and Hashmi stood there dumbfounded.

Suddenly, the rest of the boys and the two girls who had joined them all repeated the same thing into their pendants, all forfeiting their points to the project.

"The next project you invite us on better be a fun one. Perhaps one with AC and not out here in the sun, sweating our asses off," said the first boy.

"I'll see what I can do," said Jericho with his usual smile, as the rest of the group began leaving, walking across the grass back towards the campus.

Safia turned towards Jericho. "What was that about? What's going on?"

"You needed a lot of points, right? Well, all the points that they just gave up will be spread out amongst the remaining members. So, that'll be you and Hashmi. Well, Mallory too, but her points come back to you, anyway. Speaking of which—" Jericho made sure everyone else was out of earshot, before raising his own pendant and clicking on it. "I, Jericho Andrews, forfeit all the points from this current project."

"But I didn't... we didn't ask you to do this," protested Hashmi.

"You said you needed points. Well, in the next few days, you'll have a lot of points; at least a few thousand each, I think."

"And you really did all of this just because we asked you to?"

"Isn't that what friends are for?" asked Jericho. "You needed help and here I am. I'd like to think that was fairly noble of me; sacrificing my own points so that you three may survive."

"But what about the cost of lumber and stuff? Didn't you need to pay for that?"

"Nah, technically, this counted as some type of school renovation, so they paid for it. Which probably explains why they wanted it made from such cheap wood. They only make those who use supplies for their personal games pay for it."

While they were trying to think of what else to say, Nasir walked from behind the hunt with Mallory.

"Not you too," said Safia, turning towards Nasir. "Don't you need the points?"

"While a few more points would have been nice. I believe it is best to show my gratitude to you for taking care of Addison."

"What!" yelped Safia, thinking back to that morning waking up naked beside Addison. "What do you mean?" She looked around self-consciously. *Did she tell him?*

"I heard about your outburst of affection in the lunch hall. And I wanted to thank you for being Addison's friend. She doesn't exactly have many people who have taken a liking to her."

"I wonder why?" asked Hashmi, the sarcasm thick in her voice.

Nasir could help but to chuckle. "Although she'd never show it. Addison was quite excited when she told me about what happened between you two. And I know she can be a bit hard to deal with, but she really is a sweet girl after getting to know her."

"She would have more friends if she acted like a normal person," said Hashmi.

"I hope you also will get along with my girlfriend one day, Hashmi."

"I still don't know how the two of you ever became a couple. Are you sure she's not blackmailing you into a relationship? Or is it... what do they call it... Stockholm Syndrome?"

Safia thought back to every time she'd meet Addison and, true enough, every time they'd meet, she was always by herself. Even in the game night at the escape room, she was standing over in a corner alone. She'd actually never seen her around anyone else unless she was earning points. But she did seem genuinely worried about her when she tried to check on her after her fight with Dario. "Thank you, Nasir, and tell Addison to come and visit me sometime."

"Really, you can't be serious." said Hashmi.

"I will do that. Thank you, Miss Safia. I think it is good to have Addison spend time with female friends. Perhaps the company of you three can soften her up a bit."

"You expect us to succeed where so many before us have failed," said Hashmi.

"A man can always hope."

"Come on," said Jericho, wrapping an arm around Nasir's shoulders. "Let's go get us something to eat to celebrate."

"What are we celebrating?"

"Are you kidding? We built something, and we saved the girls. Me and you are the perfect example of modern, chivalrous men."

"The way you speak sometimes is really confusing. Do you know that?" asked Nasir as Jericho led him off.

"And there they go," said Hashmi as Mallory came up, stepping in beside them. "What do we do now?"

"I think I'll go have a talk with my family. It's been a while, and I want to check and see how my Papa is doing," said Safia.

"I think I'll head back to the dorm and take a shower. I've worked up quite the sweat out here in the sun," Hashmi said.

"I'm going to head to the library if that's okay with you, Miss Safia. I still have to study for my test this week," said Mallory.

"Okay," said Safia as all three girls headed back towards the campus. The walk back to the main dorm took a few minutes and then Mallory broke away, headed off towards the library.

"Have you talked to Mallory about what she's doing?" Hashmi asked.

"No, I haven't exactly found the right time to talk about it?"

"Then have you told her about wanting me to join you in the couple's scavenger hunt?"

"Not yet, but—"

"Safia, if you wish for me to help. Then I need to tell her. The last thing I wish is for her to become jealous of me over something trivial."

"I know, I know. I've just been putting it off. I'll talk to her soon, I promise."

"Alright. I trust you. I just want everything to work out. I feel like we've been very lucky since we've gotten here. Jericho said that over thirty students have already been expelled. I don't want us to add to that number."

"Me either," said Safia as they reached a fork in their path. "I'll see you back at the dorm."

"Okay. Tell your parents that I said hello."

"I will," said Safia as she and Hashmi split, and she made her way toward the communication building. She began to feel the weariness of the day in her legs as she approached the building. Raising her pendant, she began to speak, then suddenly the door opened, and she found herself standing face to face with Ricardo.

"Oh, hello Miss Safia. Have you come to speak with your family also?"

"Ah," muttered Safia, standing there holding her pendant in the air as she stared at Ricardo. "Yes. I mean, I am. Is that what you're here for?"

"Yes. I haven't seen my grandparents in two years," said Ricardo as he stepped forward with the door closing behind him. "I try to always check in on them once a month."

"Grandparents? What about your mother and father?"

"They died a little after I arrived here at the school. I only have my grandparents now."

"Oh! I'm sorry. I... I didn't know."

"It's fine. I've accepted it now. But if you wish to go in, I can call for someone to come and get you."

"Yes, thank you."

Ricardo clicked his pendant, "Safia Famosa is outside the communication building and would like to speak with her parents."

"Please wait outside. Someone will be out shortly," spoke the pendant.

"I guess we have some time," said Ricardo as he turned to stare at the small trees that had been planted near the walkway by the building. "We haven't really had much of a chance to speak to one another. Usually, Amanda has us both involved in something."

Safia watched him as he fiddled with the leaf of a tree. Being alone with him now, she couldn't help but feel a bit shy. "Ah, Ricardo. About what I said... ah, before the game night."

"It's fine, Safia," dropping his formal way of speaking again. "I didn't lie to you that night. When I look at you, I feel the same way. Amanda just has a way of picking up on things like that."

"Oh, okay." said Safia. *Dammit, I was going to say I lied. But now what do I do? Am I supposed to just act awkward around him from now on? How can he just say he likes me, like it's nothing?*

Ricardo stepped back to Safia, reaching his fingers out and placing it against the side of her face. She instinctively responded by leaning into his hand. "We can't control how we feel, but that doesn't mean we have to do what our feelings tell us. I owe Amanda a lot, and I'd hate myself if I ever did anything to hurt her."

Safia embraced the feeling of his hand for a moment longer before she stepped back, smiling at him. "I understand. I feel the same way. I owe both of you for teaching me about this school; and you for winning me those points that night."

"I was happy to help."

Safia extended her hand. "So, friends, it is then."

Ricardo took her hand in his and shook it. "Friends it is."

The door to the communication room opened and out stepped Derrick.

"Ah, hello Miss Safia. It has been a while since we've last seen each other. I do hope everything is well with you."

"Yes," said Safia, her mood instantly souring as she remembered the last time she'd spoken with Derrick in the communication room after finding out she wasn't speaking with her family.

"I suppose I should go. I'm sure I will see you again, Miss Safia," said Ricardo, his tone returning to his formal way of speaking. "I will tell Amanda you said hello."

"Are you ready, then?" asked Derrick after watching Ricardo wander off.

"Yes, I'm ready."

"Good, follow me then." He then led Safia into the checkered hall of the communication office. "I do hope you enjoyed your trip home to visit your parents. We've been keeping track of your activities on campus since you've returned and see that you've been involved in quite a few bets since you've returned."

"It's not like I have much of a choice," said Safia as she entered the first room. "Tell me, am I actually going to speak with my family this time, or will it be Champ Champ's mother again?"

Derrick raised a brow at her revelation. "Oh, so you've figured out who it was. You have been busy, haven't you? But rest assured, although they will be listening. You will indeed be speaking with your family if they answer."

"And what if I wish to speak with her? Can I do that?"

"That depends on her. You can try speaking to her if you like and see if she responds. I cannot predict her actions. But Miss Safia, you must understand she means you no ill will. Surely, you can see that we have done nothing to impede your progress on this campus. We've only watched. In fact, I believe Iris has accessed your records more than her mother."

*Iris.... Who is... No, I remember someone using that name before.* Safia searched her memory and thought back to that day she caught Killian speaking with Champ Champ. *Her real name's Iris, then? But why has she... no, she probably checks in on everything, and she's the one who called me about my father. That does make sense.*

"You can use booth number four," said Derrick, opening the door to the next room for her.

Safia stepped inside, before turning back to Derrick, who was waiting in the next room. "What? You're not going to follow behind me and listen to my conversation this time?"

Derrick just smiled, "Come now, Miss Safia. Surely you understand by now that we are always listening. We just pretend that we are not."

Safia turned away as the door closed and went over, taking a seat at the numbered booth. For the first time since arriving back at the school, she placed the phone to her ear and began dialing on the rotary phone. There was another clicking sound in her ear before she heard the phone ring. But after several rings she heard a familiar voice.

"This is Famosa's," came the voice of her father.

And suddenly Safia felt a wave of relief wash over her she didn't even know was possible. "Hey, Papa."

"Hey, it's my baby. I was wondering when you were gonna call. Yago said you were busy with classes, but I wasn't sure. You ain't got caught up with some no-good boys, have you?"

Safia couldn't help but laugh. "Why is that the first thing that comes to your mind?" Then her eyes opened wide. "Wait! You've been talking to Yago?"

"Of course, I have. He calls us every week. Unlike a certain someone who hasn't checked in on her Papa in weeks. And why, when you both call, you show up with this funny number? Where's your cell phone?"

"We... ah, don't get good signals out here. So, we use the campus phones."

"Goodness, my daughter worries her Papa. Even David calls more than you. Hey Safia, don't come home with no baby. Just because I got used to David, don't mean I'm gonna get used to no snooty uppity college boy you meet down there."

"Papa! Stop talking like that. I'm not messing with no boys here like that."

"Good. Just because I wanted your mother to have another baby, don't mean I want my baby having a baby."

Safia couldn't help but shake her head in frustration. But the common chatter with her father, even though ridiculous, made her feel more comfortable than she'd felt in a long time. "Just tell me you're okay. I heard you went back to the hospital?"

"What? Damn that Yago, I told him not to worry you. I'm fine. They're making me rest now. Got me sitting around the house doing nothing. I'm not used to this. A man should be out there providing for his family, not sitting down on the couch watching old TV shows."

"How long until they said you would be better?"

"They said I was better a week ago. But it's your mother, ya know. She's not letting me do anything. And she's got me eating all this healthy stuff. I swear, eating has become more painful than the bullet."

"Who are you talking to about my cooking?" came the distant voice of Safia's mother over the phone.

"It's Safia. She finally called. Here, talk to your daughter. Tell her not to bring home any no-good boys."

There was an audible sigh heard through the phone before Safia heard her mother's voice.

"Hey, honey. How's everything going at school?"

"Fine, Mama. Is everything okay at home?"

"Everything's fine here. Don't mind your father. He's just mad. I won't let him work in the diner for another month."

"Month?" came her father's voice in the background. "You said a week."

"Well, now it's a month because you're insensitive to your daughter. And you're gonna eat that food I made you."

There were a few inaudible words spoken in the background from her father.

"Anyway, Safia, we're all good here. David was gonna come back after he heard your father went back into the hospital, but I talked him out of it. We've got plenty of help here now since your father's insurance plan has given us enough money for it."

"Is Yago doing okay? He always sounds busy when he calls us."

"Huh, oh yeah. He's okay. We're all pretty busy here. Sorry I haven't called in a while. I've just been busy with tests and stuff. But I promise I'll call more from now on."

"That's good," said her mother as they continued to talk for another half hour, the phone switching between her mother and her father. But faster than she would have wanted, the phone conversation was over. She let the phone linger on her ear after hearing her mother say "Goodbye," and to her surprise came the sound of another voice.

"Hello there, Miss Safia. I'm happy to hear your father is doing well," came the voice of Champ Champ's mother.

Safia closed her eyes, taking a moment as she felt her mood change and a slight headache return. "What do you want?"

"Oh my. Such a hostile tone. And here I thought you would be more receptive to us ensuring that your family is being well looked after while you're away."

"Why are you doing all of this?"

"Because the school is interested in you, Miss Famosa. So, it has decided to accommodate you to a certain degree."

"You want something, right? That's usually how this goes. So, why don't you just tell me what it is?"

"No, we want... well, perhaps that isn't true. But what I want and what the school wants are two different things. I'll be in contact with you, Miss Famosa. I think it will be a pleasant change of pace for me to actually meet one of our students."

And before Safia could respond, she heard a click on the other end of the line, which was soon followed up by the dial-tone. She just sat there for a minute, confused.

*What is wrong with the people here?* She thought as she hung up the phone. *Everyone speaks in riddles and just does as they please. Is she coming here to meet me? Is she not already at the campus? What about Yago? Is he still here?* She stood up and walked over to the door, opening it to find Derrick sitting down in a chair, looking into his tablet.

"Welcome back," said Derrick. "I hope everything is going well at home."

"Like you don't know already. You've all been watching over my family."

"Them, yes, probably. But not me personally. I only do what they need me to do. Or do you think I'm secretly the mastermind behind this school?"

Safia thought for a moment, "I don't know anything anymore. But can you at least tell me if my brother is here?"

"Oh, Yago. Yes, he's here. He comes to the communication room to speak with your family about once a week or so."

"Fine, is there any way I can get you to contact me the next time he shows up?"

"Miss Safia, if your brother has been hiding from you, then I'd most likely assume he has a good reason to. Unless you both dislike each other so much that he normally avoids you."

"I know that. But he could at least have come and seen me once before he disappeared."

"I do not know your situation personally. But I imagine when he wants to be found, he will show himself. You probably just need to be patient."

"That's not so easy in this place."

"No. I imagine it isn't," said Derrick, as he stood up and turned. "Come, I'll escort you out. You probably have more things to do."

Not feeling like arguing, Safia followed behind Derrick and allowed herself to be led outside of the building.

"Did you attend this school?" asked Safia when stepped outside.

"Me? No, I'm just a friend of the family who needed a

job. Take care, Miss Safia. Whether you believe me or not, I do hope that everything works out well for you here."

The door closed on him, leaving Safia outside in the mid-day air to think about everything that happened.

She closed her eyes, taking in a deep breath. *Hope that everything works out for me? There's no way that woman wants everything to work out for me. She said it herself, that's not what the school wants; whatever that means. Everyone here does what they want, except me. I'm busy being dragged around and begging for points. Even Yago is off doing whatever he is doing. Well fine, I don't care anymore about what they want. If I'm going to be stuck here playing their games, then I'm going to start focusing more on what I want. And what I want is to be able to play the game better. And I know just who can teach me.*

Safia gripped at her pendant and clicked on the jewel.

Hours later, Safia found herself standing at the front doors of the school. The sun was low in the sky, casting an orange evening light over the school before settling down behind the mountains to bring in the nightfall. Safia opened the door and stepped inside, where she found Abigail standing by the steps wearing a long coat that covered her body.

"I wasn't expecting you to call me Miss Safia. Sorry to make you wait even though you made it sound urgent. Is something wrong?"

"I haven't seen Killian since that night in the snow. Do you know where he is? I tried contacting him, but he refuses to answer."

"Oh, so that was you," said Abigail, rubbing the side of her face. "I thought it was odd. He rarely gets messages anymore."

"So, you know where he is?"

"I do. I was with him a moment ago."

"Can you take me to him? There's something I want to

ask him."

"I can... but he doesn't really like to be bothered. He doesn't want his attention to be drawn to anything else. Are you sure you want to meet him? You might catch his attention and there's no telling what he will do then."

"That's fine. I need to ask a favor, anyway."

Abigail just stared at Safia for a moment and sighed. "Okay, follow me then," she said as she turned around and began walking up the steps to the second floor of the school.

Safia followed behind her and noticed that she was barefoot, which made me wonder even more about her attire. "Why are you wearing that coat? It's not really that cold here, is it?"

"You'll see soon enough," said Abigail as she reached the second floor and made her way down the hall. "I believe I told you about Killian and his way of thinking. Don't be surprised if he doesn't pay much attention to you. He gets like that when he's working."

"Working?" asked Safia, as they both stopped by the door. The sign above read 'Art Room'.

"He's always working in one way or another," said Abigail as she opened the door to the room and nodded for Safia to step inside.

Now feeling a bit hesitant, Safia slowly took a step inside the room. There she saw Killian sitting on a stool with a canvas in front of him. He had paint splattered all over his clothing as he stared at the painting. There were dozens of paintings laid against the wall. Some were of random things like plants, trees, a few were of the mountains that could be seen outside of the window. But a decent amount of them were of Abigail herself. A few were facial portraits; but many others were full body pieces with her in clothing from different eras, but they all looked extremely beautiful and detailed.

"I suppose it was too much to ask that you just stay away," said Killian, never taking his eyes off the piece in front of him as he dabbed his brush against it.

"You're a smart guy, right? Did you really expect me not to show up?" Safia said.

"No, when Abigail left, I figured you were who she was going to meet. You've come because you want something from me?" Killian spoke without looking up.

"I want to be able to play the game like everyone else does. No, better than everyone else does."

"And you hope I can teach you how?"

"Yes."

"Sorry, but even if that were the case, I have no reason to anymore. I don't dislike you, Miss Safia. In fact, I'm quite fond of you in relative terms. But I am a very selfish man and I'd rather just sit here with my paintings than help you." He dabbed his brush in a water bucket next to his seat and reached over, grabbing another. "Abigail, can we continue? I wish to catch the small amount of sunlight we have left. Then we can rest for the day."

Abigail locked the door behind her and removed her coat. To her surprise, Safia saw that she was wearing a see-through sheet gown. Beneath, she could see her bare breasts exposing her nipples beneath the fabric. Even her underwear was a small piece of cloth held together by a string. Abigail stepped onto a stage ahead of Killian where there sat a large red love couch. There she reached over, picked up a golden crown, and placed it atop her head. She then reached over, grabbing a replica sword, and letting it rest over the side of her body, down to the floor. The pose she made for him was both seductive and somehow power-ful at the same time as she lifted one of her arms above her.

"Thank you," said Killian.

"Is this what you do all day?" asked Safia as she stared at Abigail. "Have her pose for you?"

"Not all day, no. But sometimes yes. Although now she has grown comfortable enough that she now designs her own shows. This piece is one that Abigail decided on herself."

"I'm not sure comfortable is the right word," said Abigail. "You said you wanted something Roman, so I thought this would be appropriate."

"True. Perhaps we should have changed the clothing to an offset green and placed pieces of forestry around besides some wine vases."

"No, that would have thrown off the symmetry. You said you wanted to try a less cluttered piece. So, you should focus on the blade and how it reflects the light, rather than the environment around the main focal point."

"Perhaps. I'm just considering options."

"I don't know if you've noticed, but it's quite cold in this outfit. So, you don't have the option to change your mind. Now, hurry up before you lose the sunlight."

Killian smiled but dabbed his brush and continued to paint. "Next time, I suppose."

"Good, now back to Safia. Is there anything she can do to have you change your mind?"

"I fail to see how. Helping her would just distract me from what I need to do. I hope she succeeds here at this school, but that doesn't mean that I wish to involve myself with this school any more than I have to. You were my only goal, and I have enough points to finish my time here without being bothered."

"So, you say." said Abigail with a sigh.

Safia just stood there for a moment and watched him work. *Everyone wants something. This school has taught me that. I just need to figure out...* Safia's thoughts were halted as she noticed Abigail was staring at her. Then, when their eyes made contact, she nodded to a set of costumes on a nearby rack. *You can't be serious. You want me to put on those things.* Safia thought to herself as if she could read her teacher's mind. Abigail just gave a slight smile back at her.

"Killian, what if I become a model for you? Would that be an even trade?"

"That's very nice of you. But I have Abigail as a model. I don't see why I should have a need for two. Even with placement, all I would need would be the use of a mannequin."

"Two reasons. The first is that as I look around the room. I see you only have images of Abigail. Have you ever painted anyone else?"

"No one else has ever demanded my attention."

"I thought about that," said Safia, as she walked over to the clothing rack. "But I remember you talking about your past and how you used to paint." She reached up to the top of her shirt and began unbuttoning it, one after another. "But you said so yourself that you used to just sit up here alone until Abigail would come check on you."

"That's true. You yourself only found me because you contacted Abigail."

"What I mean is," she removed her shirt, and slipped out her skirt. "You isolate yourself from others. So doesn't that also mean that the only reason no one has ever demanded your attention is because you never allowed anyone to get near you?" Safia walked back over and stepped beyond the canvas.

"That may be the case. It's not like—" Killian turned to see Safia looking down at him. She was wearing the same sheer outfit as Abigail; her breasts clear under soft fabric and exposed to him. "Are you really trying to use sex appeal to convince me to help you?"

"No, I'm trying to use *art* to convince you to help me. Have you ever painted someone like me before? I have a lot more browns and blacks in my pallet than you have on your little art tray there. So, I'm offering you a trade. I will allow you to paint me, and while you do so. I want you to teach me about this school and how I can win here."

Killian took a look at Abigail, who smiled back at him. "Did you set this up?"

"No. And you did say that you were impressed by her. Having someone else suffer through your artistic whims would be a nice change, though."

Killian shook his head, but Safia could see the smirk on his lips as he looked at Abigail. "Fine, grab one of those stools over there and come sit by me, and I'll teach you how to paint."

Safia frowned. "Wait, paint? But I want you to show me how to play the games here."

"They are one and the same, and that's what I will teach you."

# CHAPTER 13

Safia laid in bed beside Mallory, her arms wrapped around her as she stared out the window.

*Is there anything else I can do? I have three hundred points left. There has to be something. I still don't know any of the masked people. They said they would reveal themselves to me, but that hasn't happened yet, or at least not that I noticed.* She sighed. *I need more points. Killian just keeps saying to wait. I can't believe I told him how many points I have and everything I have going on in the school. He even knows about my deal with Jericho. Was that really the right thing to do?*

Hashmi wormed around in bed for a moment before blinking her eyes against the morning sunlight. With squinted eyes, she peeked around the room and smiled as she noticed Safia looking at her.

"Don't you two look comfy over there?"

"I'm happy you think so. I'm surprised you slept in this

morning. Usually, you'd be gone for a run or off with Jericho building things."

Hashmi yawned. "He hasn't contacted me in the last few days. I just figured he was busy or something. Do you trust Killian? You've been spending a lot of time with him and Abigail lately."

"I don't know. But I trust Abigail and she trusts him."

"You do understand that you are now putting your future in the hands of the same person who you tried to sabotage four months ago? And you don't suppose that perhaps he might hold a grudge or two?"

"As I said, I trust Abigail and I'll bet on her to stop him from doing anything against me."

"Okay," said Hashmi, sitting up in bed, her hair big and poofy around her face. "So, what do we do from now on? We still haven't received the points from—"

"You have received four thousand eight hundred points," spoke Hashmi's pendant on the counter.

"You have received nine thousand six hundred points," spoke Safia's pendant across from Hashmi's.

Hashmi just stared at her pendant for a moment. "That's a lot of points."

"I guess those are the points from helping Jericho. So, what do you want to do now?"

"I would like to wait until this couple's game before I decide. Just because they said that it was not betting, that does not mean that it would not cost us points in some way. I wish to be prepared if that is the case. But afterwards if I have the points, then I will buy myself a new pair of shoes. What about you? What are your plans for today?"

"I still gotta meet with Killian."

"Really? You've been meeting with him for days now? Do you not get a break?"

"I honestly don't think he knows what that is. If anything, I'm grateful that Abigail distracts him most of the time so that I can escape for the day."

"When you say she provides a distraction—" said Hashmi, letting the insinuation hang in the hang between them for a moment.

"It's probably what you're thinking. I just don't stick around long enough to see it."

"So, has she taken a liking to him then? I mean, considering how they attained one another."

"I haven't really asked about it. But she also hasn't really asked me about Jericho, so I don't really know what to say. But when I'm there, they seem like a normal couple. They even laugh and make jokes with each other."

"Well, speaking on that," said Hashmi, her eyes drifting downward. "What about you, Miss Mallory? How long are you going to keep pretending to be asleep in Safia's arms?"

"I didn't want to interrupt you both," said Mallory unmoving, still with her eyes closed. "It's not like I can do anything to help, anyway?"

"Is that why you've been so sour lately? Do you want to help us?"

"Of course, I want to help. But what can I do? I'm just a discarded. You both are going off doing that couple's thing and you're going to leave me alone again."

"That's not—"

"Champ Champ would like to see you now," spoke Safia's pendant.

Safia sighed and reached over, clicking on her pendant, before looking out the window again. "This early in the morning?"

"See, and now you're going to go off again."

"No, that's not true. We are going to go and see what she wants."

"What?" asked Mallory, turning her head back to look at Safia. "Really?"

"Why not? We're together in this, aren't we?" said Safia, lifting herself up. "I've been trying not to worry you, but since that doesn't work. Come on, let's go and see what she wants."

They both got out of bed and after handling their morning chores, they got dressed and headed out of the dorm, leaving Hashmi to return to sleep in her bed.

"Where do we go?" asked Mallory as they stepped on to the spiral walkway.

"Let's find out," said Safia, pulling out her tablet and clicking on the map and seeing Champ Champ's location. "To the gym, apparently."

Making their way past a few of the dorms and across the campus, they eventually ended up at the gymnasium. Safia looked at her map once more and realized that Champ Champ wasn't in the gym. She was behind it. She stopped off the path and made her way over to the side and walked down the side of the building until she reached the corner and was just in time to see a male figure walk around the other end and disappear out of sight.

"Ah, there you are," said Champ Champ. "And you brought Miss Mallory. Hello there, both of you, please, come have a seat." She gestured to a bench directly in front of her.

Not seeing a reason not to, Safia did as asked.

"Who was that who just left?"

"Who? Oh, that was my husband. He had an errand to run."

Not being able to remember ever seeing the man not being asleep, Safia wanted to stand up and chase him down, but decided not to give into her urges. Instead, she couldn't help but notice that Champ Champ was in another one of her outfits. This time being a leotard with a matching headband and big fluffy socks. "Were you two back here exercising?"

"What? Oh, yes, the outfit. No, just more of my husband's teasing is all. At least this one allows me to be able to move comfortably, even if it is somewhat revealing."

"Why did you call me out here? Is everything alright

with my family?"

"Yes, everything is fine. I just figured we should have a bit of a chat. Your situation with us is very unique and I wish to make sure you're okay."

"Am I okay? Really? You think I'm okay being wrapped up in all of this mess?"

"Do you feel you've been treated unfairly?"

"It's not... I don't know. Have I?" she looked over at Mallory. "Have we?"

"What say you, Miss Mallory? I'd hazard a guess to say that you've had quite the harrowing experience here and yet you cling to stay, even though you must realize how hard it will be on you."

"Why are you still here?" asked Mallory.

"What do you mean? I'm in charge of the school. Should I not be here?"

"No, I mean. You lost to your husband, right? And now you have him. You could leave whenever you like. So, why do you stay? There must be a reason."

*I guess that is true. It's not like she's a student anymore. But she's a part of the school faculty, isn't that the reason?* Safia wondered as she looked between the two.

"Oh, now that is an interesting question. But fine, let us play a game then. I'll answer one question if you answer one question."

"But that's not—"

"Oh, come now dear, you can't start this game if you do not wish to play. Perhaps a bit of honesty between us both will teach Safia a few things about how this school works. I'm sure you've seen quite a few things under Dario."

"I don't lie to Safia."

"No, but an omission of the truth is just a different type of lie."

"What truth?" asked Safia.

"There are many truths. Come now, Miss Mallory, let us play the game. Unless you're scared your friend whom you love so much will lose faith in you."

Mallory looked to Safia and then back to Champ Champ. "Fine, I'll play. I know information isn't free. And I want to help Safia."

"Good," said Champ Champ with a smile. "Your question, I believe, was why do I still reside here at the school when I could leave? Well, that's quite simply because I'm addicted to it. Sure, I could say that I'm employed by the school, but that's only a small part of it. My husband has denied me the pleasure of subjecting others to games for my own pleasure. But I am allowed to watch as others do so. I'm not allowed to bet, so I entertain myself in little scenarios like this. Watching Safia's struggle has been especially exciting."

Safia wasn't shocked to hear what Champ Champ was saying. But it still felt hurtful to hear how she really felt.

"You see, Safia. She's not on our side. She's just on her side."

"Oh, that's not to say I don't want to see Safia succeed here. But just understand that I will always put my own pleasure before everything else. I believe I mentioned to you before that my husband wishes that I assist you. And have I not done that at every opportunity? I'm even doing so now."

"You have," said Safia. "But would you have done that if not ordered by your husband?"

"Oh, goodness no. I'd be too obsessed with myself to give you a second thought. But what's more important to you? What I would have done or what I have done? I believe the saying is actions speak louder than words."

"I can't hate you. You saved my father's life. Even if your husband made you do it."

"Exactly," said Champ Champ, turning back towards Mallory. "Now it's your turn, sweet lady. Tell us exactly what that father of yours did to you that has you so afraid to go home."

Mallory's eyes went wide.

"Don't you think—" said Safia.

"Shush, Safia," said Champ Champ, cutting Safia off, her voice stern and demanding and she leaned in, looking at Mallory. "And no omission of the truth, dear. Because, while I can't bet you directly. I can make things really hard for you and Safia. You started this game, so you better play by the rules."

Mallory took another look at Safia before dropping her head. "He's not my father. He's my stepfather. My mom married him when I was four. But he already had a daughter named Marlena."

"Yes, he did," said Champ Champ. "And doesn't your sis have a striking resemblance to someone here?"

"She… she looks like Safia."

"Good, now keep going, because we haven't even gotten to the good part yet."

"We… we became friends as we grew up. We loved each other," Mallory caught a glimpse of Champ Champ's face, narrowing her eyes at her. "I mean… I mean, we were lovers."

"And here you are trying to force that love on Safia, just because they look a little similar. It must be hard having sister-issues. But please, do keep going. Tell us about your wonderful home life."

Mallory looked up at Champ Champ with watery, hate-filled eyes. "Her father… he made her start doing online porn when she got out of school. And when she would leave… he used to make me strip down so he could wash me. I didn't want to tell her what he was doing, but she knew. Then one day, after school, she came to pick me up, saying that she'd found a way out for me. She didn't drive me home. She drove me to the airport and sent me here."

"Yes, she did. Your sister sacrificed a lot to get you here. And only for you to end up in the hands of Dario. And if you get sent back home, you'll have squandered what your wonderful sister worked so hard for you to achieve. Really, it's no wonder you try so hard not to go home. You'd have to look in your beautiful sister's face and tell her you failed. That everything that she did for you was for nothing. If I were you, I'd cling to anyone that'd let me stay. And here I thought you loved Safia."

"I do love Safia!"

"Are you sure? I thought you loved your sister. Will you abandon her?"

"What? No! I mean... I mean... that's not."

"Careful now. You must tell the truth, remember? Or you and Safia will both pay for your lies."

Mallory turned to Safia. "I'm not... You do look like her. But I know you're not her. I'm not... I'm not trying to... I mean... I don't... I don't know what I'm doing anymore." And with those words, she finally broke. Her lips began to shake as the tears started flowing down her face.

Safia didn't know what to say, so she just wrapped her arms around Mallory as she had done so many times before. After hearing all of that, Safia couldn't help but be grateful for her own simple, normal family. Even though she said so much, there had to be so much more at home that she didn't say.

"And here, I was supposed to be a therapist for you," said Champ Champ, "and look how things have turned out."

"What's that supposed to mean?"

"It means exactly that. You've been experiencing high levels of stress lately. The school noticed that you feel sympathetic around me, and I was asked to check in on you."

"How would the school even—"

Champ Champ tapped on her shoulder. "That implant you received here tracks more than your movement, Safia dear. Haven't you noticed that whenever you feel particularly stressed that I magically appear? This is the case for a few other students here as well. We must look after our prized assets, after all."

"Do you even care about us? I mean really?"

"Of course. But I do have my favorites. Some students are particularly more entertaining than others." She stood up from the bench. "Well, I can see that I'm not wanted here. I shall leave you to console what's left of Miss Palona there and have what I'm quite sure will be a much-needed discussion on misplaced affections." And with that, Champ Champ walked away, turning the corner where her husband had previously, leaving Mallory and Safia alone.

"I'm sorry," said Mallory. After some time there, she laid down on the bench, her head in Safia's lap. "I wasn't trying to hide that you looked like her."

"But I do look like your stepsister."

"Yes."

"And you are in love with her?"

Mallory was quiet.

*Well, that explains a lot of things.* "But you do know I'm not her, right?"

"I know. It's just that you take care of me like she did. I just can't help but like you. And when I see you, I just feel... well... you know. I can't help it."

"I understand, and I'm not blaming you. Trust me, I understand that you can't help how you feel about someone," said Safia, as she stroked Mallory's head. "Did your stepfather... did he ever try to have sex with you?"

"No... he said my first time would make a lot of money on camera. And Marlena would always threaten to run away if he ever did. That's why he would always wait 'til she left before... before he did anything to me."

"And you never told her?"

"No... but she knew he did other things to me. She sometimes would come into my room and catch me crying. Then she'd lay down in bed with me to try to comfort me. That's when... that's when she would kiss me and tell me it's going to be okay."

*I don't even know what to say to that. And I just so happen to look like her.* She then took a deep breath before looking up into the sky. *I can't believe I'm going to do this.* "Mallory, can I ask you for a favor?"

"Of course." said Mallory, sitting up on the bench. "Just say it. I'll do anything you want. I want to be helpful."

"Kiss me."

Mallory just stared at Safia for a moment. "What! I... I mean... are you sure?"

"I'm sure." *At this point, why not? I've kissed everyone else, apparently. And I don't even remember what I did with Addison.* "I want you to kiss me."

"Okay," said Mallory as she swallowed nervously, before sitting to her knees up on the bench and facing Safia. Reaching forward, she placed a shaky hand on Safia's face and leaned forward, slowly placing her lips against hers.

Safia closed her eyes, responding to the kiss as much as she could, trying to give Mallory what she wanted; what she felt she needed. She could feel Mallory's breath on hers as she pulled her lips away for only a second before kissing her again and then again till she'd had her fill. Then, after leaving her satisfied, she pulled herself away, her cheeks showing a bit of red as she stared into Safia's eyes. Safia then caught her own breath before nodding her head.

"There, tell me; did that feel like kissing your sister?"

Mallory bit her lip. "No, but it wasn't bad. I really do have feelings for you."

"But not the same love you have for her."

"No... it's different. I see that now."

"I'm sorry that I can't be for you what she is."

"I don't want you to be. I want... but I want... I don't know what I want anymore. Is that a bad thing?"

Safia smiled, "No, that's normal. But there's no rush. You can take your time and find out. I don't think my relationship is any better." She raised her hands to Mallory's face and began wiping the tears from her cheeks. "I swear, you're lucky you don't wear much makeup. You would have ruined it by now. Have I ever told you how I met David?"

"You mean the guy from the hotel? No."

"It was in third grade. I was fighting some boys, and they pushed me towards some steps. Well, I would have fallen, except he was coming up those steps. I crashed into him, causing him to fall down and he broke his arm. And we've been around each other ever since. We've broken up a few times, dated other people. I don't even know what we are anymore."

"He looked at me funny when we left. Do you know why that is?"

"That was my fault, I think. He might have been jealous of you since I told him how you felt about me."

"Oh."

Safia stood up from the bench and reached out her hand to Mallory. "Come on, I still have a few more errands to run. We might as well tell our depressing life stories as we get stuff done."

"Okay," said Mallory, taking Safia's hand and standing on her feet as they headed off into the campus.

*Your life's been way more messed up than mine. I used to think not working in my parent's diner was the worst thing ever. I hope being around us actually helps.* Safia thought back to Champ Champ's words. *She said she was here to provide therapy. But now, I'm not sure she meant it for me. I'll need to talk to her later. But for now, Mallory's finally opened up to me and I don't want to ruin it.*

# CHAPTER 14

Days later, in the early morning, Safia sat with Hashmi in the gazebo next to the school, where they could see the auditorium. There was a small fog covering the ground this morning, which made the rest of the campus seem calm against the early sunlight.

"We are supposed to meet them here?" asked Hashmi.

"That's what the instructions said. But I don't see anyone."

"I don't suppose they could have meant another gazebo."

"Not unless you and Jericho have been building another one in secret."

"Hardly," said Hashmi with a laugh. "He hasn't visited me since our creation of that shed. Have you spoken with him?"

"No. I haven't seen him either."

"This fog will add to the mystery of today's event, I

think," said the voice Arthur as he came into view alongside Henry and headed towards the gazebo. "Oh, Miss Safia, you're already here. What a surprise."

"We wanted to get here early. My friend Hashmi wanted to ask you a question."

"Really? Well, I'd be happy to answer any questions you have while we wait."

"I just wish to make sure that I will not be gambling of any sort in this game?"

"Oh, that. I assure you, Miss Hashmi, that we will not require you to gamble any of your points here. In fact, all the points gathered here will be my own points. Think of it as a bit of entertaining charity on my part. But I will need your consent, along with all the other participants, in order to track you and make sure no one is cheating."

"That sounds fair. I just wished to make sure before we started."

"I understand. You'd not wish to come this far and find yourself choosing between your beliefs and leaving your friend out in the cold."

"Friends are always good to have," said another familiar voice, as Safia turned to see Frilla appear behind her, outside the gazebo.

"Frilla? Why are you here?" asked Safia.

"Why wouldn't I be here? There's a bit of entertainment to be had watching this event. And speaking of which," she pointed ahead of them as Safia could see a few more shadows begin to appear through the fog headed towards them. "It seems the rest of the guests have arrived."

It wasn't long before Safia was surrounded by groups of people as they all stood in a circle outside of the gazebo with Arthur in the center.

"I'm sure you all are ready to start this game, so let's get rid of the tedious things, shall we?" He pulled out his tablet. "Each couple will walk over, placing their badges over this. It will blink and you will tap in, and that will give me permission to track your movements throughout the day."

Safia and Hashmi did as instructed, clicking their badges along with everyone one else.

"Good, now let's get on with the rules, shall we?" He smiled, before handing the tablet to his boyfriend. "Now, spread around the campus will be ten items of varying size and shape, but you shouldn't have any trouble noticing them when they're found. In each of them, you will find puzzles of increasing difficulty. When you complete the puzzle, you will be given a set of points. But keep in mind, you only have one hour to find and solve a puzzle. If you cannot, then you will be disqualified from continuing the game and the puzzle will be locked so no other team can use it."

"How will we find them?" asked a boy in the group.

"You will be able to find each of the items on your map on your tablet. But it will be only once you unlock one puzzle, then another will appear on the map for you to go and find."

"There are six groups here. So, if there are only ten puzzles, how is that fair for everyone to have the same number of puzzles?"

"No, I said when you unlock one puzzle, then another one will appear on the map. So potentially, if one group is fast enough. They can leave you all behind and solve five or more puzzle boxes themselves. Keep in mind, your points received will double every time you open a puzzle box. So, potentially you can multiply your winnings by thirty-two, although I doubt anyone here is that ridiculously adept."

Everyone's badges began to flash.

"Okay, now open the map on your tablets," said Frilla. "There you will see all the other contestants on the map. Your puzzle will appear on your screen in the image of the school's crest."

Safia opened up her tablet and saw that her puzzle was located somewhere down near the lake. *Okay, hopefully it's not something crazy hard. I wish to get* at least *one puzzle done so Hashmi can get some points.*

"Wait! That's not right. Why is our puzzle all the way on the other side of the campus?" asked a boy in the group.

"Luck is also a part of the game," said Arthur. "When it starts, I suggest you run fast. So, are there any more questions?" He looked around to silent faces and after seeing no one speak, he tapped his pendant. "Then the game has now started. Return here to retrieve your points when it's all finished."

The two boys who had said that their box was on the other side of the campus took off running while the other team just hurriedly walked to theirs. Safia and Hashmi also picked up the pace towards the lake.

"Is it in the water?" asked Hashmi, trying to look at the Safia screen. "I hadn't come prepared to go for a swim."

"No, it seems like it's in the shed."

It only took them a few minutes to make it to the lake, where they both entered the shed and began looking around.

"I don't see anything," said Hashmi.

Safia took another look at her tablet. "It moved. Now it's up ahead. But I don't..." she looked forward and saw the entrance to the tunnel where she had spent game night with its entrance closed. "I think we have to go down there."

"Are you sure?"

"No, but I don't see any things else," said Safia as she cautiously stepped forward and placed her hand on the tunnel door, lifting it open. The large metal fell hard on the other side, sounding throughout the small cabin as it rattled against the floor with its landing. Safia peered inside and saw only darkness. "How are we supposed to find anything down in there?"

"Oh," said Hashmi as she quickly squatted and began shuffling through her school bag and pulled out a flashlight, shining it down inside of the tunnel.

"Why do you have that?" asked Safia, genuinely

surprised.

Hashmi stepped down inside the tunnel. "Remember when we were helping Jericho build that other shack and went down into the tunnel there? Well, I just assumed it would be handy to have one if it happened to happen again. And it seems that I was right." She turned back around and extended a hand to Safia. "Come on. Let's find that box. I'm fairly interested in this now. Were all your games like this before?"

"I wish. But it's only just started. I'm sure something foolishly annoying is going to happen before it's all over," said Safia, as she took Hashmi's hand and followed her down into the tunnel. The steps were the same as she remembered, but the tunnel itself was completely different. Gone were the tables and furniture that had once been placed for people to relax and enjoy themselves. Now there were only barren walls and hardwood flooring as far into the darkness as she could see.

"Where does the map say it is now?"

Safia took another look at her tablet. "Not too far up ahead, we just have to take a right and go forward." Following the map, they slowly navigated through the darkness and arrived at where the next puzzle was supposed to be.

"I don't see anything," said Hashmi. "Did it change again?"

"No. It says it's here. But I don't—" Safia spotted a small chest on the floor of the tunnel. "Hashmi, here it is, I think." Safia quickly stepped over as Hashmi followed her with the light. It was a small wooden chest with the school insignia on it. She opened it, and instantly her badge glowed. "I guess that means that this is it." She reached inside and pulled out a small cypher puzzle with a bunch of letters all over it.

"What's that?"

"The puzzle, I guess," said Safia as she fiddled with the device. The letters were able to rotate back and forth around it, and each time she did, she heard a click. "I guess we're supposed to spell something for it to open." Safia looked around for a clue but didn't see one. "How are we supposed to know what the answer is?"

"I don't know. Are you sure there's nothing else in the box?" asked Hashmi as she stepped forward, shining her light downward into the chest, not seeing anything.

Safia frowned, took a breath, and leaned back. "Great, are we supposed to just guess what it—" She blinked as she started up at the ceiling. "Hashmi, turn off the light."

"What, why?"

"Look above us."

Hashmi turned around and saw above her, a green image in the shadows where the brightness of the flashlight didn't reach. Hashmi flicked the button on her flashlight as the world went dark around them except for the image above, which was now clear.

"Is that... two men having sex?" asked Hashmi, now that image was clear.

"That's what it looks like," said Safia, examining the picture. The two men wore a crown of leaves in their hair. "Although they're not having sex. You can still see their parts. Look, there's words under it." Safia pointed upward, but it was not like Hashmi could see her as it was pitch dark. "It says 'Where Greek Gods play.'"

"What does that even mean? Oh look, one of them is holding that puzzle thing in their hand." Hashmi tilted her head. "It says pride. You think that will work on the puzzle?"

"Only one way to find out."

Hashmi flicked back on the light, and in between her and Safia appeared a man. The girl's eyes went wide as they both let out a scream with Safia dropping the puzzle, grabbing Hashmi's by the hand and began to run.

"Ow, that was a loud yell," came Jericho's voice. "You have to remember your voices bounce around down here."

Safia released Hashmi's hand, stepped forward and began repeatedly slapping Jericho on his shoulder. "What the hell is wrong with you? You… stupid… jackass.”

“Ow, stop that. I was just passing by and wondered who else was down here.”

“In the dark?” She continued slapping his shoulder. “You almost… gave us both heart attacks.”

“Why are you down here?” ask Hashmi, clutching her clothing over her chest. “And how are you moving about down here with no light?”

“Oh,” said Jericho, stepping away from Safia after she had tired herself out. “I was making sure everything was ready for the next game night down here. I have special glasses that let me see in the dark. Why are you two down here?”

“Arthur has us playing another couple’s game. One of the puzzles is here.”

“So, that’s why that glow-in-the-dark graffiti was here. I thought someone was just playing some type of joke on me. Have you two figured it out yet?”

“No,” said Safia, showing him the puzzle. “We thought it would be ‘Pride’ like the image above us. But we’re a letter short?”

“Can I see it?” asked Jacob, extending his hand.

Safia looked to Hashmi for permission before handing it to Jericho, who then began messing around with the letters. “Are… are you allowed to mess with the puzzle?”

“Did they say you couldn’t receive help?”

“No.”

“Then it’s okay.” Jericho clicked around the puzzle a few more times until it read ‘Hybris’ and they all heard the puzzle click and the top release, falling off into Jericho’s hand.”

“What?” said Safia. “How did you do that?”

“Well, the image said, ‘where Greek gods play’, right? And the scroll in his hand said pride. And the Greek God of pride is named Hybris. But I’m pretty sure we could have used ‘Hubris’ as well, since that’s another word for pride.”

232

"How do they expect us to know that? Why do you even know that?"

Jericho laughed, "I'm sure they didn't expect you to know it. But you have your tablet. I'm sure you would have figured it out, eventually. I just sped things up a bit. I've never done a game like this. Is that it... have you two won?"

"No," said Safia, pulling out her tablet and seeing that a new school icon appeared in the right library. "We have to go to the next puzzle now."

"Oh, that's a shame. Well, I was happy to help. But I need to finish up down here. I hope you two win a bunch of points."

Safia just shook her head but did not want to waste time. She took Hashmi by the hand. "Come on, he's right. We should hurry before someone gets the next puzzle."

"I agree," said Hashmi, and they both left Jericho down in the darkness with the shadows slowly took his body as he waved at them.

They made their way as cautiously as they could back from where they came until they saw the daylight shining in through the exit up ahead of them. Reaching the steel steps, they went upstairs, into the shack and back out into the fresh air.

"I hope to never go back down there again," said Hashmi. "He scared the life out of me."

"I agree. Come on, let go." Quickly they hurried towards the right library. "What do you really think he was doing down there?"

"Jericho? He said he was just cleaning up, right?"

"That's what he said. But I don't know. He just always has this habit of showing up. And I gave him permission to always know where I am. So, it's not like I can hide from him. It's just too much of a coincidence to find him down there at the same time as we were."

"So, you think he came down there to help us?"

"I really don't know what to think about him anymore.

One minute makes me do some weird bets, the next he helps us get points. Then he's making me kiss him so people can see us. None of it makes any sense."

"Wait? He has permission to always find you. How did you do that?"

"That was before we went back to my home. He wanted access to the tracking chip they put in me. I didn't even know I could allow him access to that. But all I did was click the pendant, and he gained access to it."

"Safia, I think he might be getting more from that chip than just your location."

"What do you mean?"

"I mean, who knows what else that chip does? He might even be able to access those shocking features that paralyze people if he wants."

"What?"

"I'm not sure. But who knows what type of information those chips are sending out?"

"That bastard. I swear I'm..." Safia shook her head. "No, I can't think about that now. We need to get as many points as we can." Safia lifted her tablet to her face to make sure she was headed towards the right place, and she saw two other dots going in the same direction as her. "Damn," she said as she looked around. "I think someone else is heading to that puzzle, too."

"But I don't see anyone," said Hashmi, looking around. "Are they already ahead of us?"

"No," said Safia, looking down at the map. "It looks like they are right next to us."

"What?"

"I don't know what's going on, but come on, let's hurry."

In agreement, they both took off running through the campus. Safia took a few glances at the tablet as they picked up the pace and found that so two did the other two dots that were besides theirs. They ran off the pathway, making a straight line towards the right library and leaped up the steps, passing by a group of students who had just left, leaving the door open.

"Sorry," said Safia as they both passed the surprised students. They stopped in the middle hall between the aisles, and Safia took another look at her tablet. "Damn, it shows they are already here, too."

"I don't see anyone," said Hashmi, looking around frantically.

"Come on," said Safia, taking off towards the pendant's icon. She zipped through several aisles before she saw what she was looking for. Up on the third row of books, she saw the top of another chest sticking out. She looked around for a way to reach in and saw a boy about to get on a roll-ladder and ran over, shoving the boy aside.

"Hey!"

"Sorry. But it'll only take a minute. Hashmi, push me down."

Hashmi came over to the ladder and began pushing it down the aisle as Safia climbed up. As she neared it, she reached out and placed her hand on it, and her badge began to glow. Taking a sigh of relief, she glanced back down at Hashmi with a smile, but ahead of her, Safia saw another couple from the group at the start of the game looking up at her. They had frowns on their faces, but the girl raised her tablet, showing it to the boy, and they both took off running out of the library.

*Where did they come from?* Safia slowly made her way down to the floor by Hashmi. "Did you see them?"

"See who?"

"The other couple. They were in the library."

"I didn't see anyone from down here. But what's in the box?"

"Oh, yeah," said Safia, her mind coming back to the task at hand. She then walked over, placing the chest on the table and opened it. Inside there were what looked to be hundreds of keys.

"What is all this?" asked Hashmi, as she ran her hands over the plethora of keys. "And they're all different colors. It's actually beautiful, like some type of jewel box." She picked up a few before letting them drop back in the box. "Oh, some of them might be magnetic; they're sticking together." She dug her hand deep inside the box in an attempt to pick up another handful more, but instead, amongst the assortment of metal trinkets came up a large egg-shaped thing that barely fit in her hand.

"That's something," said Safia, plucking the egg from Hashmi's hand as the few remaining keys fell back into the box. "I guess this is the next puzzle." She perched the egg on her fingers, slowly rotating and examining it. Much like the keys in the box, it shined with a cornucopia of colors that reflected everything around it.

"It's very pretty," said Hashmi, the aurora reflecting off her eyes as it spun in front of her. "Oh, what's that? It has a small latch on it."

Safia rotated the egg even more, seeing the spot that Hashmi had pointed out. "I guess one of the keys goes in there." Safia took another look at the hundreds of keys in the box. "But how in the world do we pick? Are we supposed to just try them all?"

"I hope not, but there's only one way to find out," Safia picked up a random key, sliding it into the slot in the egg. She heard a click before the key locked in place. She then tugged on the key for a moment, but it wouldn't budge. "It's stuck." Then she heard the shiny egg begin ticking.

"That doesn't sound good," said Hashmi as she placed her finger on the egg. "Did you see any instructions or clues with it up there?"

"No, just the box."

"But if there are no clues, hopefully that means it should be solvable without any crazy knowledge. I just hope we can solve it before—"

There was one final click before the key went shooting

out of the egg, landing on the table.

"I guess that was the wrong key," said Safia.

"It seems so, but why did it take so long for it to reject it?"

"Probably just to waste time. Remember, we only have one hour to complete each puzzle or we're out of the game." Safia pulled out her tablet again and, ahead, it showed the time they had left. "Only fifty minutes left. I think that egg will hold on to a key for a minute."

"So, at most we can try like forty something keys before we lose," said Hashmi as she turned to look back at the box filled with hundreds of keys. "There must be a trick to it, or this is just impossible unless you are born with incredible luck."

Safia picked up the egg again and began inspecting it closer. The way the colors swirled throughout the exteriors was almost hypnotizing. It was as if she were staring into outer space. There were pinks, purples, and all other color-ful clouds and inside of them seemed to be little stars. She looked down at the keys on the table; her eyes searching for anything that would make sense. Reaching her hand into the box, she grabbed a couple of keys, laying them one by one beside each other as she sat the egg in front of them, balancing it with her index finger so it wouldn't fall over.

"What are you looking for?"

"At this point, anything. The keys are colorful, so maybe we have to match the colors up with the egg."

"But there are so many keys."

"I can't think of anything else."

Hashmi sighed, and stepped over, taking a seat beside Safia, laying her head down on the desk, and looking over the keys and eggs. "Every mistake is a minute, so we best get started."

Trying their best to match up the colors of the keys with the colors near the slot, they pushed in another. And just like before, the key locked in place, stayed in place for a minute, before the egg spat it back out.

"This is ridiculous," said Hashmi. "It's pure happenstance. The other were more trivia based, which I admit was annoying, but this... this is—"

Then came the sound click as Safia slid the next key in. Instead of only going in partly, the egg took the key in fully and this time they heard another set of clicking.

"Of course, you manage it right before I start my complaining," said Hashmi with a smile. "And it was going to be such a really good vent too."

"We had it wrong. Instead of looking at the side of the keys. I think only the end matters. We needed to finish the image that hole left open."

"Easier said than done. The details are so small, I would have to strained my eyes to death to—"

Then the sound of another click came from the egg, and both girls witnessed another small key slot open up on the egg and their faces couldn't hide their disgust at the egg.

"You can always vent now," said Safia, unable to hide her smile.

"Unfortunately, that time has passed. Am I allowed to smash it? I think that's the only form of release that shall relieve me of my current frustration."

"I wouldn't mind. But let's wait until we are out of time first."

"How much is left?"

"A little over thirty minutes."

Hashmi sighed as she grabbed another set of keys. "Then let's continue our examination then." And she lifted each one up, staring at the edge of the keys, trying to see if it matched up with the empty slots of the egg.

They would spend the next two dozen minutes slipping keys in and out of the slots of the egg. They managed to solve four more of the little key holes, and as each other key slid in, another hole opened. And each new opening built upon their frustration.

"I'm about to lose my mind," said Safia.

"It seems as if there are matching sets of keys in the pile. So, it probably isn't hundreds, maybe only a dozen or so that are just replicated over and over," said Hashmi, knocking one key off another. "I still don't see why they stick together so much." She examined the hole and looked at the key in her hand, then slid it into the slot. The egg accepted it and the key slid into place. "Wow, two in a row. I think we're getting better at this. How much time do we have left?"

"About fifteen minutes," said Safia, looking at her tablet.

Then the egg made another clicking sound, then another, and then it began shaking.

"Is it me, or is it clicking a lot more than before," said Hashmi as they both looked at the egg and watched as four different holes appeared next to each other forming an X.

"I guess we now know why the keys can attach to each other."

"Is it wrong that I am starting to feel a strong resentment towards whoever made this puzzle?"

"I think we share that emotion. But come on, this might be the last one. Then we're probably done. Seeing as we're taking so long."

Both girls began picking up keys from the already-paired sets they had made and began trying to link them together.

"They only link on the bottom, so I guess they have some sort of magnet when they line up correctly," said Safia as she linked the two together.

"Then why don't these two link?" asked Hashmi as she tried the same thing with another set of keys, but it didn't work.

"Okay, so some work and some don't. That probably is a good thing for us. It narrows down what we can use. I already have two, so let's see if we can find any more that will stick." The girls spent some time trying to get keys to attach themselves to the key link Safia already had. And after sifting through all the sets they had and a few randoms from inside to the box to make sure they didn't miss anything, they found that only four keys actually stuck together.

"No way, it's this easy," said Hashmi, eyeing the X-shape the keys had made as Safia held it in her palm.

"Only one way to find out," said Safia as she placed the keys above the hole, rotating it until it seemed as if the colors matched up. "Does this look right to you?"

"As right as I think it can be," said Hashmi, their faces pressed together as they tried eyeing down the key into the slots. "How much time do we have left?"

"Seven minutes, and there's no guarantee that this is this last one."

"Well," said Hashmi, placing her hand on top of Safia's. "Too late to turn back now." And she brought her weight down on Safia's hand, plunging the key into the egg. It shook from the impact, and then there was an assortment of clicks, then more clicks, and then silence. And finally, the keys began to descend into the egg.

"Is that it?" asked Hashmi as the egg began to shake. Then the sound of a seal being released was heard as the egg split itself in half and the tiny keys came falling out. Inside were an assortment of tiny gears, but in the center was a note that read, congratulations.

Safia looked over at her tablet and saw that the time had stopped with four minutes and thirty-two seconds left. "Oh, thank goodness. I'd rather go to class a thousand times than go through that again. Just so annoy—" Safia's eyes squinted as she saw the school symbol show up near where the school pool was. "It looks like there's another one."

"What? Are we still not done yet?" asked Hashmi as she leaned over, looking at Safia's tablet. "Goodness, what must those other puzzles be like then if there is still a third for us? Oh! Two of the dots just disappeared."

"Maybe they gave up?"

"If so, then I can't say that I blame them."

"You want to do the final one?"

"Can we just not do it?" asked Hashmi, waving her hand. "I much rather just lay my head down and forget about all this."

"I don't know. There might be some sort of penalty for not completing it after it shows up on the tablet. Maybe that's why the other two dots disappeared."

Hashmi sighed before standing up from the table. "Come on, let's go to the next puzzle. I truly hope we don't become that rare couple that Arthur spoke of earlier and have to solve five whole puzzles."

Safia grabbed the open egg and stuffed it in her bag alongside the scroll and both she and Hashmi left the library and headed across the campus towards the pool house.

"What do you think the next puzzle will be?" asked Hashmi.

"Honestly, at this point. I hope that it's a game of seeing who can sleep the longest and they have a set of beds waiting for us there."

Hashmi laughed, "We can only hope to be so fortunate. But perhaps we shall run into Jericho again and we can ask for his assistance."

"Knowing him, he's probably still down in that tunnel, digging a hole to the other side of the earth. Did I ever tell you how I met him? He was digging a hole in the ground."

"They do say the wicked shall dig their own graves."

"And here I am, doing everything the wicked tell me to do."

"Yes, and don't forget that you've even now dragged me along on this puzzle mission of yours. You should feel bad."

Safia shook her head. "You really know how to rub it in."

Hashmi laughed, wrapping her arms around Safia's. "Come along, my selfish friend. We still have another puzzle to tolerate."

With their spirits lifted a little, the girls headed on over to the pool area. Beside the door to the pool house there was a sign that read. 'Not all music is sung in verse. Pocahontas sang with the colors of the wind.'

"Pocahontas? As in the Disney movie? Are they expecting us to sing?"

"Then we will certainly lose this puzzle, since I can't sing at all," said Safia, frowning.

Hashmi laughed, "Only one way to find out. Let's go."

They entered the building, and Safia's badge changed colors again.

"I guess that means that puzzle is ours."

"I can barely contain my excitement," Safia said with a straight face.

The moment they walked through the second door, they saw something amazing. Ahead of the pool sat three tables, one in the center and two on the sides. The side tables were filled with what looked to be wooden statues and dioramas, while the center table only had a single circular shaped diorama.

"I can already feel like this is going to be needlessly complicated," said Safia as the girls made their way toward the tables.

"Safia, look," said Hashmi, tugging on her friend's arm and pointing towards the pool.

Safia turned to see a large metal box at the bottom of the pool with a lock on it. "I'm honestly not even surprised anymore. Come on, let's go and see how to drain the pool."

Both girls walked up to the three tables where Safia could see that the center table's circular diorama looked like a roman coliseum. It was very well detailed. It even had little figurines atop the stands. Behind it, against the wall, stood large pipes and on each were colorful valve wheels: green, blue, orange, and red.

Hashmi walked over, taking the piece of paper from the pink wheel. "Let power come to those who wish to have it."

"Well, that's obvious," said Safia as she looked around at the other tables. Each one housed a dozen statues of what looked to be the same man, just in unique positions. In one position, he held a scroll, in another he was holding a flute, then another he held a sword and dressed like a warrior.

"Who do you think it is?"

"I don't know, but I think that's the roman coliseum. So, maybe it was someone who competed there. But seriously, how do they expect us to know these things?"

"We don't," said Arthur as he walked out of a door to the back of the room. "Honestly, you girls are out doing all expectations. Most of us here only expected you to solve maybe one of our little toys. But look at you two go; on our third puzzle."

"Yes, I'll admit that was short-sighted on my part," said Frilla, her normal cheerful tone darker than usual as she walked out behind Arthur. "It seems her victory over the point freak might not have been luck after all."

"What are you two doing here?" asked Hashmi. "I thought we were supposed to meet up after all the games ended?"

"Well, the games have ended. You two are the only ones left. So, I suggested to Arthur that we all come to watch as you struggle on the last puzzle, rather than just looking at the screen on my tablet. Live games are always more fun."

"Yes, they almost failed the egg puzzle, but somehow managed to solve the scroll puzzle really fast. Although one has to wonder why the camera system down there was broken and we couldn't watch them actually solve it."

"Now, now, don't be a sore loser, Frilla. There's no need for that suspicion. They girls still have one last puzzle to solve before you officially lose to me. And besides, that was just a word game." Arthur placed a finger to his cheek with a smirk across his lips as he tilted his head. "But then again, if they knew something of Greek history, then perhaps they know Roman history too. It should be simple for the time they have left, considering they've gotten this far."

"What happens if we fail to solve this puzzle?" asked

Hashmi.

"Nothing. You will receive points for completing two puzzles. This competition isn't malicious in the slightest. Though I personally would be disappointed if you fail, this is simply a game to help those less fortunate than I. In fact, your dear friend Miss Safia was quite adamant about you attending with her for that very reason."

"Can we just try to finish the puzzle," said Safia, feeling a bit embarrassed.

"Yes, sorry," said Arthur as he and Frilla took a few steps up the concrete stands and sat, watching them. "Carry on. I certainly do not wish to waste your precious time."

Safia looked at her tablet once more and saw that they now only had around forty-five minutes left.

Examining the objects once again, she saw that the center table had four saucers that seemed to match the size of the base of all the figurines. "I guess we have to place the correct ones on them."

"Well, it matches up. There are four valves and four plates. So, I guess each one controls a valve," said Hashmi as she walked over, picking up a figurine. "But there's so many of them."

"And I don't suppose it's going to tell us when we get one right. So, we will probably need to get all four. What did that paper say again?"

"Let power come to those who wish to have it."

"Okay, so what statues look like they mean power," said Safia as she turned back around, searching amongst the figurines.

"I think we should sort them out as we did the keys," said Hashmi, picking up another one and comparing the two. "We need to get some type of organization amongst them, or we'll just be running back and forth."

"Okay, so we should probably read all the papers and then try to match what we think is right with the papers."

"Sounds right to me," said Hashmi, setting the figures

back down and stepping back to the main table, picking up the pieces of paper from the valves and sitting them down, matching them up with the colorful saucers on the middle table. "Okay, which one first?"

"The pink one you had before. Let's find ones that look like they want power," said Safia as she scanned over the figurines. Some were wearing fine clothing, some playing random musical instruments, and others were dressed as warriors holding weapons.

"I don't know what they mean by power," said Hashmi, poking her finger against one of the small statues. "This one has weapons, and this one is holding a crown, so I guess he's a king or something. But I guess both can mean power."

"That's something I guess. Let's put those over here."

The girls went about grabbing all the figures with crowns and weapons and placing them at the left top of the table.

"Okay, and what's the next one?"

Hashmi grabbed the paper with the green saucer. "Nothing burns hotter than the soul of an artist. For it is through their soul that change is spread."

"Okay, so art stuff?" said Safia, looking over everything again. This time she and Hashmi picked out the statues that either held musical equipment or fancy clothing.

"Next," said Hashmi, picking up the paper next to the blue saucer. "A champion must be crowned, but a champion of the people must be found." Hashmi squinted her eyes at the paper. "I wonder if they meant for that to rhyme."

"A champion. So, I guess that means the ones with weapons that look like they are fighting."

"Makes sense to me," said Safia as they separated the fighting pieces from the rest.

"So, the last one is orange, and I guess it says something about dressing nicely," said Hashmi, seeing that the only dolls they hadn't touched were the few wearing little outfits. "She reached over grabbing the orange paper. "The world's a stage and we are all its actors. Some are more dynamic than others, but we all must play our part.

"Okay, so I guess we just leave those there," said Safia, referring to the figurines in little outfits. "Which ones do you think are right?"

"You're going to make me pick?" said Hashmi with a laugh.

"Okay, you pick the green and blue, and I'll take the orange and pink."

Both girls went to the different tables and began looking over the pieces.

*Let power come to those who wish to have it.* Safia recited the quote in her mind as she looked over the pieces with the crowns. *The key has to be in how it's worded, but I just don't see a difference between them.* There were six figures all in different poses: One knelt, the crown atop his head; one other stood with his hands raised toward the sky; one leaned forward dangling the crown on his finger; one sat, the crown on the floor in front of him; and the final piece was placed with a crown on the hilt of sword embedded into the floor.

*Think Safia. Let power come to those who wish to have it. Which one of these looks like they wish to have power?* She continued looking over the piece several times. *The one kneeling looks like he is given power. The one sitting on the floor looks sad. I doubt he wishes for anything. What about the crown on the sword? He doesn't look happy. Did he take power in war?* Safia looked at the other piece, the one with its hands raised as if it were a child wanting to be picked up by its parents. Safia stared at the piece for a moment, then looked at the rest. *Wait! This one doesn't have a crown, like all the others. And it looks like he wants something or is reaching for it at least. That might count as 'wishing'.*

Safia grabbed the piece, stepping toward the center table and placing it on the pink saucer. She stared at it for a moment, but nothing happened. There was no click, or beep, or anything that signified whether she was right or wrong. *Guess it's too much to ask for any type of sign.*

She then turned back to the pieces that were dressed in odd outfits. *The world's a stage? All of these pieces look like they belong in a play.* As she stepped back to the other table, she couldn't help but look at the little clothing the figures were wearing. Some held together with string. But unlike the other pieces, these pieces had small things added to them. Two had broken pillars where one man was before pointing upward while the other statue had a man sitting on top of the pillar with his arms stretched out, much like the man from the previous set of figures. Another one had a large rock with a man on the ground before it with an arrow in his back. Of the three others; one man held a flute while wearing a feathered cap; one was a man sitting at a desk; and then finally there was a man with a bow in one hand and a quiver on his back.

*The man at the desk looks to be writing. Perhaps it's the play, and he's making it.* Safia took the piece in hand and walked back over to the table to see Hashmi herself, placing her second piece on the table.

"You think we got it?" asked Hashmi as she looked over at Safia, still holding the figure.

"Only one way to find out," said Safia, placing the little statue on the orange saucer. They stared at it for a long moment, and then over to the valves of the pool. But after a minute, nothing happened. "I guess we weren't going to become lucky on our first try."

"High hopes often have long falls. How much time do we have left?"

"A little less than thirty minutes," said Safia, looking at her tablet.

"Have I mentioned that I hope to never get involved in another puzzle again? Manual labor with Jericho doesn't seem so bad in comparison. And our chaperons over there do not help with how they are looking at us. I feel as if I'm an attraction at a menagerie."

"I don't know what a menagerie is, but just ignore them, if you can. We still have a bit of time. We should just explain to each other why we picked the pieces we did."

Hashmi nodded to the statue of the man who had two swords in his hand, raising them above his head. "'A champion must be crowned, but a champion of the people must be found' is what the note said, and doesn't this one seem as if he is celebrating?"

"Seems that way," said Safia, looking over at the other figurines. One had a shield and one had a whip spiraling around him. One had a heavy sword that looked bigger than he was, and the other two had two men in a grappling stance that Hashmi had facing each other. "I probably would have picked that one with two swords as well."

"I figured as much. None of the others seemed to fit as well," said Hashmi, moving on to her second statue. "'Nothing burns hotter than the soul of an artist. For it is through their soul that change is spread,' so I chose the figure that had the main painting. It seemed fairly obvious. Well, except for the fact that he wasn't on fire."

Safia smirked before turning back to the other table to look at the other pieces. Of the five left, there was one that sat playing a cello, one who stood on a small box with one hand one his chest and the other outstretched forward, one who held a scroll and a quill, one who played the harp, and the final one that played a flute.

"They all seem like artists to me. But I don't know which ones represent change."

"Well, I figured that they create music. But painting, while creating, is more of a change since you have to mix colors and stuff."

"That's a smarter reason than I would have come up with."

"Really? Let's go see yours then."

Safia led Hashmi over to her table and showed her the

pieces she had picked out and explained to why she chose them. Hashmi, looking at the pieces, tilted her head at one of the leftover ones on the table.

"This one," said Hashmi, pointing to the man with the crown laid on the embedded sword. "I think this one might work for my blue one. It did say 'a champion must be crowned.'" She looked over at the statue of the man kneeling with a crown on his head. "Note this one, but he doesn't have a weapon, so I doubt he's a champion." She twisted her lips, thinking. "I'm going to try it. "She took the statue with the crown on top of the sword, replacing the one that sat before on the blue saucer.

They waited for another moment, but nothing happened.

"Dang it, I really thought that was it. How much time do we have left now?"

"About fifteen minutes."

"That's enough time to keep trying. Which piece do you want to try next?"

"Wait, maybe we're missing something in the puzzle. One was a champion, the other talked about pieces in a play, then there was the one about being crowned."

"Actually," said Hashmi. "What about the musical one?"

"What musical one?"

"You know, when we entered it said that all songs are sung in verse. But I don't see any singing pieces. Only ones hold musical instruments. I don't exactly think any of them are singing. I mean, wouldn't their mouths be open?"

Safia looked over the statues again. "Yeah, and it's not like there is any music playing that they can sing for us. Everything is quiet. So exactly what verse are we..." Safia's eyes went wide as she looked over the pieces on the tables and then back to the colorful pipes, then back to the color-coded pieces they had planted on the saucers. "It's backwards. Hashmi, the colors, they're backwards."

"What? What do you mean?"

"Not in verse, as in music. Inverse as in colors. Colors can be inverted to their opposite colors." She looked over at the statues. "Blue should be orange and green should be red. We have to swap them."

"Then let's try it and see," said Hashmi, as both girls stepped back to their table and began swapping their pieces for their opposite colors. Hashmi laid down the last piece on green and they both watched for a moment until they heard a clicking sound and suddenly the diorama caught fire as the little city around it began to burn. Then came the loud sound of squeaking as both girls watched as the valves began turning, causing the water to start draining from the pool.

Then the single sound of clapping echoed over them as they turned to see Arthur with a large smile on his face as he stepped off the concrete stands and began making his way towards them from a sour-faced Frilla behind him.

"Congratulations," said Arthur. "I knew you were special. I even bet Frilla here a large number of points that you would solve this puzzle, and you even did it with over a dozen minutes to spare. Bravo, you wonderful geese."

"You were betting on us?" asked Safia.

"Oh, I thought I mentioned that earlier? Well, either way, it wasn't just us. We all were. Didn't I mention earlier how we got tired of watching you? Everyone from the upper and lower class had put points on just who in this event would come out on top. And I, Miss Safia, picked you and Miss Hashmi here as my Golden Geese, and more specifically, I selected you would manage to accomplish three puzzles."

"Yes," said Frilla, looking dejectedly over at the still burning diagram. "I suppose Rome will indeed burn today. Just how many discarded will be made because of this unforeseen turn of events? I suppose this final puzzle is quite fitting."

"I don't understand," said Hashmi. "What do you mean everyone is betting on us?"

"Didn't you find it odd that everywhere you went, you didn't see hardly any other students? The campus was empty, the library was empty, and even this pool was empty. Have you ever walked into any of these places and found them completely void of people?"

Safia began to think about their track around the campus and how it was true that the only other people they saw were the other team after getting to the library puzzle. Even Jericho only appeared down in the tunnels.

"So, everyone on the campus has been watching us?"

"Most, I would guess, ninety percent of the school are currently in the gymnasium, and would guess about half of those are crying their eyes out right now because they've won a lot of points or are trying to become someone's discarded before their time runs out."

"But... that can't be true. Who would bet that many points?"

"Oh god, the naivete. They really are adorable children," said Arthur. "How do you think we've amassed all the points we have? This is one of the few times of the year where you can bet for absurd amounts of points. Betting points on each team to win or completing so many puzzles. And wins are multipled based on which parts you get right."

"So, you mean people were betting against us?" asked Hashmi, shaking her head.

"No, some probably bet with you, like I did. But they may have still lost because they picked the wrong number of puzzles you would solve. I mean, most of the others barely completed one, if that. Truthfully, you would have another puzzle if one student hadn't smashed it in frustration after failing it. The domino effect of this is going to be quite the spectacle over the next day or so."

"But I still don't understand," said Hashmi. "Wasn't Safia supposed to be popular? Why did so many not pick her?"

"Oh, it wasn't just me. Your friend Amanda did as well. I'm sure she's grinning from ear to ear right now. But as to your question, I suppose it has to do with the numerous failings she's had since she's returned. Not to mention that absolute disaster with Dario at game night. It seems she lost a bit of her mystique during all of that."

"Then why did you pick her?"

"I told you. It's because of how badly she wanted you, her little play-pal friend, to gain some points. Usually, one's motives here are quite selfish. Even Amanda and all her charity are based on her own grandiose senses. Not many people reach our levels and still maintain that level of goody-two-shoes'ness. So, I just figured if anyone was going to do it, it would be her," said Arthur, pointing his finger at Safia, before turning back to Frilla with a mischievous smile across his face. "And now, thanks to that bit of foresight, our lovely Frilla here owes me quite a large number of points. Since she bet me personally." Arthur turned to the draining water. "Oh good, the box is revealed. Go on in ladies and claim your prize. The water's shallow enough now."

Safia looked down at the chained box in the water. *I have so many questions. But honestly, I just want this day to be over.* She then walked to the side of the pool with Hashmi, placing her hand on the railing and walked down the steps. The girls made their way over to the box, with Safia seeing a slot for her pendant. Removing it from her neck, she placed it on top and heard a seal break as the top popped open a bit. She and Hashmi then place the hands on the lid, lifting it up to reveal a dozen new colorful and ornate pendants.

"Both of you can pick one," said Arthur. "Think of them as presents and a welcoming gift. From now on, you both are going to be quite famous around the school. Safia even more so."

"What do you think?" asked Safia, looking over at Hashmi.

"I think we should just take one. While I think we have earned it, I would rather not gain any more attention from these people. So, let's take the prize and go home. The faster, the better."

Safia nodded her head and looked over the assortment of pendants, finally settling on the one shaped like a flower. Hashmi reached in and picked up a red butterfly pendant.

"The last one was broken on Dario's face. I think this will be a suitable replacement, although it's a fair amount larger, so I'm not sure I can wear it on my Hijab."

Leaving the lid open, the girls made their way back out of the pool where Arthur and Frilla were waiting on them.

"What now?" asked Safia. "Is there anything else we have to do?"

"Just receive your points. Each puzzle was worth fifty thousand points, so if you double that, twice." Arthur clicked on his pendant. "Release the points to winners of the scavenger hunt."

"You have received two-hundred thousand points," spoke both Safia and Hashmi's old pendants as they began glowing at the same time. The girl's eyes went wide at the number.

"And now for my winning," said Arthur, clicking on his pendant once more. "Now release the points of the betting on the scavenger hunt."

"You have received three million one hundred thousand points," spoke his pendant.

He looked over at Frilla with a large smile across his face. "Looks like I'm number one now, Frilla. You really should have had more faith in your little pet here. She was simply marvelous."

A begrudged smile made its way over Frilla's lips. "There are always more games. Enjoy it while you can."

"I shall," said Arthur, stepping forward and wrapping his arms around Safia. "Come ladies, I'm sure you have a lot of questions, and I am feeling oh-so generous at the moment. I shall answer them for you, as I do the gentlemanly thing, and escort you home."

Safia allowed Arthur to escort her around the pool, and

past Frilla, headed toward the door with Hashmi at their side. Safia looked back and her last sight was of the usually happy Frilla now, biting her lip and clenching her fists.

"It was Yennefer house, right?"

"Huh?" asked Safia, being brought back to reality.

"Yennefer house, that is your dorm, isn't it?"

"Oh, ah... yes."

"Right, then on our way."

"You do seem quite happy," said Hashmi to Arthur, after seeing Safia looking a bit out of it. "Were those points so important? I would imagine after getting a million, that any more would hardly matter."

"Oh, my dear. Points are power here. And now that I have the most points in the school. That means our happy Frilla, who we left back there sulking, won't be able to just do as she pleases anymore. Now, she will have to ask me nicely and I can simply deny her. Power is so wonderful when it's shared with those more deserving."

"I don't understand. So, you can't just make games? Jericho does it all the time when he has us building things around campus."

"Oh dear, Jericho's little project was hardly anything substantial. No, I'm talking about game nights. Like the one Safia and I were involved in with the escape room. You can essentially make this campus your playground. Frilla forced me and my darling man to participate in that last event but now, since I'm on top, I get to make the decisions."

"But... couldn't you just say no?"

"No, second years don't have that option. It's—"

"And since you have the most points now," said Safia, chiming in being brought back to the conversation. "That means that any bets you make with her still take priority over any bets she made beforehand."

"That's right. Well, hasn't your pretty self been paying attention," said Arthur, squeezing the Safia closer to him. "Our wonderful Miss Frilla is no longer a spectator, going out of her way to pick the selected risk-free games so that she can stay as number one. From now on, Miss High and Mighty will be forced to play the game, right along with the rest of us."

# CHAPTER 15

Safia sat up in her bed, looking at her tablet, where images of the dancing masks that she had still left to figure out appeared on the screen. *I've been so caught up in things that I haven't had time to find any more. I got one right and wrong. But weren't they supposed to show up before me? I haven't noticed anyone like that, and it's been months. Am I just not paying enough attention?*

The door opened to the room and Hashmi walked in.

"Oh, you're awake?" said Hashmi, closing the door behind her.

"Where have you been?"

"Out with Jericho, as usual. We were walking around trying to think of the next project to make on campus."

"But you have—" said Safia before closing her mouth. *I guess I should talk about it before it becomes something bigger.*

"But I have what?"

"Hashmi... are you mad at me?"

"What? No, why would you ask that?"

"I mean... they were gambling on us. And I know you said you didn't want to be involved in that and... I mean, if I would have known—"

"No, I'm not mad at you. In fact, given this school, I probably should have seen it coming. But I did not purposely take part in any gambling. I only assisted my friend in a task. What other people do with their points, well... I have no control over that. I will pray to Allah for forgiveness on my part in it, yes, but I am not responsible for the actions of others."

"Then why help Jericho now? You have a lot of points."

"Because he has come to rely on me, and I believe that his projects around the campus are doing good for others who also do not wish to gamble."

"But when we came back to the room, you didn't really speak to me?"

"I was tired. Those annoying puzzles simply wore me out. I am talking to you now, aren't I?"

Safia just shook her head and sighed. "I'm sorry. I'm focusing too much on the wrong stuff, I guess. It's just, I have to think about the games, the points, these silly masks that I have to find out, and all this other stuff. I guess I just thought too much about you being mad at me as well."

Hashmi stepped over, taking Safia's hands in hers with a smile. "It's nice that you worry about me and want to make sure we're friends. But I promise you, Safia, I am the last person you will ever have to worry about with."

"Okay," said Safia, closing her eyes. "You're right. I know that now."

"Good. Now come along, classes will be starting soon, and I'd rather not be late."

Safia turned to her side, smiling at the girl asleep beside her.

"It seems Mallory also had a long night."

"I saw. Did she say why?"

"Apparently, she was in the gymnasium watching us. She said that she screamed a lot."

Hashmi laughed, "I would have loved to have seen that. The Carnival Queen has worn herself out. But I guess that's the joy of having late classes. You can afford to sleep in."

"Well, I'm sure you can buy at least one decent grade now with your points."

"I'd rather work for it, if possible. Besides, I think that we should go shopping sometime soon. We deserve it after that mess yesterday."

"I agree," said Safia. And now feeling understood, she finished getting dressed and she and Hashmi left out of the building and headed off towards class. Safia felt an odd feeling in the air as she left her room and went down the steps of her dorm. It felt very similar to the feeling she had when she had returned to the campus from her visit home. Everyone on campus seemed to be watching her.

"I think we've become popular again," said Hashmi, echoing the thoughts that were running through her mind.

"Yes, I guess everyone really was watching us yesterday. What should we do?"

"What can we do? At least they can't make you bet any of them. You're not in your second year yet, but I don't like the look on some of their faces."

"Come on, let's not pay attention to them," said Safia as they made their way across the campus and into the school. They noticed even more students looking at them, but they quickly made their way to class, sitting down and taking their seats by the window. Looking around, Safia noticed there were a few empty chairs.

A few minutes later, their teacher walked in. "Okay class," said the older man as he plopped down his bag on the desk. "I hope everyone is ready for... Is it me or are we missing a few more students than usual?"

"They've been expelled," said another boy, turning his

attention to Safia. "They bet on the wrong people."

"Ah, I see. It's that time of the year again, is it? There's always around a few dozen that end up leveraging more than they should."

"It's not fair. My boyfriend was forced out. I couldn't afford to take him as my discarded because he owed more points than I had." She turned to Safia. "Why did you have to win? Wasn't two boxes enough?"

"Oh! Were you one of the participants?" said the older man, looking toward Safia. "And did I hear you finished three prizes? That is quite impressive. When I was here, most only ever managed two. But that was when they had someone following behind us, making sure we didn't cheat. Nowadays, we all have those little zappy chips implanted in us."

Safia lowered her head. *It's not like I knew this would all happen.*

"Don't worry, child," said the old man, seeming to notice her discomfort. "It happens every year. Dozens of students are wiped out for being too greedy on their bets. It was the scavenger hunt, yes? Tell me, what did you receive for finishing three boxes? I know that if you finish three, four, or five boxes, then you are awarded prizes, but rarely have I ever seen someone finish three, let alone five."

Safia lifted her head. "They gave us new pendants."

"Oh, may I see it?"

"I didn't bring it. I haven't had the chance to activate it yet."

"A shame. But that is understandable. But please, when you do, show it to me."

"Yes, sir."

"Good, and with that matter settled, what say we start the class, shall we? Today we are finally going to talk about the issue of how chewing gum has affected the world on a global scale. Now who here has chewed a piece of gum before?"

All the class raised their hands.

"You see, gum in the nineteen hundreds was actually advertised as a miracle drug. You need to cure your depression, chew some flavored gum. You need to lose weight, chew some gum instead of eating. You want to appear more friendly and approachable, chew some gum. Or if you want to introduce yourself to a special someone, well, a great ice breaker would be to simply offer some gum."

"That sounds just silly," said a boy in class.

"It was actually quite the ingenious way of handling a fairly cheap product. Market it at a low price so that it was easy enough for everyone to own it and suddenly you would have a company that would be in everyone's homes and, most importantly, their pockets."

"But, how did it take over the world?"

"Marketing my boy. It's what we all do, just not on such a grand scale. If you consider how the world works, most of the decisions made by consumers are based on how well something was marketed to us. Even a subpar product can and will sell better than its well-made counterpart if the advertising team does their job correctly."

"I don't get it. How does this affect the world, then?"

"Hmm, let's put it this way. How many here have purchased an item, only to find yourself days or weeks later asking the question, 'why did I purchase this? I don't even use the thing." The entire class raised their hands again. "And there you see. That was probably the example of some well-placed marketing. Something somewhere, maybe a commercial, or a picture placed in just the right location, convinced you that you needed those items just long enough to get you to buy it. But that goes far beyond just simple trinkets."

"Wait, I think I get it. So, that's what they do here. When they convince us, we need to bet. Or how, if we get more points, things will get easier. But now a lot of us are regretting it since a lot of our friends are gone or have become somebody's discarded."

"That is certainly a way of seeing things, and it is probably accurate considering the thought process of this school. But I wish to bring this around to a more historical sense; on how the world chooses to promote itself."

"The world?" asked a girl in class. "You mean like politics and such?"

"Yes, but mostly I meant in terms of their economies. Because there are different types. Democratic, socialist, dictatorships, monarchies, and a slew of others all promoting their way of doing things. Each of these are posted up on giant billboards and sold to the rest of the world, figuratively speaking."

"I don't get it. What does this have to do with chewing gum?"

"Everything. Just like there are different flavors of gum, there are different ways to brand and market each particular flavor. The same can be said for how we influence the world. For some, we advertise it as violence, other times we advertise it as compassion. The truth is that every part of all of us is for sale in some form or fashion. The real question is, how are you marketing yourself?"

"I guess that makes sense."

"Take your recent example of that young lady over there, the one who solved the puzzles. You say that she was the cause of so many students being expelled recently. Well, I ask you, what was the cause of so many people choosing to place their wagers against her? Did so much of the population here not believe her capable?"

"No, I mean, she's gotten lucky a few times. But she's never won anything big."

"Exactly, so she was marketed to you as something that was one-off, or as a failure. Even though you, yourself, just admitted that she has seen some success here. Then I dare to say that this woman has been marketed to you in such a way that you would fall victim to a grandiose error."

"That doesn't make any sense. You mean to say that she wanted us to believe that she was a failure?"

"Maybe that's not the case, but the result seems to be the same, because she opened three boxes and so many students are gone. Then that certainly means that someone or something have profited handsomely from it."

Safia thought back to Arthur. *I wonder if things are going to change now. Maybe I won't be dragged into as many games, but I still need to figure out the people under the masks.*

The class continued as the old man told them stories of how the world was influenced by advertising until the bell for class finally rang. Safia stood up from her seat, only to be bumped rather roughly by another student in passing.

"Hey!" shouted Safia. "Pay more attention to where you're going."

The girl gave her a glance but didn't say anything, just continued walking with a look of disgust in her eyes.

Safia noticed that she was the same girl from earlier who was complaining about her boyfriend being evicted from the school. Instantly, Safia knew the knock against her was intentional as her seat was two rows away and there was no need for the girl to be in her aisle.

"Just let it go for now," said Hashmi, placing a hand on Safia's shoulder before she could respond. "There's no need to involve yourself with her. Plus, we still need to go shopping, remember?"

Listening to Hashmi, Safia calmed herself down. "You're right, let's go. It'll give us something to do while Mallory is still in class."

Leaving the class, they headed back to the campus store. Still, they noticed people staring at them as they made their way across campus.

"I suppose it's too much to ask for things to go back to normal," said Hashmi as they made their way inside of the building.

"I'm hoping it calms down like last time. But I'm not

looking forward to the next few weeks until it does," said Safia as they reached the second floor and entered the store. "What do you want to buy?"

"I'm not too sure. Usually when we come here, it's because we need something. This will be the first time we are here for something other than necessity. So, I guess we just look around."

The girls browsed around the shop, but outside of a few more school supplies and handbags, there wasn't anything they needed. They did pick up a few umbrellas for the rainy days before heading up to the counter and laying everything down on the table.

"That'll be five hundred points. Oh, hello again. I see you spending those points you won during the games," said the boy behind the check-out desk.

Surprised by his friendliness, she took another look at the clerk and realized it was the boy from the cafeteria who always had on the chef's hat. "You again? Do you always work random jobs?"

"A man's gotta earn them points, ya know."

"Hey. When people get a bunch of points, what do they spend them on?"

"Oh, you're probably talking about the second-year store."

"They have a separate store for second years?"

"Well, it's more of an online thing. You've bought clothing and stuff on your tablet and had people bring it to your dorm room before, haven't you?"

"Yes."

"Well, it'll be the same during your second year, it's just that you will have more options to choose from and they will start costing a lot more."

"Stuff like what?"

"Well, I'm not a second year myself, so I don't really know. But I've heard you can buy camera footage or history of students and stuff like that. But I heard it's super expensive to do stuff like that."

"Okay," said Safia, taking her pendant and placing it over the reader. It flashed white, signaling the points for the purchase had been taken. She then stared at her pendant for a moment before turning back to the boy. "Hey. We received new pendants for the game we played. How do we activate them?"

"Oh, we can do that here. Just leave them with us overnight and you can come and pick them up in the morning."

"Thank you," said Safia. "They're back in our dorm, but we will bring them back soon."

"What about if someone wants to bet with her while she doesn't have hers?" asked Hashmi.

"Oh, then it's just postponed until the next day. It only takes a few hours to transfer the authority on it. If you prefer, you can drop it off in the morning and then pick it up in the evening. It's just that most hand it off at night and then go home and sleep."

Saying their goodbye's Safia and Hashmi exited the building and began making their way back towards the campus. They ascended the steps and headed toward their room, where they saw Amanda and Ricardo knocking at their door.

"Hey, Amanda. Why are you here? Is something wrong?"

"Ah, there she is. I was hoping I'd find you. Can we go inside and talk?"

Safia looked at Hashmi with a confused look on her face, but also asking for persimmon. Hashmi had the same look on her face but shrugged her shoulders, giving consent. Safia then opened the door and allowed them in.

"I've always liked the look of your room. It seems sop pleasant and homey" said Amanda, noticing Safia's side of the room. "I suppose having the three of your sharing this room have been it's own happy little inconvenience. Tell me, do you both still sleep together?"

"You know we do. And before you ask, no, we are not lovers."

"What? I wasn't going to ask such a thing. That would be tactless," said Amanda with a smirk across her lips. "I was just going to insinuate it and tease you a bit. But you've stolen my fun. Oh well, and where is that wonderful discarded of yours now?"

"She's probably still in class. Why are you here? You usually call me on my pendant for us to meet somewhere."

"A few things, actually. One is that I wish to congratulate and thank you for winning your event with Miss Hashmi. I didn't even realize you were attending, so imagine my surprise when you both showed up on the betting roster. It was certainly exciting watching Miss Mallory yell her little heart out when you won."

"Arthur told us that you bet on us."

"I did indeed. But it was more of a symbolic show of support. Had I known that you would actually pull off such a stunt, then perhaps I would be the leader of the campus, rather than Arthur now."

"He said that before. How does that even work? Does it mean that Frilla can't try to make me do any more of their games?"

"Yes, and no. All it really means is that not all the people in the room will go along with her plans if it's no longer in their interest. A fair trade, since she can no longer influence what type of bets they are placed in."

"I still don't understand all of this," said Safia, walking over and sitting down on her bed. "Am I supposed to listen to her now or not?"

"Yes, for most of the people on this campus, you are still a source of entertainment. So, I doubt they'd see any reason to help you in any of your endeavors. If anything, it might be in your best interest to play along now that so many on the campus dislike you for winning that game. I do believe some around the campus have started a Safia Famosa hate group."

"Great."

Amanda smiled as she had Ricardo take a seat and she took a seat in his lap. "I swear, you never cease to amaze me. I really do feel that becoming a friend of yours has been the best investment I've made since joining this school. I'd even hazard a guess to say that your direct influence of Hashmi and Mallory has been substantial. How does it feel Miss Hashmi; knowing that you will no longer have to worry about points for the rest of your tenure here? It must be a weight off your chest."

"I do admit, meeting Safia has probably been the best thing for me," said Hashmi with a smile. "I guess, I will have to thank Harmony for introducing us the next time I see her. That is, if I can pry her away from her boyfriend."

"Oh dear! So you haven't heard then?"

"Heard what?"

"Harmony has become a discarded."

"What!" said Hashmi, her eyes wide. "Why?"

"Her boyfriend bet on the game. I don't think he bet against Safia, but the margin was so wide that he couldn't pay off their debt. He was expelled this morning. Harmony should have been expelled with him, but I saw her walking around earlier, looking all gloomy faced. So, I imagined someone picked her up."

"That idiot," said Hashmi, clicking on her badge. "Give me the location of Harmony."

"Location denied, Harmony does not wish to be found," spoke the pendant after a few moments.

"I supposed she is a bit embarrassed. She may not want to be—"

"Message to Harmony," said Hashmi, clicking down hard on her pendant. "No, you do not get to run away. You are going to meet me right now, you hear me? I am going to be down by the lake, and you better be there." Hashmi stomped toward the door before turning back to Safia. "I'm sorry Safia. I need to see her."

"I understand," said Safia, a bit taken aback by Hashmi's tone. "Do you want me to come with you?"

"No, it's fine. I'll go and see her now alone. She might not talk if you're there with me." And with that, Hashmi left the room, closing the door behind me.

"Oh wow. I never knew she had that side to her," said Amanda.

"She was even worse with Dario."

"Yes, that man can bring the worst out of any of us," said Amanda, shaking her head. "But I guess, since it's just us here, I should warn you about the next game."

"What? Another one? I just finished with the last one."

"Well, it shouldn't be soon. But with so many people disliking you now, I just figured it would be nice to let you know where you stand. Most of the school hates you and the ones that don't, want to use you for their entertainment."

"Isn't that what you're doing?"

"In a way, yes. But if our relationship hasn't progressed further than that—"

"No," said Safia, changing the tone of her voice. "I didn't mean that. I'm just tired and stressed out from everything that's been happening. It's like I'm not able to catch my breath or relax before something else happens."

Amanda sighed, before standing up from Ricardo's lap. "I swear, you truly are a child in some ways. Ricardo, go over there and give our Safia a massage. Be sure to work the shoulders."

"Yes, ma'am."

"Good, now do you have any lotion? Preferably ones that absorb into the skin rather quickly?"

"What?" said Safia, pushing her hands out to halt Ricardo. "No. I'm fine. I didn't mean I wanted him to do that."

"Safia," said Amanda as she snooped around the room, looking through their toiletries. "Do you remember those favors you owe me? You know the ones you promised me. I thought we had an agreement where we help each other."

"We do. But I thought you wanted a date. Isn't that what you said?"

"This is a date. We are now at a resort spa that just so happens to be in your room. Now, take off your clothes so that Ricardo can oil you down."

"My what?" said Safia, looking over to Ricardo, who was just standing still with his arms folded in front of him.

"You've already admitted you wish to fuck my man, but now you're acting prudish about letting him touch your body. Just how many mixed signals do you wish to give us?"

"That's not... I mean—"

"Ah, this looks like it will work," said Amanda, picking up some type of ointment before dabbing it on her skin and smelling it. "Oh well, doesn't this smell lovely?" She made her way back to Safia. "Ricardo, turn around, will you? It seems my friend is a bit shy about showing her body to you."

"Yes, ma'am," said Ricardo, turning his back to them and staring at the door.

"Now, Miss Safia. Shall we start or will our friendship end here because you didn't keep your word?"

Safia looked over at Ricardo and then back to Amanda, as those crazy eyes stared back up at her. "This isn't fair."

"Yes, well, no one ever said that life was fair. Especially at this school. And it's not like I'm too ecstatic about this either. I'm using one of my favors with you for your own self help because you're so stubborn. I'm giving up a perfectly good date with you. If anything, I think I'm the one who's losing out here.

Working up a bit of nerve, Safia relented. *Killian has already seen me topless. If I got over that, then I can get over this. Out of everyone here, besides Hashmi and Mallory, they have helped me the most. I can do this. It's nothing.* Safia reached to the top of her shirt and began unbuttoning it one after the other until she had completely made her way down, revealing her bra beneath.

"Good, I'll take your clothes," said Amanda with her hand out.

Safia eyes glanced over to Ricardo once again as she clutched her shirt together.

"He won't turn around until I ask him to. Now, come along then," she raised a finger playfully. "Off with your clothes."

*That's easy for you to say. You've been naked around him before.* Trying her best to accept the awkwardness of the situation along with her own jumbled feelings, Safia slid her arms out her shirt and handed it to Amanda. She then stood and began to fiddle with the button on her skirt, loosening it and letting it fall to the floor. She then reached down, placing a thumb in her stockings, beginning to roll them down.

"Oh no, keep the stockings on. Ricardo likes when I wear them. I suspect he will feel the same about seeing you in them."

Safia's eyes went wide as she balled up her lips and stepped out of her skirt. *I hate that she's enjoying this so much. I swear, I'm going to get you back for this.* She then handed Amanda her skirt and stood there in her bra, panties, and stockings.

"There, that's better. Now give me your bra."

"What?"

"Well, you can't expect the man to work your back with that in the way. Now, hurry up, so he can get started."

Safia frowned down at those gray eyes that never took their attention off of her as she reached around and unhooked her bra, letting it slide freely from her shoulders and handed it to Amanda.

"Good, now lay down on the bed on your stomach."

Safia did as instructed, covering her breasts with her hands.

"Okay, Ricardo, you can turn around now. The only

thing you can see now is Safia's big butt and those stockings you enjoy so much."

"My butt isn't that big."

"It's bigger than mine," she examined Safia lying on the bed. "Actually, I think I remember saying how God divvies out his gifts unfairly. Everything you have is bigger than mine." She reached over, poking Safia on the side of her breast. "I'm starting to feel somewhat jealous."

"Stop that," said Safia, slapping her hand away.

"You really do enjoy your teasing," said Ricardo, shaking his head as he walked over with his hands out to Amanda.

"Well, she has become such a favorite of mine. And you know how I get," said Amanda as she placed Safia's clothing to the side and reached over, picking up the oil and placing it in Ricardo's hands. "Do take care of our friend here. Treat her as you would me. Those shoulders of hers must be so overburdened by all that stubbornness."

"Yes, ma'am," said Ricardo, shaking his head and turning towards Safia. "I'm going to start now."

"Okay," said Safia, unable to keep herself from looking back at him as he allowed a small amount of oil to leak over into his hands and began rubbing them together. *That's Hashmi's oil. I hope she's not going to be mad at me.* And before she had another chance to worry about anything else, Safia felt Ricardo's hands embrace the curvature between her back and her ass, pushing down on her slightly, causing her to arch her back a bit in response.

His oily hands were cold at first, but then quickly turned warm as they went up and down the back of her body. She couldn't help but exhale as he pressed himself into her, once at the center of her back and then upwards, lifting her hair and slowly wrapping his hands over the back of her neck. Her exhales quickly turned into moans as he made her way over to her shoulder blades.

"You really are tense," Ricardo said as he worked his way back up to her neck. "Lift your arms and place them under your face like you're going to sleep."

As if by instinct, Safia followed along with his instructions, not wanting the sensation flowing over her body to end.

"Now, Safia," said Amanda. "I've heard you've been spending some late evenings in the school with Abigal and Killian. Do you mind if I ask why?"

"Emmm," Safia moaned and took a deep breath of the scented oil. It smelled like roses and something else that was sweet. "Killian and Abigail have been... training me. Stuff... about the... school." She exhaled again as Ricardo's hands found the side of her breasts, massaging the skin just above her ribs.

"Really? That's surprising considering your last encounter. Were you so desperate to depend on him when you couldn't have just come to me?"

"Didn't... didn't want... to bother you. You've... done... so much... for me. Didn't want you to think... I was... using you."

"Hmm, and just what has Killian been teaching you?"

Safia was silent.

"I think she's asleep," said Ricardo.

"Faster than I expected," said Amanda as she stepped forward, placing a hand on Safia's face and wiping a few strands of her hair away. "You poor girl. How am I supposed to take advantage of you when you fall asleep saying things like that?"

# CHAPTER 16

Safia sat out at the gazebo outside of the school, overlooking the campus as the few remaining students walked in the sunset, making their way to wherever they were going. Breaking away from the path was another girl who stepped onto the grass and headed toward Safia. The sun behind her hid her face in darkness until she stepped up onto the platform before Safia.

"Alright, why'd you call me out here?" asked Addison.

"I just figured we haven't had the chance to talk for a while," said Safia, innocently. "I thought it would be good for us to chat."

"Bullshit, you want something. Just spit it out."

"I wanted to know if you wanted to go on an adventure with me."

"A what? What are you talking about? What do you mean 'adventure'?"

"A few days ago, I had this dream where I was walking around campus and I ended up in front of that right library," said Safia, nodding down the campus.

"Okay, what's that got to do with me? Wait, don't tell me you've been dreaming about us. Look, whatever happened that night stays between us, I haven't put all this work into Nasir just to have you come and mess it up."

"No. I haven't been thinking about you. Well, at least not in that way. It's just that when I woke up. I started remembering things about the library. The main thing is that there is a corner in that building where people keep disappearing to and I want to find out why."

"A corner?" asked Addison, squinting her eyes as she looked down at Safia. "So what? Why would I want to go searching for some mystery corner? For all I know, it could be a place that the school doesn't want us to find."

"Because I'm asking you. And we're supposed to be friends. So, I'm using our friendship to try and depend on you."

"Yeah, we're friends. But I see how people treat you on campus and it's fun messing with you and all. But why would I want to get myself involved? You've dragged along everyone you know into your ridiculous messes ever since you've gotten back. Whatever you got planned next, leave me out of it."

Safia stood up, looking Addison in her eyes. "Does that mean you won't help me?"

"I didn't say that," said Addison, looking away from Safia. "Where... where's that discarded of yours? Use her."

"I can't. She's sick. She has a cold."

"Well, what about Miss Uppity? Where is she at?"

"She's helping Jericho build something. You're the only one I can depend on." *That's not really true. They're both probably still in the dorm, but I can't risk getting them involved in this.* "Will you help me?"

Addison was quiet for a long moment. Safia could see

her face twisting as she contemplated her options.

"Fine. I guess I owe you anyway, but don't think—"

"Thank you," said Safia as she stepped forward, wrapping her arms around Addison in a hug. She felt Addison's body go rigid from the contact and Safia rubbed the side of her face against Addison's.

"Let go of me. I said I would help. You don't have to hug me, okay?"

Safia held her hug for a little while long. *I don't know why but teasing her like this is incredibly fun. I wonder why she doesn't like people touching her. But she's the one who started it by kissing me in the library. Here's a taste of your own medicine.* Safia finally let her go. "Okay, come on. There probably aren't many people left inside."

Together the two girls headed inside the library, and, to Safia's surprise, there were still more students than she'd expected. But, undeterred, she led Addison over to the side of the library where she remembered Austin and Champ Champ disappearing and reappearing from.

"It's somewhere in here," said Safia.

Addison looked around at all the books in the corner of their corner of the library. "What am I supposed to be looking for? All I see is a bunch of books."

"I don't... just something that looks weird or out of place, I guess."

"We're in a library, surrounded by books. How is a book supposed to look out of place?"

"You know what I mean."

"Sure, I do," sighed Addison as she began picking at books from the shelves.

Safia continued to scan up and down the spines of the books. They were in the history section of the library and all the books seemed to be of things that had happened long ago. *Come on Safia, think. It has to be something out of place that doesn't match up. Maybe a color that doesn't look right, or a book out of place.* Then, as if her mind channeled it, she did

274

find something that she found odd. Amongst all the history novels was a book named 'Contact by: Carl Sagan.'

"Ahh, what about this one?" said Addison.

Safia turned around, stood up and saw Addison pointing to a book named '*Rendezvous* with Rama by: Arthur C. Clark.' "I think that's it."

"Okay," said Addison as she pulled the book out and held it up. "Now what?"

"Wait, I think I heard something. Do that again."

"Do what?"

"Push the book back in and slide it out."

Addison frowned but did as asked. She pushed the book back in against the wall of the bookshelf and slowly slid it back out, listening closely. And sure enough, there was a slight clicking sound when she pulled out the book a certain amount.

"There, see. Did you hear it?"

"Yeah, but what do we do now? It's not like it did anything."

"There's another down here. Let's see if it does the same thing." Both girls squatted down to lower levels of the bookcase as Safia reached in and slowly pulled on the book. Halfway out, they both heard the sound of a click. "You heard that, right?"

"Yeah," said Addison as she turned her head, looking around the bookcases. "Okay. You got my interest now. Should we look for another one?"

"I guess so, since nothing happened," said Safia as they both stood up and Safia started to search more of the books on the shelf in front of her. She skimmed over a few rows before she felt Addison tap her on the shoulder.

"Hey. Were those books always there?"

Curiously, Safia turned to where Addison had pointed and in front of her, she saw a collection of books titled 'Dune' that she was fairly sure wasn't there before. "I don't remember them. I mean, look at the colors. I think we would have noticed them before."

"Okay then, but which one should we pick? I mean there's like fifteen books here."

"I don't know. Is there anything special about one of them that stands out?"

"No, they all look the same," said Addison as she ran her fingers over the spines of the books.

"The same?" said Safia, looking over the books. "You're right, it's not a collection of Dune. It's all the same copy of Dune."

"What, so we're supposed to pull them out at the same time? These things look heavy. I can't do that."

"Well, let's see," said Safia as she ran her hands over the books and then placed a finger on top of one, tilting it back a bit. "Well, they are separate, so it's not like that is locked in place." Safia balled up her lips, thinking. They lowered her fingers to the shelf that books were sitting on. "If we can't move the books all at one, then we can just do this." She gripped the bookshelf and slid it back towards her and then came a clicking sound.

Suddenly, the floor beneath began to lower, the motion causing them to lose their balance and grab on to each other for support. Within seconds, they were lowered over a dozen feet into a world of darkness inside of a hole, and above their head was the library, now out of reach. And just as quickly as they were lowered down, they saw the opening above them close as a sheet of some kind slid out and replaced the floor where they had been.

"The fuck was that?" said Addison in the darkness, still holding on to Safia. "Where are we?"

"I'm not sure, but probably in the tunnels underneath the school."

"What tunnels?"

"Remember those tunnels for game night? I think they go all over the school."

"Well, that's fucking great. What are we supposed to do

now? It's pitch black. I can't see shit."

"Wait," said Safia and she went fumbling around in her bag, and there she found the items she needed. She made it click, and suddenly a light shone from her hand and illuminated the area ahead of them.

"Why do you have a flashlight? Did you know this was going to happen?"

"Not really, no. But Hashmi convinced me to start carrying one or two. Here, this one's yours, just in case we get separated."

"The hell we are," said Addison, taking the other flashlight from Safia. "You're the one who dragged my ass down here. You're not just gonna dump me off and go exploring. You're gonna be stuck with me 'til you get my ass out of here. I thought you wanted to see some weird books, not go exploring under the school."

"I didn't know that would happen either. I just wondered how Austin had disappeared. Come on, there must be a way out." Looking ahead, Safia could see the walls. They were made out of ceramic blocks and so was the flooring. She made her way forward, shining her light with Addison following closely behind.

Without the sounds from up above, the tunnel there was just as quiet to Safia as before. The ominous sounds of water from a pipe above them as it dripped to the floor provided an unsettling image, as if the cave had a cold, cruel heartbeat of its own. They walked forward for several minutes until they reached a fork in their path.

"Which way should we go?" asked Safia.

"Oh no, you're not going to blame me when this all goes wrong. You pick, and I'm just going to blame you for leading me down here."

Safia smiled, turning her flashlight down the left tunnel. "I guess we will go this way, then." And both girls set off in that direction. "Addison, can I ask you a question?" Safia asked after they had made their way deeper inside.

"What?"

"Why are you with Nasir?"

"What? Are you going to complain about our relationship now? Saying how we don't match up and all that?"

"No. I'm just curious. I know you're a nice person, despite how you act. I was just curious, but I can see how much Nasir cares about you."

"Yeah... Well, what about you? People talking about you and Jericho kissing and stuff. Is he your boyfriend?"

"No. I actually have a boyfriend at home. Well, I had a boyfriend. We're on break since we're both at different colleges. We didn't want to try a long-distance relationship, figuring it would just be too hard on us."

"Probably would have been. But you know he's probably off fucking someone else, right? You expect him to just jack his dick for years until you come home."

"I try not to think about it," said Safia. She was thankful for the darkness between them, so Addison couldn't see the feelings on her face. "I don't even call him. I don't even know his number by heart. It was in my phone, which I don't have anymore. I could ask my folks for his number, but I figured it'd be too hard if I just heard his voice and couldn't touch him."

Addison sighed, "Nasir... he's an idiot like you are. Always trying to play nice with people. Dumbass doesn't even realize I'm using him."

"What? What do you mean? I thought you liked him?"

"Whether I like him or not doesn't change the fact that I'm using him. I didn't come to this school for its shitty education. I want a rich husband."

"You what? But... is Nasir rich?"

"Yeah. His family has oil money or something like that. And my family is poor as shit."

"But what about the violin? Who taught you that? Didn't you say your father paid for you to have lessons?"

"I lied. I grew up in the slums. There was a homeless

guy named Irvin who played for tips on the street. When he was finished, he'd pass the time by giving me the violin and teaching me. The truth is my father couldn't give a shit what I learned or didn't learn."

"And Nasir doesn't know this?"

"Of course, he fucking doesn't. He just thinks I'm some spoiled bitch who does what she wants."

Safia thought about everything Addison had said for a moment. "But I don't get it. Won't he find out eventually, anyway? Why did you pick him?"

"Look, it's not like I planned all this shit, alright? First this weird fucker shows up and invites me to this school. And why not? Not like I had other shit going on in my life: drunk-ass father and no mother, wearing the same clothes three times a week while some pervy assed old men show up trying to get me to suck their dicks for a hundred dollars. Fuck that! If I'm gonna whore myself out, then it's going to be to some rich fucker."

Safia had to blink her eyes and shake her head at the revelations being revealed. "Addison, I'm your friend, but why tell me all this?"

"Cause you ain't from no rich family either, right? I've heard you talk about your folks; living above some shitty diner. You know what it's like. You ever had some horny men pinch your ass while you walked by."

"I get your point," said Safia, thinking back to many times in the diner when that exact thing happened.

"Yeah, I bet you do. Just imagine what would have happened if you didn't have parents that cared about you, and you'd probably end up like me."

"But Nasir seems to care about you a lot. Wait... oh, so that's why you didn't want him finding out what happened in the escape room."

"How would your ex-long-distance-maybe-man act if he found out his girlfriend had her lips sucking on another bitch's pussy just an hour before kissing him?"

"Knowing David, he might like that."

"Yeah, well, Mr. good-ol' Muslim sensibilities wouldn't. I can promise you that. He has a hard enough time accepting how I talk now, as is."

"You do curse a lot."

"I've tried changing… I have changed," said Addison, correcting herself. "I was way worse than this. Besides, he's not here now, so I can curse as much as I like. But enough about me. Your turn again. Who have you fucked since you been here? What boys do you like?"

"What? No one?"

"None? That's boring. What about Jericho? You're with him a lot or that Mallory girl? We both know she's got the hots for you. Or that boy in the chef's hat. I saw you talking to him."

"None of them. I've been busy with all this other stuff that's going on; with points and stuff. You know, like how you get points for Nasir."

"So, you mean to tell me that while you ex is probably off fucking his way clear across campus, the only action you've gotten at this school was with me? That's sad, even if I am talking about myself."

"Well, I'm sorry I'm so boring to you. Then what are you gonna do after you graduate? Are you gonna just marry Nasir?"

"Probably. It's not like I don't like him. I just don't like the way he looks at me. He's always expecting me to be this other type of girl. Probably like Miss Uppity, wearing that Hijab and shit. Even I know I wouldn't last a day trying to be like that. My best choice is to have him love me the way I am."

"With less cursing."

"Yeah, yeah, with less cursing."

"Well, if it helps any, he really does seem to care about you. He actually asked me to look after you."

"He what? When?"

"I forgot, but it was a while ago. If he didn't care about you, I doubt he would have asked me to look after you."

"That dumbass, treating me like I'm some child. Just wait 'til I see him".

Safia wasn't sure because of the shadows, but out of the corner of her eye, she thought she saw a smile on the side of Addison's lips. *We all love in different ways, I guess. You don't like to admit it, but you do love him.*

"Hey, what's that up ahead?"

"What?" asked Safia, turning her head back and looking up ahead, as Addison reached her hand in front of the light, then clicking it to turn it off.

With the light off, Safia could see some type of blue light far up ahead.

"What's that?"

"Like I'm supposed to know. You brought me down here. Go and find out."

"Not by myself," said Safia, grabbing a hold of Addison's arms and leading her up through the darkness toward the light.

"I swear when this is over, I'm never following you anywhere," said Addison as they stepped forward.

As they got closer, they began to hear the humming of machinery. It was so thick that they could feel the vibrations of it going through the walls as they pressed their hands against it. Soon, they were near the opening and Safia saw that the light was coming from a door and was shining onto the wall ahead of them. The path looked to be normally sealed off, but for some reason, the door to the other side was open.

"I'm not liking this," whispered Addison. "Why's that door open?" Then they both saw a shadowy figure pass by the blue light that shone on the wall. "Fuck! Who's that?"

"I don't know. But I'm gonna find out."

"What? This is the stuff out of a horror movie."

"Good, if they stab me, that'll give you time to run away,"

said Safia, removing Addison's grip on her and creeping toward the door.

"Oh, for the love of—" said Addison, regretfully following behind Safia. "Don't worry, if they don't kill you, I promise I will when this is all over."

"Good, then let's go," said Safia as she peaked her head into the door. Inside, all she saw were some types of machines with fans inside spinning behind blue lights. Safia looked around, not seeing anyone, then taking a deep breath of courage, she stood and stepped inside. There, the room split off into a fork again, with both sides having the blue-lit, fanned machines going down either corridor.

"What is all of this?" asked Addison, stepping in behind Safia and looking around. "Some types of computers. Why are there so many?"

"But what are they used for?" asked Safia as she spotted something on the floor of the right-side corridor, causing her to step in that direction.

"I have an idea," said Addison as she pointed to her pendant. "All the bets we make and messages. You'd probably need a big ass computer for it."

Safia knelt down and saw that the item on the floor was a mask. Flipping it over, she found that it was the same parrot mask that she had seen in the room with the others, and the same one she found on the floor after following Hashmi into the auditorium. *Why is this here? I don't understand.* Safia stood up and walked forward through the corridor of machines.

"Hey, hey... where are you going?" whispered Addison before following behind her. "Have you forgotten we aren't supposed to be down here?"

Safia turned the corner and froze for a moment in the shadows as she stared down the next corridor at three men kneeling down at the terminals, seemingly inspecting something. And while she didn't know them, behind them was the unmistakable face of Derrick, the man who always helps the lady on the phone.

"Hey!" shouted one of the men after spotting her appearance in the shadows. "Who are you?"

*Shit!* Safia turned back and headed back down the corridor, grabbing Addison by the hand. "We gotta go."

"Fuck, I told you. I swear if you get me—"

Before Addison could finish her words, Safia spotted a dark opening between the computer and pushed her inside, squeezing herself in beside her.

"Shh!" said Safia as the three men went running past.

"Never, I'm never following you—" whispered Addison as Safia placed her hand over her mouth.

"Shh," she said again in a low tone. "You heard that?"

And soon came the sound of slow footsteps, mixing in over the humming of the machines. Slow and paced, one step, then another. Each one sounded just a bit louder as they came closer to them. Then, from the shadows, she saw Derrick appear in front of the hole between the machines they were hiding in. He looked into the shadows, a smirk seeming to come over lips before he faced forward and made his way down the cave corridor.

"The fuck was that?" said Addison in a low voice after she had felt safe. "Did he see us?"

"I don't know," said Safia, trying to peek her head out of their hidey hole, only to find herself smushed against Addison. "Can you move a bit?"

Addison shifted. "I'm trying. It's tight. Move with me."

They waddled, pressed up against each other until they were finally able to free themselves, and went spilling out into the corridor.

"Come on. Let's get out of here."

"Oh, now you wanna fucking leave?" said Addison, following behind Safia.

Knowing they couldn't go back the way they came, since the men had gone that way, they instead went forward, back down the corridor that Safia was spotted beforehand. As they made their way down, they found themselves in front of a door that just had the word "APEX' written across it and at the top was a large window to look inside.

Curiosity got the better of them; both girls peaked inside and saw a large room. The room looked to be in the shape of a circle with more of the humming machines attached to the wall. But in the center of the room was a large vat of water with what looked to be a large cube inside of it.

"The fuck is that?" said Addison.

"How the fuck am I supposed to know?"

"I swear to god if they are chopping up bodies or doing some Sci-Fi shit, I'm going to kill you before they kill us."

"Come on. There has to be a way out." Leaving the door, they continued on their way until they found another door. There wasn't a window to see inside, so Safia just placed her hand on the knob and turned it, hoping that no one was behind it. She slowly pushed it open in and peeked inside. There, through the door crack, she saw computer terminals and empty chairs ahead of her. Feeling safe, she stepped inside and began looking around.

"Where is the way out?" asked Addison as she stepped in behind Safia and began looking around. She pointed ahead to one of the monitors atop a desk. "This is how those fuckers watch us. Look, it shows the whole school on these things."

"So, this is how they always know everything," said Safia, coming over to stand beside Addison.

"I guess this is where all those cameras on campus lead back to," said Addison as she tapped the screen with her knuckle. "I wonder what kinda freaky stuff those bastards have seen just sitting here watching us all the time."

"I don't wanna think about it," said Safia, staring at the door near the back of the room. "That may be a way out."

"Hey!" shouted another guard from down the hall. "They're in the security room."

"Shit. Now what?"

"This way," said Safia as she ran forward, throwing open the door at the back of the room. Inside, they saw a spiral staircase that led upward. "This way," said Safia, closing the door after Addison came in and locking it.

Together, both girls ran up the metal stairs; their hands sliding against the cold and slippery railing as the structure shook under their hurried steps. After making it near the top, the two men forced the bottom door wide open.

"Up there," shouted a man from below before he ascended the steps.

Safia and Addison opened the door in front of them, hurrying inside.

"Now, where the fuck is this?" said Addison, looking around the room.

But to Safia, this room seemed all too familiar. Closing the door behind her, she saw that it also had letters on it that read 'Camera System'. Around the room there were steel pipes going to the wall, another spiral staircase that led to the rooftop and metal grates under their feet. She placed her hands on the railing, beginning to ascend to the rooftop, but instead stepped forward to the other door, pressing her hand on it. *Please open.*

And as if to respond to her thoughts, the door opened and Safia and Addison stepped inside, now finding themselves back inside of the school, except now the sun had gone down and the moon was out.

"Come on, I have an idea," said Safia, grabbing Addison by the hand and heading up stairs while clicking on the pendant. "Message for Champ Champ. Hello, ah, well... if you could look after us right now, I'd really appreciate it."

The girls reached the top of the steps, and Safia led Addison down the hall to the art room. She swiped her badge across the reader at the door and they heard it unlock. Quickly, they stepped inside, breathing heavily.

"What... why did we come up—" said Addison before she began looking around the room at all the art pieces.

"Why are you girls breathing so hard?" came Abigail's voice. "And why have you brought Addison with you?"

"Why are you naked," said Addison, looking over to see a half-dressed Abigail, laid across a red couch and sitting across from Killian.

"Quick, take off your clothes," said Safia, slipping out of her skirt, then reaching forward and began unbuttoning Addison's shirt.

"What? Get your hands off me," said Addison, grabbing Safia by the wrists. "Just because you got me drunk once before doesn't mean that's happening again."

"Addison!" said Safia. "Please trust me. We don't have time."

"Don't have time for what?" said Abigail, sitting up on the couch, covering her breast with the sheet that was draped over her.

"Fuck!" said Addison. "Whatever, this is better work."

A few moments later, the door to the art room opened and in walked Derrick to find Addison, Safia, and Abigail all posing in quite revealing outfits for Killian. Upon seeing him, the girls screamed, reaching for scattered clothes to cover themselves.

"What are you doing here?" said Abigail. "This is a private room. The door was locked."

"I'm sorry, Miss Abigail. I'm investigating something odd on the campus that recently happened. What's going on here?"

"Killian is painting a renaissance portrait of us. I enlisted these girls to become models for the piece."

"So, these girls and you... have been here all night?"

"For the last hour or so, yes. Why? Just what are you looking into? What happened?"

"Nothing that you need to be concerned about. Just something minor," said Derrick, looking over at the sheets of cloth covering the camera at the corners of the room. "I see you covered the cameras."

"And for good reason. Look at us. We're all barely even clothed, and we change clothing frequently. Why would we want some security personnel watching us prance about naked as we changed attire?"

"Right," said Derrick while nodding his head. "We'll, I'm sorry to have interrupted the work on your piece. I shall let you all get back to it then. Just call me if you happen to notice anything odd tonight."

"Goodbye, Mr. Derrick," said Abigail as she closed the door behind him, hearing it lock. She then turned back to the girls and walked over. "Okay, now that that's settled. I do believe that you girls owe us an explanation."

"It's her fault," said Addison, pointing a finger at Safia. "It's always her fault."

# CHAPTER 17

Down by the lake, Safia sat skipping stones over the water by herself. Not able to find one that was flat enough, they mostly just skipped three or four times before they sank to the bottom of the water.

"I see you're taking advantage of the fact that the platform still hasn't been fixed," said Champ Champ.

Safia turned around to see the headmistress walking up to her wearing an overly large sweater with a unicorn on the front that came all the way down to just above the knees and fully covered her arms to the point that the clothing was droopy over her fingers.

"I didn't know that you hadn't fixed it yet. I figured Jericho would have done it already."

"Oh, I'm sure he'll get around to it, eventually. He's been quite busy setting up all those elaborate games you've been playing in recently."

"Hopefully, I won't have to play anymore for a while. I'm not even sure I'll be able to focus, considering everything that's been happening lately."

"Speaking of which, that message you sent to me a few days ago. I imagine you must have been in quite the predicament for you to leave such a cryptic thing."

"I'm guessing since I'm not expelled, you hid the video?"

"That's just the thing. I tried to look into the time frame of when you sent the message and found that I had been locked out of the system."

"What?"

"I know. I was surprised as well. Well, needless to say, I went to the main office to find out what was going on and surprise surprise, by the time I got there, I suddenly had access again. And when I pulled up the camera system looking for you. It had all been either deleted or corrupted."

"But... if you didn't. Who did?"

"And therein lies the question. The last footage I was able to find of you was when you and Addison were standing outside of the gazebo. After that, it was you and Addison coming out of the art room late at night. So, I'm curious. What did you two manage to get yourselves into for a little over an hour?"

Safia just stared at Champ Champ for a moment. *Is it okay to tell her?*

"On the other hand, I can't blame you for not telling me. But one really has to—"

"I found the tunnel underneath the library. About how you have to move all the science books and the shelf. Me and Addison were down there exploring and Derrick saw us."

Champ Champ just stared at Safia for a moment, that pleasant smile across her face never wavering, but Safia could see that she was thinking, by the way her eyes froze on her. They moved just slightly enough to see that she was processing the information.

"Well now, haven't you been busy? And did you delete the video footage yourself?"

"No. But there was someone else down there with us. They had on a parrot mask."

"A... parrot... mask?"

"Like the one on my tablet. We tried to follow them, but that's when Derrick found us, and we ran."

"So, Derrick knows you were down there?"

"I'm not sure. But if the camera footage isn't there. So, I don't think he can prove it."

"Aaaand you're telling me all of this... because?"

Safia just slumped on the ground, hands over her knees, and looked over the water and laughed. "Who else can I tell? I can't risk getting Addison in trouble, well, not any more than I already have. It seems like no matter what I do, I find new ways to drag myself into worse and worse situations."

"Well," said Champ Champ, tucking her large sweater under her hips and sitting down beside Safia. "Your situation really isn't so bad, if you think about it."

"It's not?" asked Safia, unbelieving.

"Well, in comparison to what you've been through, it's not," said Champ Champ, picking up a stone of her own and throwing it over the water. It sank with an audible 'plop' sound, not even skipping once. "Considering the fighting with Dario, which you've done twice for that matter; or the keeping a discarded, you could have come out of it all far worse than where you are now. And as we have just discussed, there is no footage of what happened, so I imagine you're safe. But back to another topic; how is Miss Mallory? Have you two sorted out your issues yet?"

"Yes. I think so. Or at least, for now, we have. She still claims she loves me. But at least she doesn't mind talking to me about her past now," said Safia, turning to Champ Champ. "Did you really call me out just to rile her up like that, so that she would open up to me?"

"Well, I do admit, that was my most hopeful outcome,

so I'm happy it worked out that way. It was a coin toss really, but if we don't move forward in life, we're doomed to live through the same moments into infinity. And I'd imagine that her infinity would be worse than most."

"What about your mother? She talked to me again. She was saying something about talking to you. I'm not really sure about what, though?"

"Hmph. That sounds up to par with how mother works. Not even I know what she's thinking. But don't worry on that front. Our issue is less abusive parental figures and more line of succession. An issue that I know will be worked out in time, no matter how much I wish I could avoid it."

"Message form Arthur Sinclair," spoke Safia's pendant.

"I guess that's my cue to leave," said Champ Champ.

"What difference would it make? You'll find out about it anyway," said Safia, as she clicked on the pendant.

"Hello, Safia. I'm inviting you to watch the next games with us. You've been involved in so many so far, so I thought it would be a nice change of pace for you to come and sit down with me and watch. Now, doesn't that sound like fun? It'll start in two weeks, and you will meet with me in the theater building. See you then."

"Two weeks?" said Champ Champ. "I wonder what he has planned."

"You mean you don't know?"

"Not a clue. I usually don't find out about what the games are until about a day or two beforehand. Remember, I don't really bet for myself, since I'm not allowed to anymore. My husband does though."

Safia looked around. "I guess he's still sleeping."

"Yes, but this time he's sleeping because he just finished his surgery."

"Surgery? Is he okay?"

"I hope so. We won't know until he wakes up. Then there will be tests and more tests. There usually are."

"I hope it works out, and he's okay."

"Sweet words," said Champ Champ as she stood to leave. "And here comes your friends. I think I will be taking my leave. Enjoy your classes, Miss Safia."

Safia turned back to see Hashmi and Mallory making their way down towards her, dressed in their school attire.

"What were you two talking about?" asked Hashmi as they approached Safia.

"Apparently nothing," said Safia, standing up and knocking a few threads of grass from her skirt.

"I don't see why you talk to her," said Mallory. "She's just as bad as the rest of them; always messing with people."

"Maybe, but we all have our own problems we have to deal with," said Safia while watching Champ Champ step back onto the spiral walkway and head back off. She then turned back to her friends. "Come on, we're going to be late for class."

And with that, they headed back up the hill and headed off towards school. After saying goodbye to Mallory, who headed upstairs, Safia and Hashmi joined the rest of their associates at their desks.

"Okay, good morning class," said Abigail as she stopped into class, closing the door behind her. "I do hope everyone is well rested for today's discussion."

Safia noticed that her hair was loose today. It still had one of the white flowers from the crown she had worn days before. They had a difficult time explaining to her everything that had happened that night, but she patiently listened to all they had said. The odd one had been Killian, who, in return for keeping and collaborating their secret, had roped Addison into being another one of his models for the next few nights.

*I'll have to apologize to her the next time I see her.*

"Now, who here wants to explain to me the concept of value?"

"What do you mean, value?" asked another student in class.

"I mean, what things are worth.' Where does value come from?"

"You mean like money; how people make money?"

"Yes, and no. Yes, people make money, but where does the value of money come from? At the end of the day, all money is a piece of paper with ink on it or a certain number of electronic zero's you see in your bank account."

"It comes from people. People decided to make money worth something."

"There we go. That's the answer I wished to hear. And it has been a lesson that this school has been teaching you over the past year. Value: it is why we have the point system. Now, outside the confines of this school, our points are meaningless. They hold no value. But inside these walls, and around this campus, they are the measuring stick to which you all compare yourselves. Some of you have lied for points, cheated for points, or in my own case, I offered up the next six years of my life for points."

*You might as well add me to that.* Safia looked around the classroom. *But I wonder if I'm the only one. Is anyone else here like Abigail and me?*

"I decided that my sister's life had more value than twenty years of my life. And that's what I wagered. But to all of you, my sister is a stranger. Sure, you might feel sad to hear of her condition, but I doubt any of you would give up years of your life to save her? No? Then what about a year, or a month, or even one single day?" She was quiet for a moment and watched as her students thought the idea over. "And see, that is what I mean by 'value'. What you are willing to give in order to gain something that you, yourself, find worthy a part of yourself? I'm sure many of you would see value if it was your own mother or father that you would have to save?"

"Well, they're our family," said another student in the class.

"And she is mine."

Every Student has their Truth

"I don't understand. Why are we talking about this?"

"Because it's part of the principals of this school. But just recently, I've come to understand just how much value means. While I didn't think much of those years I gave away, there was a certain individual who valued me so much that they sacrificed their years here in solitude in order to buy the time I relinquished. And even after attaining his goal, that person has given into my selfish requests—" She glanced over at Safia. "In order for me to feel sympathy towards him. Yes, that person has also sacrificed a lot."

"So... you want us to understand sacrifice?"

"No. That you will understand during your second year here. I want you all to look around at the empty seats around you now. Look at those empty seats next to you of the ones who improperly misplaced their value and bet against Miss Famosa and Miss Hashmi during the last game. They are gone and you are still here. The school has been lenient on first years in terms of the games your allowed to play or in informing you just how valuable points can potentially be. And because of which, many of you have misjudged you position in this school. But, with the second year of your tutelage, fast approaching, I am here to give you an understanding of the value of your time here."

"Okay? Does that mean we don't have to attend classes anymore and we should just go out and try to get points?"

"Not quite," said Abigail with a smile across her lips. "Starting today in your classes, you all will be treated like second years. That means that any of you who have over two hundred thousand points will no longer need to attend any of your classes. You will be given an A for your final grade."

*What?* Safia's eyes went wide. *Does that mean I'm done with classes?*

"Wooo, yes," said another boy in class.

Safia was taken aback by the boy's yell. She'd never actually paid attention to him before. But his excitement
294

made the entire class take notice of him.

"Well, Mr. Richards. You do seem happy. If you wish to leave, you are free to go. You have done well."

"Thank you," said the boy as he stood up from his desk and looked around the class. "Good luck, everyone. I hope you enjoy the finals." He grabbed his bags and headed for the door, politely closing it behind him; his solitary steps outside as they echoed in the hall, sounding out in his apparent triumph.

"Well, there goes one. Is there anyone else here who wishes to leave?"

The class all shifted in their seats, looking around the room, a few of their eyes resting upon Safia and Hashmi.

"What about you two?" said another boy in class. "Didn't you win those points from that game? Aren't you both rich in points?"

"It doesn't work like that," said Safia quickly, as she, herself, watched to see if Hashmi would stand. "We just played the game. We didn't get to bet on ourselves or anything."

"So, you got all those students expelled, and you didn't even get points for it. Are you stupid or—"

"Fuck you!" said Safia, standing from her desk. "We didn't get anyone expelled. They expelled themselves. I'm tired of people blaming me because they were too fucking stupid to take responsibility for their own dumbass bets. You try running around campus playing those annoying-ass puzzles for a few thousand points and having everyone blame you and see how you feel." Safia reached down, grabbing her bag, flinging it across the room at the boy. To her surprise, it struck true and landed directly against his forehead, sending him tumbling out of his chair and down to the floor below.

"Miss Famosa! Stop!" shouted Abigail.

Seconds later, Safia felt her body lurch as she went tumbling to the floor, her body shaking uncontrollably. As she twitched on the classroom floor, her feet kicking at the chair and table near her, Safia saw Hashmi come and kneel beside her, trying to hold her down until her body finally stopped convulsing. She was saying something, but Safia was unable to hear her until...

"Safia! Safia!" scream Hashmi and she placed her hands on her shoulders, pinning her to the floor.

"How is Miss Famosa?" asked Abigail. "And Mr. Landers, I think it might serve you well to keep your mouth closed from now on, or you might end up like Miss Famosa over there."

"How is this my fault?" said the boy, standing up from the floor, his hand over the spot in his head where Safia had hit him. "She's the one who hit me." He then looked around the room to see all the girls in the class looking at him with disapproving eyes before he sat back down at his desk.

Her eyes watery as she lay on the floor, Safia struggled to gain back control of her body. But, looking ahead from her position on the floor, she caught Jericho staring back at her. His head was folding into his arms on the desk, like always. To those behind him, he looked to be asleep, but she could see it. His eyes barely open, he was staring directly at her.

"While Miss Famosa is recovering from her rash decision making, I will finish my point. As I said, those of you who have two hundred thousand points, which appears to be no one, will no longer need to appear in class. But those of you who have less than ten thousand points at the end of this semester will be automatically expelled."

"What?" said one of the female students, which was soon mimicked by the rest of the class.

"That is why there are so many freshmen and so few second-year students. This is where you will learn what is truly valuable and how much of that value you are willing to place on points. I imagine the rest of the teachers are teaching this same lesson to the other first-year students as well. And keep in mind that any students that have a discarded, they are now finding out that they will also need another ten thousand points for each discarded they may have picked up during the last campus event."

"But that's not fair. We weren't warned about this."

"I'm warning you now."

"But—"

The bell rang, signaling the end of class.

Still on the floor, Safia could easily feel the vibrations as the other students on the first floor left their classes and poured into the hallway, along with her own classmates. She could also hear their discontent from the murmurs that seeped into the classroom.

"I wish you all the best," said Abigail as she leaned against her desk. "Our next class will be next week. I hope everyone will be prepared for another lecture." Abigail watched as the rest of the class got up and left the room, but when everyone had left, she stepped away from her desk. "Are you okay?" she asked as she came over to Safia, kneeling down and placing a hand on cheek.

"I'm... I'm okay. I just... need a moment."

"I don't think I've ever seen you that mad before."

"I have," said Jericho, still looking with his head down on his arms. "Although, I guess I should count myself lucky she didn't throw anything at me. She did push me, though."

"And here I thought you were asleep," said Abigail, as she and Hashmi helped Safia back to her feet. She then turned to Jericho. "Tell me, Mr. Andrews, what goes through your mind when you look at us? Since, apparently, you seem to have a hold over Safia and I, not to mention your ongoing morning activities with Miss Hashmi."

"I'm offended by that," said Jericho as he finally rose from his desk and began to stretch. "I believe I have done nothing to deserve the looks you three are giving me now. I helped Safia stay in school, despite her best efforts to get expelled. I assisted you in an easy transfer to Killian, whom you seem to have grown fond of on your own, and for Miss

Hashmi, I've been the benefactor of points. At least she seems to have come around to at least liking me. What have I done that is so terrible? Especially considering that I could demand so much more from you."

"Then what is it you want from us?"

"See, and there we go again. I help and I help, and all I get in return is ungratefulness. What a sorry group of friends I have. And you have just given a lesson of value," Jericho gestured towards Abigail. "Well, I, for one, am able to see the value in you. I do hope that you two begin to see the value in me. Not Hashmi, of course. She's awesome." He blew a kiss at Hashmi, which made her frown and give him back a look that seemed to say she was unimpressed. And with that, Jericho gave a smile and a bow before grabbing his bag and heading out of the room.

"I don't think I will ever understand that boy," said Abigail.

"He never says what he actually thinks," said Safia, turning to look at Hashmi. "But you two really have grown close."

"We do not have a romantic relationship, if that is what you might be thinking. He just uses me to sort out some of his projects while he handles other things, since he said he doesn't have as much time to plan the campus projects anymore. Although, I'm not sure where he goes when he disappears."

"Speaking of time, will you girls continue to attend class? Surely you won't need to with the number of points you both have after completing the scavenger hunt game. I was surprised that you didn't just get up and walk out with your classmate."

"I thought about it for a moment. But I don't wanna attract any more attention than I already have. Plus, if I would have, then people would know how many points I have. And I've already been told that can be bad. And I think Hashmi will keep coming to class, so I'll be here with her.

"I do have a little over the required two-hundred thousand, but I can easily see myself falling below that if I do not continue my studies and projects around campus."

"Smart girls. Well, I must admit, having you with me for my night sessions with Killian has made the experience much more pleasant."

"I'm happy you're enjoying it. I still have to pay Addison back for that."

Abigail laughed, "Her face that night. I couldn't tell if she was angry at us or just mad at herself for following you. The way she spent that whole night pouting was surprising for someone so outspoken. But I guess being seen near-naked by Derrick and Killian wasn't exactly what she had planned for that night."

"It's not like I had planned for that either."

"What?" asked Hashmi, chiming in. "Are these those art classes you've been having at night? Why was Addison there? Why were you both naked?"

"It's not like we're always naked," said Safia. "Killian has us pose in different clothing for his pieces. Just a few days ago we were dressed as Eskimos."

"Oh Safia, you may want to skip the next few nights with Killian and I."

"What? Why's that?"

"Killian praised your effort in the last game. But I'm afraid he might be taking a larger interest in you than needed. And I'd hate for you to wind up in the same situation that I am in."

"Thanks for the warning, but without him, I wouldn't have learned so much about this school. I'll risk it for now. Thankfully, he hasn't tried to touch me or anything. Although those poses can get a little embarrassing."

"And this is for the art stuff you do with Killian at night?" asked Hashmi.

"Yeah. I'm having him and Abigail teach me about the games the school plays and how to out think them. He's the reason I knew about the inverted colors. Anyway, let's get going." said Safia, taking a few steps to make sure her feet felt solid under her and grabbed her bag.

Both Hashmi and Safia left the class and headed out of the classroom again.

"You're starting to seem really calm about all of this now," said Hashmi as they descended the steps of the building and began on their way across campus.

"About what?"

"About all of this," said Hashmi, waving her hand around at the school. "The bets, the dealing with people. Apparently being naked with Abagail Are you sure you're the same Safia who was stressing out over everything just a month ago?"

"Maybe I'm not. But I do know that in the next game, I won't have to participate. And at the moment, both me and you have a lot of points. For the first time in a long time, I don't have any bets to worry about, besides those stupid masks. So, you know what? I'm going to enjoy it."

Hashmi shook her head but smiled. "Okay then, how are we going to celebrate your freedom from the school's betting system?"

"Cake. We're going to buy some special treats from the cafeteria, take them back to our rooms, wait until night and talk about everything and anything other than this damn school system. We never could before because we always had to worry about points. But since we don't have to worry about that anymore, I think it's time we try some. My treat, of course."

"Well, if you're buying."

# CHAPTER 18

Weeks later, Safia was getting dressed in her room.

"I'm surprised they are not asking you to wear an outfit again," said Hashmi, rolling over in bed to see Safia sliding on her loafers.

"Probably since I'm not taking part in this one and just watching."

"They said no guests this time? Don't you find that a bit odd considering how I was allowed to join before?"

"I don't know. They said only those that had been selected were invited. So, I guess it's private. But Arthur said that I won't have to bet anything. So, at least there's that."

"You really think he's telling the truth?"

"No. But I'll be careful."

Safia finished getting dressed and headed out the door, making her way downstairs. She then exited the dorm, headed toward the theater where Arthur had asked for her to meet. The morning was as uneventful as usual, and there weren't many students moving throughout the campus. When compared to other events, this one seemed quieter and Safia felt less anxious.

There, outside of the event, she saw two boys standing by the door. Upon her approach they opened the door with her having to ask and she was let inside. She hadn't come back since asking Amanda for the information on the game and when she had incorrectly guessed the name of the girl who was leading the Cinderella play.

*Let's hope I don't get anything wrong today.*

She made her way up the stairs of the building and down the hall to where the opening of the theater was. There, she was let inside by another group of boys who opened the door for her. Inside, she saw a small group of people down by the stage. There was no more than a dozen. Arthur spotted her up ahead and waved her down.

"Safia, I'm glad you made it," said Arthur as she descended the aisle between the rows of chairs headed toward the stage. "Now, you will get to experience the games from the other side, which I imagine will be a wonderful change of pace for you."

"It will," said Safia, looking around. "Do I need to do anything?"

"Not at all," said Arthur as he reached over, grabbing a drink from the table and handing it to her. "Simply enjoy the show. This will probably be the first and last gaming event that I'm allowed to host."

"What do you mean?"

"I mean, Frilla is trying to regain her points. She doesn't exactly like having someone else to answer to. When you're used to being number one, it makes it hard when you're pushed to be second."

"So, Frilla will be in this game?"

"Yes, but this will be a hex game, so there will be no partner, simply a change of percentage based on the hex keys."

"I... I don't understand. What's a hex game?"

"It will be easier for you to understand when the game begins. But we still have a little while before then. So, allow me to introduce you to a few of our friends, Cinder," said Arthur, waving another girl over. "Meet Safia."

"Oh, we've met," said the woman.

Safia remembered her. She was the woman who had been instructing the ballet when she had come to the theater before. *Wait? Cinder? That's not right, she said her name was Jaqueline. But when I put that into the tablet, it said it was wrong.* "Yes, she was teaching the ballet when I saw her. I think she was instructing Cinderella."

"Cinderella?" said Arthur with a smirk on his face. "That's a bit on the nose, isn't it?"

"Oh, please. What breadcrumbs did you leave?"

"Well, something a bit less obvious than Cinderella. But I guess you were already exposed, so perhaps it didn't make a difference," said Arthur, turning back to Safia. "Well, that's fine, I guess. Oh, it seems your boyfriend has arrived."

"My what?" said Safia, turning around to see Jericho entering the room.

He looked around the room before he spotted Safia and then proceeded to make his way down the aisle.

"Well, hello there. I hope I'm not late," said Jericho as he leaned down, giving Safia a kiss on the cheek.

"No, we were just about to start."

"Why are you here?" asked Safia.

"What do you mean? I'm always around during the games. It's just that usually I'm a bit late because I'm making sure that all the equipment is working correctly. But that won't be a problem with this game since it's all taking place in the same room."

"Yes, your boyfriend here is actually invited to all games simply because he works on them. If anything were to go wrong, he would naturally be the one who knows the most about it. So, if there is a game, then naturally he'd be somewhere around."

Safia thought back to every game night she'd been in. *Yes, he has been there. Even in the last one, he was down in the tunnel and when I woke up with Addison; he was there cleaning the floor.* She looked back up at Jericho. *There has to be some more to it.*

"Oh, it looks like they're about to start," said Arthur, pointing toward one of the three large screens on the stage.

"You want to take a seat, honey?" said Jericho, taking Safia by the arm as they both sat down in the center row of stage chairs.

"I must admit, Safia, I much prefer you dating Jericho here rather than Dario."

"So do I," said Jericho. "I really have no idea what she saw in him. But you know what they say, women do like bad boys."

"I understand bad boys. I've had fun with that group. But Dario's more of a rotten boy."

The large screens on the stage came on and Safia twisted her head and squinted her eyes, trying to understand what she was looking at. There was a giant hexagon-shaped object in a room with a set of twin steps that seemed to spiral around it. At the base stood eight people in fancy clothing.

"I guess I should explain it now," said Arthur. "You see each pin inside of... well, this is a surprise," said Arthur, tilting his head in confusion, looking up at the screen, then turning to face Safia. "I thought you weren't going to participate in this, Miss Famosa?"

"What? What do you mean?" said Safia, still trying to figure out the structure.

"Correct me if I'm wrong, but isn't that your discarded in there?"

Safia's eyes glanced over to the other monitor and saw Mallory standing in between two boys. Instantly, Safia stood up. "What? But... but she's not... I mean... why is she there?"

"She's your discarded. You mean, you don't know?"

"No! The last I saw her; she was in our room."

"Well, that's not good. Considering that now that she's there, she's going to be wagering with your points."

"I have to go get her," said Safia, trying to step past Arthur, "Excuse me... I must—"

"Safia," said Arthur, reaching out and grabbing her hand. "Do you want to expel your discarded?"

"What? No?"

"Then I'm afraid that's the only way to stop her now. Once they're in that room, there's no other way out. The gym will be locked down until the game is completed."

"But!" Safia looked back to Arthur and Jericho, her eyes darting back and forth in confusion.

"Are you sure you didn't hint to Miss Mallory any sign that you wished for her to join in on this game?"

"No. I told her that I would be here but... I don't understand why she's there."

"Well, I doubt she stumbled in there looking for you. But, I must admit it's strange. There's supposed to be only eight people, and they were pre-selected. So, it looks like Mallory has taken the place of one of our other contestants. Which leads me to believe she's planned to be here for some time. And if that's the case, I'm sad to say that you've got a rogue discarded on your hands and that's a dangerous thing to have."

"Sit back down Safia," said Jericho. "It doesn't seem like there's anything you can do about it now. All we can do is watch and see what happens. But for your sake, I hope you've been treating Mallory well. Because at the moment, your life at this school is in her hands."

Taking a deep breath, Safia sat back down in the chair between the two men with a heavy feeling in her heart. *Dammit, Mallory, what are you doing there? What's going on?* She exhaled, then took a moment to close her eyes and calm before turning to Arthur. "Okay, explain the game to me."

"Yes, I guess you do have a vested interest in it now, don't you? Well, you see the giant hex thing in the middle and how it has all those little slots in all the interlocking areas? That is the point structures where you can pull out each of the orbs. Now, this part is very easy and yet complicated. Each time they insert a new orb into the hex slot, they will gain, or lose, a set of points."

"How many points?"

"Depends on the point they inserted the key into."

"Wait, then what are those orbs along the base, the red ones?"

"If one is willing, they can insert that into one of the points and they will lose a certain percentage or multiply the number of points they lose."

"You mean the points they make in the game?"

"No, I mean in general. This isn't a charity game like the one you and Hashmi played. They aren't just gaining points here. They are risking all the points they all have in general. So, if you see a number, then they are adding that percentage to their amount, or subtracting that percentage from the account. And not just theirs, but from the adjacent accounts with orbs nearby. But it's able to steal a certain percentage if another hex key is near."

"Wait, so you mean I am playing with all the points I have?"

"Essentially, yes."

"So, I can lose everything?"

"That is true but divided up amongst those eight people. It's almost impossible for some to lose everything. A person would truly have to be mad and just constantly grab those red keys and—oh, they're starting."

They all watched as one of the four boys was selected to go first. He walked over, grabbing one of the blue keys, walking up the steps to the second row of slots and inserting it into a slow on the second. A screen on the orb lit up, and it flashed several numbers until it stayed on the number two.

"See, that means his overall points are set to go up by two percent," said Arthur.

Next on the screen, Frilla walked over grabbing a slot key, taking it in both hands and walked over by the same steps as the boy before and then slid her key into one of the base slots, near the previous boy's. It flashed its own set of numbers before stopping on a three, then it flashed green, turning into a four and the previous boy's orb changed from a two into a one.

"You see, it stole a percentage of his points. And every time another orb is hit, the number taken will double. First it was one, then it will be two, then it will be four. And you get the idea, how it can get out of control very fast, and you can find yourself actually doubling your points, but you would have to plan that out well, since everyone will try to outplay you so that they can get all of the points. Think of it as a more complicated version of tic-tac-toe."

"So, they can also steal percentages?"

"Exactly. So, imagine if all your orbs are placed in the wrong place and they constantly get attacked. Well, you could find yourself becoming destitute very fast." He smiled and pointed up at the screen. "Oh look, speaking of destitute, it seems your little discarded is about to have her turn. Let's see if she's figured it out."

Safia couldn't help but stare at the screen as Mallory began walking over to the orbs. *Mallory, I don't know why you're there,* but *do your best. Whatever it is we can—* Safia's mind went blank as she saw Mallory walk past the blue orbs and reach over, grabbing one of the red orbs. She took it in her hands and began walking back to the staircase with the audible complaints of her competitors. Ascending the steps, she walked over the platform to a slot adjacent to the one where the boy and Frilla orbs were, then slid in her key. The red orb lit up, but the number didn't flash, instead it just showed a solid two. And then Frilla and the boy's orbs beside hers also turned red and changed numbers.

The boy's number changed to a negative two, while Frilla's changed to a negative eight.

"Oh my," said Arthur, with a disturbingly huge grin on his face as he clenched the armrest of his chair. "What do we have here?"

Then, before anyone could speak, they heard Mallory's voice over the speakers. She stood on the platform, looking down at the rest of the contestants.

"I'm tired of this damned school and I'm sick of being a discarded. I'm sick of how Dario used me, and all of you just watched him do it. I'm sick of how Safia treats me. And most of all, I'm sick of how all of you look at me. But now the game has changed and now, for the first time since I became a discarded, I have a say in what I do. And what I plan to do is have all of you expelled along with me and Safia, so you all can feel what I feel every day on this shit campus, alone!"

"Oh my god, I think she's actually serious," said Arthur, standing up from his seat. The grin on his face somehow managed to get even bigger. He then turned and looked to see the horror on Safia's face. "Oh my, it's true. You really had no idea. Your little discarded is actually serious." He stepped forward, snatching his tablet from the side of the stage and began flicking away at the screen. "Oh no, this is just too good. I can't let this opportunity just slip by."

"What are you doing?" asked Safia.

"I'm making sure the campus knows about this. There's no way we can just keep something this good to ourselves." He tapped on his pendant. "I, Arthur, ask to issue an emergency request to have our private match streamed to every TV and tablet of the campus with footage starting back to the beginning of the match."

"You can do that?" asked Jericho.

"I'm the campus leader," said Arthur, "It's going to cost me some points, sure. But there is no way what happens here stays between us."

"Point cost for special request will be one point five million with a ten percent inclusion of any bets made during the event," spoke Arthur's pendant.

"Yes, yes, I accept," he said as he clicked on his pendant. "Take whatever you like."

"Acceptance received, you will now be streamed across campus in five, four, three, two, one."

"Oh, this is marvelous. I swear, Miss Safia, you are an absolute diamond of entertainment. Even when you're not involved, you and your little friends are the gift that keeps on giving."

"Uh-oh," said Jericho, pointing back to the screen. "It looks like Mallory might be in a bit of trouble." On the screen, they could see a blonde-haired boy making his way over to Mallory as she came down the steps.

"You little bitch," he said as he grabbed Mallory by the collar of her dress and lifted her off her feet and caused her shoes to slip, falling to the floor below. "If you think you can just ruin all the work I've—"

And those were his final words before he dropped Mallory, causing her to fall on her bottom as the blonde-haired boy began twitching and dropped to the floor, shaking uncontrollably.

Then, from the monitor, they heard the sound of Champ Champ's voice. "We are monitoring this match closely at the request of Mallory Polana. Any violent action we see against her for the duration of this game will be met with immediate expulsion from the school. All of you will follow the rules of the game and play it out to completion, or none of you will have a future in the world after leaving that room."

Mallory then stood up, wiping off the fluffy dress that she was wearing and noticing that it now had a bit of a sag as it was torn on the left side, exposing her shoulder. Then, with the biggest smile Safia had ever seen on the young girl's face, she stood proudly, looking over the rest of the group.

"I've spent the last year scared to death of being sent

home, of going back to the hell I came from. Now it's my turn to show all of you what that feels like."

Suddenly Safia heard her name being called, only to see Frilla yelling for her.

"Safia, stop this mess. Expel this discarded right now. This is not how the game is played. Safia! You hear me, Safia? Safia!"

"I guess that is an option," said Jericho. "But can you expel someone in the middle of a game? I mean, technically, she doesn't represent you. So, I guess you can—"

"It doesn't matter," said Safia as calmly as she had ever spoken anything ever before. In a mix of emotion, she felt her own lip curl up into a smile as a tear leaked from her eye. "I wouldn't expel her for anything in the world."

Arthur glanced down at his tablet and his eyes went wide. "It seems people are now watching the game." He laughed, holding the tablet above his head, and spinning around as a slew of numbers began to scroll past. "Look at all the bets coming in."

The blonde-haired boy who had grabbed Mallory was now slowly picking himself up off the floor.

"To ensure fair play, the time limit of this game has been reduced from one hour to thirty minutes," said Champ Champ over the system. "Anyone found to be holding up the game will be expelled. You all will play this out seriously into fruition. Good luck." And with the muffled sound of a speaker being closed off, the game was now back on.

With wide eyes, the next boy looked around at the rest of the group. Seeing no way out from the others, he stepped over and begrudgingly stepped to another blue orb from the table. Although now, not wanting anything to do with the revealed antics of Mallory, he took the steps on the opposite of the hex structure up to the top and inserted his key on the fifth row of orbs.

"This is ridiculous," said Frilla, stepping forward. "Don't you see what they're doing? She is trying to make us play oddly. All we need to do is figure out how to play in order to beat her. She can't take us all down."

"And do you think we can figure that out in thirty minutes?" said another boy, looking up at the structure. "Because I sure as hell can't. I just joined because I thought it'd be an easy way to boost my points up a few numbers, but to be here risking it all to some lunatic discarded; this is just absurd." He walked over, grabbing his own blue orb and walked over to the base of the game and inserted his orb adjacent to Frilla's. They all watched as his pieces glowed and began to change numbers before finally stopping on a positive three. Then Frilla's number became a negative five, while the number on the other boy's cube became a positive five. "What in the world? Why did that happen?"

"You see," said Frilla. "We don't have to be at the mercy of Safia's discarded. We can fight back. We can dig ourselves out of this if we work together."

Mallory just smiled. "You all think you're so smart. Well fine, maybe I can get all of you, but the higher those numbers get, I can at least get one or two of you. And who knows, if one or two of you make a mistake, or maybe betray one another, then maybe I can get more. Either way, one of you will be expelled with me."

"Don't listen to her," said Frilla. "We can win if we just place our pieces in the right spaces."

"I'll trust Frilla," said the next girl. "There's no way she can get us if we just keep boosting numbers and work together. We all might lose points, but we won't be expelled." She then took a blue orb of her own and walked to another slot that was adjacent to the Frilla's and two other boys, before raising up on her toes to reach it and sliding her orb into the second layer slot next to theirs. The number inside began to spin before finally landing on four. She looked at the other numbers, watching them drop as her four went up to twelve. But what was surprising was that Frilla's number went from a negative five to a negative one.

"You see," said Frilla, pointing towards the game. "It works. We might all lose. But there has to be a limit to how much she can take from us."

Feeling a bit of hope, the next four went inserting their rods across the orb, countering Mallory's red orb so that she was the only person with negative points.

Then it was Frilla's turn as she walked over to the blue orbs, taking hers and lifting it into her arms. "Sorry," said Frilla as she walked by Mallory with a smug look on her face. "Whatever it is that you and Safia had planned is not going to work. But when this is over, I'll see to it that she regrets ever picking you up. You should have stayed as Dario's little pet and been a good little girl." She then slid with her orb on the third floor, causing it to change the numbers beside it and leaving them all in the positive.

Mallory dropped her head, staying silent as Frilla made her way back down the steps.

"It seems your discarded has gotten you even more unwanted attention, Safia," said Arthur, shaking his head.

Safia was silent as she just stared up at the screen.

In it, Mallory was just as silent as she walked over, grabbing another red orb from the table. Again, she made her way to the steps and upward to the second row till she was adjacent to her previous red orb. Then, raising her head, she looked down at them with an evil grin spread across her face.

"You all really should have paid more attention to the rules of the game. Like all games, as long as the game is going, I can lose more than one hundred percent of my points. I can lose a thousand percent and they won't drag me out of here until the game is finished and all the slots are filled. So, if you thought all you had to do was out last me, well too bad for you."

"Wait? Is that true?" said one of the boys down below.

"I don't know. I've never played this before."

"So what?" said Frilla. "That still doesn't mean you can

have any of us expelled. That just means you get to stay here and watch us beat you."

"You really don't listen, do you? I just told you that none of you know all the rules of the game. Like you know that you add numbers to blue and subtract numbers for red. But when you slide two reds next to each other," she slides in her orb adjacent to her previous one. "It's no longer additional or subtractive for the nearby positive orbs. It becomes multiplicative." Mallory's orb flashed five and then her other orb adjacent orb with two began to flash and both turned into a negative ten. But the adjacent two orbs at the top and bottom that were attached to both orbs went from a three percent to a negative thirty percent and from a four to a negative forty percent.

"Argh!" scream one of the boys alongside a girl as he dropped to his knees. "Thirty percent. I just lost over a million points. Do you know how long it took for me to get that, you bitch?"

"Screw that, I just lost forty," said the girl. "That's nearly half." She then turned toward Frilla, pointing her finger. "This is your fault. You said she wouldn't be able to do anything if we worked together. Well, Frilla, it certainly looks like she's doing something."

"Did you know about this, Safia?" asked Arthur, his eyes wide.

"Me? What? No, I didn't even know this game existed until I got here. I still don't even know what she's doing?"

"I mean, I just thought they might lose ten or twenty percent if things went really wrong. But to lose almost half your points off one play. That's just ridiculous," said Arthur as he began to laugh. "Thank goodness, I didn't include myself in this." He looked down at his tablet as the numbers began to scroll even faster. "This is the best. It looks like everyone on campus is betting on this. No one knows who's going to survive. This just might be the best event ever."

"I don't understand," said Jericho. "Is there nothing they

can do to stop it?"

"Even if they could, they only have like fifteen minutes left to figure it out. I'm afraid Miss Mallory has got them in between a rock and a hard place. This game has turned into a death trap for all those inside and it seems Safia's little discarded is on a suicide mission. And since she has nothing to lose, she essentially has them at her mercy."

And once again, their eyes fell back on the screen.

"You bitch. You set this up from the start," yelled the blonde-haired boy.

"That right," said Mallory as she made her way down the stairs, stopping before the group and looking between both the boy and girl that she had trapped. "I might not be able to get Frilla anymore. But I've got both of you now. And both of you will be expelled, along with anyone else that I can drag down with me, but you two for certain are mine now. I'll just keep attacking you until you can't come back."

"Why are you doing this?" said the blonde-haired boy on his knees before Mallory as she came back down the stairs. "The fuck is wrong with you?"

"It doesn't matter anymore," said Mallory as she walked away from him and over to another red orb. "There are only a few minutes left. All you bastards hurry up, so I finish them off."

"No, that's not right," said Frilla. "There must be a way—"

"Fuck this," said the blonde-haired boy, who had lost his points as he stood to his feet. "I'm not going to be the only one who gets expelled because of some stupid discarded." He walked over to the red orb table, taking one and walked up the stair where he saw the most cluster of blue orbs.

"No, wait," said Frilla. "What are you doing? Stop. This is what she—"

"I'm done listening to you. It's your fault I'm in this mess," he said, and with a hard slam, he lodged the red orb into place as it began to light up, stopping on the number two and the adjacent four blue orbs all turned negative. "There

314

are only so many red orbs she can use. I'll be damned if she uses them all on me. Pick someone else, you dumb bitch."

Over half the players in the game began screaming up at him.

"It looks like it's over," said Arthur.

"What do you mean?" asked Jericho.

"They might have found a way to fend her off if they continued to work together. But now, no one is thinking clearly. They will be lucky if any of them have half the points they came in with after this. It seems this will be the end of our dear Miss Frilla's dreams of regaining her number one spot in the academy."

"It's at times like this that I'm glad that I just build the game and don't participate in them," said Jericho.

"Ha!" laughed Arthur. "I must admit, this has turned out to be quite the spectacle. It seems your discarded there will be responsible for the largest point loss in this school history. If I had to guess, there's twenty million points on the line in that room alone."

"What happens to the points if no one wins them? Where do they go?" asked Jericho.

"You know, I actually have no idea. I just assumed they flowed back to the school since there is on one to retrieve them."

"I think from now on we should give proper respect to Miss Mallory," said Jericho as he pointed up the screen. "I can't think anyone watching this right now has ever seen this school's elite down on their knees begging before."

"Please, don't do this," said one of the boys, holding onto Mallory's dress.

"Let go of me. Or do you want to get shocked like he did?"

"You've already taken seventy percent of my points," said the blond-haired boy. "If you do this, all three of us will be expelled. What have I ever done to you? I don't even hang around Dario. Expel them," he pointed to the two girls who were crying over at the side of the room. "They're the ones who hang out with Dario."

"What? How dare you!" yelled one of the girls. "Aren't you supposed to be a man?"

"Shut up. If you two would have gotten rid of Dario. This never would have happened. This is all because you couldn't do your job."

"What do you mean, 'their job'?" asked Mallory.

"We've been trying to get rid of Dario all year. But he's always been involved with different games. So, we couldn't trap him. And then he was in that match with Safia, so we couldn't touch him then either. No one actually likes Dario, but he has too many points, so we couldn't do anything."

"You're lying," said Mallory.

"We're not," said one of the girls, walking over. "I'll even let you check my betting history. You'll see. All our games were declined."

"You can check mine too," said the other girl, coming over.

"Oh wow, they certainly are burning bridges, aren't they?" asked Arthur, shaking his head. "I'm sure Dario won't take this lying down if they make it out of there."

"What do you mean?" asked Safia.

"They just admitted to trying to get rid of a student. And both you and I are well aware of just how spiteful our dear Dario can be. How do you think he's going to act when he finds out a certain group of his so-called friends have been trying to get rid of him?"

"I see your point," said a solemn-faced Safia.

"You seem very calm, for a person who's discarded is about to have her expelled."

"Am I?" asked Safia. "Out of all the times I've almost been expelled, this doesn't feel like that, and if it happens, there's nothing I can do about it. This is Mallory's decision to make."

"You're both crazy," said Arthur with a laugh. "An owner

willing to be expelled over the whims of their discarded. No wonder you both are so fun. Who would ever do such a thing?"

Mallory snatched her dress away, freeing herself from the blonde-haired boy's desperate grip and up to the steps where a large group cluster of reds were near one another. There with the numbers sitting well over fifty percent, she could wipe out at least three of the participants by inserting it into the space between them. But instead, she walked past that opening, taking her ball, she walked past it up to the fifth level and stood next to an opening near two of Frilla's orbs.

"I knew it," said Frilla. "Don't think you and Safia are going to get away with this. This isn't over."

"Safia's my friend and you should have left us alone," said Mallory before shoving her final red key in the slot. There, both of the orbs beside Mallory's flashed and showed that while Safia now sat at a negative seventy six percent, Frilla was sitting at a negative eighty-five percent.

"Oh wow," said Arthur, "So, she was targeting Frilla the whole time. Or did she just decide to go after her at some point in the game?" Arthur turned back to Safia. "Either way. Whether it's what you wanted or not, you've most certainly made an enemy out of that woman. I mean, she was a bit upset before, but now. She's going to be... well, I have no idea what she's going to do."

"Is it over?" asked Safia, standing up from her seat. "Can I go see her now?"

"There are still four orbs left but seeing as they are all blue. Not much will change now. So, by the time you make it over there. I suppose they should be coming out."

Safia excused herself, stepping out from the room of seats and hurried back up the aisle and out of the door. She then broke out into a run through the hall and down the stairs, making her way outside of the building. Not breaking her stride, she barreled across the grass and over the campus.

It wasn't long before she was standing in front of the locked door to the gymnasium, and it was shorter still before she heard the sound of a click and saw the completely drained faces of two of the players exit out into the light. But she paid them no mind as soon as Mallory stepped out.

One of the boys went sprinting out of the building and running across campus, zipping past Mallory and everyone else.

Mallory squinted her eyes as the sun hit her face, but after a few blinks she noticed Safia ahead of her and dropped her arms, slumping her shoulders. Then, with her head lowered, she stepped out and walked over to her. Standing before Safia, Mallory couldn't seem to bring herself to look into Safia's eyes. She kept her head down.

"I'm... I'm sorry I should have—"

Mallory words were cut off as Safia wrapped her arms around her friend, pulling her close and squeezing her face against her chest.

"You did good," said Safia. "I'm so proud of you."

"But... your points... I lost... I lost so many."

"It's fine. We'll make them back. Everything's going to be fine," said Safia as she began rubbing the back of Mallory's head. Ahead of her, standing in the shadows of the door of the gymnasium, Safia saw Frilla staring back out at her. The unmistakable look of hate was written across her face. Safia kissed Mallory on the side of the head, never taking her eyes off Frilla. "Don't worry, everything's going to be fine."

# CHAPTER 19

Safia was on the second floor of the school, in the art class, next to Abigail. They both wore seventies-era style dresses with Safia wearing a blue long button up dress with Abigail sitting beside her wearing a pinkish two-piece version of the same outfit. Between them was a small table where an old rotary phone sat, which Abigail had posed against her ear.

"You seem to be distracted today," said Killian, from his position ahead of them as he continued the workings of his piece, dabbing his brush against the canvas.

"Oh, sorry." said Safia as she tried to continue to hold a friendly face for the portrait.

"No need to hold that face now. I'm still trying to find the correct shading for the Abigail's dress. So, tell us, what has your mind preoccupied today?"

"I'm just thinking. Everything was going so well." She

shook her head. "Okay, maybe it wasn't, but at least I was learning to manage everything. And now, I think Frilla wants to kill me, and I'm not sure what to do about it."

"You mean after the Mallory incident in the hex game?" asked Abigail, placing the phone on her lap. "We saw that when it happened. I really didn't know what to think about that when it happened, and I truly don't understand it now. Did you send her off to do that?"

"No. I had no idea."

"Well, someone did," said Killian. "And they succeeded in their goal."

"You know what they wanted?" asked Safia.

"I have a reasonable guess. To me, it seems that someone wanted to wipe out the points of all the higher second-class students. But the real question is why more than who."

"I don't understand. Isn't 'who' more important?"

"In some cases, it would be. But in this one, if you find out why it was done, then it will most certainly lead back to the who. Have you asked Miss Mallory herself why she participated?"

"She just keeps saying she was trying to help me."

"In her own way, I'm sure she thought so," said Abigail.

"Well, considering that everyone in that room now hates you or hates Mallory and, by extension, hates you, I can see how the situation isn't promising. But I'd be more concerned with the fact that someone else on campus might have the ability to control your discarded other than you. They could force her to act against you and have you both expelled."

"Mallory would do that?"

"I mean, she wouldn't do that knowingly. But if someone were to trick her into it, then that's another story altogether."

"Then what am I supposed to do, because I'm not going to expel her," said Safia, the tone of her voice growing harsher. "I won't be the one who—"

"Miss Safia, come here for a moment, please."

"What? Why?"

"Think of it as part of your education."

Safia glanced over at Abigail, who shrugged her shoulders and, with a smirk, just nodded over to where Killian was sitting. She then reluctantly stood up and made her way over to Killian, taking a seat on the extra stool next to him, as she had done many times before.

"You've seen several attempts at my painting so far. Tell me, what do you see when you look at this one? What am I trying to do here?"

Safia sighed, then stared at the painting half-heartedly. "I don't know. You're still trying to fill in the colors, but they don't match up yet. The pink on the top and the pink on the bottom of Abigail's outfits don't match."

"That's correct. And how am I going to fix it?"

"You're going to use lighter colors, probably a white to lighten the pinks until they match properly," said Safia, her voice showing her weariness of it all.

"And why am I going to do that?"

"What? I don't... look, just tell me what you want me to do. I'm really tired of all this right now. I know I promised to help if you taught me, but I really don't understand what you want me to—"

"Control, Safia," said Killian, cutting her off. "Look at this half-finished painting. That's all art is. I'm trying to control the outcome of all of these black, whites, and other colors, to the point where it looks like something that isn't a complete mess. Everyone here is doing the same thing."

"I don't... so I should learn to control things?"

Killian's sighed as he looked up at Safia. "I can see you truly are tired. You usually catch on faster than this." He took the brush and set it down on the ease in front of him, before turning his chair towards her. "Go home and rest, Miss Safia, and think on what I said. I'm sure you will understand soon enough."

Safia scratched at her head. "Look, I'm sorry. I didn't

mean to. I'm not feeling well today."

"And that's why I am telling you to go home and rest. I can't say that I know what you are feeling, but I can say that rest is good for the mind. So, go home and rest. We can pick this back up later."

"Alright, I get it," said Safia as she turned and headed toward the clothing rack and began to unbutton her outfit.

"Just keep it on," said Abigail. "I'll have your clothing delivered to your room."

"Thank you," said Safia as she nodded and headed towards the door. She exited the room and made her way downstairs and left the school. The weather outside was chilly as the moon sat high in the sky above her, the clouds slowly drifting around it. The path-lights once again lighting the patch back towards her dorm, she placed one foot in front of the other and began the trip back across campus.

On the way, she couldn't help but think over what Killian had said. But she couldn't really focus on anything as it felt like she'd been away for days and her mind was just a random assortment of thoughts, not being able to focus on anything.

Although the campus was mostly empty at this time of night, Safia saw someone up ahead looking at one of the path-lights next to a bench as if inspecting it. As she got closer, she was surprised to see that it was Harmony, the woman who first showed her around campus.

Harmony couldn't hide the surprise on her face when she saw Safia approaching.

"Hey, ahh... long time no see," said Harmony as Safia came and stood before her.

"Yeah... wha... what are you doing out here?"

"Me, oh... Nothing. I was just staring at the light."

"In the middle of the night?"

"What can I say? You know me. I guess I'm just a ditz. I mean, look at me now. Things are a whole lot different now, right? I mean, who'd have guessed I'd be a discarded and look at you, you're like the queen of the campus now or something."

"I'm sorry about that. I heard that your boyfriend became a discarded."

"Yeah, we backed the wrong horse. All things considered; we probably should have bet on you."

"Look, Harmony, I know it might not be right to ask. But... but do you blame me for... for what happened?"

"What? No, I mean, okay yeah, I kinda did at first. But I was mad, you know. And I had just become friends again with Hashmi and, well... it wasn't your fault. I was stupid and listened to my boyfriend and bet more than I should have. But hey, at least Hashmi still talks to me. Sometimes we even sing together."

Safia found herself cracking a smile at the thought of them singing together. "I didn't know that."

"Yeah, well. Don't tell her I told you that. She gets embarrassed about it now. But she meets me once a week and we sing songs together outside where no one can hear us down by the water."

"I promise I won't tell her."

"Good. Anyway, I should get going. Gotta get some sleep before classes tomorrow."

Both girls waved their goodbyes as they left, walking back off into the darkness of the campus. Safia stood there for a moment underneath the street light with her eyes closed. *At least there's some people on the campus who don't hate me completely.* She then began to head back off towards her dorm when, as she opened her eyes again, there off in the distance was the building where Mallory had played her hex game.

Safia found herself drawn back to it as she stepped off the walkway and made her way over the grass until she was standing in front of its door. She placed her hands on the door and found that it was still unlocked. Opening it, she stepped into the darkness of the building that was only illuminated by the moonlight that streamed in through the windows. And ahead of her was the hex shaped structure with the spiraling staircases around it.

She stepped forward, looking over the structure before spotting a row of nearby chairs. Walking over and taking a seat, she just observed the structure; how it was bolted together, how all the orbs fit into each of the slots and stayed in place; it looked like something out of some weird type of futuristic game show.

*How do they even build this? Who comes up with it? Do the students? I remember them saying that sometimes they think of these games, but they can't think of all of it, can they? I mean, who can think of all of this? It's crazy just looking at it.* Safia began to rub her own fingers together in thought. *But Mallory was able to figure it out. Did someone tell her? Will she really even tell me the truth if I asked her that? And what would I even do if she didn't?*

These thoughts ran through Safia's mind for over an hour as she sat there in the dark looking up at the hex shaped structure. The cold silence of the room seemed to match the stoicism of the cold metal that towered in front of her. Those numbered orbs that had decided the fate of those who were involved had long since lost their light, leaving only darkened globes at the joints of the structure.

*I still can't figure it out. Why would she risk everything and join this game?* Mallory had been tightlipped about why she was involved in the game. *She needed to do it. She needed to do it. Why is that all she's willing to tell me? Does she not feel that can trust me? Even after everything we've been through? I just don't get it. What did she mean by 'needed to prove to herself that she deserved to be here?' But that doesn't make any sense. I'm not sure anyone deserves to be at this school. And now, on top of the school hating me, no one's seen Frilla since the game. And the way she looked at us. There's no way she leaves us alone now.*

Suddenly, the sound of metal piercing the quiet

atmosphere took Safia from her own mind as she turned to look at the entrance to the building. She had to squint a bit at the light from outside irritating her eyes and through the light stepped in Jericho wearing a yellow hard hat. He looked around before letting the door close behind him and began walking over to where Safia knew the light switches for the building were. But on the way, he stopped when he noticed her sitting down in a chair alone.

"Sa... Safia? Is that you?"

"It's me. Have you come to take this down?"

"That was the plan," said Jericho as she began walking over to her. "Or at least it will be. I have everyone coming over sometime tomarrow and we will start breaking it all down." He stood in front of her, looking down at the expression clear on her face. "I see you're back in one of your droopy moods again."

"You weren't there. You didn't see how Frilla looked at me. Not even Dario looked at me with that much hatred. And now it's not like I have a bunch of points left to fight against her for whatever stupid idea she comes up with."

Jericho plopped down in the chair beside her and stretched out his arms. "I'll admit, even without my help, you managed to find yourself in all kinda of stupid situations."

Safia just shook her head. "If I could hate you, I would. But honestly, I just don't have the energy anymore."

"Good. Friends shouldn't hate each other."

Safia couldn't help but laugh. "Friends, that really is all you ever talk about. Then fine, 'friend'. Help me get out of this mess like you did last time. Isn't that how this is supposed to work? I do what you tell me, and you look after me?"

"Except that I haven't really told you to do anything yet. Well, nothing significant at least. And when I asked you to attend that gathering, you didn't even show up. Because of that, I actually spend more time with Hashmi than I do with you these days. Unlike you, she actually listens to me."

"So, that's it. You're saying you're not going to help me? You're done with me."

"No, I'm saying I just haven't thought of how I can help you. This isn't such a quick fix like before, where I could manipulate Killian and Abigail. You and your infinite powers of misfortune have managed to piss off almost every second and third-year student at the school. Honestly, I'm surprised they haven't formed some sort of Anti-Safia Society and started protesting to have you removed from the school just out of sheer fear of you. Do you know that over forty students have been expelled because of you now? That's not to mention the discarded. You've probably forced the school to double their recruitment next semester."

"You're no help, and you're an idiot."

"Okay, now that's hurtful. And I fail to see how any of that will help."

"You want to help?" said Safia, standing up from her chair. She then reached over, grabbing Jericho by the collar.

"Hey, what are you—," said Jericho before he found himself dragged out on his chair and down on the floor. "Agrh... have you lost—"

"Shut up," said Safia and she straddled herself on top of him, before she then laid herself down, pressing her head against his chest and in the quiet began to listen to his heartbeat. Even through his clothes, she could feel and hear it. It pounded heavily inside of his chest, but the rhythm of it provided a sense of calmness to her.

"This is... different. I don't suppose you're going to explain to me what—"

"Shut up, David."

"David? Who on earth is—"

"You are. For as long as I need you to be. Now shut up and let me have this. I need it." Safia closed her eyes, trying to find a place of peace within herself. An effort that would be helped along just a few moments later as a soft hand found its way over her back and then another and they wrapped themselves around her. A sigh of relief came over her with the embrace. "Thank you. I have a favor I need to ask of you."

"I'm all ears."

# CHAPTER 20

Days later, the evening sun shone over the campus as Safia stood at the entrance of the school, looking up at its walls. She closed her eyes for a moment, taking in a deep breath. And with a heavy sigh, she placed her foot on the steps and entered the building. Many times, she'd walked these quiet marble floors that, when cleaned properly, reflected the sparking chandeliers overhead. But after the day's classes, it was hard to see anything other than the dirty footprints of a hundred students that had tracked past it.

She stepped forward, passing the steps that led to the second floor. The cool air of the school tingled against her skin as she passed by the empty classrooms until she made her way down to the end of the hall and stood before the wood-painted metal door. Placing her hand against it, the lingering cold flowed into her fingers as she heard a clicking sound and felt the door give way.

A gust of cold air flowed over her skin as she stepped beyond the door into the familiar room of steel pipes and iron grates beneath her feet. But this time, as she stared straight ahead at the door in front of her, she knew what was behind led to an underground tunnel that she and Addison had escaped from.

Stepping forward, she placed her hand on the spiral stairwell and began to ascend to the rooftop of the school. The humming of the machinery beneath her was still so thick that she could feel the vibrations against her body as she made her way upward. And there she would find the same wooden door as before. The strong sense of Deja Vu came to hear as she opened the door and peered out to the campus around her. And there, just as the time before, sat Champ Champ with her husband, asleep on her lap as she looked out over the campus.

"Welcome back to my favorite place, Safia."

"I would prefer to not be here," she said as she stepped out from beyond the door and over the rooftop to stand next to the two. "But I have questions for you."

"I'm sure you do," said Champ Champ as she gazed out over the campus. "Has it really been almost a year since you first came to me begging me to save your family? Time really does fly when you are busy."

"You sent Mallory there, didn't you?"

"Did I?"

"That dress that she wore during that game. It was yours. The same one that I met you in, under the tree when I first came here."

"Yes. Although she is a bit taller than I, it seemed to fit her better than it did me. A shame it was ruined when that boy grabbed her."

"Why did you send her there? What are you trying to—"

Champ Champ raised her hands and sighed, "I had hoped that spending time with Killian would have taught you better than to think on just emotion. I merely lent

Miss Mallory my dress. She is the one who came to me asking for entry into the game. I told her that the game was already filled. So, imagine my surprise when she informed me that one of the people involved had decided to forfeit their participation. So, I think the question is, why did that person give up their spot for Mallory?"

Safia thought back to the game and remembered the surprise on Arthur's face when he saw Mallory appear on the screen. *But if he didn't know she would be there, then did she do it herself? But that doesn't make sense. How did she convince someone to drop out? She doesn't have anything to trade in order to convince someone to do that.* "Do you know the name of the boy who dropped out?"

"Yes."

"Will you tell me?"

Champ Champ just stared up at Safia for a moment.

"It's alright," said The Husband, laying on Champ Champ's lap. "I think telling her will provide us with a bit of entertainment." Startled by the sudden deep voice of the man before her, Safia stepped back as the man lifted himself from and stood up, looking down at her. "Hello, Miss Famosa, it is good to see you again."

"What? You're awake?" said Safia, staring up at him, only now noticing there was a fresh new scar on his face that went opposite the other two, stopping beneath his eye.

"I am awake," said The Husband, reaching up to the side of his face, tapping his finger on the scar. "And for the first time in a very long time, relatively pain free. My wife has told me that she's been taking good care of you. Is your father well?"

"Yes, he's fine. They released him from the hospital," said Safia. She was feeling a bit intimidated by the man before her, who easily stood near a half a foot taller than her. The way his eyes stared down at her felt more unsettling than she had ever felt before.

"I'm glad to hear it. The pain of you losing a father is

something we would like to avoid, if at all possible. But to answer your question, I believe you know the fellow. He's Mauricio Astudillo, I believe he's always doing odd jobs around campus, although you might remember him from wearing that chef's hat every month when validating your food pass."

"You always were the generous type," said Champ Champ, as she stood up and took a step to stand beside her husband placing her hand in his.

"It's our job to be generous to those who are desperately trying to survive here," he said, not taking his eyes off Safia. "And what about you, Miss Famosa? Are you feeling desperate at the moment?"

As Champ Champ and her husband both stared at her, she had to admit, desperate was the right word. She desperately wanted to be anywhere else than having these two take any more interest in her than they already have.

"I... I... can I go now? I need to... to find Mauricio."

"Of course," said Champ Champ. "You are free to leave."

*This isn't good. Nothing about this is good.* Safia turned around, heading back and placed her hand on the door.

"Oh, and Safia dear," said Champ Champ. "Try not to worry too much. Both me and my husband both want you to succeed here. So, we will be watching you and your family very closely from now on."

An uncontrollable shiver took over Safia after hearing those words. Closing the door behind her, she made her back down the stairs and through the door into the school. *I feel like things are going to get worse. That man... the way he looked at me. It felt... something felt off about it.*

She exited the school and clicked on her badge. "I would like the location of Mauricio Astudillo."

"Location granted," spoke the pendant after a few moments.

But Safia realized she didn't have her tablet on her to see the location on the map. So, she clicked on the pendant again. "Where is Mauricio Astudillo?" *Will this even work?*

"You've received a message from Mauricio Astudillo."

Safia clicked on the pendant again.

"Hey Safia, I figured you might be calling me sooner or later. I'll meet you by the bench in the middle of the campus. The one along the walkway near the light post."

Having an idea which bench he was talking about, Safia set out on her way. The sun was quickly fading from the horizon as she stepped on the winding walkways on the school. So much that the lamps that she usually would focus her attention on flickered before illuminating her path forward. And just as she had assumed, it was to be the correct bench, there she saw Mauricio sitting under the streetlight waiting for her arrival.

"How did you know I would be—"

Mauricio smiled while holding up a parrot's mask. The same parrots mask that she had seen several times since she'd come back to the school.

"You? You're the one who's been following me around campus?"

"Not me, sorry. I'm just as stumped as you are. I received this mask along with a message that asked me to drop out of the game."

"And you just did it, no questions asked?"

"I don't know what type of games you play here. But I'm not into all the mess they have going on. I go to class and do my little jobs and then head back to my dorm. I don't want any part of whatever this is," he said while waving the mask around. "But when I saw your discarded had taken my spot and the mess that happened on the screen all over campus. I figured it'd only be a matter of time before people came around asking questions."

"People. So, someone else came?"

"Yeah. First it was Dario, then Frilla came. And I don't want those two giving me any more of their attention."

"Why Dario?"

"I decided it wasn't in my best interest to ask questions."

Safia shook her head and took a seat on the bench beside him. "Yeah, well, I wish I had that option. I feel like all I can do is ask questions."

"Are things always like this around you?"

"Unfortunately, yes. It's been like this ever since I got here. Tell me, did Dario or Frilla say anything when you told them?"

"Frilla did. But she wasn't all too happy with the answers I gave her."

"What about Dario?"

"Dario didn't say anything. The moment I showed him the mask, he got this weird look on his face and just turned around and left."

Safia dropped her head, looking down at her shadow being cast by the light. "Well, that doesn't help much."

"Sorry. I wish I could help, but—"

"No, I understand. I guess I just can't assume for all the answers to just fall into my lap. There's just so much happening around me and I feel like I can't control any of it."

"Honestly, I'm surprised you're even trying. If I were you, I feel like I would have just given up and run away."

Saifa laughed, "That would be nice. If I could just give up and run away and it didn't hurt anyone else for me to do so, then I would have done it a long time ago." Safia nodded her head and then stood up. "It's getting late, so I should probably just head back."

"Good night, Safia."

"Good night, Mauricio." And with that Safia headed back to the dorm, leaving him sitting on the bench next to the mask. By now, the moon was high enough in the sky for Safia to see clearly as it peaked out from behind the mountains. The way it shined on the purple flowers at the steps of her dorm gave off a more mysterious appeal than they probably intended. She made her way up the steps and saw Austin sitting at the front desk reading a book.

"Welcome back."

"Thanks," said Safia as she walked over, placing her rand on the railing leading upstairs. "Hey, Austin, do you like it here?"

Austin stared at her for a moment. "Well, it's much quieter since a third of our dorm's been expelled. But yeah, I do. It's not so bad here as long as you don't get too wrapped up in the craziness."

Safia looked around, noticing the lack of people in the common area and the overall quietness of the dorm. "And do you blame me? For all those people getting expelled, I mean."

"Me? They chose to make the bets. They have to live with the consequences," he smiled as he waved his book at her. "But maybe I'm a little biased. I mean, I did bet on you after all."

"Really? Why?"

"We look alike. Well, your skin is a bit lighter, but that's close enough."

"Really, you voted for me because my mother is black?"

"Maybe, but remember, I'm from Texas. There are a lot of Latino's in Texas."

Safia shook her head, "I've never been to Texas, so I'll take your word for it."

"Truthfully, I just didn't like the idea of betting against some from our dorm. Plus, I've seen you run before, remember? I figured if you did well, you would be sprinting across campus in no time."

Safia couldn't help but smile. "Good night, Austin."

Austin opened back up his book and flipped the page. "Good night, Safia."

Taking her time as she went upstairs, Safia thought about everything that had happened so far. But the closer she came to her doom, the heavier her feet felt. Placing her hand on the knob, she opened the door. Inside, she saw the welcoming faces of Hashmi and Mallory waiting for her, but there was also another that sat in a chair in the middle of the room. A face Safia had seen a few times before.

"Hello, Miss Safia, we were wondering when you would arrive," said Jaqueline, the girl who had organized the ballerina practices she had attended with Amanda.

Safia stepped into the room, closing the door behind her. "Hello? Why are you here?"

"I've come to talk to you. It seems you've found yourself in more trouble than you'd like and could use another ally."

*I guess I can't just say 'I'm tired, please go away.'* Safia narrowed her eyes, stepping fully inside and locking the door behind her. She then walked over and grabbed another chair and took a seat in front of the woman. "Someone just recently told me that I can never have enough friends."

"Sounds like a smart friend."

"He's an idiot who just happens to be right from time to time. Now, tell me what you mean. Why would you try to be my friend? Aren't you with Frilla?"

"I am. But Frilla's lost her mind and isn't thinking clearly. It seems you've really gotten to her. She's been trying to make us bet her in these ridiculously one-sided games."

"And what do you want me to do about it?"

"Take her place."

"What?"

"I'm sure you've noticed that a select few of us, mostly those that were in that room, are able to decide what activities are set out on the campus. Well, we want you to take Frilla's place in our little group. You've certainly earned it, given all you've been through.

Safia glanced at Mallory and Hashmi after hearing the girl's proposal. "And what do you two think?"

"At first I didn't like it," said Hashmi. "But given how they've been treating you, it might be the best option to not have all these crazy games keep repeating themselves every semester. It hasn't exactly been easy on any of us."

"I don't know," said Mallory. "But I'll go along with whatever you want to do."

Safia looked back to Jaqueline, "How do I know this isn't some crazy plan by Frilla to get me expelled?"

"You don't. And it's not as if there aren't any risks involved for us either. As you can see, I'm the only one who dared to show their face here. You have this interesting habit of getting those who bet against you expelled, or haven't you realized?"

"Fine. So, what are you trying to get me to do?"

"Nothing, at the moment. But we will announce the final game of the semester soon. And we'd like to ensure that we survive it or at the very least survive you. None of us have put up with this school for as long as we have just to get expelled weeks before an acceptable graduation. So, when it is announced, we will help you expel Frilla and you will take her place and we all will live happily ever after."

Safia stared at the woman for a while before biting her lip. "Fine. I'll take Frilla's place. Just make sure you do your part."

"Then it sounds like we have a deal," said Jaqueline, as she stood up from her seat and headed for the door.

"Hey," said Safia, not even turning around to look at her. "Is your name really Jacqueline?"

"It is. But that's only one of my names. And probably not the one you need. But I guess you've been a little too busy to put much thought into our other little game." She then opened the door and left the room.

Safia slumped herself in the chair when they were finally alone. "It feels like every day is like this."

Hashmi laid back in bed taking a deep breath as she stared up at the ceiling. "I must admit, this isn't how I imagined our time at this school would go. Where have you been today? She was here for at least an hour waiting for you."

"I was trying to figure things out on my own. But that

didn't really work out too well. Oh, but remember Champ Champ's husband? I talked to him."

"Wait, was he actually awake? How did he look?"

"Scary... very scary."

# CHAPTER 21

Safia awoke in her bed next to Mallory. She looked over to see Hashmi brushing her hair in the morning sun.

"I'm surprised you're here. You're usually off helping, Jericho."

"I actually went out to meet him already. But he said that there's nothing to be done until the next game is announced, so he asked that I return here and look after you. It seems that he's worried you might do something reckless."

"Yeah, well, I might have given him the wrong impression yesterday," said Safia as she released herself from Mallory's arms and sat up in bed. "I kinda was feeling a bit low yesterday."

"Do you wish to talk about it?" asked Hashmi, as she lowered her brush to her knees and turned toward Safia.

"Would you mind if I asked what you would do if you were in my situation?"

"What? You mean besides crying constantly?"

"Yes," said Safia with genuine laughter. "Besides that."

"I suppose you have a responsibility to see this through. Actually, I think we all do. Mallory and myself included. I know we can't really help, considering how things are, but we will do what we can."

"I really think that's what I'm doing; whatever I can."

"We do have help. That woman from last night seemed adamant about helping you. And then there's Amanda and Jericho, although we have yet to understand why he is doing what he is doing. But I'm sure there are others."

Safia laughed again. "Are you sure? Because without you two, I'd start to feel alone, really fast."

"True," said Hashmi as she placed her brush on the windowsill and walked over to her closet, searching for something. "I admit they are not exactly the most trustful individuals to have supporting you, but it could always be worse. You could have Dario as a partner again."

"Emm, good morning," said Mallory, awaking from her slumber.

"No, thank you," said Safia, shaking her head and lowering her left to the floor. "I've already gone down that road. I'd rather not have to suffer through that again if I can help it." She looked over at Mallory and smiled. "Wow, you have a terrible bed head. Why didn't you wrap your hair last night?"

"I was tired... I forgot," said Mallory, rubbing her eyes.

Safia stepped over, taking the brush from the windowsill and patted her hand against the chair Hashmi was just in. "Come on, I'll brush your hair before we go to breakfast."

"Hey," said Hashmi, holding up a bottle. "What happened to all my oil?"

"Oh," said Safia, as she grimaced. "Sorry about that. I may have used a bit a little while ago."

"A bit? There's barely any left," said Hashmi as she turned the bottle upside down, bumping it against her palm. "There was over half a bottle left."

"Yeah, I might have gone a bit overboard."

Hashmi laughed while pointing the bottle at Safia. "You're going to buy me another bottle from the store after breakfast."

They finished their morning routine and finished getting dressed before heading out the door and towards the cafeteria. There they meet Mauricio in his usual chef's hat as he stood waving people in after taking their monthly points.

"How ya feeling?" he asked when they finally arrived at the front of the line.

"Better than yesterday," said Safia, as she raised her badge and allowed him to scan.

"That's good. Then hopefully tomorrow will be better than today," he said as the badge flashed colors, and Safia stepped forward. He then swiped Mallory's badge and both she and Safia's badges flashed together. "You three enjoy your breakfast."

"What was that about?" asked Hashmi as they entered the cafeteria and took up their trays.

"For me, nothing, But I think he likes you."

"Funny."

"Hey down there," came Amanda's voice.

Safia looked around for a moment before noticing Amanda and Ricardo up above them on the second floor of the building. Feeling a bit embarrassed at being called out in the crowd, she reluctantly waved back.

"Speaking of someone liking us," said Hashmi, raising an eyebrow and nodding up towards Ricardo. "What about him?"

"What about him?"

"Are you really going to pretend you're not interested?"

"I'm going to pretend we're not having this conversation."

"Come join us," yelled Amanda.

Safia nervously smiled but nodded her consent. "God

help me."

After receiving their food, the three girls made their way upstairs, sitting down at the table with Ricardo and Amanda.

"I heard you've been having quite the exciting time," said Amanda, glancing between Mallory and Safia. "Whatever possessed you to pull off that stunt together? For a moment, I really thought you two were trying to get yourselves expelled. And here I was thinking that I needed to babysit you during these events."

"I didn't exactly plan for what happened to actually happen," said Safia, glancing at Mallory, who lowered her head.

"What? You mean your discarded did all of that on her own, really?" asked Amanda, giving her attention to Mallory. "Oh my, you've certainly come a long way, haven't you? From cowering beneath Dario to expelling a second year."

Safia was surprised to see Mallory somehow appear smaller than she was as she brought her legs together and placed her hands between her thighs.

*She's actually embarrassed.*

"Tell me," said Amanda, "how did you figure out where to place the orbs? I must admit, I didn't understand what you were doing until you had already done it. I, myself, have never actually played that particular game. How did you know about the red orbs? That when they clashed that they would multiply?"

"I... I guessed. It reminded me of a game I used to play. So, I thought it would. Like how the blue one would subtract from each other, and how red and blue would double theirs and yours. It seemed like the reds would just bounce off each other."

"I'm having a hard time keeping up with your logic," said Amanda with furrowed brows as she tried to understand.

"And the Carnival Queen strikes again," said Hashmi,

shaking her head and waving her hands in dismissal. "Don't try to interpret how Mallory's mind works. Safia and I have just given up trying and decided to name it 'Florida Magic.' She did the same thing at last semester's Winter Games."

"Did she now? Well, I'm sad to hear that I missed out on such an event. But Jericho and I had our hands full with the event, so neither of us were provided much leisure time then. Did you know he made a small mountain out of snow and named it after himself? A true narcissist if there ever was one. But, I suppose I'm not one to talk."

"He renamed it Killian's Mountain after someone was hurt on it," said Safia, shaking her head.

"Of course, he did. All that does is further solidify my point. Tell me, Safia, what absolutely wonderful mess do you have planned to send us all spiraling into next? This time I'd prefer to have front row seats if possible."

"Oh," said Safia, remembering the past day's events. "Amanda, can I ask you something?"

"I'd like to think you can."

"I mean, you're a second a second year, right? But I've never seen you hanging with Frilla or the rest. Why?"

"A fair question, I guess. I supposed the short answer is: I never wanted to. I stay out of their business, and they leave me alone to my concerns. Plus, I'm not the type to just blindly follow behind someone. I don't know if you've noticed Safia, but I really am a selfish person. As much as I dislike the thought, Dario and I have that in common. He, himself, has often been at odds with their little group."

"Dario is at odds with everyone," said Hashmi.

"I can't argue with that, but the point remains. There are some here who just do not fit into their little social circle. But why the question? Has Frilla convinced you to become her acolyte?"

"No, it was Jacqueline... I mean, the girl from the ballet that you introduced me to. She came to my room last night and asked for my help to have Frilla expelled."

"Well, considering the grudge she has for you at the moment, I'd imagine that would be in your best interest. Someone like her isn't exactly the type to forgive a slight the likes of which Miss Mallory pulled off. I might not know the points she had, but you both lost around eighty percent of your points if I remember correctly. I'd imagine she's the type to hold a grudge against you for that."

"So, you think I should do it?"

"Safia, my wonderful dear. I don't think you have a choice. But at least you won't have to guess when it will happen. There's only one major game night left this semester and given your popularity, or should I say infamy, around campus, I hardly think Arthur is likely to leave you out of it."

"Do you think he would help Frilla?"

"Who? Arthur? No, there's no love lost there. Plus, it wouldn't be wise for him to. While manipulation of a game does happen amongst players, can you imagine if a game master was found to have cheated? They'd probably forbid their entire family from attending this school, not to mention the connections involved. No, I can't think of any faster way to become destitute than that. You've seen how this school treats their games. They are deadly serious when it comes to keeping things as fair as they can."

Safia sighed while rubbing at her face. "Alright, I guess all I have to do—"

"You have a message from Arthur," spoke Safia's pendant.

"Well," said Amanda. "Speak of the devil."

Safia frowned but clicked on her pendant. "Hello, Miss Safia, I hope everything is going well for you. I'm here to tell you the next game has been decided and it will be next week. I just need to work everything out with Jericho and the school. But spoiling it over this message is no fun. Come see me at that spot near the edge of the school grounds. You know the one. See you there."

"I guess I should—"

"You've received a message from Jericho Andrews,"

spoke Hashmi's badge.

"Well now," said Amanda, looking back and forth between Safia and Hashmi. "I suppose you girls are going to be busy."

"I'll guess. I'll go and see him. It's a long walk out there."

"Where?" asked Mallory.

"You can come along if you like."

"Okay."

The three girls stood from the table.

"Thanks, Amanda," said Safia, glancing over at Ricardo before heading back downstairs with Hashmi and Mallory and leaving the cafeteria.

"I'll see you two later then," said Hashmi as she waved to her friends and then headed off towards the other side of the campus.

Safia and Mallory began making the long trip to their destination. They stepped off the walkway and headed off past the building. This time, off in the distance, Safia could see the machines that they used to mow lawns of the campus all coming down in a line. For such large machinery, they were surprisingly quiet.

"Where are we headed?" asked Mallory, noticing the grass getting taller as they went out.

"It's still a while to go. If you squint your eyes, you can see him out there waiting for us. I think he has an umbrella this time. Thankfully, it's not in the midday or it would be hot outside."

"Way out there?" asked Mallory, squinting her eyes and pointing ahead of them.

"Yeah. Out there."

They both paced themselves, walking for about fifteen minutes before they finally reached their destination, and stood before Arthur as he laid across the bench, his head over his partner's lap. His partner held an umbrella to shelter them from the sun.

"Greetings, Miss Safia. I hope you're enjoying your day."

"I was. Then, I was asked to walk over a mile out in the middle of nowhere," said Safia, looking over and spotting an extra umbrella. "May I?"

"Oh, be my guest."

Safia took the umbrella, opening it up above her head, stepped over, and sat on the bench to the left of Arthur and Henry with Mallory. She then patted her lap. "Well come on Mallory, you might as well rest your head like it is. One of us should at least be comfortable."

"Ah… okay," said Mallory a little shyly as she stretched herself out on the bench, laying her head on Safia's lap and looking out over the campus. "The school. It looks so pretty from out here like this."

"Doesn't it?" said Arthur in agreement. "This is where I come to rest my mind when I'm thinking about things. You and Safia are welcome to start using it together."

"I'll start doing that. It seems I've had a lot to think about lately."

Arthur laughed, "Oh, I bet. But sadly, I'll have to add to that. The final game has been decided."

"And what is it? Will you have us bungee jumping from the rooftops of the school, solving puzzles on the way down?"

"I don't think the school would allow that," said Arthur, continuing his laughter. "No, for the last one of the seasons. I decided that it would be best to keep it simple. Plus, I think we've been overworking our little builder boy Jericho. So, instead of some grand event, I'd decided on a just a simple murder mystery."

"You mean, like those old fashion movies?"

"Exactly. I will place eight people in the school and decorate each room and it will be up to everyone to figure out who amongst them committed the murder. The theme will be in the eighteen hundreds, Victorian era, so dress accordingly." There was a long moment of silence between them. "What, nothing to say? I thought you would have more of a reaction."

"No," said Saifa as she gently stroked Mallory's head. She looked down and found that her friend had already gone to sleep in her lap. "I was just taking this time to relax and look over the school. I'll ask Amanda to help me pick out an outfit and I will be there. Forgive me. It's nothing."

"Can you answer me something?"

"Of course."

"This school only has three years. But you can graduate after two. Why do people stay past the two?"

"Power, mostly. A lot of them, coming from rich homes, don't really have a sense of who they are when they are at home. You're a trojan, right? So, your parents probably just want you to live a happy life, and that's it. You don't have a father or mother who controls every aspect of your existence. From the moment you can walk, they are telling you what to do and how to do and even when you try your best, nothing's ever good enough."

"Is that you?"

"A little bit, yes," said Arthur as he reached up, rubbing his partner on the chin. "But I've been disappointing my father for a few years now. My mother, not so much. We all have our own problems. And running away here has been an option. But then again, there's always Killian, who apparently came here for a wife."

"Will you stay for a third year, then?"

"Probably. It's not like I'm just so excited to return. But what about you? You've done a lot as a first year. If you survive the game, then you'll soon become a second year. You'll be one of us."

"I'm so excited," said Safia, a reluctant droll in her voice.

"Yes," said Arthur with another chuckle. "I'm sure you can't wait. Safia, I'm curious. Do you remember the first time we met?"

Safia thought back. "That was in the escape room, right? Or do you mean in the room when you were wearing one of those masks?"

"No, it was much earlier than that. But it's fine if you don't remember," He smiled. "I just suddenly had the memory of you with a surprised look on your face come to my mind. And looking at you now. I think you are incredible to come to this school and still remain who you were when first got here."

"I think you're wrong about that," said Safia as she continued to gently stroke the side of Mallory's head, before narrowing her eyes as she looked out over the school. "I really do feel like I've become a much different person."

# CHAPTER 22

The night of the game, the girls stood with confused looks on their faces as they looked down at a box that laid on Safia bed. Inside, sat another dress with more complicated looking designs that they had ever seen before.

"Well, at least this covers you up for the most part," said Hashmi, rubbing her hand over the ensemble. "At least the fabric is made well. It even comes with a corset." She picked it up and examined the waist. "That's not going to be pleasant squeezing into."

Mallory reached in and lifted the top piece out of the box. The piece was large and was mostly black with golden and velvet that ran down insides and into the wrists. "It reminds me of the outfit Champ Champ lent me. I didn't understand how to put it on, so she had to help me with it."

There was a sudden crack of thunder from outside their window.

"I do hope it doesn't rain before you get there. I can't imagine how annoying it would be to wear that in a heavy downpour. It looks heavy enough without it being soaked in water."

Safia sighed. "Let's just get this over with. Will you two help me with it?"

The girls helped Safia into the outfit, as she slid her arms into the sleeves. "I think I'm getting tired of my clothing needing to come with instruction manuals." After slipping on the shift, she then placed her hands over her breasts as the girls fit her for her corset, fitting the back as best they could. "That's a bit too tight," said Safia as she found herself having a bit too much trouble attempting to breathe.

Then came the under blouse and something Safia didn't even know how to describe. It appeared to be a bunch of loops that looked to make a shell of some sort.

"What is that for?" asked Safia, looking over the thing as the girls grabbed it.

"I forget the name," said Hashmi, "but it's supposed to make your butt look bigger I guess." She took another look at Safia. "But, I guess you don't need help with that."

"Oh, ha ha," said Safia, shaking her head. "No, thank you, that thing looks like a bunch of hula-hoops. You can keep it off."

"Are you sure? I think the dress is designed for it to be on."

Safia sighed, "Fine, let's just get this over with."

They lifted over her head, draping over her body and made it appear as in she had on a shell or a cone that wrapped around her waist

"This is actually kinda fun," said Hashmi. "I've always wanted to try one of these on. You're going to look like a duchess or someone else who should be living in a castle."

"I think I remember that they also used to keep prisoners in castles. And this thing feels like a cage."

Next came the undergarment that would drape over her

shoulders and spread out over the cone around her hips. Then to be followed by the last piece of the actual dress and the blouse above. All in all, the outfit took a little over half an hour for the girls to figure out, barring a few mistakes.

"So, how's it feel?" asked Hashmi when it was all done.

"I feel one of the hoops on my ass."

"That is the price we pay for beauty."

"I can't believe people used to dress like this all the time. No wonder they all had maids back then. Who would deal with this alone every day?" asked Safia as she took the shoes from the box, dropping them boy by one to the floor as she wiggled her feet into them. "Am I missing anything?"

"Just the umbrella and the hat," said Hashmi as she picked up the hat. "Although, it's quite small for; oh it comes with pins beneath it. So, it's to be treated as an ornament then. Come here, I'll set it for you."

Safia knelt a bit as she fit the small hat on her head. Afterwards, she spun on her heels, letting them both get a good look at her outfit.

"You look lovely."

There was a knock at the door a few minutes later.

"Come in," said Safia.

The door slowly opened as a hand stuck itself inside, holding another box in its hand. "Am I allowed to come in?" came the voice of Ricardo from behind the door.

"Yes," said Hashmi. "We are all properly dressed now."

Ricardo stepped into the room, holding two boxes in his hand. "Sorry for being late, but the order took some time getting here." He walked over and handed the box to Hashmi.

"Thank you."

"Are you sure you don't mind coming with me again?" asked Safia.

"Not at all. I'm going as a guest and won't be betting. I'll just be helping you solve a puzzle like last time."

Ricardo left the room for the girls to finish getting

dressed.

Hashmi opened the box to see that her outfit was a long-hemmed dress. There was a loose-fitting blouse with a puffy neckerchief. But the outfit also came with a long-sleeved dress coat. "I must admit, I've never worn anything like this before. But it seems as if it will cover everything up well."

"What's in this one?" asked Mallory as she opened up the other box to reveal a green satin hijab that seemed to shimmer in the room's light. It appeared to match another overcoat that was given to her.

"Well, this is certainly pretty," said Hashmi as she took the cloth and ran it across her fingers. "I actually don't have one in this color."

"Good, then it's your turn to suffer with putting one of these things on," said Safia, to the applause of the thunder outside.

"I don't like the way you both are looking at me," said Hashmi, taking a step back.

"It's too late to run away now. You promised to join me and I'm going to hold you to it."

There was a crackle of lightning outside of the window as both Mallory and Safia both descended upon her.

Around half an hour later, both girls were dressed and ready, stepping out of the door to meet Ricardo. But just in case, Safia brought her school bag with her.

"You ladies look lovely. I feel bad for not dressing up myself this time," said Ricardo as they all headed downstairs and out of the building.

"It's fine," said Safia, as she let Ricardo take her hand. "You're not the one who has to perform tonight. I just hope everything works out."

"It will. You both are smart women, and apparently, so is Miss Mallory. I'm surprised she didn't ask to come tonight."

"Well, I'm only allowed one guest. And after the fun she had in that hex game, she said she would gladly just wait for us to come back."

"Amanda, herself, tried to join tonight's game, but unfortunately all the spots were taken. But I think they didn't allow her to join because she was friends with you."

"Sounds like my luck," said Safia as they reached the steps of the school where two boys were standing outside, dressed in sir-coats and masks while guarding the door.

Ricardo patted her hand and leaned forward, giving her a kiss on the cheek. "Good luck, Miss Safia. Amanda and I will be watching you from our room and wishing you the best." He then turned to Hashmi and nodded. "You two, Miss Hashmi. I hope tonight you both kick ass." He took a few steps back, smiling at both the girls before turning his back to them and walking back off into the shadows of the night, being dimly lit by the streetlights as he faded into the night.

"He really is a well-mannered man. If he wasn't with Amanda, I'd think he had a crush on you."

"He's just a friend. But he is nice to look at. You know, in a friendly way, of course," said Safia with a smirk across her lips as she looked at Hashmi. "But thank you for being here tonight. I know you had to turn down working on this project with Jericho to help me. I... I appreciate that."

"Well, I think he needs someone to tell him no every now and then. Or else he might become spoiled," said Hashmi, linking arms with Safia. "But come on. Let us see this game that they've made to catch you." And together the doors to the school were opened to them by the men standing ahead, allowing them to walk inside.

As they made their way up the steps, the first thing they noticed was the thick gray fog that poured out over the floor of the school. It covered their feet so completely that they couldn't see the actual floor itself. Looking around, the girls could see that the entire first floor had been outfitted in the theme of what looked to be an old building.

"How did they get all this done so fast?"

"I honestly don't know," said Hashmi, as she knelt, running her hands along the fog and scooping it up in her hands and watching it run between her fingers. "I'm starting to feel a little bad about not helping him."

There were old planks of wood leaning against the walls as green vines layered themselves across them. Some veins were even hanging down so low that the girls needed to brush them aside as they passed. Going forward, they saw that the doors to all the rooms had been removed and they could see inside of them. One room looked like it had a garden inside of it. Another, that still had its door, looked to house a suit of armor. Ahead, they saw the sign that read, 'Welcome' next to Abigail's room.

"I guess we go in," said Safia, and she and Hashmi walked into the room.

The room itself was dressed out in a lavish Victorian setting with bookshelves, which Safia guessed were imported from one of the libraries. There was also furniture spread about, some of which Safia remembered from the game down in the tunnel. Over on one of the loveseats, she saw one of the costumed guests asleep with his back turned to the rest of the room.

"Welcome, Safia," said Arthur, breaking away from the other guests as he noticed them enter the room. His outfit was of a long blue tailcoat and top hat with a doublet underneath. "Everyone is almost here. Just a few stragglers, I assume. But don't you two look absolutely amazing. Despite the circumstances of tonight, I hope you two enjoy yourself at tonight's game."

"We shall try," said Safia as she nodded over to an older woman who was sitting up on the table, talking to one of the boys in the room. She was in a pure white sleeveless evening gown. But the thing that drew her attention was the large red bloat above her right breast and the knife in her hand. "I guess that she will be the dead body that we are going to have to figure out what happened to?"

"Yes. Everything is already planned out. We are just waiting for the rest to arrive before we get started."

"It seems that someone over there couldn't wait," said Hashmi as she nodded over to the boy who was asleep on the love seat.

"Oh, that's Jericho. You didn't notice him with his back turned and the way he's dressed. We may have overworked him a bit, getting everything together in such a short order. In truth, he had only finished setting up the final parts of the puzzle an hour or so before everyone arrived."

"Now, I really am feeling a little bad about not helping," said Hashmi as she stepped over, and began looking down at him, inspecting him.

"Your friend seems to have taken a fond liking to our builder boy," said Arthur.

"It seems so," said Safia, as she watched Hashmi squat down beside Jericho, shaking her head in disapproval. "They have been working together a lot." Safia noticed Jaqueline over in a corner talking to two boys. Jaqueline also saw her and nodded before continuing her conversation with her companions.

A moment later, Safia saw Frilla enter the room and, to her surprise, her partner that came into the room was Dario. They instantly spotted each other, and Frilla and company immediately made their way over.

"Hello there, Safia. I hope everything has been going well for you," said Frilla as she began looking over the room. "And look, you even brought your Muslim friend to help you. I had hoped I'd get to meet with your discarded again. But I guess I can just see her off when she's expelled."

"That won't happen. Or haven't you noticed that, apparently, I'm quite hard to get rid of?"

"Yes," said Frilla, the smile leaving her face. "That is the case with most fungus."

Safia then turned to Dario, "Why are you even here? Don't you have anything better to do than follow me around?"

"Anytime I can get to see that bitchy face of yours in pain, is a chance I refuse to pass up. Or do you not remember the last time we weren't together? Because I remember your face pressed against the wall, begging for me to let you go."

"And I remember your face bloody. It's nice to see that the scar left a mark. How does it feel to remember me every time you look in the mirror?"

"How's it feel to remember me every time you sit down?"

"Fuck off."

"Ladies and so-called gentlemen, please!" said Arthur, interrupting the two's banter. "Save the energy for the game. The last thing I need is for you two to start destroying things when the game starts. So, at the very least, play nice until tonight is over."

"We're fine," said Frilla. "Just a bit of friendly rivalry is all. Come Dario, let's go and talk to the people who actually belong here." She then took Dario by the arm and walked off to entertain herself with the rest of the crowd, but Safia couldn't help but notice that she immediately made her way to Jacqueline.

"That didn't seem fun," said Hashmi, coming back over, standing beside Safia.

"It wasn't. How's Jericho?"

"Dead to the world. I called his name a few times, but he didn't wake up. So, I decided it's best to just let him sleep."

A little while later and everyone had arrived with their partners and Safia saw the woman in white laydown on the table holding the blade over her chest in both hands before closing her eyes.

"Okay everyone, come join me by the body so that I may inform you of the rules," said Arthur as he stood beside the table. "In this room are five teams of two. One better and their partner. All of you will be handed a list with ten pieces of information on it. These will help you narrow down who the killer is mostly likely to be. And at the top of the paper, you will see just which character of the game you are."

*So, I'm the Mistress?* Safia looked down at the paper that was handed to her.

"How the points will work is that you must correctly solve the puzzle in order to receive points. And at the end of the night you will be asked five questions. For each question you get right, you will receive twenty percent of the amount you bet. Get all the questions right, then you will double the number of points you bet. Get all the questions wrong and you will lose everything you bet. But after solving the puzzle, you will have the option to keep your points or subtract those points from someone else in this room."

"How many points are we allowed to bet?"

"As many as you like. But not more than you actually have. While I don't particularly like these rules, it was suggested and approved by the committee. So, we all will have to live with the consequences at the end of the night."

"That's fine with me," said Frilla.

"Okay everyone, take your turn and walk over to the edge of the table and swipe your badge over the school's crest. There is a keypad there where you can type in the number of points you wish to wager. There is a little privacy shield so that no one else can see what you type in. Miss Hashmi, of course, being our only Muslim guest, is allowed to not wager, and consequently, you will not be allowed to attack her points or donate points to her at the end of the game."

Hashmi smiled and nodded to Arthur.

Then one by one, each and every one of the contestants made their way and input their numbers into the system.

"Okay then," said Arthur. "There are four other rooms on the first floor. You will have one hour to explore all of them in any order that you prefer, and then after you will all come back here, and you will figure out who was the killer. You will find clues in every room that will lead you to the culprit. Most clues cannot be moved, but for the ones that can, please place them back in their original positions when done."

And with that, Arthur stepped to the side and pulled out his tablet.

As a few others left the room or began scanning their papers. Safia began looking over the dead woman's body. She was barefooted, and one of her feet was dirty. The blade in her hand didn't have any blood on it, but the spot on her chest looked like blood. One of her eyelashes was missing, and she had a bruise underneath the same eye. She looked her over once again, but besides seeing a small wrapping on one of her fingers, she didn't see anything else that stood out.

Following her look of the body, she and Hashmi both left the room and headed to the right most room near the entrance of the school. Inside, the room looked like it was some sort of garden. There were fruit plants spread out through the room, along with gardening equipment that poked out of the fog on the floor.

"I must admit that this is better than what I thought it would be," said Hashmi as she poked her finger at a pumpkin. "It's fake. I guess that makes sense. Where would they get pumpkins from?"

"I'm more concerned about the fog," said Safia, kicking her foot forward. "We can even see the floor."

"I think that might be the point. But I'm not going to get on all fours and start checking every square inch of the floor."

Safia continued to look around the room as a flash of lighting came through the windows, followed by the feel of a thunder that vibrated through the walls into them. "That doesn't sound good," said Safia as she walked up to the wall, where a scarecrow was planted with his arms stretched out. There were large lumps of dirt beneath where it looked to just have been planted, along with vegetables beside a slew of gardening tools. Some of the plants were still in pots, while others were surrounding the scarecrow.

*Were they putting the plants in the ground or taking them out?*

"I don't suppose the paper says what clues match up to which room," said Hashmi, coming back to Safia.

"No, but apparently I'm the mistress," said Safia, handing the paper to her.

"So, the five possible killers are, The Husband, The Banker, The Mistress, The Butler, and The Reporter." She flipped the paper over, but it was blank on the other side.

"Sounds like a soap opera, doesn't it?"

"True. But it does sound a bit interesting."

Safia saw something shining between the vegetables, reaching her hand in, moving the greenery aside. It was there that she found an old broken camera half covered up by the dirt. "I guess this means something," she said as she reached her hand in, trying to take the camera. But it was solidly locked in place. "I guess that is what he meant when he said most clues are locked down."

Hashmi walked around the other side, moving the brush on her side, and examining the camera from the back. "There's something caught on the back of the camera. It looks like a bracelet. Did the body look like it was missing one?"

"I don't know. I didn't look at her wrists. We'll have to go back and check."

Hashmi quickly stepped back and began examining a nearby table as the door to the room opened and in walked a boy and girl couples from the game.

"Hey there," said the boy as they walked into the room and began looking around. "Find anything interesting yet?"

"Not yet," said Safia, stepping away from the camera in between the plants. "But I'm pretty sure we aren't supposed to be sharing with each other."

"No, we can. Sharing information doesn't necessarily mean we will come to the same conclusion," said the boy as he stepped towards Safia. "Hello, I am The Butler, apparently, according to this paper. And who might you be?"

Safia looked at the boy's paper as he waved it in front of her and, sure enough, it did read 'The Butler' across the top. "I'm the mistress. But I don't see how that helps us solve the puzzle."

"It probably doesn't, but I think introductions are important. And you are very famous," he looked over at the plants. "I see they have dirt in here, too. So, I guess that cancels out my idea that she was killed in the dining hall."

"Why the dining hall?" asked Hashmi from over by the clock in the corner.

"There's a large plant in there in a vase. But the vase that it's in was broken, so the soil had spilled to the floor."

"I don't see why you're sharing this with them," said the girl that he was with as she knelt down, examining a wheelbarrow.

Safia looked at the boy for a moment before nodding over to the plants. "Inside that garden, over there is a camera. There's a bracelet stuck to the back. It probably means something."

"Thank you," said the boy, looking over at his partner. "See, a little kindness can go a long way."

"Do you remember if the body had any markings on his bracelet?"

"Nah, we didn't look at it," said the boy as he walked over to the patch and looked at the camera. "But after we snoop around a bit more, we'll probably head back there to check."

"Good luck with that," said Safia as she walked back over to Hashmi, who had moved to investigate the side of the clock.

"There's a hole here like it had been cut open," whispered Hashmi. "It might have something to do with the knife the girl was holding."

"You're right," said Safia, rubbing her hand over the side

of the clock.

"Are you going to tell them about this, too?"

Safia glanced back before turning back to Hashmi. "He gave us a clue, and we gave them one. I'd say we're even now. Come on, I want to see the dining room he mentioned." Then both girls left the room, saying their goodbyes to the other couple.

"Which room is supposed to be the dining hall?" asked Hashmi when they both stepped out into the corridor. They stepped forward and looked over into the next class where they saw what looked to be a child's daycare room. "On second thought, let's go in here."

In agreement, both girls opened the door, stepping into the nursery. In the center of the room, there was a large cradle that sat next to a rocking chair where two feeding bottles sat. On the table next to it, lay a thread of yarn with a set of children's clothes next to it. Around the room there were dolls and small children's toys to play with. Safia looked into the cradle and there was a note alongside another set of clothing. Safia reached in, picking up the note.

"Feb 1st, 1966"

*My dearest love, how I have missed being away from you. It has been over a year now and coming home to you is the only thing that keeps me sane out here. The war drags on day by day and the men that I serve with often brag about the ones they left behind. You often heard the stories of the horrors of war, and I wish to tell you that they are true. The things that we must do to our fellow man are the things that I am sure will haunt my dreams until my dying day. Be well, my lady, for surely, I shall return to you. Sincerely yours, Hector.*

"Well, that was sad," said Safia, putting the letter back down into the crib.

"Really, it seemed romantic to me. He was a man who missed his wife."

Safia walked around the room and saw a painting of the supposed couple sitting above the fireplace. They were dressed in fine clothing and stood holding each other's hand. "It looks like someone got Killian involved in this game."

"What do you mean?" asked Hashmi, walking over to her.

"That's his painting. I can tell by the style of it and the paints used."

"You really have been spending a lot of time around him," said Hashmi before looking up at the painting again. "Oh, look," she said as she pointed up to the painting. Look at his wrist. Isn't that the bracelet from the garden?"

"Wow, it is. So, it wasn't the wife's bracelet then?" asked Safia, her face twisting in thought. "Then why was it around the broken camera?"

"It really is starting to feel like a mystery now," said Hashmi as she turned back around and began snooping around the room. "I wonder what other clues we're missing."

Suddenly, with another crackle of thunder from outside, they both began to hear the unrelenting sounds of the rain that began to pour down on the window outside.

"That startled me," said Hashmi, with her hands covering her chest.

"Yeah," said Safia, also feeling startled as she looked outside of the window. "But you gotta admit that this is the perfect weather for this type of game."

"Maybe so," said Hashmi as she reached under the picture and began to fiddle with a music box. "Oh, it doesn't work. I guess it doesn't matter, anyway. It's not like I would be able to hear anything over the sounds of the rain outside."

"Come on," said Safia, as she headed for the door. "We only had an hour. Let's go and check the other two rooms. We can always come back if we have the time." Together, both girls left the nursery and headed down the hall and entered another room. This time, they indeed found the dining room that was mentioned earlier. They could tell from the silverware and plates that sat on the table in the center of the room.

"So, I guess we look around," said Hashmi as she stepped into the room.

Looking over the room, there were a few things that caught Safia's eye. The most obvious being the dining room table itself. As she made her way over, she could see that only the table had been set for three. But the food that sat at the tables had been left mostly uneaten except for the head of the table, which had a whole slice of pie left, and the only piece that was missing was still on the fork on the side of the plate.

The head of the table's chair had also been the only one that had been turned over and laid on its side on the floor.

"Well, something happened here," said Safia, as she placed a finger on the side of the plate and found that it didn't tilt, but instead was solidly attached to the table.

"Yes," said Hashmi, as she stood over by a large broken vase in the corner of the room. "It seems they weren't lying. The vase is broken and there's dirt all over the floor over here."

Ahead of them there was another fireplace, but above it, there were no pictures, instead there were several books all stacked neatly beside one another. Although, Safia couldn't help but see that one of the books was missing, leaving a noticeable hole in the uniformity of the shelf.

She began to look around the room, but finally saw the half-charred book sitting in the fireplace and sticking out of one of its pages was a piece of yarn. She tried reaching down to pick it up but noticed that it was also solidly attached to the fireplace.

*That's weird. So, the camera, the book, and probably the food over there are stuck in place, but they allowed me to move the paper? I wonder if that means anything.* Safia turned around and began heading back over to Hashmi. "Find anything?"

"I'm not sure," said Hashmi, looking over a suit of armor by the door that held a sword in his hands with the tip heading down before his feet. She made a fist and then tapped on the figure, hearing the distant sound of hollow metal. "It's a real statue, and it looks like there is a bit of blood or something on the arm."

Safia could see the spot about which Hashmi spoke. There was what looked to be blood on the armor right next to the elbow and beside it stood a long piece of wood leaning against the wall. "I still don't see how all of this adds up. Cameras, bracelets, and suits of armor with blood on them."

"Well, if it isn't the beggars," said Frilla as she entered the room. "I do hope you're enjoying your last puzzle here. It'd be a shame for you to be sent home without at least enjoying your final moments here."

"Where's Dario? Did he get tired of you and leave you already?"

"Hardly. We've decided to search each room separately and save time. We'll share details and form our conclusion together. You know, something smart people would do," said Frilla as she looked over at Hashmi. "But I suppose you wouldn't understand with all the help you've been receiving."

"You can be as bitter as you like, but the truth is you'd never be in this situation if you would have left me alone. Mallory was right. What happened to you is your fault."

"That is where you are wrong. No matter who you are, you should have long since become discarded like all the rest. But you have someone helping you, I know you do. I thought it was Builder Boy, since he makes all the puzzles. But, I've had the school watch him along with others and he hasn't left this school since he started the game. They even took his badge away. But that's fine. When I get you expelled, I'll find out who it is that keeps getting in my way. None of you are smart enough to have pulled this off on your own."

"Let's go Hashmi, for as smart as she claims to be, she's

too stupid to understand."

"What I understand is that you should never have been here."

The girls left the dining room and made their way down the hall to the final room, opening the door. Inside was a kitchen and along all of its walls was a countertop that housed an assortment of items, finally meeting up at the center of the back wall to what looked to be a brick oven. But they stopped at the door before they entered the room because ahead of them, they saw Dario looking over a set of knives that hung from the wall.

Sighing and shaking her head, Safia stepped into the room with Hashmi following behind her and intentionally going to the opposite side of the room from Dario. She could hear him tapping his hand on the kitchen counter as he thought. She wanted to turn around and take another look at what he was staring at, but her pride wouldn't let her.

Instead, she and Hashmi looked over the counter at their side of the room. There were bags of flour and wheat, along with several rolling pins. She could see that one of the flour bags had a hole somewhere in it, as there was a large pile of white powder sitting next to it.

At the corner of the room, underneath the countertop, were several wooden barrels. Safia knelt beside them and noticed a small pry bar, but she didn't need to use it as the barrels had already been opened. Leaning one on its side, she rolled it out towards her, peering inside. There was some odd liquid that Safia couldn't place. She slid her finger across the top of it before placing it to her nose.

"I don't know what this is. Do you Hashmi?"

"Probably butter or cooking grease of some sort."

Safia frowned before rolling the barrel back into place and placing the lid back. She then stood, looking over the room again before walking over by the oven. Dario, seeming to have finished his investigation, turned and left the room without speaking to them. But as he left, Safia could see him glance at her from the side of his eye.

"I think that's the first time he's ever been silent. I much prefer him that way."

"Yeah, well. I'd much prefer it if I didn't have to see him at all."

"I doubt he'd miss the chance to have you expelled."

"Yeah, I figured as much." Safia shook her head. "It doesn't matter, and I'd prefer not to think about him." She then began inspecting the oven area. Nearby, she could see a bag of flour and a rolling pin along with a piece of crust from the pie she saw in the dining room.

*I don't understand what any of this has to do with anything.* Safia continued to look around the kitchen, walking over to where Dario was standing, inspecting the knives. They were all in order, from smallest to largest, with the middle one missing. Safia guessed that the missing one was the blade that was held by the faux corpse in the starting room.

But below the kitchen cutlery, Safia could see small traces of blood still on the counter. To the side of her was a waste bin. Looking down into it, she saw a single item. She knelt, peering inside, and saw that it was a ring with a blue jewel at its center.

"There's a ring in here," said Safia as she reached into the pickup and found it solidly attached to the bottom of the bin.

"What type of ring is it?"

"It looks expensive. Maybe a wedding ring?"

"I can't say that this particular puzzle is fun," said Hashmi, as she began opening the cupboard doors, exposing a slew of pots, pans, and jars. "What's this?" She asked as she reached in, pulling out a jar with the letters 'As' on it.

"I don't know. It's in a kitchen, so, something to cook with, I guess."

Hashmi twisted her lips, looking at the jar as she twirled it around in her finger, but then something caught her eye behind it. "What a minute." She reached in and pulled out a glove, holding it up. "This looks like it might belong to the butler or someone else who is probably well dressed. It even has a button on it."

"Are there any stains on it?" asked Safia as she came over to look.

"Not that I can tell," said Hashmi, rubbing her finger across the glove. "Although there's some sort of white powder on it." She began rubbing the residue of the powder between her fingers before smelling it. "Flour, maybe?"

"Maybe. That would explain why that flour bag over there had a hole in it. But I still don't understand how it all comes together. See anything else?"

"Not at the moment, no."

"Then let's head back to the room with the body. We can see if we missed anything."

Together, both girls left the kitchen and, after visiting all four rooms, they walked back into the main room where Arthur was sitting down looking over his tablet and Jericho was continuing his unconsciousness over on the love seat.

They immediately walked back out into the corridor and spotted Dario standing in the middle of the hall. He wasn't doing anything in particular, just standing still between the dangling vines above him and the fog filled floor.

They made their way past him and into the first room, then over to the body and began inspecting it again. The first thing Safia did was inspect her wrist, remembering the bracelet that was latched onto the back of the camera. Looking over her wrists, Safia saw nothing that would indicate that the bracelet was hers.

*Okay, so I guess it belonged to the guy in the picture then. But what about the rest of it? She has dirt on her feet, so she was either in the garden or it came from the broken plant vase. There was also that letter to his wife... wait? Maybe the letter wasn't for his wife. I don't remember it saying anything about her specifically. Maybe it was for his mistress.*

"Safia, have you figured something out?" asked Hashmi.

"What... oh, maybe. The letter, I was just thinking it might have been for his mistress and not his wife. So, maybe they both had a mistress."

"Oh, that's right," said Hashmi, looking down at the woman's hands. "Safia, look, she doesn't have a ring on, and she has an imprint of her finger. So maybe it was her wedding ring."

"Okay, so maybe she found out about the affair as well. That's probably the reason she's dead."

"But we still don't know who did it."

"Maybe the husband?"

"That's who I would guess. But with how things are and considering that this is a game from the school. I wouldn't be surprised if they told me the dog did it."

Hashmi laughed as she looked over at the woman again. "Hmm, is she one of the second-year teachers? I don't remember ever seeing her near one of our classes. Or even around campus."

"Probably. Mallory said they had two female teachers for the second-year students, but I've never seen any of them."

"Hmm, one of her earrings is missing. Did you see it anywhere while we were looking?"

"Not that I remember," said Safia, looking around the room.

"Actually, wasn't there a picture of the husband and wife in the nursery?"

"Yeah, why?"

"I want to check something. Can we go back?"

"Sure," said Safia, following Hashmi back out of the room and over into the nursery. But this time, they weren't alone. Instead, there were two other groups in the room, including Jaqueline. Both groups were hovering over the cradle as Jaqueline read the paper out loud.

"Well, look who it is. Have you figured out the mystery yet?"

"No," said Safia, "we're still figuring it out."

"So are we. Would you like to join us in figuring out this room?"

Safia stepped forward, "I'll trade you; you tell us something and we'll tell you something."

Jaqueline smiled, "I see you've learned something since coming here. Alright, how about over in the garden area, a few of the leaves are cut and there's a hole in the clock that is nearby? We think there may have been a fight. The woman was probably trying to stab someone and then ended up getting stabbed herself."

*I didn't notice any of the plants being cut. But if that's the case, then it explains the dirty foot if she was in the garden fighting. But only one foot was dirty.* Safia smiled back at Jacqueline. "Fine, in the kitchen, there's a trash can with a ring inside of it. It's stuck to the corner side of it, so looking straight down into it, you wouldn't see it unless you were on the other side of it. We think she was wearing it because of the grove on her finger. So maybe she took it off in a rage after finding out her husband was cheating."

"A ring?" said Jaqueline as she turned back to a boy in their group. "Did you see a ring?"

"No. But I just looked down at it from above since it was in a corner. If it's stuck to the side, then I might have missed it," said the boy with a frown. "I'll go check and see. I'll be right back." He then stepped out of the room, headed toward the kitchen.

"See," said Jaqueline. "Isn't sharing wonderful? Are you sure you don't want to join us? Frilla has Dario with her. We didn't expect that, so getting rid of her might be harder than we thought."

"No, thanks. I don't exactly trust you all either. I want to believe what you're saying, but this school doesn't exactly promote helping each other. In fact, I think it encourages the opposite."

"That's a fair point," said Jaqueline as she stepped away,

headed back to her group, "But remember, we're not the one that Frilla is after."

Safia watched her leave before turning back to Hashmi and they stepped over to the side of the room and began pretending to inspect a tabletop.

"What did you want to come back for, Hashmi?" asked Safia, as she picked up a nursery book from the table.

"The picture of the family. Doesn't it look strange to you?"

Safia glanced back at the picture above the fireplace. "Not, really. What's so odd about it?"

"The husband and the wife have black hair. But the baby's hair is brown?"

"That's true. I didn't pay attention to that. So, you think that she cheated on her husband?"

"I mean, your paper says that you are the mistress. Who's to say that she didn't have other lovers besides him?"

"So, we just have a house of everyone fucking everyone else then? Who knows, maybe the butler is the father, and that is why he took off his gloves and she took off her ring." She shook her head. "This is becoming way more complicated than it needs to be. Okay, so let's say that the baby wasn't his," said Safia, keeping her voice low so that the others couldn't hear her. "Let's go somewhere else for a bit."

And with that, they both left the room and headed back out into the corridor. They headed over to the dining room, but through the closed window, Safia spotted Dario inside and decided not to enter. So instead, they walked over to the garden area once again and saw that it was empty and went inside.

"Well, at least we're starting to figure things out," said Safia, as she looked up at the clock on the wall. "We only have around fifteen minutes left to figure out as much as we can."

"I dislike how they only give you an hour to try to figure everything out," said Hashmi as she walked over to the plant near the clock. "Well, it looks like she wasn't lying. The plants over here have been cut." She picked up a few of the cut off leaves and held them up for Safia to see. "I wonder how we missed it. Some of them even looked crushed and the dirt's all scattered."

"So, something else to figure out," said Safia, as she looked down at the paper again and began reading over the names. "Actually, I wonder what happened to the baby."

"What do you mean?"

"I mean, everyone else is on the paper, right? The Husband, Photographer, and all that. But I don't see the baby anywhere. You'd think they'd have put in the doll of a baby doll or something."

"That is a good point. When you consider everything else they've added. They even have a suit of armor. If they can drag all that in here, then they could..." Hashmi's eyes went wide. "Hey, what if the baby is dead or you know, someone might have murdered their baby?"

"Yes, and maybe their father found out. But why and who? Oh! The photographer, that's why the father's bracelet is stuck to the camera," said Safia as she walked towards the cut off plants. "Maybe they were fighting over here. Someone had the knife. That's why the plants were cut and why the clock has that hole in it."

"Okay, then, but who was fighting? And how did the wife get stabbed? We know that the husband and the photographer were here. Does that mean that their wife was also here?"

Safia rubbed her face in frustration. "Ahhh, we need more time to figure all this out. It isn't making any sense yet. The only thing we know is that they were all here," she said, then looked up to the clock and saw that now only ten minutes were remaining.

"So, what do we do now?" asked Hashmi as she stepped over, looking at the turned over wheelbarrow. "Should we go to another room?"

Safia sighed. "I guess we can head back to the dining room and see if we missed anything."

In agreement, both girls left the room and headed back to the dining room. Both were relieved to see that Dario was now gone.

Safia walked back over to the dining table, looking over the three plates with their pieces of pie. Looking closer, she studied how the two seats opposite each other had pieces of pie scattered around their plates, while the plate at the center of the table didn't have any mess around it. It just had its piece of pie still sitting on its fork.

"We still can't explain why the blood is on the armor," said Hashmi as she stood over in the door frame reexamining the statue. "We already figured out that the fight took place in the garden, so why would she stumble all the way over here first, then head over to the first room?"

"To check on the baby, maybe? But why was the vase broken unless she fell or something?" said Safia as she walked over to the vase, trying to imagine what would have happened. "I don't get it, there's no blood. So, maybe she didn't break the..." Safia squinted her eyes and there, in the dirt above the fog, she saw something. Reaching down, she cleared away some of the dirt and revealed a child's shoe. "It was the child who broke the vase, not the mother."

"How can you be so sure... oh," said Hashmi, coming over and spotting the top of the child's shoe poking out of the dirt. "You know, I wonder how much of this even matters?"

"What do you mean?"

"I mean, surely, not all the things we found to be clues matter. They must have just put some things here to trick us or confuse us, so we come to the wrong conclusion."

"Well, not like it matters anymore," said Safia, looking up at the clock on the wall and seeing that they only had a minute left. "I guess we should head back."

"Yeah. Sorry, I wasn't much help on this one."

"Are you joking? I can't imagine how frustrating it would

have been to do this without you, and I doubt any of them managed to figure out more than we did in the time we had."

Both girls then left the room and headed back into the main room. Within seconds of them entering, so did all the rest of the participants, as they all came to stand around the body.

"I do hope all of you enjoyed your time in tonight's game," said Arthur as he came over to the group.

"I'd hardly think of this game as anything enjoyable," said the boy who gave Safia the clue earlier. "Why were we only given an hour? That's hardly enough time to figure out anything. Games like this should last the entire night."

"Because rarely in life are we ever given enough time to do anything that we want. That is something you should have figured out from all of the games you've played here. None of us ever really has enough time. So, we simply must make the most out of the time we have."

"Fine," said one of the girls that was with Jaqueline. "How are we going to figure out who won?"

"That's simple," said Arthur as he walked over to a shelf and grabbed five electronic tablets and began handing them out to the groups.

"On the screen, you and your partner will just answer the questions. It is that simple. And the percentage of the questions that you both answer correctly will be the percentage of the points you wagered that you will be able to add or subtract to yourself or to any other participant in this room, besides Miss Hashmi, of course. So, if you would please, you will have ten minutes."

Safia and Hashmi walked over and sat down on one of the loveseats and began looking over the first question on the screen.

*1. Who was the killer? The Husband, The Banker, The Wife, The Mistress, The Butler, or The Photographer.*

"You wanna take a guess?" said Safia, turning to Hashmi with a hopeless smirk on her face.

"Well, I don't remember seeing anything that mentioned the banker, so I guess we missed whatever clues were meant for him. So, I think it was either the husband or the wife who killed herself."

"I thought the same. But since the husband was fighting with the photographer. Wait, actually, I know it sounds silly, but can a mistress be a man?"

"What do you mean?"

"I mean, I guess the male term would be her lover or something?"

"I actually don't know. But I've never heard of a mistress being the male counterpart to cheating. But I guess it could be."

"You know what, no. I'm overthinking things. I'm going to say that the wife killed herself," said Safia as she clicked on 'The Wife.'

The screen then faded away as the second question appeared on the screen.

2. *Who was the accomplice to the murder?* The Husband, The Banker, The Wife, The Mistress, The Butler, The Reporter, or There was no accomplice.

"There was an accomplice?" asked Safia, shaking her head. "I didn't even think of that."

"I'm the same," said Hashmi, shaking her head. "I didn't think about that either."

"Okay, so we're probably going to get this one wrong. Want to help me guess?"

Hashmi laughed, "I feel like we're back in class trying to bluff our way through a test."

"We are back in class taking a test," said Safia, looking over the room. "It's just that class looks a lot different now that it's all dressed up."

"Then, in the spirit of guessing, I want to pick the Husband. I mean, why wouldn't he? They were married, after all. But this whole time I kept thinking it might be the butler. I mean, we did find his glove and her wedding ring in the same room."

"We're only two questions in and I already feel like an idiot," said Safia as she tapped on 'The Butler.' and the screen faded and up popped the next question.

3. *How many people were killed?* One, two, three, four, five.

"Two," said Safia, looking to Hashmi for agreement, "right?"

"Yes. I would say two. The mother and her child, the one from the portrait. Although we still didn't find the body. It could have been in one of the other barrels in the kitchen. We didn't pop open all of those," said Hashmi with eyes wide. "Oh, we found the butler's glove in there, right? Maybe he put the child's body in a barrel."

"Wow, I didn't think of that either," said Safia, looking back down at the screen. "Suddenly I'm feeling a bit more confident in our random choices."

"See, we aren't doing so bad. Even if we're having to guess our way through it. Our answers are making sense."

Safia sighed. "I guess we're going with two." Then she tapped on the screen and waited for the next question.

4. *Where did the murder take place?* In the Kitchen, In the Dining Room, In the Garden, In the Nursery, In the Main Room.

"There was blood in the kitchen, but I think she just cut her finger in there," said Safia, "and then there was the blood on the suit of armor in the dining room."

"I still believe that the murder took place in the garden. We didn't see any blood, but we couldn't see the floor because of the fog. So, someone could have been there."

"The Garden it is," said Safia, clicking one again on the screen and then the final question appeared.

5. *Why did the murder happen?* Jealousy, Shame, Love, Rage, or Power.

"Don't tests like these usually have a final option that says: 'All of the Above?' Because I'm sure all of these were involved."

"I think they mean which was the catalyst of the event which led to the murder."

"Jealousy? Maybe?"

"Probably. But it could also be love. I don't know how we are supposed to differentiate between the two. I don't think it could be power, because we haven't seen anything relating to money or control since we got here."

"Yeah. And rage is what killed them, but it's not what started it. Shame, maybe? But they both had lovers so... I wonder if they knew about each other's cheating."

"Well, the wife certainly did if the wedding ring was in the trash can. Maybe she cheated because he cheated, so hers came after."

"That makes sense. So, we were probably right about the letter that we found in the nursery being meant for the mistress and not the wife then."

"Sooooooo... are we going with jealousy, then?" asked Hashmi, balling her lips in contemplation.

"I think it's the best option," said Safia, taking a deep breath before pressing down on the final answer and watching the screen fade away and then go black.

Afterwards, both the girls sat there for a moment until the ten minutes were up and Arthur came around, picking up his tablet. He then brought them to his boyfriend Henry, who walked over, sitting them down back on the shelf.

"Okay, come around everyone," said Arthur with a wide smile on his face as he held up his tablet. "The scores are in and it's time for the moment of truth."

"Let's get this over with," said Dario. "I want this bitch expelled, so I get on to more important things."

"Why are you like this," said Safia. "At first, I just thought you were just an ass. But it's something else, isn't it? Did your mother not give you enough kisses when you were a child? Is that why you hate women?"

"I love women, but only the ones who listen and know

their place. You don't belong here and no matter what you do, and no matter how lucky you think you are; you can't beat me. You have never beaten me. The only reason you're still here is because I want you to suffer."

"Stop," said Arthur, stepping in between the two. "We will not be having a repeat of the escape room here. If you two wish to go at it, then I suggest doing so after the game has finished."

Dario just smirked at Safia before turning his back to her.

"You two really don't seem to get along," said Frilla. "And here I thought I hated you, but it seems your ex-lover—"

"We were never lovers. I would never let someone like him even touch me."

Dario smiled, "I'm so glad to hear you say that."

"Either way, whatever you both were to each other, it seems we are in agreement that you simply must go, Safia. At first your disruptions were an amusement. But now they have become an annoyance. And not just for myself. I'd imagine much of the campus now sees you and your friends as a much unwanted eyesore."

"If I may be allowed to continue," said Arthur, raising his tablet. "It seems that only one couple managed to acquire a perfect score," He sighed while shaking his head. "I would love to drag this out and build the suspense, but after the antics of Dario and Safia, I'd figure it's best to rip the band-aid off. Dario and Frilla scored a perfect score, getting all the answers correct."

"Of course, we did," said Dario. "Now let's get this over with. I've been waiting for this."

"No. First, since you were the only ones to get everything correct, it is your duty to explain how the events of the night unfolded, guiding us along your train of thought."

"We would love to," said Frilla as she leaned on Dario, patting him on the arm. "It would be a good send off to the loser over there to walk around with her and show her exactly everywhere that she failed. Can we go now?"

"Of course," said Arthur. "But, first tell us who was the killer."

"The killer was the wife herself," said Frilla, pointing a finger to the body lying before them. "But sadly, I have to admit that Dario figured out where it happened. I wasn't able to figure that out."

"Good, now show us where the bodies are," said Arthur.

"Follow along then," said Frilla as she led the group out of the room and over to the garden. There were a lot of clues here, but only one of them was important. There's the camera underneath the brush over there where the husband and the photographer were fighting, but the key lies with Mr. Scarecrow here." She walked over to the piles of dirt underneath the scarecrow and began brushing it away, revealing two faux bodies of a little boy and girl."

"Wait," said one of the boys with them. "So, there were two babies?"

"Yes," said Frilla. "The clues were there. In the nursery, there were two sets of children's clothing, along with two bottles. But there were also other clues, such as the setting of the plates in the dining hall. How one of the two of the plates had messy eaters and much smaller portions of pie. The wife's children both sat there."

"Well done," said Arthur. "Those were indeed all the clues. Then on to the second question: who was the accomplice to the murder?"

"There's no accomplice. Or at least not a willing accomplice. The butler showed her where the arsenic was that she used to poison her children."

"Okay, I'm confused. How did she..." said a girl, her eyes going wide. "She put the poison in the food there. That explains why the pie at the head of the table still had the food sitting on the fork."

"Yes. She probably couldn't force herself to eat something that she knew was poisoned."

"Wait, then why'd she have the knife?"

"I assumed she took it from her husband while trying to stop him from killing her lover, who was, in fact, the photographer. But the husband also had a mistress of his own. Even so, men can be quite possessive."

"Don't I know it," said Arthur looking over at his boyfriend. "Well, the third question was how many people were killed, but as you all can see, it was three. Unless you wish to count the dead rat behind the barrels. So, we will skip question number four, which was already answered by Miss Frilla, thus spoiling the fun. But come, let us head to the dining room, but I'll take this with me. I do so love visual aids." She stepped over, grabbing one of the fake pumpkins from the garden.

They all left the garden and made their way over, entering the room and standing by the table.

"Wait, so all the murders took place in this room?" asked the boy from before. "I get the kids, but you said the wife didn't eat the poisoned food. And she didn't stab herself with the knife. Then how did she die?"

Dario looked over at the door to the room. "She killed herself on the statue."

"What?" said the boy. "How? I mean it has blood on it, but how did she kill herself on the statue?

"Oh, let me explain it. Even I admit, I was surprised when you showed it to me," said Frilla as she walked over to the door. "Did any of you pay attention that this room is the only room that has a door on it?"

"Actually, no. But I guess you're right. But they left it open, anyway. So, why's that matter?"

"The real question is why did it matter to the game that they would remove all the other doors in the first place," said Dario. "They have this damn fog filling up the halls and every other room." He nodded to Frilla. "But since they left the door on, what happens when you close the door?"

After his words, Frilla closed the door to the room,

locking the fog outside. And slowly, the thick gray fog at the feet began to fade away. Then to their surprise, at the base of the statue, between his legs, the sword was dyed in red.

"What? Do you mean that she took the sword and stabbed herself with it, then placed it back in the statue? That's ridiculous."

"We already established that the woman was a coward who couldn't die with her children. That's why she didn't eat the pie," said Dario as he walked over and picked up a long piece of wood. He then raised the arms of the statue that held the sword and propped the wood underneath.

Frilla then placed the fake pumpkin that she had brought with her at the feet of the statue. And with a tap of his hand, he knocked the board loose, sending the sword coming back down to its feet and stabbing the Pumping down the center.

"And now we have our murderer," said Frilla, "Assisted suicide via suit of armor. "I must admit, I didn't think about the door, so it was a good idea for me to have Dario as my partner."

"And thus, the mystery of murder is solved," said Arthur as he clapped his hands. "Thank you for explaining this to us." He then turned to Frilla. "I suppose you've won and will be taking your spot at the top of our little group again. That is, of course, if you wagered enough points."

"Yes, but not in the way you think," said Frilla, looking over at Frilla and clicking her badge. "I, Frilla Santiago, wish to subtract the one million points I wagered from Safia Famosa's account. I told you I'd get you and since both I, and that stupid discarded of your both lost the same points, there's no way you have a million points left," she waved her hand in disgust as she looked Safia up and down. "If you ever had that many points in the first place."

Safia took a deep breath while closing her eyes, letting it all sink in. *I lost. I don't have a damn million points.* She looked over and saw Jacqueline shake her head. *Fat lot of good that did. Looks like I'm on my own. But that's fine. If it doesn't work out, then Mallory's old enough. I can have her come live with me if we need to. Or maybe we can both work for the school if they have me become a teacher here. I doubt they'd say no to that.*

"Judging by the look on your face," said Dario as she stepped closer to Safia. "I don't think you do."

"Let's just get this over with. So, I can be expelled. At least then I won't have to look in that stupid face of yours any longer."

"Yeah, about that?" said Dario as he leaned in close to whisper in her ear. "A friend of mine told me about that little deal you have with the school. You're going to owe them ten years of your life, just like Abigail. So, tell me what happens to that wonderful Papa of yours when I buy those years from the school."

Safia's eyes went wide as she stared up at Dario, her lips beginning to shake.

"And there it is," said Dario and he stepped back with a wide smile across his face. "That's the look I've wanted. It's true. That means you're going to become my new Mallory whether you like it or not."

"You... there's no way you have enough points to..." said Safia as she pointed at Dario before she bit on her lip. "No... how much did you—"

"All of it," said Dario, unable to control his laughter as he placed his hands over his face, pulling on his chin. "Unlike you fuckers, I went 'All In.'" He turned to Arthur. "Go on. Say the number, fruit boy."

Arthur just shook his head and then looked down at his screen. "Dario wagered six million nine hundred and seventy-six thousand points."

"The fuck?" said another boy in the room. "You have almost seven million points?"

"Oh no," said Dario, as he raised back up to his full height to look down at Safia. "I *had* almost 7 million points. I just doubled them in this game. So that means I have almost fourteen million points. And I'm pretty sure that'll be more than enough to get what I want. And one of the things I want is to have my own little pet, Safia, to walk about and bark whenever I tell her to."

"I'd still say you should expel her," said Frilla. "Even if it is you. She'll be sure to cause you trouble."

"Oh, no... she won't do a thing. She knows how this school treats people who don't hold up their end of the bargain. But don't worry, I think Safia is going to listen to me now. Maybe my first command should be to have her start calling me Papa."

Safia thought back to her time in the class, about how Abigail had told her that she had to stay at the school in order to protect her family. *And my family is already poor. What would happen if the school stopped giving them money? Papa still goes to the hospital. Who's going to keep paying for that? Or the diner. That's where we live. He's right. I wouldn't have a choice..*

"I swear, there's nothing more beautiful in the world than when you finally break someone. Now come here Safia. Let's see if you can follow directions. Come and stand beside your new master."

"Dario!" shouted Arthur, "Enough. She won't be expelled until the game is officially over. Don't you think—"

"Shut it, fruit boy. I've been waiting for this for a full year. And I'll be damned if anyone ruins it for me." He turned back to Safia. "Now come, and show everyone how good you listen because, what you don't pay for, your family will."

With clenched teeth, Safia balled up her lips and stepped forward. Only to have Hashmi grab onto her arm.

"Safia... don't."

She glanced back at Hashmi. "It's okay. We tried." She then gently removed Hashmi's hand from her shoulder and went over and stood in front of Dario. "You win. Are you happy now?"

"Oh, more than you can possibly imagine," said Dario as he placed his hands on Safia's shoulders and spun her around, facing the rest of the crowd. He then reached his hand around her waist, bringing her in tight and holding her against him.

"Now what?" said Safia, a snarl of disgust on her lips as she felt Dario's hand make its way up her side before patting her on her chest before squeezing one of her breasts.

"Oh, soft. I think that after this, me and you are going to continue where we left off that night when you took Mallory from me."

"Well, I am surprised. She can be a good little girl and listen. Just make sure you keep that one on a leash. We can't have her acting as recklessly as that last thing you called a discarded."

"Yeah," said Dario as he gazed over the ground before whispering in Safia's ear again, before shifting his weight, turning her to look directly at Frilla. "Be thankful for this bitch." He then kissed her on the neck before looking over at Frilla. "I, Dario, subtract my six million nine hundred and seventy-six thousand points from Frilla Santiago."

And from her viewpoint of being wrapped up in Dario's arms, Safia was able to watch as Frilla's smug face slowly morphed from a sense of joy into fear and horror. Her body began to shake as both her eyes and her mouth opened so wide that they seemed to stretch her face.

"What!" shouted Frilla. "What are you doing? This wasn't our agreement."

"What agreement?" said Dario. "I only have one agreement. And it's not with you."

"No..." said Frilla, looking around the room. "You bastard. This isn't right."

"Hey," said Dario, still clutching onto a shocked Safia, "If you don't like it. You can always find someone to give the points. Now, I'm guessing you had around three million points. So that only means you need to find someone here who has an extra four million. So, look around and think hard. There's no other way out of this, because the moment the game ends and your account goes negative. Well, you know what's going to happen."

"No, but that's..." Frilla looked around the room at all the other participants. "Look at them. None of these idiots have four million damned points. I order you to rescind that bet immediately."

"Oh no, that time has ended. You think I wouldn't find out that it was you who started all that bullshit against me? Well, don't worry, you won't be ordering me around anymore," said Dario as he glanced over at Arthur. "And that includes you too, fruit boy. If you even think about making me do any of these shitty games that I don't decide on myself, then you'll be heading out the door just like she is."

"Noted," said Arthur, giving a chuckle. "But don't you think this is a bit excessive, even for you?"

"No one tells me what to do and gets away with it."

"Oh, the hypocrisy. Didn't you just do the same thing to Safia?"

"If she has a problem with it, then she needs to do something about it. But speaking of which." He spun Safia back around, and before she knew what was happening, for the third time since coming to this school. She felt Dario's lips on hers. Stunned, Safia froze up, clenching her fist at her sides as she let him do what he wanted. He then stepped away from her, spun her around and, with a huge swing of his arm, slapped Safia on her ass so hard that she skipped a few steps forward. She was about to fall over, but Hashmi stepped in front of her, catching her and holding her up.

"What is wrong with you?" screamed Hashmi. "Do you really enjoy tormenting people so much?"

Dario laughed, "You're damn right, I do. That's what power is. Allow me to demonstrate." said Dario as he turned to Arthur and the rest of the group. "Alright, let's skip the other bullshit with fruit boy. Everyone here who won some points, give your points to my little pet over there. I know there's at least two million points between all you fuckers."

"What? Why would we—"

"Because if you don't, then I'll come after you. So, here's how this is going to go. If she's expelled, then I won't be able to play with my favorite toy anymore. So, that means all of you will be my new toys and I still have a whole year left, so I want you to think about everything you just saw me do to her and now imagine what I'll do to you. And if you think I'm lying, then take a look at that sad sack of shit on the floor then," he said, pointing to Frilla, who had fallen to her knees after realizing her situation. "If I can do that to her, then just wait and see what I do to you."

There was a slight moment of silence in the room before.

"Wait, can we do that? I mean, she doesn't have points right?" asked the boy.

"Well technically, Safia is probably in a state of limbo at the moment," said Arthur, rubbing his chin. "The points taken from her won't become active until the game ends. So honestly, if she were to receive an influx of points before the game ends, then she wouldn't be expelled. All that's matters is that she has a positive supply of points at the end of the game.

"Exactly," said Dario with a smirk on his lips. "A shame so many idiots here don't understand how the point system works. But the more you don't know the more of an advantage I have. So hurry up and get this over with."

"I give all my three hundred thousand points to Safia Famosa," said the boy. "Or whatever, twenty percent of that is, since I only got three answers right."

"I give my hundred thousand points to Safia Famosa," said the girl next to him.

"I give my two hundred and eighty thousand points to Safia Famosa," said another boy.

And at the end, the final person, who Safia saw had a smile on her face, was Jacqueline.

"I, Jacquiline, give my five hundred thousand points to Safia Famosa. At least I think that's the correct number."

"Okay," said Arthur, looking at his tablet. "All together, that means that Safia Famosa leaves this game with four hundred thousand more points than when she entered. So that means she is safe and since there are no more contestants. I, now declare the game over."

Instantly after the game was over, Frilla's badge began to flash a multitude of colors against the floor.

"Frilla Santiago," spoke her badge. "You are now three million two hundred and fifty thousand points in debt to the school. You must find someone to take responsibility for this debt and your future here at this school, or you will be expelled. This must be done within the next ten minutes."

"Ten minutes," said Frilla, looking around the room with watery eyes. "You can't do this. I can't be expelled. Not when I've come so far. I can't. I'll be disowned if I don't graduate from here. My inheritance, all of it. You can't!" She stood to her feet, walking over to Dario, grabbing him by his shirt collar. "You... you have the points. You're going to take responsibility for this."

"And there you go, trying to order me around again. You should have taken a lesson from Safia. When you lose, you should admit it and submit. But it's too late. Looks like you'll be joining all those other losers who went home."

"No... you bastard," said Frilla as she began walking to the other participants. "Someone here must have enough points. I... I'm not useless. There's a reason I became number one on the campus. I can help any one of you. You can't just send me home." She then spotted Arthur. "You... you took my place. I know you have the points. You can make me your discarded. I can help you. You know how good I am."

"Sorry, Frilla," said Arthur. "We were never really

friends. And honestly, I prefer to not have to worry about you or any schemes you think up. So, bye-bye. I hope things work out."

"Are you fucking serious?" asked Frilla, spinning around. "Are all of you fucking serious? What have I done that is so bad? I made life here interesting, and this is how you treat me? You ungrateful cowards. I swear, I hope all of you drop dead on the floor right here, so help me—"

Suddenly there was a loud thud that sounded over the room, which was then followed up by the sound of coughing. Everyone's attention turned to the back of the room as they saw Jericho on the floor. He had fallen off the love seat from his sleep and had hit his head. He didn't even attempt to get up, and he stretched out on the floor before rubbing the side of his head and looking over the room and seeing everyone staring at him.

"Is... is it over?" said Jericho, whipping at his eyes, then trying to blink the sleepiness away. He still had dark spots under his eyelids from the lack of sleep. "Why is everyone looking at me like that?"

"You're a sleepy idiot," said Dario, shaking his head.

"Well, excuse me," said Jericho, sitting up and leaning his back against the cushion of the love seat, still whipping at his eyes. "It's not like I've spent the last five days organizing this damn game for all of you. Or that my little assistant decided to not help me so that she could participate. Let's see you organize, plan, and build and all this stuff. Then we'll see how you look after five days."

Frilla's eyes went wide as she pushed Dario to the side, hurrying over to Jericho and dropping to her knees beside him.

"You, Builder Boy, how many points do you have?"

"What? I'm not going to answer that?"

"Fine, then tell me. Do you have more than four million points?"

Jericho narrowed his already tired eyes even more at

Frilla. "Why?" he said with a long drool as he turned his head and narrowed his eyes at Frilla.

"Holy shit, you do. Look, you have to take me as your discarded."

"What? The fuck I do? Wait!" said Jericho, finally realizing who was in front of him. "Frilla! What's going on? I told you, I'm not getting involved in whatever games you got going on. We made a deal; I build the stuff you want, and you leave me alone."

"That deals off. So, I'm making a new deal with you. You make me your discarded and I will help you build stuff. You said you needed an assistant right; I can be that for you. You know what I can do. I'd be much better than your last one."

"Yeah, maybe. But that's not worth all my points. And why are you a discarded now, anyway? What the hell happened while I was asleep?"

"You have two minutes to find a caretaker, or you will be expelled," spoke Frilla's pendant.

"That's not important now," said Frila as she began to shake the barely conscious Jericho. "Just hurry up and make me your discarded."

"Fine... fine... just.... Stop... shaking me," said Jericho, grabbing at his head again. He reached for his badge and clicked it. "I, Jericho Andrews, take up the burden of becoming Frilla Santiago's caretaker." He shook his head in disgust. "For four million fucking points. God, I must be an idiot. He then slowly lifted himself from the floor. "You better be ready to work, Frilla. I didn't just waste..." He grabbed at his head after standing up and stumbled. "Okay, I stood too fast." He headed toward the door on shaky legs. "That's it. I'm headed back to the dorm. Arthur, I'll get some people from around the campus to help clean all this mess up when I wake up. But I'm going to sleep now."

"Yes... yes, I'll walk you home," said Frilla, placing herself under one of Jericho's arms. She glowered back at the rest of the room before turning back to Jericho and leading him out of the room.

The room was silent for another long moment.

"The fuck was that?" asked Dario.

"It seems our wonderful obnoxious Miss Frilla managed to survive. Although now, since she's attached herself to our lovely Builder Boy, I do wonder if things are going to become more difficult for us."

"What the fuck can she do now? She has to listen to him. He's probably gonna have her building his little toy houses clear into the next year. She won't even have time to deal with us."

"True, but there are cases of discarded acting on their own accord, without their owner's permission. We just had such an incident with Miss Mallory that was broadcasted across the whole school. If Frilla somehow manages to seduce Builder Boy, I can't imagine she wouldn't use whatever resources he has against us."

"Let her try. I'll crush them both if I have to," said Dario with the same smug look on his face as he'd always had as he turned to leave, only to see Safia standing before him.

"What now? You want another spanking?"

"Why? You could have expelled me. Why didn't you?"

"Because where would the fun be in that? I don't want you expelled. I want you down on your knees begging me to stop. And now..." He tugged at his shirt collar. "I have a whole other year to find new and exciting ways to fuck with you. And nothing will give me more pleasure than watching you go through it."

Safia turned her head in disgust. "I won't say thank you. Not for you, never."

Dario just smiled and leaned forward, still looking down at her. "Ya, know," he said in a low voice while looking around. "You kinda just did." And with the most prideful walk, Safia watched as Dario smugly strutted himself out of the room.

"I... I don't know what to say," said Hashmi, just shaking

her head.

Safia turned to her head. "You know what? I don't even care anymore. All that matters is that it's over and— ahh!" Safia yelled as she stumbled forward, falling to her hands and knees on the floor. A sharp pain coursing through her backside. From the floor, she turned around to see Dario waving his hand at her.

"And there you are. Just like I said. Down on your knees and I can't wait for the day you start begging."

"You stupid son of a bitch," said Safia as she hopped back up and ran at him, only to beheld back Hashmi and Jaqueline.

"Safia, stop," said Jacqueline. "You know what's going to happen if you attack him."

"Attack him? What about me?" said Safia, trying to reach out and grab Dario by the neck.

Jacqueline turned her head to face Dario. "That is a good question. Why are you not down on the floor shaking? You shouldn't be able to just strike her as you did. What's going on?"

"Figure it out yourselves," said Dario in another fit of laughter as she turned around and left the room again.

"I hate him. I hate him so much," said Safia, as her eyes began to water from either the pain on her rear end or the emotion of the humiliation she was going through.

"Safia, calm down," said Jacqueline. "You won. Frilla lost and you're still here. Don't ruin the night by thinking about that jackass, Dario."

Safia bit down on her lip, trying to contain herself, and began pacing back and forth, before coming back to Jacqueline. "Did you... did you know he was going to do that? That he was going to turn on Frilla?"

"No. I had no idea. My plan was to have myself and the three others who agreed to help balance out the points after everything was settled. How could I have known that Dario would even be here, let alone bet everything he had to bring down Frilla. No one could have predicted that."

Safia continued to calm herself, taking another deep breath and exhaling." "Fine. It doesn't matter. I'm just going to go home and forget this day ever happened."

"That sounds like the best idea," said Hashmi as she grabbed Safia's schoolbag, handing it to her and led her out of the room, leaving the rest behind. They made their way down the still fog filled hallway and out of the door. Thankfully, while they could still see thunder in the distant sky, the rain stopped. "You were really impressive back there."

"How?" said Safia with a reluctant laugh. "The way I failed the game or the way I fell to the floor with my ass on fire."

"Before the ass on fire part. We actually managed to get three of the five questions right."

"Yeah, but some we got them right for the wrong reasons."

"A right answer is still a right answer?" said Hashmi, sliding her tongue and through her smiling lips in a silly manner.

Safia laughed. "I guess there's a bright side to everything. But now, the only side I want to see is the side of my pillow. This night has just been way too much."

"I can't argue that," said Hashmi as they continued their way through the campus. It took a few minutes, but eventually they made their way back to Yennefer house.

"Actually, that reminds me, did you ever say where your points went?"

"No. So much happened, I just forgot."

"Hmm. I wonder what happened to the points you bet."

"I'll ask Arthur tomorrow. I'm done thinking about that game now. All that matter is that I and Mallory are safe."

They made their way up one level of the steps before Safia's badge began to glow.

"Jericho Andrews has sent you a message," spoke the

pendant.

"Oh my god, will this night not end?" said Safia as she tapped on her pendant.

"Hey, Safia. Come see me. We need to talk. I'm outside of the auditorium."

Safia turned back around, looking all the way across campus to the school they had just left. "I know he did this on purpose. He waited 'til I was almost free and now he is asking me to walk all the way back down there?"

Now it was Hashmi's turn to sigh. "I guess we should start making our way back."

"No," said Safia. "I'm the one he made the deal with. He probably has something else he wants me to do. With any luck, he has Frilla running around the campus screaming his name."

"Oh! I just thought about something. Actually, both you and Frilla are now being used by Jericho. We'll technically you aren't his discarded officially like Frilla now is. He's just black mailing you."

"Yeah... that somehow escaped my mind as well. Thanks for bringing it up."

"Sorry. But Jericho doesn't seem like he's taking advantage of you like I thought he would when you first told us what was going on. I'm glad for that. I've actually started to like him. Well, you know what I mean," said Hashmi with a pitying smile across her face as she reached over and gave Safia a hug. "I'll go in and tell Mallory what happened, so she won't bug you when you get back. Try not to get caught out in the rain."

"Thanks," said Safia, embracing the hug from her friend and then turning to make her way back across the campus. The road back was just as dark as the streetlights flickered as lighting stretched across the sky. Alone, walking at night, the school seemed eerie behind the backdrop of a half-hidden moon.

But, stepping off the path, she made her way around the

school and saw Jericho sitting down in a chair in front of the door. There was another chair opposite him, which she assumed was for her.

As she stepped forward, another boy stepped out of the building. His blonde hair and face looked familiar to her, then she realized that he was the same boy from the hexagon game. The boy who had gotten angry and picked Mallory off the ground. He said something to Jericho that she couldn't hear and then left, walking toward Safia as she approached. He nodded to her but didn't say anything as he went on his way.

"Welcome," said Jericho, rubbing the side of his face. "I hope you enjoyed the games."

"No. But I survived, and that's all that matters," said Safia, as she came and stood in front of him.

"Take a seat," he said, gesturing to the chair. "We have a lot to talk about."

Safia took one look at the hard metal chair. "No, thank you. I think I'll stand."

Jericho laughed. "Did he really hit you that hard?"

"You try having someone almost twice your size constantly smacking your ass as hard as he can and then you try sitting down right after."

Jericho raised his hand, unable to wipe the smirk off his face. "I'll take your word for it. But it was your idea. You had to know that something wouldn't work out the way you planned."

"So what? Am I going to have to spend the whole next year constantly in fear of random ass slaps?"

"No," he said, continuing his laughter. "I only gave him access to you for the night. Tomorrow, your booty will be just as safe as it always was. But tell me, how did you know he wouldn't expel you?"

"What you mean besides the fact that he wants to fuck me?"

"Yes, besides that?"

"Dario gets off on control. That's something I know a lot about, since I'm pretty much the same."

"Yes, I remember you telling me of your particular fetish."

"Well, after our fight that night in the escape room, I realized just how much he got off on it. He could have beaten my ass in that little box elevator. But he couldn't help but feel me up. He's smart, but also stupid in that way. So, I wondered what he would do if he had control over me while at the same time was about to lose that control because I was going to be expelled. Well, his pride wouldn't let me just walk away."

"So, you purposely lost all your points to Frilla?"

"I couldn't be sure Frilla would come after me first. But I was mostly sure he would wait to see how everything played out. Dario knew there'd be no way in hell I'd willingly make myself his discarded. So, he would choose the second-best option. He'd keep me here and find other ways of trying to control me."

"So, that's why you had me approach him and offer him access to touching you without having to worry about the school's pesky safety system."

"If he could hurt me and not have to worry about it being expelled, there's no way he was going to turn that down. Especially after that night in the elevator. His pride wouldn't let that night go. And if it came from you, his friend, then all the better. And everyone on this campus already thinks I'm your girlfriend or whatever, so I didn't think he'd go that far. But even then, I hated having that bastard touch me."

"Still, wasn't there a risk involved with having me tell him about your father?"

"Everyone already knew I left the school. There was no harm in telling him why at that point. Plus, I knew he'd use it to try and have something to hold over my head. He wanted more power over me, so I gave it to him."

"And in return, you took care of Frilla and tricked Dario

into protecting you."

"I'd say that's more than worth the price of a few fake tears and two ass slaps, even if they were painful."

Jericho clapped his hands. "Well, all I can say is congratulations. Your plan worked almost exactly as you said it would."

Safia placed her hand on the chair, squeezing her fingers against the metal as she stood looking down at Jericho. "I just realized it was you who sent Mallory down into that hex game."

"Yes," he waved his hands, adding on. "Well, not completely. I had a bit of help. But in order to break Frilla down to the point where I could force her into being a discarded, I needed to do a lot of things to make that happen. I asked Mallory not to tell you because that would ruin my plans."

"Did you ask, or did you threaten her?"

"I asked. I told her that what I was doing was to help and that I would protect you if it all went south. And seeing as how that's all I've done; she had no reason not to believe me. That girl really does have an interesting fascination with you." Jericho smiled at her, while waving a finger. "But I told her if you compelled her to speak using your caretaker rights, then she should tell you and I'd work around it. But we both knew that's something you would never do."

"Fine," said Safia, releasing the chair and taking a breath. "And what about your plan? Why did you want Frilla so badly?"

"Yes, I guess I should come clean about that," said Jericho, looking up into the sky. "My brother attended this school some years ago. Well, turns out he wasn't good at the games they played here so he ended up becoming a discarded. You know that they only allow you to transfer discarded once, right? Well, my brother is the reason for that. They treated him like shit, passing him back and forth to the point where he ended up taking his own life when he finally quit and came home. And it just so happens that our lovely Frilla was one of the ones involved in that mess."

"I'm sorry to hear that."

"It's fine. I came to terms with it some time ago. But that doesn't mean that I'm the type to forgive her."

"So, what happens now?"

"Now," said Jericho as he lifted himself from his seat, and folded both chairs, taking them in his hand. "We go inside. There's still a bit of work for you to do." He opened the door and stepped inside, with Safia following behind him.

After entering, the door closed, leaving them both in complete darkness, as Safia heard the door locked behind them.

"I can't see anything," said Safia, freezing in the dark, but reaching her hand forward trying to feel for anything around her. "What's going on?"

"Sorry, but I needed to black out the windows so that no one could look in. Just give me a second to turn on the lights," said Jericho as his footsteps echoed in the darkness. Then came the sound of a flick as several lights turned on, partially illuminating the room.

And before her, Safia saw Frilla standing up in the middle of the room. Her makeup had run down her face from the tears she'd shed. But the shock was that she was being held up by leather shackles over her wrists that had ropes attached to them that hung from the roof. And around her mouth was a cloth gag. She twitched when the lights came on as her eyes began to adjust.

"She's hasn't been standing like this long," said Jericho. "Only a little after we left the game. My first command was for her to stay silent until you arrived. She's doing well so far."

Safia swallowed nervously and she lowered her school bag to the floor. "What are you going to do with her?"

"Me?" asked Jericho as he took one of the chairs and

placed it in front of Frilla, before walking over to the wall and grabbing a paddle. He then slapped his hand with it before walking over and holding it out for Safia to take. "I tried to get a whip also, but it didn't make it in time. I hope this works."

Safia looked at the paddle and then looked over, seeing the fear in Frilla's eyes as she moaned. "And what if I don't want to do this?"

"Safia, dear. You don't have a choice. I told you I'd help you in this school and I have. I've saved you numerous times. Now it's time to pay up." He then walked behind Safia, then reached forward, placing his hand under her chin and tilted her face so that she looked over at Frilla. "But be honest with yourself. You know you want to do this."

Safia was quiet for a moment before looking down at the paddle. "And you're going to take responsibility for what happens here."

"I've been taking responsibility for you since we met in front of the communication room. I see no reason to stop now."

Safia then closed her eyes before taking a deep breath and gave another look over at Frilla, her facial expression more serious than before. "Then let's get started."

Jericho clicked on his pendant while looking directly into Frilla's eyes. "I wish to share my caretaker rights with Safia Famosa."

"Jericho Andrews wishes to share the caretaker rights of Frilla Santiago with you. Do you accept?" spoke her pendant.

Safia tapped her pendant while staring back into Jericho's eyes. "I do."

"Caretaker privileges are now shared."

"I didn't realize you could share rights."

"Another lesson I learned from my brother," said Jericho, never taking his eyes off Frilla. "Before he died, oh, he told me a bunch of things." He leaned forward in his seat. "And slowly I am going to make sure she experiences every one."

"Sounds like you've been thinking about this for a while."

"I have, but enough about me. Now, you can do whatever you want to her and not have to worry about what the school has to say about it."

Safia closed her eyes and took a deep breath, rocking her head back and forth for a few moments. "Not like this," said Safia as she knelt, lowering the paddle to the floor, before placing her hands on her dress and began to unbutton the top of her dress, then when finished she tossed into the floor, revealing the corset underneath. She then looked over at Jericho. "You mind helping me with the rest of it?"

"How can I say no?" said Jericho, as he stood and walked over helping her remove her clothing piece by piece until Safia stood before him wearing nothing but a black corset, black panties, and cream stockings. "I'm sure this is a fetish for someone."

"I'm sure," said Safia, extending the palm of her hand to him. "If you would be so kind."

Jericho knelt, picking up the paddle and placing it in Safia's hand. "I look forward to it."

"Okay, let's get this started." She walked over, placing the paddle on Jericho's lap. "Hold this for a moment." Walking over, she stepped in beside Frilla, reached up, removing the gag from her mouth.

She began to cough. "Safia, I'm sorry, I'm sorry. I promise I won't bother you any—"

"Shhh!" whispered Safia as she placed a finger on Frilla's lips to silence her. "Listen… listen. For the rest of the night, you will call me Mistress."

"Safia, please, you don't have to do this. I promise. I… I can help you. I can help both of you. You know—"

"That's a shame. You didn't listen," said Safia as she reached down, undoing the two buttons on Frillas skirt, before letting it fall to the floor and exposing her panties as her shirt draped over them.

"Please… please," begged Frilla as she wormed around

in her shackles. "You don't have to... you... don't..." was all she could muster before she began to start crying again.

Safia then took her time, placing her hand on a specific area of Frilla's behind and began rubbing the spot gently, as if letting her know exactly where she would hit her. Then she took the paddle and began rubbing that same spot and she watched as Frilla dropped her head, squinting her eyes and began trying to control her breathing for what she knew was coming. Safia then pulled the paddle back before swinging it down as hard as she could.

"Ahhhhh!" screamed Frilla as the paddle made contact on her ass, causing her to shuffle in her bindings as she broke down, letting the weight of her body hang on her bindings.

The sound of Frilla's scream shook Safia. It felt as if she could breathe it in. The power she felt wasn't trilling, it was intoxicating. Safia took a finger and began to gently run it over the red spot of Frilla's ass, just around the rim of her panties. The way her soft skin sank in just ever so slightly to the way her finger moved up and down it. Just how much more of herself would she give?

*All of it. I want all of it.* Safia licked her lips as stared into the tired, exhausted face of Frilla. *More.*

She then stepped back and raised the paddle high above her head before once again bringing it down hard on Frilla's backside. She screamed again, her body quivering and her legs shuffling back and forth. Only to then have Safia step behind her and wrap her free arm around Frilla, her hand over her body.

"Come on," said Safia, as she let her finger roam over the navel. "Tell me. Who's a good little girl?"

"I.,, I... am... I'm a... good girl."

Jericho gave a smile as he crossed his leg and leaned back on the chair, watching Safia work.

"See. You do learn, don't you?" said Safia, as she placed her cheek on Frilla's shoulder exhaling into her ear. Then she moved her hand upward, allowing her fingers to slide under Frilla's bra, cupping her breast in her hand, before taking the paddle and sliding it between her legs. "Now, what do we say?"

"I'm... I'm so sorry."

"That's a shame," said Safia, removing her hand from Frilla's exposed breast and taking a step back. "You didn't say my name."

"Wha... No... I'm so sorry, Mistre— Ahhhh!" she screamed again as she brought down the paddle again, causing Frilla to shake in her binding. Not once, not twice, but three times, as hard as she could, she brought down the paddle on Frilla's body. And each time it was as if the two were exchanging Frilla's pain for Safia's pleasure. It felt as if jolts of electricity flew through her with every swing.

It was as if she couldn't get enough. One swing after another, Safia brought down the paddle on Frilla's backside, every time harder than before, and once again Frilla screamed in pain as her body shivered in response.

Jericho's eyes never wavered in watching the show. He tilted his head as Safia noticed him rubbing the thumb and index finger of his hand together as he bit his lip. The slight curl of a smile still on his face as his chest heaved. It seemed as if he was breathing in the moment, holding it inside himself and savoring it.

*Show me.* Safia stepped around in front of Frilla. *Show me how you look when you're broken.* Safia then took the girl's chin in her hand, forcing her to look at her through watery eyes. *Yes, this is what I want. More of this. All of this. This beautiful face and body that is barely able to stand.*

"I'm... sorry. I'm sorry," murmured Frilla under her voice in a whimper. "Mistress"

"That's it, say my name again."

"Ma... Ma... Mistress."

"That's a good girl," said Safia. "Now this is what's going to happen." She slid her hand down to Frilla's body, letting it stop on her hip as if comforting her. "I'm going to punish you."

"No... no... please," said Frilla, in her whimpers.

"Yes. Yes, I am," said Safia, as stepped to the side, allowing her fingers to slide over Frilla's belly. "And when I punish you, you're going to thank me for it. Because if you don't, I'm going to hit you again and again until you do. And if that doesn't work, then I'm going to have Jericho come and do it and, since he's a man, that probably means he's a lot stronger than me, so who knows how more that will hurt? What did you call him? Oh, right, Builder Boy? Well, I imagine Builder Boy has strong muscles from doing all your dirty work. Do you understand?"

Frilla's body shook as if in response to the thought of what Safia was saying, but eventually she nodded her head as the water began to leak out of her nose.

"See, you're already listening. But don't worry. I'll give you a reward after."

As if in agreement, the sound of thunder came, which was followed up by the sounds of hard rain against the windows and on the roof of the building.

"Well, I guess we won't have to worry about anyone hearing you scream now, will we?"

What would come next were the sound of a hundred thank you's where, at the end, even through the cloth Safia could easily see the redness of her skin from where she had struck her. Now Frilla's body hung near lifeless, with her knees having long since buckled under her weight as she gently swayed back and forth in her shackles.

"And now here's your reward," said Safia, grabbing Frilla back the back of the head, lifting her face and staring down on a helpless and defeated Frilla and leaned forward, kissing her on the lips, tasting the salt from the tears that had run their way down her face. While kissing her, she took in a deep breath, as if taking in all the emotion and pain from what had just happened, before pulling herself back and releasing Frilla's head and watching her lifeless face fall back down. "You did good. You can rest now." She then turned around and stepped back to Jericho, dropping the paddle on the floor.

"That was quite the show," said Jericho, looking up at Safia from his chair as she came to him. "Well done, you can leave now if you—"

Safia lifted a foot, rubbing it over Jericho's crotch.

"Well, this is unexpected," said Jericho as Safia raised her foot even higher to his chest. "But I'm not exactly interested in—shit!" He yelped as Safia pushed him back onto her foot, sending him tumbling over to the floor.

"What is with you pushing me to the floor?" said Jericho, grabbing the back of his head.

Safia walked over to him, tossing the paddle to the floor before standing over him, a foot on each side. She then lowered herself, straddling him above his crotch before leaning herself down and pressing her mouth against his. She took him, tasted him, that damned wood smell he always had on him. All of it as she ran her finger through his hair before gripping it tightly and pinning his head down against the floor as she lifted herself, breathing heavily as she stared back down at him.

"I'm starting to feel as if I'm not going to have a say in what's about to happen," said Jericho as he glanced up at Safia, noticing how she was looking down at him.

"I asked if you were going to take responsibility for what was about to happen. And do you remember what you said?"

"I do, although I think I'm just now understanding the scope of what that meant," said Jericho as Safia began undoing her shirt. "Are you sure you want me? I remember you having a fondness for that fellow Ricardo."

"Well," said Safia as she undid only two of the buttons before ripping the other buttons off completely, as she tore open the shirt and started unfastening his belt. "Ricardo's nice, but I won't risk falling in love with someone else while

I'm here. There's only one man I want to love, and you remind me of him. So, either I fuck you, who I already have a relationship with, or I fuck Dario. And I'll die before I let him have me."

"Great, I'm the winner by default. Lucky me."

"Shut up and take off your pants."

# CHAPTER 23

Safia awoke underneath a bundle of clothes with her face resting on Jericho's chest. She moaned as she felt the heat from him and wrapped herself more into his presence, squeezing him tightly to ignore the coldness around them.

"Good morning," said Jericho. "Did you sleep well?"

"Well enough, I guess," said Safia, looking up at him as he stared up at the ceiling. Safia then glanced over to where Frilla was and noticed that she was gone. All that was left were the leather bracelets that hung from the ceiling. "Where's your newest play toy?"

"I let her go sometime after you closed your eyes. I started feeling bad for her. Plus, it was hard to sleep over the sound of her crying in the middle of the night."

"I didn't expect you to have sympathy, considering what you said she did to your brother."

"My brother had his problems before he came to

this school. And after coming here myself, I knew it was something he'd probably brought on himself."

"Then why all the—"

"Just because I understand, doesn't mean she's without blame. And I plan to use her like I do everyone else."

"Including me?"

"Including you. And it's not as if you haven't used me. That's what people do here."

"About that? What are your plans with Hashmi?"

"What do you mean?"

"You like her, don't you? I see the way you look at her. That's why you kept inviting her to help you with all those projects. You're not the type to do that."

"I was helping you by not having you worry about your friend's need for points."

"I'm not blind. There's more to it than that."

"Yeah, well. Too bad, I have no intention of acting on it. I enjoy being around her, that's true. But it's not going farther than that. I have other things to worry about."

"Good, because if you were trying to hurt or use her, I was going to come after you."

Jericho laughed, "Yeah. I figured as much. You seemed fond of your little friend group."

"Hashmi and Mallory are nice people. They aren't like us."

"Us? So, you're not a good person?"

"If I was, I'm certainly not anymore."

"Then all I can say is 'Welcome to the Apex Academy.' I'm glad you came to join us in our wallowing around in bullshit."

Safia found herself laughing despite herself. She then reached over Jericho, spotting her bag nearby. She then flipped the flap on it and reached in, pulling out her tablet.

"Now, what are you doing?"

"I had an idea about that stupid name game Frilla lured me into. I couldn't figure out everyone's name, but last night

404

I saw Jacqueline wearing the same crown she had on from the ballet, then it hit me that all the names on the list are from Disney movies."

"What list?"

"It's a long story," said Safia as she turned on the tablet and tapped her finger on the screen until she reached the screen with the masked icons. She then clicked on the image of the deer mask that Jacqueline had worn and typed in the name 'Cinderella.' The area turned green, and a green check mark appeared over the mask even though it was still grayed out. "I probably should have figured this out sooner, but I've just been so busy."

"So, you have to just figure out which fairy tale princesses they are?"

"No, it can be anyone in the story. They've introduced themselves in some way to me by giving me the right name to use. Except one, the person who wore the parrot mask, and I think I know why. And now I have the points to test out if I'm right. In the movie Aladdin there's a parrot. Do you remember what his name is?"

"Iago, I think."

"Yes, and my brother's name is Yago."

"You think it's that simple?"

"Let's find out," said Safia as she typed Iago into the tablet and watched as the green check mark appeared over the parrot mask. Then she laid the tablet on Jericho's chest as she sighed and shook her head.

"Yago Famosa has sent you a message," spoke Safia's pendant from somewhere nearby.

"I'm going to kill him."

"So, what happens now?"

Safia sighed, before raising herself up from Jericho as she began to look around their area for her clothing. "Now, we get up and enjoy the last week of the semester. I will have a month of no tests and hopefully no stupid game nights to worry about. So, I'm going to try to spend that time with my friends and beating up my dumbass brother whenever I find him."

"Sounds like fun," said Jericho as she stood up, sliding back on his underwear and pants.

"I remember you said... Wait... where are my clothes?"

"Look ahead," said Jericho with a nod to where a new set of school clothes sat for Safia to wear.

"You have been busy."

"I had someone bring them to me. I figured you wouldn't really be too excited to be putting back on that outfit. It took us long enough to get you out of it."

"Wait, you had someone bring them? Did they see us?"

"I met them at the door. So, what were you saying?"

Safia reached over, grabbing her new clothing, and slid on her underwear. "I remember when we first met, you said you had a sister? Do you ever talk to her?" She then slid on her bra as Jericho handed her a button-up shirt.

"Yes, I call her about once a month or so. She just had her daughter. She's about three months old now," said Jericho, noticing Safia fidgeting with the buttons on her shirt. "Here, let me."

Safia lifted her hair out of the way as she let Jericho fasten the buttons. "So, you're uncle Jericho then?" When finished, she stepped into her skirt, reached down, and slid her skirt up to her waist inside the hem, trying to look presentable.

"Apparently," so said Jericho as he allowed Safia to do the same to him as he began to button up his own shirt. "How do I look?"

"Like we never fucked. And me?"

"As beautiful as ever." said Jericho as he walked to the door. "Come on, let's go get this shit started." He said as she walked over to the door.

Safia put on her shoes and followed behind him as they both left out of the auditorium into the daylight. They both tried to shield their eyes for a moment in the morning sun as they walked over to the spiral walkway and headed back across campus. About halfway, they split up with each other.

"Good luck with that brother of yours," said Jericho.

"And good luck with Frilla," said Safia as she headed back through the walkway, only to slow down when she saw someone sitting down on the bench ahead of her.

"Hello there, Miss Safia," said the woman in a friendly manner as Safia approached.

Safia stopped for a moment, realizing that she recognized the woman, then with realization she stepped back.

"You're the woman from the game last night, the body that held the knife."

"I am. But I also have a major influence on this campus. Although you might just remember me from my voice over the phone."

"Over the..." Safia's eyes went wide as she began to remember the voice of the woman. "You're Champ Champ's mother."

"I am indeed, and you are quite the interesting young lady. That plan you cooked with Jericho in order to use Dario's petty grievances against him and then to take down Frilla. I must say that it was masterfully executed."

"You know about that, huh? I guess I shouldn't be surprised."

"Don't worry, I won't spill your secret. It's just so rare that I'm allowed to have a bit of freedom around campus, let alone participate in a game night. I just started to feel a little nostalgic and wish to have a little talk. Have a seat.

"I'd rather not."

"Yes, I suppose not after Dario's assault on your behind," said the woman, placing a finger to her lips as a sly smile came to the corner of her mouth that reminded her of a certain annoying and confusing smaller version of her. "Although, you didn't seem so averse to the assault of your hind region when it was Jericho behind you. I even remember you asking for it."

Safia sighed, "Just say why you're here."

"I want your help with a task that I'm not allowed to interfere with."

"What?"

"I want you to expel someone for me. Someone I'm not allowed to touch."

*I don't have time for this. And I most certainly am not going to get myself involved with this woman.* Safia looked back at the woman. "And who is that?"

"Malik Freeman."

"Who?" asked Safia, not able to recognize the name.

"Oh, forgive me. You probably know him under the moniker of "The Husband.""

"Wait! You want me to expel your daughter's partner?" asked Safia, remembering the scary-looking man that loomed over her above the school.

"Yes. That's right."

"I'm going to have to decline. Despite her methods, your daughter has looked after me and helped me a lot since being here. I'm not going to turn my back on her because you say so."

"Oh well, I tried," said the woman. "But I think you will soon come to see things my way. It will be the start of a new year soon and once you become a second year; you might be surprised with how much things change."

Safia stepped forward, continuing on her way to Yennefer House where she caught Mallory and Hashmi just coming down the steps.

"There she is," said Mallory, coming over and giving Safia a hug. "We were worried about you. Hashmi told me about everything that happened. Why were you out all night? Were you building something with Jericho?"

"That's a lot of questions. I'm not sure how to answer them all," said Safia with a smile.

"I think the most important question to ask would be, is everything okay?"

"Yeah," said Safia with a nod. "I think so."

"Then let's go and get something to eat and you can tell us about it."

"Actually, I really want to take a bath. After spending all night out, I really need one. You all can go ahead without me."

"Go ahead without you?" asked Mallory, letting go of Safia and stepping back. "There's no way I'm going to wait any longer. I want you to tell me about everything that happened."

"I thought Hashmi told you everything?"

"She did, but now you can tell me. I want to hear your side of everything."

"Fine," said Safia, shaking her head with a laugh. "Let's go back inside."

And together, both girls headed back into Yennefer House and up the stairs to the second floor. They made their way down to their room, and Safia opened the door to see a young man sitting in a chair in the middle of their room.

"Hey Saffy, how ya been?" asked Yago.

Teddy Baire

Thank you for reading

# Every Student has their Truth

This is book #4 in the Teddy Baire 10 book project.
If you've enjoyed this novel, please leave us a Review.
Everyone helps.

More Reviews, More Free Ebooks.

And if you interested in Teddy Baire's 10 book project.
Please visit the web site.
www.teddybaire.com
and see what other novels have been written.

Teddy Baire